THE
Spite House

THE
Spite House

JOHNNY COMPTON

NIGHTFIRE

TOR PUBLISHING GROUP
NEW YORK

THE SPITE HOUSE

A Nightfire Book
Published by Tom Doherty Associates / Tor Publishing Group
120 Broadway
New York, NY 10271

www.tornightfire.com

Nightfire™ is a trademark of Macmillan Publishing Group, LLC.

Library of Congress Cataloging-in-Publication Data

Names: Compton, Johnny, author.
Title: The spite house : a novel / Johnny Compton.
Description: First edition. | New York : Nightfire, 2023. |
Identifiers: LCCN 2022034342 (print) | LCCN 2022034343 (ebook) |
    ISBN 9781250841414 (hardcover) | ISBN 9781250891952 (Canadian) | ISBN
    9781250841421 (ebook)
Subjects: LCGFT: Ghost stories. | Horror fiction. | Novels.
Classification: LCC PS3603.O4865 S65 2023 (print) | LCC PS3603.O4865 (ebook) |
    DDC 813/.6—dc23/eng/20220719
LC record available at https://lccn.loc.gov/2022034342
LC ebook record available at https://lccn.loc.gov/2022034343

Our books may be purchased in bulk for promotional, educational, or business use. Please contact your local bookseller or the Macmillan Corporate and Premium Sales Department at 1-800-221-7945, extension 5442, or by email at MacmillanSpecialMarkets@macmillan.com.

First U.S. Edition: 2023
First Canadian Edition: 2023

Printed in the United States of America

0 9 8 7 6 5 4 3 2 1

To Sister Gayle, Mr. Comer, and Mrs. Doke,
who taught me I was good enough to get better

THE
Spite House

Eric

The Masson House of Degener, Texas, was like the corpse of an old monster, too strange and feared for most to approach it, much less attempt to bury it. After all, it might be feigning death or dormant.

In the primary photograph of the full-page ad, the house's rectangular windows reflected the sun. Behind the house, the treetops looked close enough to brush the walls of the second floor when the wind blew. It was gaunt and gray, old and sickly. Four stories tall and narrow enough to be mistaken for an optical illusion, like the photographer was one step to the left or right away from revealing the other half or two-thirds of the house they had skillfully hidden.

Another picture showed the house overlooking a shallow valley and three buildings that, according to the description beneath the photo, once comprised an orphanage, and before that a family estate.

Eric Ross could not find much more about the house online. A wiki of "The Most Haunted Places in Texas" stated, "If the Masson House came to life one night and climbed down the hill to destroy that old orphanage, no one in Degener would be quite as shocked as you'd think." Eric wondered whether he should share this part with his older daughter, Dess, or just show her the ad, keeping to himself the quick research he was doing in the motel's "complimentary office"—a small, doorless closet with a sluggish computer. He valued Dess's input—had she objected to them leaving home and pursuing a fugitive path, they might still be in Maryland—but he felt the need to steer her in a certain direction. Not manipulate or misinform her, but guide her, as a father should. In this case, that guidance would come by way of what he withheld.

The daily effort of finding a semblance of "real work" was exhausting him. Eight months of driving from one new place to another, from one new job to another, starting over again and again, it was unsustainable. There were only so many cash-payment construction, security, or dubious sales jobs to be found, and they all came with significant risk. More than once he'd been asked to do something of questionable legality. One of his supervisors had told him to dump trash in an unspoiled wooded area where no one needed a sign saying NO DUMPING ALLOWED to know that there was probably no dumping allowed. At one "security" job he discovered too late that he and his six coworkers had been hired to look intimidating while their boss negotiated with a prospective partner, who at one point threatened to call the cops, saying, "I don't feel safe here."

In other instances, the person who hired him took advantage of his situation and tried to stiff Eric when it came time to pay up. In both of those cases Eric had to make a decision—live with wasted efforts and a shorted budget, or do what would have made his grandfather Frederick smile and say, "That's my boy's boy." Twice he chose to ignore the examples his father had set for him, to be the figurative bigger man and walk away, and instead mimicked what he'd once seen his grandfather do when he was a boy— take advantage of being the literal bigger man. Each time, he squared up and stepped closer to the men trying to cheat him, saying, "It'll cost you a lot more not to pay me." It always felt like the right thing to do, and filled him with a fire that burned out too fast. It also felt like a trick he couldn't keep getting away with. He was a few inches shorter than his grandfather, at least fifty pounds lighter, and far less comfortable wielding a size advantage when he had it.

Frederick Emerson was six foot two and built like God considered making him a wall before making him a man. His hands were so large and heavy they seemed the sole reason his shoulders rounded slightly. As imposing as his frame was, his reputation is what really made people think twice about crossing him. People knew not to get on "Ol' Fred's" bad side. "He could just look at you the wrong way and buzzards would start following you," Eric once heard his grandfather's barber say of him, and everyone at the shop had laughed, including Ol' Fred himself. It hadn't quite sounded like a joke to Eric, though. He repeated it to his father later on, hoping to make him laugh, which would reassure him that it wasn't serious, but his father just shook his head. "Bet your grandpa thought it was funny, huh?" he said. "You shouldn't be hearing stuff like that."

Eric didn't have his grandfather's reputation or imposing stature, but he had an unwavering obligation to his daughters, and a desperate desire to right his upturned life. That must have put something in his eyes—some of his grandfather's spirit—because on the occasions he made a veiled threat in order to get paid, the men who owed him gave him what he'd earned. After the last time, about five months ago, he started budgeting to account for the possibility that he might be tricked or coerced into working for free. Just in case. It hadn't happened again, which, to Eric, just meant that when it happened next, it would happen two or three times in a row.

The offer in the ad for the Masson House promised "high six figures at minimum upon completion of the assignment, with a much larger upside for the qualifying candidate." Even if the true payout ended up being half that—a quarter of it—it was far better than anything he could get anywhere else. Enough money to set them up for at least a year, more if they stayed frugal. All for staying rent-free in a place that was—again, according to the ad—"the site of pronounced paranormal activity."

The pictures of the spite house certainly made it look uninviting. One taken from a low angle emphasized how tall and thin it was, and captured a dark sea of clouds above it. Eric could not tell whether this was intended to attract or dissuade the curious. Widen or shrink the applicant pool. Its appearance might entice those earnestly interested in experiencing the unusual, or intimidate those who might otherwise be casually interested. He could not know what it would mean for his competition and therefore his chances, but he couldn't concern himself with that. The only way to win the job was to apply.

The newspaper rested beside the keyboard on the narrow desk. Eric took out his prepaid phone and called the number on the ad. He would ask for Dess's thoughts and permission later, and if she didn't grant the latter he'd just ask her forgiveness. But he couldn't wait.

The call went to voicemail, a professional-sounding woman saying, "Thank you for your call. I must stress that we are interested in serious candidates only. Please leave your name, contact information, and an explanation as to why we should consider you. If we intend to follow up, we will reach out to you. Thank you."

"Thank you for taking my call," he said right away, as though speaking to an actual person. A little decorum could still be effective, couldn't it? Especially here in Texas. His grandparents and even great-grandparents—all Texas natives—had told him this years ago, when he used to visit them. "A simple thank-you goes a long way. Even when you don't want to say it, find a way to say it." He had encountered enough bigots in Maryland and elsewhere in the Northeast, to say nothing of a few rancorous idiots in West Texas in his early teens, to disabuse him of this. Nonetheless, he was in no position to be anything but presumptively grateful now.

"I'm no ghost hunter or anything," he went on. "I'm a father of two looking for work and a place to stay. Me and my daughters have been on the go for a while and work isn't easy for me to come by in my situation. I can explain further if you like, but right now I just want to say how much I would appreciate this chance. I can promise you that whatever you need done, I'll find a way to do it." He gave his name and number, said "Thank you" again before hanging up. Afterward he held his head low for just long enough to remember the house back home.

Two stories and in a wonderful neighborhood. Not exactly "Black Beverly Hills" but as close to it as he cared to get. A few of his neighbors were even parents of journeymen professional athletes. Given his humbler roots, there was something immensely satisfying about taking the trash down the driveway to wave at the mother of a onetime NBA All-Star who was out for a morning stroll. Now he was pleading his case to stay in a house that—despite being twice as tall—might have half the living space of what he and his wife had worked so hard to obtain in Maryland. Possibly less than that. A house that must have something terribly wrong with it for its owners to offer so much money for a temporary resident.

He logged off the computer and left the office, waving to the clerk, who barely nodded his way. Eric would call the number in the ad again if he didn't hear back by noon tomorrow. He believed in persistence. That was how he'd gotten his foot in the door with the cybersecurity firm he had built his career with back in Maryland. That was how he would win this job, too. He would show them that he would work the hardest, that he would be the most dedicated. And if they still passed on him, he'd give it another week here before moving on.

With continued luck and care they could avoid getting pulled over, avoid anyone who might be searching for them, and make it to his grandparents' old house in West Texas, which, based on a quick check of online listings, was still as it had been when he'd looked it up before they left Maryland. More than a bit the worse for wear, though not uninhabitable, still unable to find a buyer despite being on the market for close to a year. While he had nowhere near enough money to buy it now, maybe its owners would agree to an "off-the-books" deal. Some work and payment arrangement that would be unfavorable to him but would at least give him a chance. There were a lot of "ifs" that needed to go his way for that to work: if he could find a steadier job locally, if he could convince the sellers, if the house didn't require too many repairs to be livable, if the neighbors didn't become suspicious or even hostile toward him and his daughters. If all of those things worked out, then it could be a viable, if difficult, solution, a better prospect than being on the run forever.

Considering all those "ifs," the Degener spite house offer was much more appealing. It had only two significant "what-ifs," as far as he could tell. First: "What if it's a bogus offer?" What if this was yet another person looking to get a week or two of free work from someone too desperate to turn it down? He had tried to account for that in his recent spending, and had his guard up about such a thing, but even if he fell for it this time, he would at least get some free lodging for himself and his girls out of the deal. That wasn't payment, but it was more than nothing.

The second question was "What if the house really is haunted?" He was in no position to discount this but didn't see it as a threat sufficient to make him think twice. What harm could a ghost do?

He took one more look over his shoulder as he walked down the hall, checking to see if the clerk had her phone to her ear, or was eyeing him in a way that should make him wary. He knew that her lack of response to his wave likely didn't mean she was hiding anything, or was suspicious of him, or recognized him from some article he didn't even know about out there on the internet. Nothing unexpected or alarming about him had come up when he'd searched on the computer. Some dead links to his de-activated social media profiles. An old picture showing him as employee of the month at a sales job he'd left years ago, which barely looked like him since he'd shaved his beard and head. Likewise, his daughters' names didn't bring up any concerning search results. Still, he had cause to believe they might be followed, and he knew enough about the web to know that the obvious and well-known sites and search engines weren't necessarily the ones with the information that should worry you. For all he knew his disappearing act—despite not being newsworthy—could have gone viral and the clerk was just waiting for him to get out of earshot before calling someone to report that she'd seen him. He knew how unlikely that was, but it couldn't hurt to be a bit paranoid. It kept him alert.

Behind her counter, the clerk slouched in her chair and stared at her phone, the light of its screen reflected in her glasses. He could turn back around and talk to her now and she might greet him like it was her first time seeing him today.

He entered his motel room expecting to see his daughters but found it empty. There was a note on his pillow.

> *STACY WANTED PANCAKES. TOOK HER DOWN THE STREET. IF YOU DON'T SHOW, I'LL BRING BACK SOME CHICKEN STRIPS.—DESS.*

He took out his phone to call her, to ask her how she had enough money to dine out, and it vibrated in his hand before he could dial. He knew the number on the screen; he had read it several times today and had just called it a few minutes ago.

"Hello," he said, conscious of not wanting to sound surprised to have been called back so soon.

"May I speak to Eric Ross," a woman said.

"Speaking." He sat on the bed. He'd known many people who could stand or even pace a room and still sound composed when talking business, but he'd never even liked calling customer service to dispute a charge without sitting down first, much less discuss something this important.

"Mr. Ross, my name is Dana Cantu. I just listened to the message you left expressing interest in the house. I'd like to talk to you about scheduling a face-to-face and some other prescreening items if you have a moment."

"I do," he said, and pressed the speaker button on his phone. There was a pen on the nightstand, beside his bed. He flipped Dess's note over to take notes of his own, starting with the name "Dana Cantu" written at the top of the page. Most of what he wrote during the call, however, did not pertain to what she told him, but to what he told her. He had a strong memory when it came to the things people said to him but struggled to keep up with his lies if he didn't put them to paper.

Dess

Two hundred miles to the west was the birthplace of her great-grandparents.

Her father held a fondness for Odessa, Texas, that she found strange. He'd been there fairly often as a boy, to visit his grandparents, but from what Dess knew of her father, she didn't think the city as a whole appealed to him. It certainly wasn't attractive to her, not the parts of it she remembered from the few trips she'd taken with him and Mom to see her great-grandparents. She was much happier when Pa-Pa Fred and Ma-Ma Nelle came up to see them in Maryland, and was sure that Dad felt the same. Nonetheless, since his grandparents had passed, Dad had often spoken of his dream to buy their former home in Odessa from the people his father sold it to.

"Your pa-pa Fred basically built that house," he had told her. "It should have stayed with the family."

Now they were closer to Odessa, Texas, than they'd ever been in her life, and her father's dream had never been more futile. Dess thought she ought to feel something about that but couldn't muster a meaningful emotion.

For the third time that day, she turned the television on and skipped through channels too quickly to see if anything might hold her attention. She didn't dare hope to be entertained, merely occupied. She used to have a taste for television, but spending so much time staring at the same shows over and over for the past eight months had soured her on it. She had four paperbacks in her backpack, and had read through three of them more than once, but hadn't been able to muscle past chapter three of the remaining novel. It was written well enough but opened with and lingered on the disappearance of a young girl, something the blurb on the back had not hinted at, and that Dess found too difficult to read about.

She glanced to her left, where Stacy sat at the motel room's small desk, her legs swinging above the floor. Her doll, Miss Happy, a cotton-stuffed rag with no mouth, black ink dots for eyes, and glued-on straw for hair, sat on the table. Stacy had assisted her mother in making the doll a few years ago, and she took great care of it. Its fabric was marginally frayed, but none of the seams had come loose enough for it to be in danger of spilling its insides. Stacy's box of colored pencils rested against Miss Happy, and once in a while she would thank her doll for helping her.

Having filled up the latest coloring books Dad bought for her at a dollar store, Stacy had decided to create her own coloring book using stapled sheets of printing paper donated by the motel's clerk. She was on her third page of outlines, waiting to fill in her drawings later. Dess had looked over the first page of drawings when Stacy had finished them. It wasn't the work of an artistic prodigy, but smiling bears looked like smiling cartoon bears, dogs like friendly dogs. Houses didn't lean, and trees weren't misshapen. For an untrained seven-year-old, it was solid work.

"How did you get so good at drawing?" Dess had asked her, more a statement of encouragement than a genuine question.

Stacy had shrugged. "Pa-Pa Fred always said we could do whatever we wanted, we just have to make it happen, remember? I just kept trying because I wanted to get better."

As a big sister, Dess knew she'd had it easy when it came to helping Stacy learn her arts and crafts, the alphabet, her numbers, and anything else. She used to joke with her parents that her brilliant teaching was responsible for Stacy being ahead of most kids her age, but the truth was that Stacy was a fast and determined learner. Gifted, even. She had uncanny patience for someone her age and didn't get discouraged by failure. Any mistake was just something to learn from, and she didn't repeat most of them.

Dess glanced at the clock. Six thirty. Dad hadn't called the room to check in on them in close to two hours. Whatever he was looking into today, he was lost in it. She had the feeling it was something major, some big, wild idea, and the more she sat around thinking about it the more restless she became. She turned the television off, got up from the bed, and walked to where Stacy sat drawing and humming to herself.

"Hey Staze," Dess said, "let's get some pancakes. That little diner down the street has a sign that says, 'Breakfast All Day.'"

Stacy turned to her sister so fast she almost fell from the chair. "Really? I thought we didn't have money."

"I've got a little extra." Last night, shortly after the others had fallen asleep, Dess had snuck out and earned one hundred dollars by making a delivery run on foot, relying on speed and conditioning she'd cultivated in three years on the varsity track team. Her father wasn't the only one finding work wherever he could get it, although she found hers on considerably less reputable websites than he did. It was dicey, but necessary, she believed. Dad hadn't refilled her emergency fund in weeks. If anything should happen to him while he was out on a job, that fund was supposed to buy her time to think. There was a plan in place for what she was to do if he went out and couldn't make it back, but she didn't agree with it. They had left home for a reason. Going back wasn't a legitimate option. Plus she was eighteen now. She'd grown up a lot in the last year and a half, especially since they'd been on the road. If it came to it, she was confident she could take care of Stacy on her own.

Granted, spending any of what she had to treat the kid to some pancakes—and herself to a cheeseburger and fries—could be taken as proof that her confidence was undeserved. They had bread, cold cuts, and chips in the room. That was good enough for lunch and dinner every other day the last two weeks, and it would have been good enough tonight. But she was sick of ham sandwiches and store-brand chips, and had a little over five hundred dollars in her secret stash. She could afford to splurge at a roadside diner, even accounting for the tip.

"Don't we have to wait for Dad?" Stacy said, still in a bit of disbelief.

"Nah. We'll bring him something back. Come on."

Stacy smiled, clapped her hands once, and held them close to her chin as though saying a thankful prayer. "You think they'll have blueberries?"

"They better, or I'll tell them to go pick some, because my sister loves blueberries. But if that doesn't work, I'll let you use extra syrup, just this once. Now get your shoes on. Grab your sweater, too, in case it's chilly in there."

Dess opened the motel room door and peeked outside like a lookout, something she'd got some practice doing in her after-hours work. After confirming their father wasn't near, she hustled Stacy out in an exaggerated fashion, pointing her toward the same side door she had used the night before to avoid coming and going through the lobby.

Should have brought my own sweater, Dess thought. At Stacy's behest, they sat at a booth near the windows that faced the frontage road and highway. Hardly any of the warmth from outside penetrated the glass, however. The restaurant seemed to be overcompensating for the eighty-degree October day, as if it could be an indoor haven for autumn-seekers. She had almost broken a sweat between the diner and the motel.

Turning from the window, she scanned the restaurant as though she were one of the properly paranoid spies in her favorite novel. She looked at the other patrons scattered across the dining room, looked at the wait-staff and hostess, and wondered if she was able to read anything in their faces. Had anyone watched her and Stacy enter? Not simply seen them, but *watched* them? Were any of them watching now? Did anyone look like they were trying not to look, or trying not to get caught? Was anyone there liable to give them any trouble?

Dess tried not to presume prejudice in the people who lived here simply because this was small-town Texas, but it was what it was, and they were the only black girls in the dining area. Possibly the only darker-skinned people in the building. When one of the waitresses exited the kitchen, Dess looked through the swinging door and thought she saw a cook who might have been Hispanic or mixed, or at least had a deep tan. That was it. Everyone else she saw was white, and most were in their fifties at least. Even when they didn't look at her at all, she sensed that they wanted to, and maybe do more, such as approach and ask questions that masked warnings that doubled as threats. Or maybe not. Being one of only two or three nonwhite people in a restaurant or store was something she was still adjusting to. It wasn't a common occurrence for her back in Maryland, on the outskirts of D.C.

Their waitress—Tanya, per her name tag—came to take their order.

"Can I have pancakes with blueberries, please?" Stacy said.

"You sure can," Tanya said. She had a tune-up twang in her voice that, to Dess, made her sound a little naïve, but also kind of condescending. Dess knew that to native ears it probably didn't sound like anything.

"And what can I get you, dear?"

"Cheeseburger, medium well, please, but no onions. Some fries and a couple of waters. Thanks."

As Tanya jotted the order in her notepad, Dess thought she noticed a woman in a blue shirt and a man in plaid staring at them from a few tables over. When she looked over at them, they both looked down at their menus.

A current of anxiousness made her skin tingle. She managed to redirect it into a fist clenched under the table. This could be nothing—sometimes people didn't even realize they'd been staring until they got caught—and she didn't want to worry Stacy if that was the case. Even if it was something, it would be better for Stacy to see her big sister unflustered.

"Hungry?" she said to Stacy.

Stacy smiled back and nodded as though she'd be denied her food if she didn't show the appropriate enthusiasm.

Dess looked around the dining area once more. Maybe coming here had been a mistake. They had dined out only a handful of times since they had left home, and almost exclusively in towns and cities with a more diverse racial makeup than this. Even then, in places where they thought they could better blend in, Dess had always been a little uneasy, measuring her surroundings like a secret agent who could never sit with their back to the door, who always knew where all the exits were.

Here they were surrounded by strangers, any one of whom might have seen a picture of them in a story online that reported them as "missing." Presuming such a story even existed, to say nothing of it being important to anyone this far south. As far as Dess knew, they hadn't made any headlines in the D.C. area. Maybe they'd pulled their escape off as well as they'd hoped. Or it was possible that none of their family or friends could get anyone else to care. One of the few things they had going for them, she figured, was that missing black people weren't all that newsworthy, or much of a priority to the authorities. Fugitive black people, sure. But missing? That wasn't going to lead the news any night of the week.

Nonetheless, she knew as well as her dad that it could still circulate in other ways. Church flyers, emails, true crime blogs, or YouTube channels that specialized in unexplained vanishings. It was at least possible, then, that one of the other patrons in the diner was, at this moment, trying to recall where they'd seen these two black girls. Yes, Dess and her father had been careful, and had been fortunate to get as far they had. But one unlucky day or careless moment could undo all of that, and she wasn't being careful right now.

Stay cool. It's okay. If it's nothing and you turn it into something and get caught because you panicked, you're going to feel dumb. You're a normal girl having a normal meal with your sister. That's all they see, and if that's all you show them that's all they'll know.

Dess unclenched her fist and hoped her silence hadn't made her sister worry. Stacy appeared not to have noticed. She was busy twisting and folding a handful of paper napkins into flowers. She had already finished a carnation and had rolled the stem for what Dess expected would be an attempt at a rose.

"All right, Staze, pop quiz time," Dess said.

Stacy looked up and set her craftwork aside. "Uh-oh."

"Don't worry, this should be easy. What does 'run' mean?"

Stacy put on her serious face, which might look like a mockery to anyone who didn't know her. "'Run' means run and hide."

"Yeah. From who?"

"Everyone but you and Dad. Even police or firefighters."

"And then?"

"Stay hidden until you or Dad come find me, or until I count to a thousand."

"And how do you do that?"

"Count to ten, ten times on my fingers. Then count that as 'one,' and start over until I do the whole thing ten times."

Dess nodded and smiled. Things were probably fine. They had been so far. True, their ultimate contingency plan wasn't much of a plan at all, but it was better than nothing. As a last resort, if they were close to being caught by someone, they'd shout for Stacy to run and then Dess and her father would split up, if possible. Hopefully neither would be caught, but if one of them was, the other would track Stacy down, counting on her to evade any pursuers herself and then find a suitable hiding place that would hold for at least fifteen minutes. The reason they thought she had even the slightest chance of doing this was that she seemed able to do almost anything she really put her mind to.

They had put slim, circular GPS trackers originally designed as dog tags under the soles of her shoes. They weren't thin enough for Stacy not to feel them, but she never complained about them or walked differently because of them. The trackers advertised a relatively limited range, and they hadn't tested the tracking app's reliability much out of reluctance to use a location feature on their phones. Still, the limited tests they had performed showed some promise.

During practice runs Stacy had found hiding places not too far from where she'd started, which was good, but she hadn't hidden herself too well, either, so losing her was less of a concern than her being found by someone canvassing the area. Again, it was only for emergencies, and was mostly there to give them a semblance of control, a sense of preparedness for the worst, even if it had little chance of success.

Tanya returned with the waters and let out a small gasp at Stacy's handiwork.

"Look at that. Aren't you creative? Where'd you learn how to do that?"

"I saw someone else doing it one time," Stacy said, her smile having returned, "so I taught myself."

Tanya's eyebrows lifted like she'd seen a minor yet impressive coin trick. "Can you make a bow?"

"I think I can."

"Can you make one for me? I have a little girl at home who loves bows. She'd get a kick out of it."

"Yes, ma'am," Stacy said, and set aside the stem she had been working on to fulfill this new request.

Dess's phone buzzed with a text from her father. *On my way*, it read. She had hoped he wouldn't join them. He had to be wondering how she got the money to dine out, and that would lead to a conversation she would rather avoid. At least she doubted he would bring it up in front of Stacy. Still, if he was coming, there had to be something he wanted to talk about that couldn't wait.

She took a deep breath and tried to relax, tried to enjoy as much of the moment as she could, to feel normal for a while before Dad arrived. She was in a restaurant with her baby sister. The place smelled like fried food that probably had way more salt and butter than her old track coach would have approved of, and she loved it. Not half as much as the smell of the kitchen back home when Mom and Dad were cooking dinner two or three nights a week. Not a tenth as much as that, but that was long gone, so she had to do like that old song said and love what she was with, as much as she could.

Across the highway there were trees that hadn't changed color or lost any leaves yet. Dad had told her when they passed through Austin that the fall barely touched most of Texas, and the parts that did get some color and coolness didn't get it the same way Maryland did. That made sense, of course, but it was one thing to know it, another to see it and feel it and miss home that much more because of it. When they had left, she'd thought of other, more immediate things she would miss. Mom most of all, even though she had already had time to miss her before they moved. Then there were her cousins, aunties, and uncles. School, too. Not friends, so much. Most of them had peeled away in the months before they'd had to leave. Not the old house all that much either, or so she'd thought at the time. In hindsight, she'd been fooling herself, but in the moment the house had been attached to so much sadness, and then strangeness, that she thought it would be good to get away. What she hadn't considered was how much she would miss the first September chill. Red, orange, and yellow leaves. Pinecones on the ground. Across the street she saw greens and browns that lasted into the winter. This made her sadder than it should have, and she shook her head to snap out of it.

Dess didn't know exactly how long she had spaced out, but when she looked at her sister she saw that Stacy had already made the bow Tanya had requested. Dess remembered when she had shown Stacy the video of someone making the napkin flowers and other simple decorations. It had been a quick tutorial, and the woman in the video had also used proper supplies, including tape, twine, and scissors. Stacy didn't need any of that. She tore one napkin to strips and used them to tie tight, unobtrusive knots. It only took her a minute or two longer than the woman from the video to make her bow.

Stacy held it up. "You think she'll like it?"

"Bet. I think she'll love it."

Out of the corner of her eye, through the window, Dess saw someone approaching the restaurant. She turned, saw that it was her father. When he waved at her, she looked away as though she could undo being seen. She chuckled at this, recalling one of her last happy memories among friends before her world changed. During a lock-in with the track team she and a few others snuck out after lights out, just to hang out and talk. After a while one of the coaches heard them and when she approached, Dess and her teammates fell silent as if Coach wouldn't be able see them if she couldn't hear them. Coach walked up and stared at them, and Dess knew she had to speak up first before someone else tried to come up with a bullshit explanation that would get them in more trouble. So she said, "We were all just out here praying for you, Coach. No lie."

That got a laugh out of everyone, Coach included, and Dess was sure that her desperate little joke had shaved a few laps off their punishment.

She was still smiling when her dad joined them. He sat next to Stacy in the booth, and she beamed at him. He put the jobs page of the local newspaper on the table. The photograph of a house on the page that was faceup drew her attention. For a second she thought it was just *part* of a house, the improbably freestanding ruin left over after a storm or fire took the rest away. Then she saw where it was built, at the edge of a hill, and realized it must have been built as thin as it was on purpose to fit on the strip of land between the slope in front of the house and the trees behind it.

It looked like something left behind after a disaster. She'd seen a video online a couple of years ago that told the story of an old dam that collapsed in California. An enormous wave had rushed through a valley and killed hundreds. The biggest remnant of the dam was a slab that locals called "the tombstone." It hadn't been nearly as tall as the dam had been but was still tall enough that a fall from it would kill you. That was exactly what happened to some unfortunate sightseer who climbed it years later. That last death had been enough to make city officials blow up the tombstone and keep that old, failed dam from killing anyone else. Dess had a feeling that someone should have done the same thing to this strange old house. They should have blown it up years ago.

God, why did she think that? Yeah, it looked weird, but it was still just a house, wasn't it? She blinked and brought the paper up for a closer look, but leaned back away from the picture as she did so. It was the sort of thing she used to tease her mom for doing when she didn't have her glasses on, except Dess wasn't tilting back because the image suddenly went blurry. She did so reflexively, like she was scared of seeing something she didn't want to. A face in a window maybe. Or something worse.

Dess rubbed at the imaginary bug crawling on her neck, and was glad when Stacy broke the silence.

"Look, Dad," Stacy said, showing off her bow and flowers.

"I see," Eric said. "What's all this for?"

"The waitress lady saw me making flowers and asked me to make a bow for her daughter."

"That's so cool," Eric said. He looked at Dess. "Waitress sounds friendly."

Dess said, "Yeah, but I think it's ninety-nine percent the accent, though. Everybody down here sounds like they want to call me 'sugar.'"

"They don't all sound like that, believe me."

"Yeah, nah. I'm going to keep thinking it's all 'howdy' and 'sweetie' and all that other stuff. Especially since we're probably going to be here awhile, right? Even if we went straight through it still takes like five years to get out of Texas, don't it?"

"Five years?" Stacy said.

"I'm being silly," Dess told her sister. "It would take us a while, though."

"And we might be here longer than you think," Eric said. He took the newspaper from her hands and tapped a finger on the headline of the ad beneath the picture of the strange, narrow house.

Paranormal documentarian needed.
Serious inquiries only. No experience required.

Dess shook her head. "This isn't for real, is it?"

"I just called and talked to them about it. They seem sincere. Urgent, too. They want to interview me tomorrow. I told them I needed to check with my daughter to see if it was okay first, and they were good with that."

"Okay, hold up, wait. This is wild. So you talked to somebody already? When did that happen?"

"Maybe ten minutes ago. I called them and they called right back."

"And we're just gonna go there? Where's it at?" Dess checked the ad again. "Where is Degener?"

"About two hours away. Not that far."

"What if these people are like, you know . . ." She glanced at Stacy and tried to think of how to say what she wanted to say without scaring her. Then she thought, screw it, they'd been in survival mode since they had hit the road and Stacy was a part of that. There were certain risks and concerns she needed to understand. "Do they know what we look like?"

"I brought it up," Eric said. "The lady I talked to, her last name is Cantu, so that made me feel better already. She just kind of chuckled when I mentioned it and said it's not an issue."

Dess's eyes widened a little. "First off, she could've married and divorced that last name and be a whole damn racist by now. And she laughed when you brought it up? Dad, that sounds suspect as hell."

"It wasn't an evil laugh from a movie villain, Dess. It was more, 'Oh, that's nothing.' And then she said, 'That's not an issue at all.' That's a direct quote."

Dess shook her head and checked to see if Stacy understood the conversation they were having. She'd been paying attention to them but wasn't the type of kid to speak up just to be heard. She had a question in her eyes, though, Dess saw.

"What does 'paranormal' mean?" Stacy said.

"It means, um, unusual," Eric answered. He threw a look across the table at Dess that she read to mean, *Don't mention ghosts.* She tossed a look back that she hoped said, *Yeah, nah, I'm not stupid.*

"Are they talking about the house? Why do they say it's unusual? Because it's so skinny?" Stacy said.

"I think so," Eric said.

"Why is it like that?"

"That's a good question. I don't know. You want to go there and find out?"

Stacy tapped her chin like she was thinking it over, then nodded and grinned. Eric smiled and looked at Dess, who was about to accuse him of playing dirty, getting Stacy interested in this weird place before they had a chance to talk it all the way through, when Tanya returned to take Eric's order—chicken strips, fries, water with lemon. Tanya saw the bow Stacy had made and thanked her. "What's your name, darling?"

"Stacy."

"Oh, I love that name. Well my little girl is named Libby, and she is going to love this. And I am going to make sure she thanks you by name when she says her prayers tonight."

"Thank you," Stacy said.

After Tanya left, Eric said, "Maybe Degener's full of people like that."

The ad had stolen Dess's attention again, so while she heard him, she didn't react to what he said. She was fixated on the promised payout upon "completion of the assignment." Six figures at minimum, with the potential for more. "There has to be a catch, right? I mean, I know it says we don't need experience, but this is a lot of money. Why would they pick us? What do we even know about these people?"

He slid two more pages across the table, an article with the title "Merchant Saint and Mercurial Queen of the Hill Country."

"It doesn't go into detail about it," Eric said, "but that mentions that the house is owned by a very rich woman named Eunice Houghton."

"You think this is real?" Dess said while scanning the article.

"It all checks out so far as I can tell. I even looked up the lady who wrote the piece. She's worked for major publishers, won a bunch of awards. It's not just something off a random blog."

Dess's eyes floated to the byline. Emily Steen. She wanted to say something about not recognizing the name, as if that might mean something to her father, but held off. It wasn't like she had off-top knowledge of renowned journalists. Instead she focused on what she picked up about the house's owner. Eunice Houghton was a benevolent multimillionaire—if one could truly be such a thing—and founder of something called ValTuf Wellness, which had apparently been around for decades. They specialized in fitness electronics and personal health monitors that had begun as exclusives for professional trainers and trendy gyms before gradually becoming available to consumers directly. They owned patents that they licensed to better-known brands, which in turn used ValTuf components in their higher-end devices.

This was all well and good until Dess read how the original manufacturing site and headquarters in Degener had so tied Eunice to the local economy that she effectively owned the town. The money she brought in had benefits, as did the people she brought in from other manufacturing sites in larger cities. The financial viability and influx of out-of-towners contributed to Degener being an "oddly progressive anomaly for the area," according to the article. But that was only part of it. Apparently, people in town feared angering Eunice or even her subordinates. She influenced the local school's curriculum, particularly when it came to local history and ensuring it didn't gloss over certain ugly events in America's past, a good thing, but not something Eunice should have had a say in.

Similarly, years ago, she had all but ordered the mayor to declare Juneteenth an unofficial holiday, complete with a small carnival, and strongly "encouraged" any inessential businesses in town to shut down for the day. No one dared to object. Emily Steen applauded the outcome, but questioned the process that created it, which wasn't really a process at all, just the whim of one powerful person. The story then ventured into Eunice's ownership of the spite house, and the strangers she'd paid to live in the house—who never lasted very long.

"Dad, this lady seems a little bit out there, doesn't she?"

"She built a tech empire. How out there can she be?"

Dess stared at her father like he'd suggested she pet a snake because "How venomous could it be?" He stared back for a few seconds before cracking a smile that let her know he knew how absurd his comment was.

"So you talked to her, too?" Dess said.

"No, just Dana. But I was invited to talk to Eunice tomorrow. In person."

"You must have made a great first impression," Dess said. "How much did you tell?"

Her father smiled in a sad way that stabbed at her heart. "I told her about the places we've been staying. A general—if inexact—idea of where we're from, how far we've come, and how limited our options are. I took a gamble that it wouldn't scare her off. I think it worked."

Dess nodded, but still had a sour taste in her mouth. "I still don't know. I think it's weird."

"It definitely is," Eric said, "but it also might be a chance. We should at least check it out, see if it's legit, don't you think? Unless you know about some money coming in that I don't know about."

That statement—the way he said it—brought Dess back to her younger days, to when she was a little older than her sister was now, and a lot more rambunctious. Sometimes, when she'd really gotten out of hand at school, she would come home and Mom would ask, "Anything particularly interesting happen today?" Which was different from her usual "How was school?" or "Have fun at school?" When Dess would shake her head to say no, nothing interesting had happened, Dad would follow up with, "You're sure? Nothing you think we ought to know about?" And that was when she would know that the teacher had already called and told one of them, who had then told the other, and they were just giving her a chance to confess, which she would typically turn down, because there was always a chance they were bluffing, right? Sure, she was probably already caught, but she always had to try.

"Hey, Dess," Stacy said.

"What's up, Staze?"

"If you're worried about the house because it looks weird, you don't have to be. It's okay. I figured out why it's so skinny."

"Yeah? Why?"

Stacy snickered, then said, "Because it hasn't had enough to eat." Then she laughed like she'd told the best joke she'd ever tell.

CHAPTER 3

Eric

Hours later, at the motel, as soon as he was sure that Stacy was asleep, Eric said to Dess, "Since when do you have money to take her to eat?"

It would have been easier to leave the subject untouched, at least until tomorrow if not indefinitely. His distrust of anything that struck him as easy encouraged him to broach it now.

"I found an extra twenty, that's all," Dess said.

"Mm-hm."

"If it's that big of a deal to you I can just give you what I have now."

"It's not about that, and you know it," Eric said. "And if twenty was all the extra you 'found,' you'd have held on to it."

"You want to know how much I've got?"

"You don't have to tell me if you don't want to. I just need to know you're not doing anything wild out there."

"I'm not, like, charging randos fifty bucks a kiss if that's what you mean."

"There's a lot of other stuff you could be doing that I would hope you wouldn't do."

"Such as?"

He leaned forward, pressed his stubborn gaze against hers, and lowered his voice. "Anything that could circle back to you and be a problem we can't fix."

Dess shook her head and lay back in bed. "I hate when you do that."

"Remind you of something you should already know?"

She rolled her eyes. "No. When you sound like Pa-Pa Fred. Put on your deep voice and your super serious face. It freaks me out."

"Well, if he was here he would . . ." Eric trailed off.

"You were about to lie and say he'd say the same thing you were saying," Dess said.

Eric couldn't help but smile. "I was. Truth is, he'd probably be proud of you. Except he'd probably be upset you weren't carrying a knife or a little baby pistol, just in case you needed it for whatever."

"Yeah, in case I needed to 'make something happen,' instead of just letting it happen."

They both laughed quietly, though neither found it very funny, as if Frederick could hear them and they were being polite.

After a sigh, Dess said, "Dad, I think we're already in the middle of a problem we can't fix."

"Maybe we can with this new opportunity. The thing in Degener. I think we've got a real shot here. After the talk we had today I've just got a feeling. That lady Dana could have just told me, 'Thanks, but no thanks,' or not even called me back, but she told me to come in. There has to be a reason for that. I think I have a shot at this. I really do."

Dess looked at Stacy again, and Eric wondered if she was reminding herself why they were where they were, the decisions they had made, what was at stake. "I've been pretty careful, Dad, just for the record. I might be even smarter than you always say I think I am."

At this, he smirked, as did she. Both smiles disappeared in a couple of seconds.

"I had to do something," Dess said. "You were barely finding any jobs."

"I know, I know. I understand. But whatever you've been doing, you don't have to anymore. Look, driving to Degener won't set us back any, right? I do this interview, they either make an offer or they don't. If they don't, we come back, we stick to the plan. I know it's been a little sketchy but, believe it or not, it's been working for us so far. On the other hand, if they give me the job, she said we'd get an advance just for moving in. Then we stay there, we power through it, I do the work, and we're set. They want to hear about knocks and footsteps at night, I'll tell them about everything I hear. It's an old place, I'm sure I won't have to lie about it. And afterward we should have enough money to probably get a house with some land and space. Hell, probably enough where neither of us would have to look for work for a while, let alone take a job that might be trouble."

"Hm. You know, if I said something like that to you, you'd be like"—

she deepened her voice, clasped her hands across her chest, and raised one eyebrow—"I heard a 'should' and a 'probably' just a few words apart."

"That impression isn't getting any better. You don't work on it at all when I'm not around, do you?"

"It's like ninety-nine percent there. I did the eyebrow and hand thing and everything. For a sec *you* almost thought I was you."

They shared a laugh, with Eric's being a little louder than it had to be. Part of him wanted to at least see Stacy stir at the sound of it. He never liked how deeply she could sleep. She didn't budge, though, and he said to Dess, "Let's call it a night. We got a drive tomorrow. And if the house actually has anything weird going on with it, besides the way it looks, this could be our last chance to get some decent sleep for a while."

Dess shut her eyes. "You really think there could be something there?"

"Probably not. Hopefully not." He waited for Dess to tease him about his choice of words one more time, but she didn't say anything. Eric stayed awake a few more minutes, listening for Dess's breathing to steady itself. It gradually did, settling into a rhythm that almost matched Stacy's. After he was sure she was asleep, he laid his head on his pillow.

As was his custom since they'd been on the road, he slept fully clothed— keys and phone in his right pocket, wallet in his left—in case something happened that demanded a quick exit.

Stacy

Stacy heard her name in her sleep and knew that the person who said it was a little girl named Libby who was the daughter of the nice waitress lady. Libby had thanked Stacy in her prayers, just like her mother had said she would, and now Stacy could see her. Libby slept with a night-light. She slept in a bed with purple sheets. She slept on her side with the paper bow Stacy had made for her clipped to her blond hair.

Stacy couldn't see into Libby's room until after she heard her name, and it must have taken her some time to get there, because when she did, Libby woke up like she heard someone come through the door. Libby wiped at her eyes and looked around, then rested her head on her pillow with her eyes open.

Stacy got bored soon, watching Libby for a long time, feeling every second of it and wishing something interesting would happen. When the door creaked open, though, Stacy immediately wished she could go back to when nothing was happening. Something was wrong, now. Someone was there who shouldn't be. She couldn't see them, but she could smell them. Flowers and spice. It would have been pleasant if there weren't so much of it. Libby smelled it too. She pulled her covers over her nose.

That someone carried a cold with them that made Stacy wish she had a coat. They moved to the bed and whispered to Libby in an old woman's voice. "Hey there, sweetie. I missed you."

Libby whined and shook her head.

"Why are you acting like that?" they said. "Aren't you glad to see me?"

Something brushed Libby's hair, carrying the locks that held her paper bow into the air for a second before letting them fall.

Libby shook her head again. "You're not real."

"That's not nice to say," the old woman said. "Your mother should have raised you better than to talk back like that."

For a moment, Stacy felt a small bit of pride, knowing that she was the reason it was possible. That the bow she made created a way for the old woman to be here, and not just in the room, but in this world. Stacy felt good until she realized how scared Libby was, and she felt sick. It didn't matter that this was just a dream, she didn't like making anyone feel scared.

Breathing heavily now, Libby was able to calm down enough to say, "If you're really Grandma, then what's my favorite story?"

The old woman laughed in a way that made Stacy want to run. "'The Golden Arm,'" she said. "Do you want me to tell it now?"

"No. No! I told you—"

"Oh, you always told me to read something else, but that story taught you not to be greedy, didn't it?"

"Why were you so mean?" Libby said.

"I was no such thing," the woman said, her voice gaining an edge. "You watch what you say about me, young lady."

"You never liked me."

"Adults don't have to like little children. Especially rude little girls spoiled by their mothers." The woman's voice changed to something sweeter before she spoke again, like she was a monster wearing a fairy costume. "We're supposed to *love* you. And I did. Part of loving someone is teaching them things, even if they don't want to learn. That's why I read that story, remember?"

"You just liked scaring me," Libby said.

"No, I wanted to tell you about what happens to greedy, selfish people who take things without thinking of giving to others. That's what that story is really about."

"I want you to go away."

If Stacy could have turned herself into a bigger, scarier monster and shown herself to the invisible old woman, she would have. She felt responsible even if she didn't understand why.

Something brushed against the little girl's hair again. This time, Libby sat up and pulled the paper bow from her head. Libby eyed it like it was dangerous. Like a small, cute animal that could bite one of her fingers off. Stacy recognized it, too. Stacy knew that if Libby got rid of the bow— ripped it up, burned it, or threw it out of her window—the old woman would go away. The bow had some kind of magic in it, like the old hat that brought Frosty to life in the song, but the wrong kind of magic, like if the hat made Frosty into a giant beast with icicle teeth. Stacy didn't know how she made such a thing, and part of her wanted Libby to give the bow back to her so she could take it to her dad or Dess, see if they knew why it was the way it was, but the bigger part of her wanted Libby to do whatever she needed to do to make the old woman leave.

"You be careful with that, Libby," the woman said of the bow. "Someone made that for you, didn't they? It was a gift, and you're thinking of doing who knows what to it. I see that look in your eye, young lady. I know you better than your own mother knows you. I know what kind of mischief gets into that head of yours, and I will not stand—"

Libby tore the bow in half and the woman stopped talking.

The next thing Stacy saw was the morning. Her sister and father were already up and getting themselves ready for the road. They were going somewhere today, she remembered. Where was it? Oh, right, the skinny house from the newspaper.

Dess

They had come up with a game for the road that Stacy called "ABC's." It differed from the more commonly known road trip game where one went through the alphabet by spotting signs along the road that started with the letter A, then B, then on through the rest of the alphabet. Stacy didn't enjoy that one as much. Dess thought it was because the game only consisted of spotting signs. You needed to be alert, but you didn't have to think. Stacy liked to stretch her brain and come up with things on her own. So Dess had helped her come up with their family's version of the ABC's.

The first person would say a word starting with "A," the next person would say one starting with "B," then "C," and so on. The rules were that your word had to be somehow related to the previous word, but not related in the same way as the previous word was related to *its* previous word. If you couldn't change the relationship, or couldn't think of a word, you would lose a point.

Early in their drive to Degener, when Stacy, who had the backseat to herself, said she wanted to play, she started with the word "apple." Dess said, "Banana," since they were both fruits. Their father couldn't say another fruit, like "cherry," so he went with "canary," a yellow bird to match the yellow banana peel, which led Stacy to say, "Dolphin," and Dess to say, "Evian," and Eric to say, "Fire hydrant," which was doubly wrong since it was two words and still water related. Stacy had still seemed a bit drowsy at the time, but perked up when she got to exclaim, "Daddy loses a point!"

"That's right," Dess said.

Eric put up a mock protest that "fire hydrant" was hyphenated and that since fire was the opposite of water he shouldn't lose a point, but the sisters stuck together in judging that his score was down to four while they each still had five.

"You should have just said 'fire,'" Stacy said, giggling.

"Oh man, you're right," Eric said. "Why didn't I just say that?" After a quick wink to Dess he picked the game back up at the letter "G."

If nothing else, the game gave Dess something to do besides stare out the window as the scenery passed, singing songs to herself to pass the minutes. There was only so much she could discuss with her dad when Stacy was awake. She had tried to get into other things such as writing and sketching, but those things didn't appeal to her. The only peaceful, sit-down solo activity she enjoyed was reading, and even that she preferred to do outside of the car, as she was prone to mild car sickness and could never fully focus on what she was reading anyway.

She missed being more active. More than that, she missed being a leader. She hadn't been All-State or even All-City, and wouldn't have been up for a track scholarship, but she'd won her share of meets, and Coach had once confided that she was the most valuable person on the team. Even as a sophomore on varsity she'd had upperclassmen who came to her for advice, though most were too prideful to directly ask for it. That was okay. It gave her a chance to exercise her charisma and empathy, understand what her teammates were asking for without them having to say it, and then suggest a solution without sounding like she was trying to give orders. She didn't like telling people what to do, but she loved being recognized as reliable.

On the road, when she looked out the window, she often saw herself running alongside the car, her stride graceful and measured, less powerful and urgent than rhythmic, and that image would soothe her for a little while, until it depressed her. The first time she had snuck out of a motel a couple of hours past midnight, they had been near Charlotte, and she'd done it because the image of her running had gotten stuck in a loop in her head for several nights in a row, and she had struggled to sleep because of it. She hadn't gone out looking for a shady way to make a little extra money, she had gone to an open field she had spotted nearby, one that kept its lights on all night, and had run the length of it, back and forth, just to feel the air rush by and her heart pumping.

She wasn't as afraid of encountering anyone as she probably should have been. She was sure she could outrun the average person who posed a threat. If it came to a fight, it depended on who her attacker was. One-on-one with a girl her size, or even one slightly bigger, she loved her chances. Even if it was two-on-one, she thought she could do enough damage early to make them see it wasn't worth it. If it was a guy, her best bet was to play helpless long enough for him to let his guard down, then go for something sensitive, like her great-grandfather told her.

"The eyes are a good place to start," Pa-Pa Fred had said. "Everybody's scared of losing an eye. You have to really go for it, though, like you're planning to put it in your pocket for later. Don't be afraid to use your teeth. Bite a nose, bite their ears. I've seen pro boxers who can take a hundred punches freak out when someone bit a piece of their ear off. You've got to go after whatever you can get to. That's how you avoid being someone who let something bad happen to you. Instead you make it happen to them."

She'd been too young for this lesson, just ten years old, but he'd given it to her one summer while they were visiting him and Ma-Ma Nelle in Odessa. She came home from the park that afternoon with scratches on her arms. She could have told any of the other adults in the house about the older boy who picked on her for "not being from here," pulling her hair, shoving her to the ground, but she somehow knew the boy would get into more trouble if she told Pa-Pa Fred. She didn't realize how much trouble that would be until later.

She described the boy to her great-grandfather, and he nodded and said, "I know who that is. I'll take care of it." Then he was gone for about an hour or so. Later that evening, there was a knock at the door. Pa-Pa Fred brought her out to the porch to see the boy who had picked on her, his father standing next to him. Pa-Pa Fred stood behind Dess, his shadow blotting out the porch light, darkening the two people in front of her. Still, she saw the struggle between worry and anger in the father's eyes, and the bewildered fear in the face of the boy, who looked much younger and smaller here than he had at the park.

"Go on," the father said to his son. "Tell her."

"I-I-I'm sorry," the boy said. His father immediately smacked him hard on the back of his neck. The boy bit down on a cry of pain.

"Sorry for what," the father said. "You better say it how I told you."

The boy took two hitching breaths to compose himself. It seemed like he wanted to cry but had already done too much of it earlier, and didn't have any tears or energy left for it. "I'm sorry for being mean and hurting you today," he said softly.

His father looked at Pa-Pa Fred and for a moment his eyes bulged. He swallowed. Whatever he saw in Pa-Pa Fred's face made him forget to breathe for a second. Dess almost looked back at her great-grandfather, but her insides got watery at the thought of it. She didn't want to see him the way this other man was seeing him. For some reason she didn't think he would look stern or angry. She thought he would be smiling.

The father smacked the boy again, harder this time, knocking his son off-balance. The sound of it shocked Dess and made her want to cover her ears, but she didn't dare move. She knew her great-grandfather would disapprove of any show of sympathy.

"Speak up and say it like you mean it, damn it," the father said, his voice cracking and his lip quivering for half a second. For an instant he looked even more distraught than his son.

"I'm sorry that I was mean to you," the boy almost shouted. "I'm really sorry. I promise I won't do it again."

The father looked again at Pa-Pa Fred, a grimace on his face, pleading in his eyes.

Pa-Pa Fred said, "Well, what do you say, baby girl? Do you accept his apology?"

Dess nodded quickly, and the father hustled his boy away from the house and to their car parked at the curb.

When they got back in the house, Dess could tell that her parents, Grandpa, and Ma-Ma Nelle had heard everything and were upset, but none of them challenged Pa-Pa Fred about it. Grandpa looked like he might say something when Pa-Pa Fred said he was going to teach her to fight, but Pa-Pa Fred cut him off. "Not gonna let my great-granddaughter get shoved around by anybody. I won't always be there to deal with things like this, and it doesn't look like any of y'all want to take care of it."

Mom asked if she could join the lesson and Pa-Pa Fred said, "Sure." Later, Mom said it was actually good for Dess to learn how to defend herself. It was practical. Even then, though, Dess knew Dad's feelings were hurt by the suggestion that he couldn't care for his child.

Now, Dess couldn't help but be somewhat grateful for that early training, even if the memory of what prompted it made her feel like she was floating, and not in a good way, but like she was a stiff breeze away from never touching the ground again. She didn't want to think of herself as capable of doing what Pa-Pa Fred did to that boy and his father. She hoped she'd never have to employ his lessons about fighting, either. But if it really came to it, she knew she had at least a little bit of the old man in her. She had, after all, effectively adapted his little philosophy. "You either let things happen, or you make them happen." The former was how you ended up a victim, according to Pa-Pa Fred. The latter was how you stayed ahead of a world that was out to get you. Sitting back while Dad struggled to find work, hoping the money wouldn't dry up, that was letting things happen. Getting out there and finding an alternate means of income was making something happen.

When a group of teenagers showed up her second night of running at the field, she eyed them carefully for a while. They were loud and a little obnoxious, but there were more girls than boys in the group, and they were a mixed bunch—black and white and one Asian girl, and one kid who mixed a few Spanish words in when he spoke. All of which made her feel a little safer. One of the boys carried a skateboard with him in a way that made Dess think all he ever did was carry it. They were like a small-town version of the group of kids smiling at the camera on a college brochure. Instead of gathering for a study group, they had snuck out to drink and smoke. Except, Dess overheard, the one in charge of bringing the weed only brought enough for himself, and none of them wanted to walk back to buy more from the boy's older brother.

"Hey, I'll do it for you," Dess said before she could talk herself out of it.

They looked at her like she was one of their teachers who'd just used some slang incorrectly. *I'm barely a year older than any of you, at most,* she thought. But the last year had probably aged her in ways that she couldn't sense the way they could.

"You'll do what?" the kid with the skateboard said.

"Run back and buy you your smokes."

After a brief back-and-forth during which they first expressed skepticism over Dess's seriousness, then half-heartedly accused her of wanting to run off with their money, they finally agreed to pay her if she'd make the literal run for them. That was when Dess discovered she could make an extra forty bucks or more just for running.

She wondered if such opportunities would exist in Degener. Maybe it wouldn't be necessary if Dad's deal was legit. She'd believe that when they actually got paid. Until then, she had to think ahead, consider the next

move, weigh the pros and cons. It was dangerous to be out at night running petty-criminal errands, especially in some of these small towns where
"Teenage Stranger Caught with Weed" might be the biggest story of the
week behind the score of the recent high school football game. But was it
that much more dangerous than sitting back and doing nothing until they
ran out of money?

After four rounds of ABC's in the car, three of which Stacy won, with
Dess winning one to make sure Stacy didn't suspect that they were letting
her win, Stacy said, "Me and Miss Happy are going to color some." She
got out her book and crayons, and Dad turned the radio up after finding
the local NPR affiliate.

Dess eventually saw her phantom running up and around decent-sized
hills. What she'd seen of Texas so far—by way of Houston, then heading
northwest—had been low and flat, its trees unremarkable, the occasional
lake or river providing a slight change-up. From what her father had told
her, his grandparents' hometown was more of the same, except drier, and
with even fewer trees. What she saw now had some genuine beauty to
it. Broad hills that seemed to have been imported from elsewhere. Big
trees, wider at the top than they were tall, but still notable, especially the
ones that stood alone, like they'd stretched out their limbs and chased all
the others off. They didn't have quite as much character as the ones back
home, or some of the mossy trees she'd seen in Mississippi or Georgia, or
the ones coming up out of that swamp basin they'd driven over in Louisi-
ana, but they were still a sight.

"You see this, Staze?" Dess said. "All the hills?"

"Uh-huh. It's nice," Stacy said, sounding far less enamored than her
sister. Dess glanced back at her and saw that the ride was lulling Stacy to
sleep.

"I'll be fine if you want to grab a quick nap, too," her father said.

Dess shook her head. "Yeah, nah. I'm okay." She didn't sleep while her
dad was driving, just like he didn't let himself sleep on the rare occasions
when he let her drive. It was important to have more than one set of eyes
on the road, especially when driving through what they termed "the Red."
Places where WE BACK THE BLUE bumper stickers or star-spangled Punisher
skull decals and the like became more prevalent. Places they wanted to get
through as quickly as possible, but where they absolutely couldn't afford to
drive too fast or even too slowly.

They didn't exactly have a set strategy for evading a squad car if lights started flashing directly behind them. Their plan was simply to stay out of trouble, so it was important for the passenger to remain reasonably attentive in case the driver had missed a speed-limit sign or might be succumbing to highway hypnosis that could cause them to drift out of their lane. Nothing but luck could keep them from getting pulled over by an officer determined to pull over some black or brown people for no reason, but for those who needed a reason, they would deny them one by keeping careful.

Still, even while trying to remain vigilant, a little bit of daydreaming was permissible. Dess was glad to have a chance to do that now. Picture herself running the hills, not toward any destination or for any preset distance or time. Carrying nothing but her own weight, no anxiety or responsibility. For a few seconds at a time, between glances into the rearview and side mirrors and through the front windshield, she could almost feel what it might be like to have a normal life again.

Just before they passed the big, rustic sign that welcomed travelers to Degener, Texas, Dess noticed without commenting that the cars here were different than they had been ten or so miles back. Not all of them, or even most, but enough to stand out. There were fewer pickup trucks and more entry-level luxury cars. Far fewer bumper stickers, more cars adorned with a simple magnetic cross on the back, if anything at all. These were the kinds of cars her crew back home used to talk about buying after they graduated and "made it." Not the super exclusive foreign ones certain rappers bragged about, but the ones driven by a friend's oldest brother, or your homegirl's cousin who was making so much money as a nurse it made you think about majoring in medicine. The one difference between these cars near Degener and the dream cars her friends had talked about was that these Cadillacs and BMWs and Infinitis were all either silver, black, or white. "Adulting" colors, she thought. Not a sports-car red in the bunch, much less a yellow, blue, or—the color she'd have picked for her first Lexus—pink.

As they made their way deeper through Degener, Dess noticed how clean and kempt and similar the houses were. Throughout the South she'd gotten used to seeing a fair share of proudly weathered little houses sitting on about half a football field of land, septic tank in plain sight, an old truck around the side, maybe. A fence up, possibly a flag or two as well, either celebrating the country they lived in or the rebel army that lost to said country two hundred years ago, or, incongruously, both. Some of those houses looked nicer than their brethren, but they all had a fair amount of age and even more character. Those houses didn't appear to exist in Degener, or at least not in the part they were driving through. On the edges of town, maybe, but every house visible in every direction off Main Street fit the description of neat, tidy, pleasant enough, and unremarkable. She wondered how much of it was really like this but knew her curiosity would go unsatisfied. They weren't here to tour the town, just to get a look at the spite house prior to her father's interview.

They were leaving the more congested and developed part of Degener when she finally said, "This place is different."

"I think I see it too," her father said. "It's a good sign, isn't it? Should mean the money is real."

Dess nodded, but didn't really feel the same way. She didn't find what she saw directly suspicious, either. She didn't quite know what to make of it, except that it was unexpected, and they both knew well that the unexpected could be a curse or a blessing.

The directions her father had printed took them four more miles down Main before they took a right onto a road that wound toward two hills in the distance. Once they cleared an initial canopy of trees they got a clearer view of the hills and saw that the one to the left, the taller of the two, had a house on top, right at the lip of its slope, like it wanted to lean over for a look but was a little too scared. That was how it looked to Dess, anyway, and thinking of it being scared instead of being scary kept her stomach from completely rolling over at the sight of it. Because its strangeness was otherwise as off-putting as it was magnetic, even at a distance. She had figured the picture was exaggerating to some degree, making the house seem leaner and more bizarre than it really was. Really it was the opposite. What she felt now was the difference between seeing a photo of a house fire and witnessing the flames in person.

"There it is," her dad said.

"Yeah."

Marked with signs reading PRIVATE PROPERTY, the road snaked one way then back the other multiple times during the remaining fifteen minutes of the drive. Despite those many turns, the thin house high above never seemed to move far from the center frame of the windshield.

They did not drive fully onto the site, stopping short when the road forked just before the valley. Dess glanced at the buildings to their right, down below, but they couldn't hold more than a second of her attention. She couldn't even remember what her dad had said about them yesterday. They didn't matter. It was the place where they might live, the oddity up above them, that held her.

This close, she could see something that hadn't been present in the picture. A bulge in the building that ran broadside along the third floor, like a long balcony that had been walled up ages ago. Goose bumps rose on her arms.

Her father looked back at Stacy and said, "Think I should wake her up? Might be better for her to see it earlier instead of later."

"I don't know," Dess said. "I don't know, Dad. I don't know anything. I don't know about this."

"What's wrong?"

She shook her head. "This just feels really too real right now. I guess I thought it would look more like a goofy tourist trap or something. Like the pictures might look one way, but then in person it wouldn't be *this*. It's just wrong, right? I mean who builds a house like that? What kind of house did you say it is again?"

"A spite house," her dad said. "That's what it said on the sites I went to."

"What does that even mean?"

"Pretty much what you think. A place built just to make someone upset or show the world how pissed you are. Apparently, there are several of them."

"Here?"

Her dad laughed. "No, sorry. I meant around the country. Even the world from the little bit I read. Don't think any of the others look quite like this though. This had to be put where it is and built how it is for a reason."

"What reason?"

Her dad shrugged.

"You couldn't find that out when you were looking stuff up?"

He smiled. "It's like those stories your mom used to tell you about that old hospital in Mississippi. There are still some stories that only make it about halfway to the internet."

Dess nodded, even though she felt like this was different. Her mother's tales of the haunted hospital in Biloxi, where she'd grown up, had felt a little too personal to be part of internet lore. The reason why this spite house had been built felt more like something that should have belonged to the historical record unless it was being deliberately suppressed. Then she remembered Emily Steen all but accusing Eunice of just that—suppression of information—in that article. Just the idea made her about as uneasy as the idea of spending the night in that house.

"You're sure about this?" Dess asked her father.

"I'm sure that we at least need to try. I think this is our best chance."

She started to ask, *What about Pa-Pa Fred's house?* Once they'd left Virginia, after their early scare with almost being spotted Dad had doubled down about where they should end up if another, better opportunity didn't fall in their laps. Odessa, Texas. The house his grandfather had rebuilt after it had burned down. He'd talked about it like there was something important there. A secret stash of money under a floorboard? His grandmother's jewels hidden in the walls? No, something more precious than that. She hadn't asked precisely what. She trusted that he would tell her when the time was right, though if he held out much longer, she'd take the initiative to try to get it out of him.

For now, she held her tongue. She knew she wouldn't be able to mask any sarcasm and suspicion in her voice. The last thing she wanted to do now was invite an argument between them, however mild. They needed to support each other, they were all that they had, and he had something important to do today. Regardless of her concerns and skepticism, she agreed with him that this was an opportunity they couldn't ignore.

CHAPTER 6

Eunice

The interview was running long, despite Eunice knowing within the first few sentences that this four-person "paranormal investigative team" wouldn't be any more suitable for the job than any of the others she'd met with in recent days. It was running long, and it was her own fault, but she couldn't help herself.

This group of four comprised three men and one woman. The one who sat closest to Eunice's desk, in the center chair of the row arranged in her mansion's sizable office chamber, was a stout bald man with a goatee. Beside him, on his right, was the "cool geek" of the crew, something Eunice was used to seeing. Younger than the leader, with hair dyed a harsh blond and arms sleeved in tattoos. He was the one who went into false depths every time the bald man pitched him a look that gave him the green light to speak. To the bald man's left were the big guy and the woman of their group. The big guy, well-muscled and wearing a shirt that had to be a size too small, looked like a bouncer on loan. He was working hard to hold his smile. The woman, Meredith, the only name Eunice really tried to retain, was doing a much better job of maintaining her practiced enthusiasm than the big guy was. Eunice wasn't sure what role either of these two had in this party, but if they fit the mold of most of the others that had come in before them, the woman was supposed to be the reasonable one, while the big guy was there to be surprisingly easy to scare when the cameras were on.

They were the fourteenth such group to waste her time since she'd given Dana approval to place the ad. Given that there were more than forty of these groups in Texas alone, and how many Dana had already filtered out through phone interviews, she supposed she should count herself lucky. Each of them had spoken of temperature-fluctuation measurement and electromagnetic-field recorders, and other equipment that was part of the professional-ghost-hunting charade, as though they'd be the first ones to tell her about these things, even though they all said something to the effect of "I'm sure you've heard of this, but . . ." before going into their sell.

They were somewhat inoffensive considering their intent was to effectively cheat her out of money and time while boosting their careers. The money, she didn't mind. If they stayed in the house, they would earn it whether they meant to or not. The house would not let them live there without them doing what they were paid to do. The question was whether the money would be enough of a compensation for what the house might do to them. Eunice's previous tenants in the Masson House—Jane and Max Renner—could attest to that, presuming Max cared to ever resurface and Jane regained the ability to speak.

Although money was no concern, time was another matter. She couldn't make more of that. She was in her early eighties, still sharp, still astute, and still susceptible, now and then, to certain indulgences, one of her favorites being calling someone out on a lie when she could easily let it go. She'd let thirteen other groups pass politely unchallenged in the last few days, so she had multiple, recent examples that proved she could resist if she really wanted to. Right now, she just didn't want to.

"Hold on, dear," Eunice said, raising a hand and silencing the tech kid just as he'd finished talking up his "high-grade infrared thermometers that can pick up and isolate any cold spots that are sort of like chemtrails for unseen spirits."

She checked her smartwatch, which housed several components built in the factory she owned at the south end of town. She already knew the time from the large clock on the far wall. She was checking her pulse to confirm what she already suspected. Her heart rate was up a bit. Not nearly as high as it would be when she was warming up on her treadmill or taking a walk along the property's trail, but still ten beats per minute higher than it should have been when she was sitting down. She suspected she'd heard the term "cold spots" one time too many to remain calm.

She glanced at Lafonda, who sat in a corner of the room. Lafonda gave her a small headshake that she had to have known wouldn't dissuade her, and Eunice answered with a faint smile. Then she stood up, walked to the front of her desk, and leaned back on it.

"I must tell you all, I actually have a friend who used to host a show a bit like the ones you say you put on, although his was focused on the debunking side of things. Have any of you heard of Neal Lassiter before?"

"That jackass," the bald man said.

"Did you not just hear me call him a friend?" Eunice said.

The bald man's mouth slacked and skin blanched, and Eunice could see his thoughts working overtime to salvage this interview and the potential payday and exposure that came with it. "I-I'm sorry, that was inappropriate. I thought you meant it, like, sarcastically. Like you didn't really like him. I didn't mean any offense by it, really."

Her stare told him how much of a fool he was to think he could presume she meant anything other than what she'd said, much less the opposite of what she'd said. In the back, Lafonda snickered, and Eunice had to clear her throat to keep from laughing in kind and lessening the gravity she'd just brought into the room.

"My friend Neal and I don't see eye to eye on matters of the paranormal. He thinks I'm wasting my time. Nonetheless, he has agreed to come here as soon as I give him the call to tell him that I'm ready. That I'm sure I can prove something is in that house, because I brought in the right people—serious people—who have made me sure. Do you think you're going to be the ones to do that, talking to me about the same things that I see in these silly little television shows that my friend Neal regularly eviscerates in two sentences or less?"

The others looked to the bald man, who shifted in his chair and started to answer before Eunice cut him off with, "That was rhetorical. You've had your chance, now I would like to speak. I don't know how sincere you may be or not. I don't know what any of you has or hasn't experienced with regard to spirits. What I know is what I've experienced, and why it leads me to believe that most people who talk about 'cold spots' and the like probably haven't been in the presence of the dead. Now I've just given you some time to share some things with me, you'll do me the same courtesy, won't you?"

The men hesitated to answer, no doubt wondering if this might be another rhetorical question, but Meredith spoke up and said, "Yes."

"Thank you," Eunice said. "When I was ten years old, I had a favorite aunt. Her name was Val. She was tall and wide and strong and loud. She seemed to me like someone out of a tall tale. My very own Paul Bunyan. Technically she was my cousin, my grandpa's brother's daughter. Some family members would correct me when I called her my aunt, but she was too old to me to be my cousin, and I minded her like an elder. Not that she was the fussy sort. She didn't have to be. She'd ask or suggest, and I'd take it as an order. Whenever I was being stubborn with my mother, she'd only have to say, 'What do you think Val would say about this?' and that would be enough. I loved my mother, but Aunt Val was my hero.

"She lived and worked in San Antonio, but she would stay with us most summers and on the big holidays too, and we kept a bedroom reserved for her here. During the summers we used to walk up Luger Hill before it was officially a park. We made some of its trails. We had a favorite path up to the top and we hiked it two or three times a week. She'd let me get closer to the edges and drops than my daddy or mother ever would. Everyone else in the family was so protective and gloomy so much of the time. Acted like I'd break in the breeze if it blew enough to fly a kite. God forbid I should ever fall when I was out playing. When I came home with scrapes it led to a talk from my parents about how I had to be more careful. But Val would tell them the same thing she told me when I picked up a cut or a bruise during our hikes. 'No one ever got tough without getting hurt first.' Then she'd have to argue with my parents about the benefits of young girls growing up to be tough. She never had to convince me, though.

"Aunt Val and I were on Luger Hill on the last Saturday of May in 1948. It was a little warmer than usual for that time of year, but not too bad. Birds were singing, and you didn't have to stop and smell the flowers to smell them. It was wonderful. Just a wonderful day. We were at one of our favorite spots, a lookout point above a rocky hollow. When it rained, a little thin waterfall would flow down the side and into a tiny baby of a creek below. Lot of green among the rocks, but not so much that it crowded the view the way it did with some of the other spots on the hill. There were other drop-offs on the hill that looked so flat and smooth you would think you could slide all the way down and not hit anything. Those made me more nervous than the others because a part of me always felt a little tempted to slide down, even though I knew it was dangerous, and I was more worried about me just suddenly doing it one day than anything else, so I'd stay away from those edges. But with this one, it was so rocky and harsh that I didn't mind getting up close, because I knew how careful I had to be around it. That probably sounds backwards. Probably *is* backwards, but that's how I felt.

"It had rained pretty heavily off and on for about a week before we'd gone up, so even though it had been sunny for the past couple of days, the little waterfall was there, and it was nice and peaceful to sit there and listen to it. My last pleasant memory of my favorite aunt, loud and talkative as she could be, didn't involve her saying a word. I stood there listening to the waterfall and the birds and the breeze, and I watched her crouch near that edge to pick up pebbles and bounce them down the side, and I was happy.

"And then two things happened. Val stood and put her hand up against her chest. I looked at her face and saw her eyes and jaw were tight from pain. She reached out for me, grabbed my shoulder to steady herself, and I stood there confused. She was a big woman, like I said. Almost overgrown in a way. To me she looked as hale and healthy as anybody could be. And she was only fifty-five, which was old to me—older than my parents—but not that old. Not dying old. But, as I'm sure you've figured out, she was having a heart attack. Right there at one of our favorite places to be."

Eunice sighed and stopped simply to take a break. She checked her watch again. Her pulse had slowed, albeit not quite down to her healthy, resting rate. So there was a tangible benefit to recounting this awful memory. That was good. She hadn't spoken of this aloud in a long time, not since she'd hired Lafonda. It was always there, but now it was in the air, and each time she'd told it before—to Lafonda, to Dana, and to Emily—it seemed to invite things that might be present in the mansion's many rooms to become more active.

Lost for a moment in these thoughts, she almost forgot that the foursome before her were in the room until Meredith said, "What happened then?"

Eunice said, "Well, the second thing to happen, immediately following her heart attack, was that the temperature dropped. This was not a cold spot. It was not a chill. This was like the sun had retreated.

"Let me tell you what I learned that day about the cold. For one, there's more coldness in nature than there is anything else. When I say 'nature' you probably think of the woods, the fields, maybe mountains and deserts. You're forgetting, first off, about the parts of the sea that have never seen daylight. Then there's all the air around the tops of mountains, and then above them, up into and past the clouds. Miles of it, and it's all too cold to be lived in. And that's before you get out into space. It's cold out there in ways that we can put a number on but can't really fathom. Negative four hundred fifty-five degrees Fahrenheit, approximately. That's the temperature in space when you're clear from any stars. What does that number even mean? That's not something any living thing is designed to feel. But what about the ones done with living? They don't have any use for heat anymore. How deep is the cold they carry with them? I'll tell you. Imagine your bones turning to ice so fast you don't have time to scream. Imagine a cold so deep it makes the day grayer without a cloud in the sky. Hard to imagine, isn't it?"

Meredith and the big man nodded. The techie seemed transfixed. The bald man looked more confused, like he was still working out how to make up for his earlier mistake.

"That's the cold that blew through while my aunt Val had her heart attack," Eunice said. "Not a 'chill.' Not a spot. Nothing as safe or stationary as that. This felt like the end of the world, except personal. It didn't belong to anyone else. It was there for us. It came to us.

"Aunt Val had her hand on my shoulder, like I said, and she pulled me in close so fast and so hard that I was sure she meant to hurt me. For a second, I was sure she was going to throw me over the edge like she'd been doing those pebbles. And she was sure strong enough. She could have launched me clear with just the one arm and I'd have been falling, and then hitting those rocks, again and again, breaking apart a little more and more all the way to the bottom. I thought of that as she held on to me. I called her name over and over and told her mine too, quickly as I could, to remind her of who she was and that she knew me and loved me, in case all she needed was reminding. I asked her what was wrong. I looked at her, but she wouldn't look at me. She was staring out at something in the woods. I tried to see what it was but there wasn't anything there. Nothing but trees and the trail.

"Val grunted and staggered, and I could tell something was really wrong, and that frightened me. Her strength frightened me. Not knowing why she wouldn't answer me or look at me frightened me. And the cold. That horrible, unnatural cold. But the worst came when Val shouted at whatever she was looking at, 'You can't have her! You can't have her!'" Eunice shouted the words like she needed to be heard a block away. Her interviewees all flinched. Eunice saw that even Lafonda, who had to know this moment was coming, shuddered a little, although that might have been due to the shrillness of Eunice's voice.

"I can't do it justice," Eunice said. "Think of a voice heavier and heartier than mine, and much angrier. I've had cause to be angry in my life, but I've never sounded like she did. Never that frantic, either. She was using her last breaths on those screams. It was an effort just to get the words out, I could tell, much less to have them come out so forcefully. She sounded like she was on the verge of tears, but at the same time like she could kill an army with her bare hands if she had to. Or she'd at least give it an honest try.

"Then the cold started to move. It closed in like it knew it had us trapped. I heard this raspy, growling sound. Low and threatening. I heard it all around us, heard it through my skin as much as in my ears. Val screamed one more time and pushed me down so hard my chin hit the ground, but I didn't feel any pain at the time. I was too cold to feel pain, and I was distracted. Val's voice was trailing off. Or falling off, more appropriately. Falling away, following her down the hillside. The cold followed her too, and the rasping voices that came with it. It all went over the edge, still lingering with me for a second, but soon everything was quiet again, and the sunlight was warming me, and the world seemed like it had gone back to normal.

"I didn't want to look back, because I knew what I would see if I did, so I just stayed there on my hands and knees. I thought of my scraped chin and the sun being on me, and I tried to think of Aunt Val being right behind me, about to put a hand on my shoulder, but gentler this time. Back to being herself. She'd ask me if I was okay, check on my scrape, tell me not to cry, that I was tougher than a little ol' scratch on the chin, and everything would be normal again. She wouldn't have to explain herself to me. I wouldn't care what had caused her to act that way, I'd only care that she was alive and herself again. All I wanted was for the truth to be a lie, because the truth was that she was at the bottom of that rocky hillside.

"She wasn't shouting any instructions up at me, so how could I know what to do to help her? That's if she was even alive, and if she was, how much longer could she hold on? I had to get someone to help her. I had to go fast. I ran as hard as I could and I was a lot less careful around some ledges and declines than I'd ever been before, and rolled my ankle pretty bad once, but I could be tougher than a little ol' sprained ankle for my aunt's sake. When I got home, I went to my mom and dad, who were with my uncle and a few older cousins, and I told them Aunt Val had fallen.

"They had to bring me along for the rescue so I could show them where

Aunt Val went over, but when we got there, they didn't let me look past the edge. My mother took me away even though I was shouting at her to let me see if Val was okay. I knew she wasn't. Something had gone wrong with her before she'd gone over, and then she'd fallen, and now they weren't telling me if she was okay or not. All of that let me know everything there was to know. But I still wanted to see her. She must have hit those rocks pretty bad because her funeral was closed-casket. Besides pictures, the last time I saw her face was when she was yelling at something only she could see.

"A few days after we buried Aunt Val, my mother came to my room. I was crying again, even though I knew Aunt Val would want me to be tougher than that, which just made me sadder. Anyway, my mother sat at the foot of my bed, patted my legs for a while, then told me she had an important question, and that it was very important for me to be honest with her. She asked me if I'd felt anything strange while Val was having her heart attack, before she'd fallen. I told her about the cold, which I hadn't mentioned before because I thought everyone would think I was making it up, and because it didn't seem all that important. But my mother nodded when I told her about it, and I knew she believed me. Then she took a big breath, straightened her posture, and told me that my beloved aunt was the latest victim of a family curse that stretched back to the nineteenth century. She'd hoped to spare me that news until I was older, but I was going to find out sooner rather than later, anyway. Val wasn't my only relative to die when I was young, and I've been living with that over my head since I was a little girl. So you can probably imagine why I'm more compelled than just curious to uncover certain mysteries of the hereafter. I have quite a bit at stake. I'd rather pass more peacefully than Val, and I'd much rather find out ahead of time if dying is where the agony ends or just begins. Now, be honest, do you think yourselves up to the task of helping me make this discovery?"

The ghost hunters stared at Eunice a moment, again unsure if she actually wanted them to answer, then jumped when they heard a knock behind them. They turned to see Dana in the doorway.

"Sorry to interrupt," Dana said, "but your one o'clock is already here, Mrs. Houghton. Just wanted to be sure you knew."

"Oh. Good on them getting here so early," Eunice said. "Thank you, Dana. We're done here anyway."

She motioned for the interviewees to follow Dana out of the room. They hesitated, and she could tell they wanted her to finish her story. She told them, "Thank you for listening. I appreciate your courtesy. If we're interested, you'll hear from us. Have a pleasant rest of your day."

"Right this way, please," Dana said. Then the four of them stood and followed Dana, shuffling out in silence as though they had just received terrible news and were still processing it. After they were gone, Lafonda approached and said, "How are you feeling?"

"Not bad. My blood was up for a moment."

"I saw."

"You could read my watch from way over there?"

"I could read your face."

"Oh? What's it saying now?"

"'Damn Lafonda and her perceptiveness. I know that's a big part of why I hired her, but I kind of hate how good she is.'"

Eunice laughed, then said, "Would you mind helping Dana with our next group. I believe it's the father with his two girls."

"Oh, right."

"You're sure you're okay with keeping the girls occupied? It shouldn't take very long, but I can ask Dana to trade places with you, if you like."

"No, no," Lafonda said. "She's probably already mad I let you go so long with this last one. Anyway, I already wear a hundred other hats in this house. I don't think a little babysitting will kill me."

"As always, I appreciate your efforts, Miss Lafonda."

"And as always, I appreciate my healthy salary, Miss Eunice."

They shared a small, quiet laugh, Eunice knowing better than anyone how her family home's acoustics could carry a sound even all the way down the stairs and up to the front door. She didn't want Dana to hear the two of them joking any more than Lafonda wanted that. It was liable to put Dana in a mood and they would have to meet after this last interview to discuss next steps. Eunice did not want to spend any time this afternoon listening to Dana sigh, suck her teeth, and answer any request for her opinion with, "It's really your decision, Eunice."

Before she left, Lafonda said, "I'm changing the routine this evening. Just warning you now—"

"Don't you dare," Eunice said.

"—so I don't have to hear you complain later. Well, not as much."

"I want to hit the bag. I've been looking forward to it. I need to hit the bag."

"You need to relax."

"That does help me relax."

"Not as much as the yoga. We have stats on that, you know. The lady who pays me runs a whole big company built around that kind of thing."

Eunice frowned. "We'll talk about this later, but I'm boxing tonight."

Lafonda waved as she exited the office. Eunice went behind her desk, put on her glasses, and woke up her laptop—docked to large dual monitors—to check her notes for the next interview. She worked almost as hard on remaining computer literate these days as she did on remaining as fit as feasible, in no small part because of situations like this. She'd forgotten the name of the person she was to meet with. There it was on the screen, though, in her business notes app. Eric Ross. Beneath his name, a few things about him she'd documented while quietly listening in on his prescreening call with Dana.

> *2 daughters—did not volunteer names.*
>
> *From "northeast area." When pressed, claimed from "near Phila-delphia." No accent?*
>
> *Why is he living out of motels with his girls? He did not say. Messaged Dana not to ask. Don't want to scare him off.*
>
> *Sounds sincere. Clearly hiding something. Might be running from something. Fugitive? Will have Dana check background to be sure it's nothing serious. Otherwise, this could make him more likely to stay. Could be an ideal candidate. Should have thought of someone like this before.*
>
> *Question: Should I tell him what happened to Jane and Max? Leaning toward yes, for the sake of his girls. We'll see how I feel in the moment.*

She reread the last lines a few more times, determining how she felt now that the moment was here.

Eric

It surprised him that there was no gate or guard in place to keep out trespassers. He followed the directions Dana gave him yesterday after retracing his path back from the site of the spite house to the sign that welcomed people to Degener. From there he headed north, toward the even more scenic and less densely populated part of town. After passing a couple of ranches, the road rounded into a large hollow where a monstrous mansion stood in the middle of several lush acres.

"Wow, it's like a castle," Stacy said. Eric jumped a little at the sound of her voice. He hadn't realized she had woken up.

"Yeah, it is," Dess said to her sister.

Eunice Houghton's estate was almost overstuffed with natural niceties and man-made outdoor amenities. After turning onto a long cobblestone driveway that looked too nice to be driven on, Eric passed large trees that must have been hundreds of years old. There were multiple benches and picnic tables, isolated gardens, two small ponds (both of which featured a walkway leading to an island gazebo), an atrium, and an encompassing trail that looked to be made of the same synthetic material Dess would run on at her track meets.

The trail created an informal border that marked the end of the more "civilized" section of the Houghton Estate. Beyond it on three sides lay the wilds. Clustered trees, tall grasses, small hills, and the sounds of the animals and insects that occupied that land. Eric did not know where Miss Houghton's property truly ended, but believed you could lose yourself for at least half a day finding your way out of the surrounding woods after walking in.

He tried to imagine owning even a tenth of this property. The privacy it could afford them. He imagined that people who lived in such places did so specifically to have some space, enjoy some seclusion.

A black-haired woman in a dress suit stood a few feet from the steps leading to the mansion's front entrance. He parked the car several feet away from her, and by the time he and the girls walked close enough to be within comfortable speaking distance, the first woman was joined by a black woman dressed more like she was about to run a few errands. The first woman extended her hand and said, "Welcome, Mr. Ross. I'm Dana. We spoke yesterday. This is Lafonda, my colleague."

Eric shook hands and introduced his daughters. "This is Odessa, and this is Stacy."

Lafonda said, "Well, young ladies, it's my pleasure to meet you. You're going to hang out with me for a bit while your dad talks to my boss, if that's cool."

"Sounds good," Dess said.

"Do you live here?" Stacy said.

"I do," Lafonda said. "Come on. I'll show you around some."

Eric and his girls followed Dana and Lafonda into the house, first passing through a foyer that was larger than many of the motel rooms they'd stayed in, then parting ways at the crest in the marbled floor of the main hall. Lafonda said to Eric, "If you need me, have Miss Eunice page me," then took the girls with her to the right, toward what appeared to be a huge sunroom.

Dana said, "This way, please, she's waiting for you in her office," then escorted him up the hall's staircase, which reminded Eric of the stairs in the film *Titanic*. Midway up the stairs he started to feel dizzy. This place was too large to be thought of as anyone's home. The house back in Maryland—which Tab had convinced him was the one, even though he'd been a little unsure due to its price tag—had been more than enough for his family. Four bedrooms, a decent little office, a dining room and breakfast nook, a den and living room. Very nice, and it could fit in Eunice Houghton's home at least ten times over.

"You live here, too?" he said to Dana, staring up at the ceiling that seemed closer to the clouds than the dirt.

"No, my husband and I live closer to the town proper," Dana said. "Puts me closer to the plant and campus for work. I go in just about every day so Eunice doesn't have to. I'm presuming you've done some homework about her."

"What makes you think that?" he said, still trying to take in the mansion's sprawling three stories from a vantage point that barely let him process one.

"You sounded smart on the phone. Smart people do homework."

He looked at her, tried to gauge whether this was a continuation of the prescreening. "I did a little."

"Good." At the top of the stairs they went down the left hallway, and to Eric the mansion increasingly became more of a museum. The halls were wide enough to bring a tour group through, eleven or twelve feet tall, he couldn't quite tell, and lined with impressive art pieces. Paintings primarily, with a few engravings and large photographs—some portraits, some candids—spread throughout. One at the end of the hall captured a woman with a smile big enough for two. She looked to be about a second away from laughing, and Eric almost expected her to come alive within the frame and do just that.

"Right here," Dana said, stopping in front of a closed door. "For whatever it's worth, I'm pulling for you. The others that have come through, I haven't been a fan. You? You're not claiming to be some amateur expert in an unscientific field. At least, I don't think so. You've got that going for you."

"So don't be an expert," he said. "Got it."

Dana's smile changed, like she might be impressed but also a bit wary. "I'm not giving you pointers, just pointing something out. There's a difference."

"I agree."

"Just be yourself."

"I'll do my best."

The smile shifted again, in which direction he couldn't tell. *You're getting cute*, he thought. *Don't blow this before you even get to it, for God's sake.*

Dana opened the door, brought him in, introduced him to Eunice. The older woman got up from her desk, and the thing that struck Eric most about her was her posture. She was in no way bent or stooped, and didn't appear to be trying hard—if at all—to stand so erect.

"Mr. Ross, please have a seat," Eunice said.

Dana told him, "Good luck," then left him alone with the rich woman who owned a strange house she believed to be haunted, and lived in a mansion that would make kings envious. His girls were elsewhere in this house, in the care of someone he'd just met. It occurred to him that all of this should have made him more anxious or suspicious, but the past year and a half had numbed him somewhat. The immensity of the manor was something else, something new, but the rest of it, the need to have some measure of faith in strangers if he had any chance of earning some money, finding some shelter, he'd grown accustomed to that.

Eunice's gray eyes were closer to the color of steel than storms. She had them open wide, like she was looking for more of him than was there. "I hope you found us without any trouble."

"I did," he said.

"Good. Unfortunately, that's all the small talk I have for you. It's been quite the day, and I think I've used up about all the charm I can muster. I hope you understand."

"That's fine by me."

"Good. Good. Then, to begin with, I must ask what's brought you to where you are? Not the physical space you're in, but the general condition of your life. My first impression of you, based on appearances, is that you don't come across as a neglectful or irresponsible man. But here you are, living out of a motel and desperate for stable employment. That's questionable enough on its own, but with one school-aged child and another who's barely an adult . . . How on earth did you get here?"

Despite saying he was fine with skipping small talk, Eric had counted on using it to warm Eunice up to him. Make it evident that he was a decent, reliable person, regardless of his circumstances. Then, he figured, he'd have some leeway to be vague about what they had left behind and why. Now a small lie might be in order. He took a breath, not wanting to get started before his brain had enough of a head start to keep him from stammering.

"Back home, back in Philadelphia, there was a situation. Something to do with family. We had to get away. Nothing criminal, but, well, there were elements involved that didn't have my kids' best interest at heart. There were dangers involved in staying home. I wish I could tell you more—"

"You could."

"I really can't. You said I don't look irresponsible. I can assure you it would be extremely irresponsible of me to say more than I'm saying. For the sake of my daughters."

Eunice gave a perfunctory nod. "Well, look at it from my perspective, Mr. Ross. I'm going to be giving someone a place to stay and money to live there. I need to know they're not some fugitive from justice. I need to know they won't be bringing anything unsavory to my property. In short, I need to know this is someone I can rely on. If you can't tell me anything of significance about where you're from and why you're apparently on the run, I can't imagine what you could tell me to make me trust you."

Before he could second-guess himself, Eric said, "I can tell you about something I haven't shared with anyone else in years. And it's relevant to the job, too. I never even told my wife—*ex*-wife—about this, or told my kids. If I trusted you with that, would it help you trust me a little?"

"Relevant to the job? Sounds like you're going to tell me a ghost story, Mr. Ross."

"I don't know what to call it, exactly. But it's a real thing that happened to me, I promise you that."

Eunice sat back. She already looked unimpressed, and Eric felt fear fluttering in his chest, expecting her to cut the interview short and send him on his way, having wasted his chance, wasted a day he could have spent seeking real work. Instead she raised a hand that invited him to speak.

"My grandparents had a house in Odessa, Texas," he said. "I visited a lot when I was a kid, over holidays and a few summers. I loved that house, and I'm actually hoping to buy it back someday if I can get my money right. Not just for nostalgia's sake. There's something there, maybe, that can give me some answers I'm looking for. At least, I hope. I'm sorry, let me just get to it.

"I'd heard at first, growing up, that my grandfather built that house. That wasn't the whole truth. His parents had bought it and moved in when he was still a teenager. He *re*built it after it burned down when he was maybe about twenty or so, and still living there, along with his new wife, my grandmother, Nelle. This would've been in the early fifties, and uh, you know, there were incidents back then. Not that there aren't anymore, but you know."

"I do. Unfortunately, I do," Eunice said.

"So, they lived south of the tracks, the black side of town, but that didn't make them safe there. I never got the full story behind how the house burned. I never knew about the fire at all until I was twelve years old, visiting them one summer. I used to sleep in the back-corner room, and I started having these episodes where I'd wake up in the dead of night and I'd smell smoke, and I'd hear flames eating up the wood. The first time it happened I tried to tell myself it was a dream, but I was never one of those people who could tell they were dreaming, so the fact that I was even thinking of that let me know I was awake. And I knew I needed to get up and get everybody else up outside because the house was on fire. But I didn't want to move because it felt like there was somebody else in the room with me."

He took a deep breath, remembering. "That first time it happened, the moonlight was bright enough that I should've been able to see somebody there with me but I couldn't. I could sense them, though. Sense their fear. I could put two and two together and tell they were frantic because of the fire, even though I didn't hear them say anything. Then I felt this incredible rush of anger that I knew came from the other person. It was a hundred times more intense than the fire. It was like the harshest, most blinding light imaginable paired with the loudest scream ever heard. I couldn't see or hear anything past that anger for what felt like forever. Then it was all gone, and I was by myself again, wondering what the hell just happened. It's not easy, going through something like that . . ."

"I agree," Eunice said. She sounded somewhat distant, but not uninterested.

"So, that first time it happened, I stayed awake for the whole night, too scared to move to even save myself. When enough of the day came to chase it all away, I finally got up and walked around the house to be sure nothing had burned up. Everything was fine. I figured my imagination had gotten the best of me and I just kept it to myself. A couple of days went by before it happened again. Then it happened a third time a couple days after that and by then I was so tired I almost fell asleep at the dinner table, and that's when my grandma made me tell her what was wrong. I told her about it, but I said it was a dream even though I knew it wasn't one. She looked at my grandfather and said, 'You want to tell him?' He pulled me aside, told me about the fire, and how he'd been in that back-corner room when it started. Him and Grandma had argued that night, and she and my great-grandparents all agreed he should sleep off his anger in there.

"He didn't say what they fought about, but apparently he had a rep for getting into it with some of the people north of the tracks. Sometimes he had a response for when they threw a slur at him. They were used to black and brown people just keeping quiet, never standing up or pushing back. That wasn't his nature. I've got a hunch that it was all related. The fight with my grandmother, his confrontations on the northside, the fire. Maybe Grandma had been telling him he needed to be more cautious, think of everybody else in the house before he got into it with somebody north of the tracks who might take things too far. Not knowing that some of them were already on their way to take it too far.

"Anyway, my grandfather said he never remembered making it out of that room. He remembered being surrounded by flames and choking on smoke and then he must have passed out. The next thing he knew he was in a hospital bed. No one ever told him how he got out. His mom and pops and my grandma just said it was a miracle. God had delivered him. Didn't even have a mark on him. And he was on his feet and better than ever sooner than expected. The rest of them wanted to move, find some other town, but Grandpa said hell no. They stayed with some friends while he got to work rebuilding the place. His dad was a little too worn down to be much help, but they had some cousins and neighbors who pitched in some. A little later when I asked around town about it, some of the old-timers would tell me it was mostly my grandfather's work. One of them said that he worked like a man possessed. They wouldn't tell me much else, except for one other big thing. Nobody north of the tracks ever so much as side-eyed him or the family again. He got some kind of rep after all of that, I guess. And with all respect to my own pops, that story solidified my grandfather as my hero.

"But it didn't explain what had happened to me in that room. That's why I don't call it a ghost story. Like I said, I don't know what to call it. I've looked up theories over the years and the only one that kind of makes sense to me is that sometimes the past has sort of an echo that catches up to the present. It's not a standardized thing, it doesn't happen on specific anniversaries or anything like that. It's random, and sometimes people are there to see it or hear it, and sometimes not. Anyway, that's my experience, Miss Houghton. You're the first person I've ever told that story to."

Eunice said, "I appreciate you sharing that with me, Mr. Ross. It did indeed help. I have one follow-up question, if you don't mind."

"I don't."

"You said you smelled the smoke and heard flames. Did you feel the fire, too? I'm just wondering."

A short laugh hopped from his throat, and Eric said, "No, actually. It was cold as hell. Cold as I've ever been, and I've lived up north, as I told you. I've been through some ugly winters, but that room in West Texas, of all places, in the summer, was the coldest place I've ever been in. It was like being on the dark side of the moon or something."

Eunice looked somewhat startled at that, and Eric thought he saw something close to excitement come to the front of her eyes. Maybe even a little smile threatening to cross her face.

"Well then, Mr. Ross, my next question is do you have time now to do a walk-through of the house you'll be staying in."

"Are you offering me the job?"

"I'd like you to take a look inside the house first," she said, "be sure you know what you're literally getting into. Then, if you're still agreeable to it, yes, I'm offering you the position."

"I . . . I wasn't expecting that. Thank you. This means so much. Thank you."

"Don't thank me yet. Take a look at the house first. I'll have Dana take you. Lafonda and I will keep your girls company. Lafonda's a medical professional. And chef, and physical therapist, and maybe a superhero when I'm not around. Point being she's great at taking care of people. She and I will take the girls on a little shopping trip downtown, with your approval. I'm presuming you-all didn't bring any clothes to stay here overnight. Here in this house, I mean. Not the other one. We'll need a day to get that properly arranged for you."

"Um, you're right. We didn't think to bring clothes. Sorry, we weren't expecting to get this invitation."

"I wasn't sure I'd extend it," Eunice said. "But you've made an impression. If nothing else, I believe you're sincere. You're here to earn money, not just get it. Even if you change your mind after the walk-through, the offer to stay tonight stands. You came this far, you shouldn't have to drive back today."

"I appreciate that," Eric said. "So you're going with Lafonda? Just me and Dana in the spite house?"

Eunice came half an inch closer to smiling. "Mr. Ross, if I was comfortable at all with being in that house, I'd stay there myself instead of paying someone to do it for me."

He was still a little light-headed from the buzz of knowing the job—the money—was there if he said yes to it. Nonetheless, he'd been sharp enough to see the red flag that Eunice just waved in front of him.

"Is it dangerous?" he said. "I'm bringing my girls in there with me. I should know if it's even a little—"

"It's fine," Eunice said. "It just takes a certain amount of energy to deal with it. As spry as I feel some days, I'm under no delusion about my age and what I can take."

"Understandable," he said, hoping his skepticism hadn't crept into his tone. "I guess, now that I'm really going to be doing this, I'm starting to wonder why nobody else worked out for you. I mean, this isn't the first time you've tried this, is it?"

"You're right, it's not. But think of the story you just told me. Imagine the average person experiencing that. Some professed 'ghost hunter' who's expecting to hear a few innocuous noises in the night that they'll amplify later, when they're adding shadows and editing their footage to make it seem like there was something there when there really wasn't. That's what the people who I've hired before went in expecting, and when they encounter something even close to what you did, they panic. They don't analyze whether it's an echo or a spirit or anything. They run away. I've had so-called experts and researchers leave after the first shadow they thought they saw or first whisper they thought they heard. I've had others stay a day or two longer, but they all leave far too early to give me anything solid. I'm of the belief now that you won't. And if you're worried about your girls, we can discuss those details later. Suffice to say, they'll always be welcome in my house if you're comfortable with that. Although I'm confident it won't come to that. I know something is in that house, but I don't have any reason to believe it's hostile."

Her assurance sounded rehearsed to him, but he didn't think that necessarily made it disingenuous. He'd been on the other side of the desk in job interviews before and he'd had prepared statements on those occasions. They hadn't been half-truths just because they'd been written or practiced. He should give Eunice the same benefit of the doubt.

Except he sensed she was keeping something from him. To be fair, he was keeping things from her as well, but being fair wasn't close to a priority for him. There was an imbalance of power here as it was. She could move on to another candidate, even if they were less ideal than he was, far more easily than he could move on to the next eccentric millionaire willing to part with a small fortune. That made this opportunity too good to let a little suspicion obstruct his path to it. And he'd kept Dess and Stacy safe so far, hadn't he? Kept them protected from real-world threats. He could do the same when it came to otherworldly ones, especially considering he had recent reason to believe that the dead meant no harm, irrespective of his doubts about that.

"Well then," he said, "as long as the walls don't start bleeding or something on this first visit, I'm letting you know now that I accept."

Eunice said, "Considering nothing like that's happened yet, if it does now then I'm going to think it was in response to you. And if that's the case, I'll be more than happy to increase my offer enough to change a 'no' to a 'yes.'"

Dana

The first floor of the Masson House—the spite house—was effectively one long corridor, nine feet wide, barely over seven feet from floor to ceiling. A spiral staircase waited at the far end. A compact sofa, a small, padded chair, and an end table lined the wall opposite the windows, further thinning the walking space. A few framed floral paintings filled out the décor.

"This isn't impossible," Eric said. "We can make this work."

She took him upstairs. The kitchen, with its refrigerator, its two-burner stove and half-sized oven, occupied half of the second floor.

"Newer appliances," Eric said, gesturing toward the oven.

Dana said, "As much as we'd have preferred to keep the originals, it was determined the safety hazard wasn't worth the risk. The entire house was rewired as carefully as possible once Miss Houghton started seeking tenants."

There was a pantry beside the refrigerator. Three shelves, not very deep. Past the pantry, behind a closed door, was a compact laundry room furnished with a stacked washer-and-dryer unit.

As they walked back to the stairs to move to the third floor, Dana said, "The bathroom and bedroom situation up next is a little bit awkward."

A closed white door faced the stairway on the third floor. Another door, this one ashen brown—almost the same color as the wall—was to the right of the stairs.

"I'm sure you noticed the bulge in the building from the outside. The jetty? That's the bathroom hallway. The original owner had it added after his niece and nephew moved in, when he converted this floor to their living space. Before that, this floor was his own bedroom, and the top floor was supposed to be his workshop. I'll take you down the hall on the way back. Follow me."

Eric said, "There were kids living here back then?"

Dana hesitated. "Miss Houghton didn't tell you that?"

Eric shook his head. Dana inhaled a hiss and thumped herself lightly on the forehead. "Well, shit. Could you do me a favor and not tell her that I told you?"

"Sure," Eric said. "How old were they? The niece and nephew."

"Young. That's honestly about all I can tell you. I don't really know much of the history. I'm not from here. In fact I'm from the Philadelphia area myself. Have to admit, nice as the weather is here, I do miss home sometimes, don't you?"

"Sometimes," Eric said, and turned his head slightly as he smiled, as if to inspect something on the bare wall. He wasn't really from Philadelphia. She'd suspected it before, when she spoke to him over the phone, and her bluff now made her certain of it. Not that she was looking to catch him in a lie about his background. That wasn't her job. They had people looking into his past, starting with learning his real name. She'd let those experts do what they were paid to do. All she'd wanted was to keep him from asking her about things she wasn't supposed to tell him.

She opened the white door and walked him through the first empty bedroom, then through a second door and into the adjoining, second bedroom. Each had a single window facing the valley and enough room for a full bed, a dresser, and an armoire, all of which were set to be delivered on less than a day's notice as soon as the decision was made on who would occupy the house.

"And here's the full bath," Dana said, opening the door to an intrusive enclosure in the second bedroom. "I know it's small, but everything works as well as you need it to."

The space was barely big enough to turn around in. It somehow contained a toilet, sink, and small bathtub. To the right of the sink was another door that looked like it had been made at a time when tall or broad people didn't exist.

What lay beyond that door was the floating addendum of a hallway. The overhang she had mentioned a moment ago. She had never liked this part of the walk-through, even before what happened to the Renners. This was her first time in the house since that couple had left and they had found Jane's journal, which contained multiple references to the hallway being "the darkest part of this place."

"Will that hall hold up?" Eric asked. "You said it was a late add-on."

"It was. But it's sturdier than you'd think," Dana said.

"Sturdier than I think isn't necessarily sturdy."

She nodded and opened the hallway door. "I'll go first, you follow. If it can hold the two of us, your daughters will be able to walk it safely, too."

"And if it doesn't hold us?"

"You'll get to say 'I told you so' all the way down."

She flipped the light switch and went in first. The floating hall was an import from a claustrophobe's nightmare. Dana did not look back to verify it, but she was sure there wasn't enough room for Eric to put his hands on his hips without his elbows stubbing the walls, and he wasn't a particularly outsized man. She was a little more than half his size and even she felt squeezed in.

At the center of this narrow space was a light bulb fixed to the ceiling. Its yellow light barely brushed the shadows at each end of the hall. Its thinly stretched efforts felt worse, in the moment, than the idea of total darkness. It provided just enough light for Dana to begin to think she could see something down the hall. A lean, largely featureless shape that should not have looked familiar. This was a shade that was almost there. At most a remnant someone had left behind, which Dana should have found doubly harmless because, for one, she couldn't really see it, her imagination was only working to make her see something, and secondly, even if it were there—which it wasn't—it was insubstantial. As imposing and tangible as a memory.

Another line from Jane's journal came to mind. The last line, spread across several pages. "Something here has taken part of me and won't give it back."

Eric's increasingly heavy footsteps brought her back to the here and now. Made the nothing at the end of the hall stop pretending to be something in her head.

Even in sneakers his steps overpowered the sound of her heels stabbing the floorboards. Did he want to shake the hall apart? Not that he could even if he jumped up and down, but did he have to test it? That was all he was doing, she told herself. Testing how much the floor could withstand before his girls had to use it, the little one possibly running its length at some point, to avoid having an accident. It was understandable for him to want to see how sturdy it was, then, but she would have appreciated him conducting his heavy-footed test after letting her get to the end of the hall. Instead of telling him as much, though, she just walked faster. For some reason she made a conscious decision not to speak when she came through here, as if afraid someone who wasn't supposed to be there might respond to her.

When they got to the end, she barely tried to hide her relief when she looked at him. "Not quite as bad as it could be, is it?"

"A little better than I expected," he said, coming out behind her and taking a couple of extra steps away from the door. He sounded a little out of breath, like he might have had a small panic attack.

"You're okay?" she asked.

He nodded, but said, "Wish there was a different way."

"You'll get used to it," she said, then brought him up the last flight of steps.

The empty master bedroom took up the top floor. The waning daylight still warmed the color of the room. Dark curtains were drawn back from each of the room's four tall windows, and through the windows you could see the orphanage's large, Georgian country house. Its red bricks were faded and bleached by time, and even from this distance Eric could see that its front door was missing, which made it slightly resemble a startled face, mouth agape. Adjacent to its north wing was a small chapel whose cross was missing. Behind this church was a modest, forsaken playground largely overtaken by weeds.

Not far beyond the building, the church, and the playground, there stood a shorter but broader hill, which delayed the sunrise by at least half an hour during part of the year, just as the Masson House, atop the hill to the west, could sometimes pitch its shadow across the buildings below to hasten the sunset.

The windows in the house all faced east. Dana watched Eric approach them and wondered what he must be thinking. He seemed smart, and she believed he could add up certain facts—such as the house being called a spite house and its station on the hill—to determine why it was built where it was, and who exactly it had been meant to upset. She let him take in the view and didn't make a sound or gesture that might steal his attention.

When he turned to her he said, "I'll be sleeping up here?"

"Your choice. This is the room where the original owner slept, and where our previous tenants have slept, but you can stay anywhere else in the house if you prefer, as long as you're getting your work done."

"What happened with the previous tenants?"

"Eunice didn't tell you?"

"She said they got spooked before they could finish the job."

"That's pretty much all there is to tell."

"Really?" he said. "It's a lot of money to just walk away from because you're a little scared."

"I don't think they were just a 'little' scared."

"I guess it's just hard for me to see what could scare someone away from getting paid if it's not really dangerous here."

Dana chuckled. "You know, Mr. Ross, when I was a girl, my father thought he could sort of buy out my fear of roaches. I have it to this day, so bad that I get chills seeing one on TV in a commercial for bug spray. When I was a kid sometimes we'd get them in the house and I'd have to leave the house until it was, in my mind, 'safe' to go back in. My dad didn't understand it because it's not like they're poisonous or they can attack you or anything. He thought he could fix my fear by offering to pay me twice my monthly allowance that I got for doing chores if I would just hold a roach in my hand for five seconds. I can barely get that sentence out of my mouth without wanting to scratch my palm. I told him no. I didn't even try. I told him I'd rather do double the chores to make double the money. In fact I'd have rather done triple the chores for a lower allowance than touch one of those disgusting things for a second. Now, if I had literally no other choice, if it were the only way I could make a living now as an adult, I think I could fight through the fear, but never as long as I've got other options. It doesn't matter that they're basically harmless."

Eric nodded. "It does make a difference if you have fewer choices."

"Or if you just don't scare as easily."

"True. So what exactly would I be doing on the job, here? Is that something you can tell me?"

"I can. I'm just surprised you didn't ask Miss Houghton," Dana said.

"I probably got a little too excited when she said I basically had the job. So I just, what, report back if I see or hear anything notable?"

"That's it in a nutshell. Miss Houghton has certain preferences. She likes things handwritten. She's the oldest techie I've ever met but that's the one thing she gets a little romantic about. But she'll give you a journal and provide the details on that later."

"Okay," Eric said. "Can I ask one more question?"

"I can't promise to have an answer, but sure."

"Do you believe in it?"

Dana furrowed her brow. "Now you're just seeing if you can skip ahead in the process, aren't you? It doesn't matter what I believe. The whole point of this is to record the observations of someone with no skin in the game."

"I understand. It's just, I'm moving my kids in here," Eric said, "and I'm not doing it for kicks. I know you're not supposed to say too much, but I don't think it's saying too much to give me your general opinion. You've been in here often enough. I'm not asking you to tell me about a specific time you saw a ghost or heard rattling chains or anything like that. Just whether you believe in it? Any of it?"

Dana mulled her answer. It occurred to her that no other prospective or accepted resident had asked her this. Probably because they never entertained the possibility of it being real. Now it seemed so obvious a question that, in hindsight, she thought less of the ones who'd failed to ask. The grain of guilt she kept for never trying to dissuade anyone from staying in the house—the Renners especially—lost some of the small thorns and edges that made it tough to ignore. It wasn't like they had ever considered the house a legitimate threat and she had talked them out of it.

That made this situation different, made her consider her answer a moment, deciding how best to word it. She didn't want to lie and claim to believe in things that didn't exist just to be able to say she tried to persuade Eric Ross to decline Eunice's offer. At the same time, if he or one of his daughters ended up like Jane Renner, her guilt was going to regain its recently lost hooks and edges, and blow up to one hundred times its current size.

"I've personally never encountered anything to make me a believer," Dana said. "But, again, you're not the first person to accept this offer. If you stayed, you'd be the first to see it through. Now, none of the others suffered any physical injuries, I can't stress that enough, but I also can't pretend to know what made them leave. Whether it was anything real or just in their heads. If we knew that, one way or another, we wouldn't be hiring you to find out for us. What about you? Do you get the impression that something is here? Or do you think it's just easy money?"

"I'm trying not to make any assumptions," Eric said, "least of all that it's going to be easy. If anything I'll assume it's going to be the opposite. But I think it's doable."

"That's a good approach to take. Sounds like you're on board, then."

"Like I said, my options are pretty limited. I'm guessing that's what made me the favorite."

She almost said, *You guessed right*, as a joke, but thought it might sound cruel, so instead she said, "Let's get back and give Eunice the good news. I bet your girls will be happy to hear it, too. I have a family of my own, and for whatever it's worth, weird as this house looks, if I had to choose between living here or living out of sketchy motels with God-knows-who as your neighbors, I'd pick here ten times out of ten."

Even knowing what happened to the people who were here just before you, she thought, but kept to herself. Because she ultimately didn't know what had happened to Jane and Max Renner. Part of her believed it couldn't have been that bad. In Dana's opinion, the house's strange architecture and location just wore on people. The close walls, its placement on the hill, the sounds it must make at night, the way it must feel when a strong enough wind blew, like it might topple. All of that combined to tear people down, especially those who hadn't mentally or emotionally girded themselves for how strange it would be. Even Dana, disbeliever that she was, had almost convinced herself just a moment ago that there was a third person with them in the floating hallway. How much worse did it get staying here overnight? Or, in the Renners' case, three and a half weeks?

Eric Ross was different, though. He was a serious person, a single parent already dealing with an unknown, stressful situation. He wasn't going to crack just because his confines were too narrow or because his footsteps echoed strangely in a hall. And he also didn't strike her as the type to ignore the signs that things were getting worse without doing anything to help himself, blinded by a quest for fame like Max and Jane Renner. He would get his kids out if things got bad for them, and give himself a break if it came to it. If he had the foresight to ask Dana what she thought of the house, he would also think to ask Eunice about taking a night or two off if he needed it. He was the type of candidate they should have been looking for all along. Of all the people she and Eunice had met with about the job, Dana had the most faith in him to see it through.

Stacy

What excited Stacy the most about Miss Houghton's gigantic house was that it had its own library. Stacy had asked to see it earlier, but Miss Lafonda told her they couldn't go upstairs today.

"I'll show you later, promise," Miss Lafonda said, which kept Stacy from getting to sleep after dinner, despite her being in the biggest, softest bed she'd ever been in. Her sister was next to her and didn't answer the few times Stacy said her name. The first couple of times she had wanted to talk to her about the library. How many books would it have? Would it have any books for kids?

Even if it didn't, that would be okay. Stacy had started reading just before she turned five and liked the challenge of trying to read grown-up books, but it would be nice to have something she could read all the way through without having to ask what certain words meant. She had read the few books she brought when they left home so many times she had them all but memorized and wanted something new. Dad wouldn't let her go to a bookstore since they left home, though, and they couldn't go to a library either. She told him that she wouldn't take too long to pick a book out at a store, not like she would have back home when she went book shopping with Mom. She knew that was why he wouldn't take her to a store now. They had to do things in more of a hurry, and he trusted her to go faster with a lot of things, but not with looking for something new and fun to read.

Her mom used to read to her and liked to tell her that books were full of "secrets and wonders." Having a whole library inside your house was something Mom would have really liked, she thought. She wondered if Mom would get to come live with them again now that they were going to have a real place to stay. Dad announced they would move into the skinny house during the dinner Miss Houghton and Miss Lafonda cooked for them. That made Stacy happy, but she'd be happier if Mom were going to join them. She still didn't understand why Mom wasn't with them, and whenever she brought it up, Dess and Dad just said, "She just can't be around us now, but maybe later."

If Dess was awake now, though, Stacy wouldn't ask her about Mom again. She didn't want to ask her questions about the library anymore, either. Now she just wanted to know if her sister could also hear people talking even though they weren't really there.

Miss Lafonda told her that the two ladies had the giant house all to themselves, which made it a lot different from the other places they had been staying in. In the motels, Stacy had often heard people talking, laughing, crying, or sometimes shouting through the walls, and even heard voices that sounded like they could be in the same room as her. Sometimes they sounded like real, normal people, but other times they were echoey and whispery.

This was different. She heard a group of people talking here, and she couldn't pick out exactly what they were saying since they were talking over each other, talking fast like they were excited. One moment they seemed to be upstairs on the third floor, and then a little later like they were down on the first, and sometimes it sounded like they were going from room to room, a little bit lost. But even though she couldn't pick out their words, she could hear the echo and the weird softness that still felt ugly in her.

From a couple of the books about haunted places and scary legends she liked to read—the ones Mom stopped letting her check out from the library because they gave Stacy strange dreams, and inspired drawings that made Mom look worried—Stacy was sure that she heard ghosts. That was what ghosts sounded like according to the books, far away and whispery, but still harsh. Listening to the voices didn't bother her that much as long as they didn't come close, and even then, she knew she had Dess and Dad to protect her. What bugged her was not really knowing what any of it was. Mom would have told her it was just her imagination, and Dad would have said it was "Just the wind," or "Just air flowing." They had to be wrong, but they were older and had done things that she hadn't yet, so maybe they knew better.

She tried to wake Dess up one more time, yawning as she did, and when it didn't work, she knew it was time to stop thinking about those strange voices, who they might belong to and what they were talking about, or anything else that would keep her up. It had been an amazing day—they had met new, nice people and she was spending the night in a castle like a princess—and tomorrow they would go to the new house. The skinny house. Dad said she would even have her own room there. The sooner she went to sleep, the sooner tomorrow would come, and she wanted that more than she wanted to stay awake listening.

She shut her eyes, thought of how she didn't want to open them again until it was the morning, and was asleep within a minute.

Eric

The movers brought furniture to the third-floor bedrooms after yesterday's walk-through. They placed an armoire in Dess's room, and a small purple wardrobe in the corner of Stacy's room, beside the twin bed that was made up with white and pink covers and pillows, as well as two white stuffed bears wearing pink bow ties.

Stacy's face lit up when she entered her room. "This is mine?"

"All yours," Eric said.

"I have my own room again!"

Eric pictured Stacy's empty room back in Maryland. The memory pushed a knot into his throat, and he had to clear it before saying, "Your very own room. Just like before we moved."

Stacy squealed as she ran to her bed—a short sprint in such a small space—and jumped onto it.

Two of the movers hung back near the stairs, along with Dana. One of the men rocked side to side like an inverted pendulum and hummed softly. The other, arms crossed over his chest, shuffled forward then backward and looked around the room like he couldn't remember where he had left something. Next to them, Dana looked like a statue. "Thanks again," Eric said.

They just smiled at him but looked to Dana for apparent confirmation that they were done. She nodded at them and they left in a noticeable hurry.

Eric glanced back to see Stacy holding Miss Happy in one hand and

THE SPITE HOUSE • 69

pulling Dess along with her other hand, giving her big sister a tour of her tiny room. Dess glanced at her father, a question reflecting curiosity more than concern on her face. She must have also noticed how fidgety the movers were, how they had rushed out of the house.

Eric said to Dana, "Can we go over one last thing, if you don't mind?"

"Absolutely," she said.

Dess read her cue and told Stacy she wanted to show her the bigger room and led her there, where she couldn't eavesdrop. Eric stepped into the stairwell with Dana and partially closed the door to Stacy's room, leaving it ajar in case the girls called for him.

"Those guys are true believers, huh?" he said.

Dana laughed. "There's a reason we have to bring people in from out of town to stay here."

"I see. You know, I noticed when I was looking up info on the house before I came here, there's actually not much about it online. Are people here just that afraid to talk about it or write about it? Or is that maybe Eunice's influence? I read an article that said she basically has a stranglehold on the town."

"Really? Do you remember who wrote it? I'm sure Miss Houghton would like to have them assassinated, being the tyrant that she is."

"I'm serious."

"You're overthinking it," Dana said. "She has some sway. She has a big voice and likes to be heard, metaphorically speaking. But she doesn't have to tell people not to talk about one thing or another, and this house, especially. The town came to that agreement all on its own even before she was born."

You're either not telling the whole truth, or that means these people are hiding something. Ashamed of something, he thought. "Okay, okay. I'm sorry if I sounded a little suspicious."

"More than a little."

"Again, I'm sorry," he said. "I think it's just really hitting me right now that I'm committing to this. You see some guys who can't stand to be in here another minute, it makes the idea of spending several weeks here a bit daunting."

"Listen, Miss Houghton gave all of our phone numbers to you, right? She didn't do that just to do it," Dana said. "Call her anytime, I mean it. God knows she'll call you or Odessa anytime she might feel like it, at least if she treats you two how she treats me. Seriously, if it's an emergency, if you're concerned, or if you just want to run something by her, call. She'd rather you do that than walk off the job. And if it's something urgent, if she doesn't answer, call me. If I don't answer, call Lafonda."

"And if none of you answers, that's when I have permission to call the police?"

Dana shook her head and told him, "We both know that the only one who'll keep you from calling the cops is you."

The lack of any threat in her tone or expression made her sound more dangerous and knowing. Like it would be routine for her to turn any information she had on him against him. She didn't need to have much, just the confidence that he was wary of involving law enforcement. He'd told Eunice that he wasn't running from anything criminal in his past, but if Eunice had shared that with Dana, Dana clearly disbelieved it. Now she had effectively called him out.

"Do you think you're good from here?" she said, as friendly as when she'd introduced herself yesterday. "You've got your debit cards, you've got our numbers, am I forgetting anything? Our other guys should have all your things from the motel here in about an hour. I'd stay but business calls."

"We're good," he said.

"If you do need anything, like I said, just call and someone'll be here."

He walked her downstairs and to the front door, a minor courtesy he thought necessary after their exchange. He was walking a line so thin it might not even be there. He wanted Eunice and her partners to believe he wasn't as bound to this situation as they might have thought. It was the best opportunity for them, but not something he wouldn't give up if he absolutely had to. At the same time he needed Eunice's trust, and needed to be more careful going forward with what he said, or insinuated, to Dana.

What if she reported back to Eunice that he had accused her of being Degener's despot? What if Eunice was so offended she evicted them? What then? They had an agreement, but not a contract. Nothing in writing, and even if they'd had one, who would he go to, to have it enforced? He had no recourse. They would be back on the road, he would be back to hunting for off-the-books jobs, never knowing when the money might dry up, or when they might get pulled over, or when they'd be found out. If that happened, he wouldn't be able to protect Stacy, not if other people knew the truth about her. She would be taken away, treated like a lost child at best, an object to be studied at worst.

As he returned to the third floor he heard a door creak and close. Stacy's bedroom door was partially open, as he'd left it, but the door to the "floating" hallway that led to the bathroom was shut. It must have been Dess. She had come down the hall to see if he was still there talking to Dana, probably to eavesdrop as well.

He couldn't be upset with her for it. It was the prudent thing to do. Not that he had kept anything too important from her since they had left home. Hiding the depth of their money troubles was the only major, true deceit that came to mind, and he knew now that had been a mistake, though he hadn't admitted it to her yet. The other things he hadn't told her about—his grandfather's grim past, and why he actually wanted to return to the city of Odessa—weren't her burden to bear. Once he found out more, and if he could break those secrets down into smaller, lighter fragments, then he might share them with her.

Still, he couldn't blame her for having suspicions when he had so many as well. Later, probably after Stacy was asleep, he would talk with Dess and reassure her that he would never—

No footsteps.

The thought clicked into place and took prominence in his mind, though he could not quite understand why.

I walked that hall with Dana yesterday and heard every step clear as day. If Dess was just in there—

She's smaller than me. She's quieter.

Not that small. Not even Stacy's that small.

Well, if it wasn't her, who or what was it?

Eric had little difficulty believing that something unseen could be with him and his daughters in this house. Life experience had taught him to keep his mind open to possibilities that rational people had every reason to dismiss. Part of him even hoped, for selfish reasons, that the house was indeed as haunted as Eunice wanted him to prove it to be. But he found it hard to believe it would manifest itself so soon. Perhaps because he dared not think that whatever else was here would make it so easy for him.

The money Eunice agreed to advance him for living here was a comparative stipend. The true reward awaited once he brought her enough stories for her to feel satisfied that he'd really walked and talked with the house's spirits, and unearthed the Masson House's buried secrets. What she meant to do with that satisfaction, she hadn't shared, and he didn't really care as long as the money was real. Eric had steeled himself to be here for several weeks, perhaps even a few months. It seemed impossible to him that any activity might start before noon on his first day here. At that rate, he might only have to subject his girls to this for one or two weeks at most.

The warmth of anticipation and hopefulness kindled in his chest. He shook his head and grunted disapprovingly at himself. He could not trust optimism. He knew better.

He went to the door of the adjunct hallway, opened it, and looked inside. The walls were thin enough for him to hear Stacy talking to Miss Happy, back in her room now. Eric found the light switch along the wall and flipped it. The bulb in the center of the hall lit up, but its light could not penetrate the thick darkness at the other end of the hallway.

Have to ask for a brighter bulb to be put in here, he thought. *Don't forget—*

The thought retreated as his eyes adjusted. Was there someone standing at the end of the hall? He sensed this more than he saw it, like the air had shifted closer to him. It brought up the gooseflesh on his arms. He saw a small figure within the darkness, like a body pressing against a thick, black curtain. Was it facing him? Facing the wall? He could not tell. The longer he stared, the more convinced he was of the shape's presence. His imagination would have swayed the figure one way or the other, moved it closer or farther away, stretched or compressed its height. It wouldn't have been able to hold the form so rigidly, he thought. And he was sure the hall had grown colder than it had been a few seconds earlier.

He surprised himself when he spoke aloud without a second thought.

"Hello," he said to whoever he saw at the end of the hall.

The bathroom door opened slowly, as if whatever opened it wanted to peek first at what was on the other side. Daylight from the small bathroom window seeped into the end of the hall, just enough to illuminate that no one was there.

"Dad." It was Dess. She had been in the second bedroom, the room that the door at the end of the hall led into. Eric heard her leave the room, go through Stacy's room, and enter the foyer. He lingered in the hall an extra second to be sure that whatever had been at the end of the hall was truly gone, then stepped back into the foyer, where Dess was waiting for him. She looked like she had seen a car drive off a bridge but was just barely calm enough to give a solid account of it to first responders. Before she said anything, she turned to shut Stacy's door.

"That wasn't you, was it?" she said. "The bathroom door opened just now."

"I know."

"And it couldn't have been you, because you were over here, right?"

"It wasn't me," Eric said.

"All right. Do you think that was a thing or not? Like, could it have just been this weirdo house being uneven or something?"

"I don't know, Dess. I guess it could be that."

"It has to be that, right? I mean we just got here. Anything weird would take longer to start up if it was going to happen, right?"

"I wish I knew, Dess. I feel like maybe I saw something, but maybe not."

"Okay. Oookay." She put her hands behind her head and nibbled the inside of her bottom lip, a nervous habit she'd picked up from her mother. "So, that either happened or it didn't. I mean it did, but it was either real or it wasn't. Which is pretty obvi when I say it like that, but that's what it is, right? It either is or it isn't. Shit, I feel like I'm not saying what I want to say."

Eric put his hands on her shoulders, and her light tremors gave him an extra measure of calm. His sense of fatherly responsibility activated and demanded he be strong for her despite his own anxiousness over what he did or didn't see in the hallway.

"I understand. I know what you're trying to say."

Dess shook her head. "No, no, no. Dad, you don't. You can't because I'm not saying it right. What I'm saying is what if that is a ghost or something? I know what we do if it's not, but what do we do if it is?"

"I just write it down, that's all. That's what she's paying me for. And if it really is something, we'll be fine. It can't hurt us."

"How do you know that? There's no way you know that."

"Listen, if you don't want to stay, I can ask Eunice to take you and Stacy in. She's already agreed to that."

"And you would just stay here by yourself?" Dess said, her voice rising for the first time.

"Keep it down. You'll worry your sister."

Dess inhaled deeply and shut her eyes for a moment of micromeditation. "Sorry."

"It's okay. It's all going to be okay. This is what we signed up for. We knew that this was at least possible, right?"

"I just didn't think anything would happen this soon."

Eric nodded and forced a smile. He didn't want her to see anything other than confidence in him. She was scared, and he was forgetting to be her father. He'd asked so much of her, lately. In moments like this he realized he had to remember how young she still was, despite all she'd been through and the extraordinary growth she'd undergone. She had not, in fact, signed up for any of this.

Still, he didn't want to say anything that might put her off this opportunity entirely. Not after what he might have just seen in the hall. For the first time since they'd had to leave home, since he'd started pondering what all he might have inherited from his grandfather, he thought he might finally get some answers. That they might be near, right here in this house.

"I get you," he said. "I thought we'd at least have to wait a few nights for anything weird to happen. But hey, maybe it was nothing, right? Like you said, it could just be the way this old house is built. Doors might kind of swing a little bit or we might hear the house settling, all that stuff. Remember our old place, how some of the doors slammed when we turned on the AC? Maybe there's a draft that does the same thing here. There's probably some regular explanation for this. And if not, it could be for the best that it starts up sooner, so we can get right into it. Like tearing off a Band-Aid fast instead of slow. Or just jumping right in—"

—*the water*, he was going to say, but he locked the words in his throat. He winced like he'd plucked a thorn from his fingertip, then forced the memory of Stacy playing in the water from his thoughts.

"Jumping right to the end," Dess said.

"Exactly. But listen to me, and I mean this. If you don't want to stay here you have to tell me. I'll be fine on my own."

"If it gets to be too much for Staze, then we'll talk about it," Dess said.

Eric said, "Or if it gets to be too much for you too."

She wanted to push back at this, he could see it. She wanted to tell him that she wasn't anywhere near that scared yet, but the lie wouldn't leave her lips. Dess turned and joined Stacy in her room, asked her if she could help her do some coloring.

Eric stood alone in the foyer. Troubled as he was by the prospect of staying here by himself, he was more troubled by the anxiousness he'd seen on Dess's face, and troubled most by the fact that the best he could do for his girls was to have them live with a stranger who was willing to spend a fortune seeking evidence of an afterlife. He had no reason to suspect Eunice of anything thus far, but he'd known her for less than a day. He needed to trust her, but was distantly aware of the possibility that her benevolence was an act.

Max Renner

*M*ore than one doctor implied that Jane Renner was acting, especially after finding out what she and Max used to do. The job that brought his wife to this state was actually hindering the quality of the medical care she received. A job that she hadn't been enthusiastic about, despite supporting his efforts to make it their long-term career.

"Husband and Wife Paranormal Researchers" was how they promoted themselves. Privately, they considered themselves "Stealth Skeptic Parodists," patterned after a television program Max enjoyed, hosted by Neal Lassiter. Max and Jane visited many supposedly haunted locations and went through the same motions as any other "ghost hunting" team, while slyly highlighting the absurdity of jumping at shadows and sounds and shuddering at indecipherable EVP recordings, many of which were added during postproduction. That was supposed to be what set them apart from the countless others doing the same thing on the internet.

They found decent success. Fourteen thousand followers was a tiny fraction of what the most popular people in the field had, but Max did the math. If they got ten percent of those people to donate an average of five dollars a month they'd be doing well enough. Cover their business expenses, pay their personal bills, and have more than enough left over to treat themselves. And their numbers had been creeping upward for a year before they went to Degener.

People enjoyed their banter. Commenters on their videos said they came off as a couple hosting a home-remodeling show rather than a ghost-hunting show. Many hardcore ghost-hunting fans didn't like their irreverence or playfulness, but others found it refreshing. Their core audience either didn't notice how staged it all was or just didn't care. Maybe they tuned in specifically to watch such shamelessness.

There had been nothing staged about that last night in the spite house. If Max had any of the video or audio recordings from that night, or the three weeks that preceded it, he could share them with some of the doctors to prove Jane wasn't faking anything. It wouldn't necessarily be enough to convince them ghosts were real, but it would convince them that the Renners had been through something. They'd see what weeks inside the spite house had done to them, the before and after. Max left all of that equipment behind, though, and hadn't saved anything to a cloud or put it online before leaving. Eunice Houghton probably kept it in a vault somewhere. He didn't want to see it anyway. It was bad enough when he relived that night in his mind.

Jane had broken his grip as he tried to drag her out of the house. "I can't leave me behind," she screamed, scratching and punching him. "It has me and won't give me back. I can't leave without getting me back!"

She had run upstairs, and the days of hardly sleeping or eating had left Max so weak he could only crawl after her. He almost didn't do that. He almost left her. By the time he got to Jane in the floating hallway, where it was so cold he felt like he'd been buried naked in snow, she was unconscious on the floor. He gathered her up and managed to carry her downstairs despite feeling like he could hardly carry his own weight. As he got through the front door and brought her to the car, he heard someone who sounded like Jane screaming from inside the house. But he had her in his arms, where she was dead quiet, so it couldn't have been her, even though it sounded like her, even though in his soul he knew it had to be her and that if he went back he'd find the part of her that she'd gone back for. The part she said the house had taken. Screaming for help while he pretended not to hear it.

Eric

Eric found himself on an unknown dirt road, struggling to make sense of two competing memories. The last thing he remembered was checking in on Stacy and Dess before going upstairs to go to sleep in the master bedroom of the spite house. But he also had a memory that couldn't be his. The memory of a battlefield filled with a mind-altering quantity of violence. It couldn't have been from a movie he'd seen or book he'd read, because the unspeakable smell of it still lingered with him. Burning, rancid, metallic, and vulgar, it was a merciless and unshakable smell. The noise of it all, too, was fixed in his mind as though he had lived it. So he must have been there. But he had never been to war, or been in the service. Hell, Eric had never been in a fistfight. But when he looked down he saw that he wore boots and pants caked in mud, and a darkened khaki service coat.

He noticed that his hands were not his; they were white.

This was a dream, then. He shut his eyes for a moment, then checked his clothes and hands again when he reopened them. Nothing had changed. The road ahead looked the same, tree-lined. The clouds in the sky hadn't darkened or departed.

He shut his eyes once again, and this time he saw the memory of combat that part of him had tried to stave off. A field that warfare had turned into a deforested bog. Sucking mud where he'd gotten his feet stuck and been hit with something, where he'd glimpsed his insides spilling out below his waist, his lower half absent. He heard the deafening storm of exploding mortar shells. There had been an alarming absence of pain. He should have been in a world of agony. His legs were gone, his guts sliding out. Why hadn't he felt any of that?

Against his will, he recalled those final moments as he fought for each breath and held on for as long as he could before he fell deep into blackness and infinite coldness. He'd been in that void for an unknown time, the only thing keeping him partially afloat being his desire to go home. There was an unfathomable multitude with him. More than it was possible to estimate, much less count. Several worlds' worth of people, it seemed. Many, like him, stayed afloat because they wanted to get back to something, return to a place or work left unfinished, loved ones left unprotected. He sensed almost all of them succumbing to acceptance, though. Gradually, they sank to the bottom of this void. There were very few like him, exceptions who refused to sink deeper, refused to believe this was the end. Some loved their lives too much to surrender them, but most who had the strength and will to fight did so for the same core reason. Less for want of living than the hatred of dying. Hatred of losing. Of allowing others to take what was theirs.

After some time, the soldier rose higher, and the darkness faded. And now, eyes open again, he walked. Whoever he was—for Eric was not himself here—he walked like he could outpace his past.

He passed a wooden signpost that displayed the name of a French village not far ahead. Once he got there, he'd have to find someone who would pardon his meager French and who spoke enough English to help him. *I am an American. Private Pete Masson of the 144th Ambulance Company. Is there an army post nearby?*

He found people who understood him and were willing to help in the tiny commune of Montfaucon. The looks they gave him when he explained who he was prompted him to ask something else. "What month is it?"

Août.

August? The last he remembered it had been September. "What is the year?"

Dix-neuf cent dix-neuf.

1919.

He had lost almost an entire year. How? Where had he been in this time?

It doesn't matter. Get home.

But they must have reported him missing by now. He'd have to explain where he'd been. What if they thought he had deserted? What if they somehow thought he had died?

Stop it. Why would they think that? Of course I didn't die. I'm here, I couldn't have died. I'm getting home. I've got to get back. I've got to—

"—get back."

Was that a woman's voice that had awakened him? Where the hell was he now? Why was everything so dark?

Eric grabbed the sheets on the bed. An array of emotions invaded him. A cocktail of grief and fear and anger. He reached for the lamp beside the bed and found the switch to turn it on. Even with the room lit, he struggled to believe he was back in the house, back in his own body, not trapped in another man's life in the past. Something still didn't seem right. The bedroom curtains were open. Hadn't he closed them before going to bed? He must have. He never liked sleeping in a room with an uncovered window. Still, the day had been busy between deliveries and getting settled in and simply remembering to feed himself and the girls. He could have forgotten to close the curtains.

The night was dark enough for such an oversight to be possible. Not quite impenetrable, but close to it. Lights from Degener's Main Street shops and restaurants traveled just far enough to prevent the dark's absolute dominion. Eric was sure that those buildings in town kept their lights on through the night to warn the spite house that it could not sneak into town unseen, or open its door to draw people inside. Eat them. Hadn't Stacy inadvertently suggested that a couple of nights ago? She'd said the house was skinny because it hadn't eaten enough. What else would a house like this feed on but lives? All of Degener knew it, too, but they had let him come here with his children, hadn't even tried to warn him, they had just let him—

He shook his head, freeing himself from as much of this paranoia as he could, and rubbed his eyes hard with his palms. He still wasn't awake enough to think clearly. When he was young, when the nearly living memory of the ghost fire at his grandparents' house would follow him wherever he rested his head, he would fend off the visitation by getting out of bed to get a glass of water or a snack. Something to anchor him to reality.

Eric slid out of bed like he didn't want to wake a partner beside him. Part of him remembered how unfamiliar this house was to him. In the moment, he could hardly remember how many floors this house had, three or four, much less which one had the kitchen and sink where he could get some water.

Just leave, then, he thought. *Get the hell out. Get in the car. Drive. Get away.*

He moved quickly to the bedroom door and froze just before opening it. His chest felt empty, and he thought he might get sick. The impulse that had just guided him to the door through the darkness hadn't reminded him to get Dess and Stacy on his way out. Had he followed it, he'd have left them. He might have been in the car and halfway down the road heading into town—or away from it—before he remembered.

The house, or whatever powered it, was more formidable than he could have guessed. It hadn't directly attacked him yet. Maybe it couldn't, or didn't want to. Still, it wasn't something he could take lightly. Not when it could fill his head and overtake him like this. If he was lucky, though, he was the focus of all of its energy, and it was leaving the girls alone. He'd check on them after he managed to calm himself. He didn't want to wake them up and freak them out, or worse, bring the energy that had briefly possessed him into their rooms.

He turned around to see if there was anything behind him, but he only saw the bed, the room. For a moment, as he held his breath, he felt as if he were in a cave no one had ever set foot in. A place underground that you could discover and die in, and where your remains would go undisturbed for as long as civilization lasted. A place where a ghost could stay lost for eternity.

Eric thought he heard laughter from elsewhere in the house. Or was it a scream? He couldn't tell if it came from a man or a woman, an adult or a child. What he did know was that the temperature in the room had fallen considerably, a familiar iciness he hadn't felt since he was a boy. He could sense a presence, just as he had when he was young. It was larger this time, filling most of the room, making him feel trapped, like if he tried to step too far in one direction or another, he would bump into a wall of ice. It didn't want him in the room, but also seemed reluctant to let him leave. Maybe because "it" wasn't a single thing, but competing forces.

He opened the bedroom door, backed out, and shut it quickly behind him as if to keep anything from following him out.

Dess

She hadn't expected to miss a motel room, but she couldn't sleep in this bizarre house. When they had first hit the road, it had taken her some time to get used to the noisiness of the places they stayed in. Neighbors one room over would turn the volume up too loud on their televisions, or play music late after dark, or stay up drinking and talking and screwing until well past midnight. Dess and Eric never risked raising a fuss with the front desk, because they feared the situation might escalate to a point where police might be called.

Stacy could sleep through almost any amount of racket when she was tired enough, and Dad willed himself to sleep with relative ease. For Dess, the process of adapting to the regular commotion had taken longer. That was one reason why she'd found herself sneaking out and finding ways to make money. She couldn't sleep and needed something to do.

In the past few weeks she'd trained herself to fall asleep beside Stacy each night despite the racket of footsteps in tiled hallways or inebriated singing coming through walls. But now she found it impossible to even be tired in a bed she had to herself, particularly in a house that was too silent on top of being too narrow.

From the outside the house looked like something you'd want to take a picture in front of, post to social, get a few laughs and likes. #CrazyAssTexas. #DontSlowDownHere. Spending the night inside, even trying to, instantly made it clear that this house wasn't really designed to be lived in. A man with means and resources, who could have built a decent house anywhere else, had gone out of his way to put this strange, emaciated thing on this precarious spot on this hill, looking down on those other buildings in the valley. *Just to make someone upset or show the world how pissed you are,* Dad had said. That was why the person who built it put it here. It wasn't just an eyesore, it was a statement. She couldn't imagine how mad or disturbed you'd have to be to build a house like this.

Dess wished she had someone to talk to. She missed having friends, although she'd lost many of them well before she and her dad and Stacy had hit the road. It wasn't anyone's fault. Her grief and depression just put distance between them, and the business of getting their futures together— applying for scholarships and financial aid, weighing whether to join the military, and in one case making postgraduation wedding plans—added to the gulf between them. Still, Dess wondered what they were up to. She wondered what they'd say about this house, about her life, about what she was going to eventually do with herself, because she couldn't spend the rest of her life doing this, right? She'd have to get back to something close to normal someday, wouldn't she?

Yeah, nah, she would say to them. *Normal is out the window,* and she'd have to leave it at that because she couldn't tell them why. They might be right, though, about how long she could keep this up. She had no timeline set, but at some point, she'd have to see the rest of her family again. Her mother if no one else.

Thinking of her mother and the way they had left her behind, what she might be thinking of them, or worse, that she might *not* be thinking of them much at all, turned Dess's stomach over. Why did she have to think of her mother tonight? She'd done well to keep memories and thoughts of her mom locked in a box in the corner of her mind that she'd only open about once a week at most, just often enough to keep it from hurting too bad when she did, and she always braced herself for it. She had practiced preventing thoughts of her mother from getting loose when she was already in her feelings, which was where she was tonight. She missed home, was frustrated about having no future in sight, and was, she could at last admit, afraid to fall asleep. Fear was an underrated emotion, she thought. It was the original alarm system. Tonight it was ringing several bells that called for her to stay alert, even if it meant keeping her eyes open until sunrise.

Beyond the darkness that sat in the room like a lazy fog, eating most of what little light tried to come in through the window, and beyond the too-close walls, particularly the wall opposite the bed, there was the fact that Stacy was sleeping in a separate room. It was the first time Dess or her father had let Stacy stay out of their sight for more than enough time to use the bathroom. This made Dess as anxious as anything else, and part of what kept her awake was the idea that she needed to be able to hear if Stacy called out to her, in case.

In case what?

She felt for the key-chain flashlight on her nightstand. When she found it, she turned it on, got out of bed, and walked to the adjoining door. The worst-case scenario that had just crossed her mind was worse than the idea of Stacy screaming for her big sister's help in the dead of night.

Dess opened the door to the first room and was startled to see Stacy sitting at the edge of her bed, facing her. Stacy had her back to the door that led to the stairs. She clutched Miss Happy like she wanted to squeeze the breath out of the doll. Stacy lifted her head to face Dess, her eyes initially full of concern that looked out of place before a familiar relief came over her.

"Are you okay?" Dess said, remaining in the doorway. Before Stacy could answer, Dess added, "Why is it so cold in here?"

"I don't know," Stacy said.

"You want to come to my room?"

Stacy nodded.

"What's wrong?" Dess said.

"I heard somebody."

"What?"

"I heard a boy talking to me. He woke me up. He told me something bad."

"Okay. Okay, let's—"

"He said the house can make people disappear," Stacy said, her voice quivering. "And then he said that was a secret, and since he told me a secret, I had to tell him mine. But I didn't know what he was talking about. I told him that and he called me a liar and went over there."

She turned and pointed toward the corner of the room by the door to the stairs. Dess's flashlight was already bright enough to reveal that no one else was in the room, but she aimed the light at the corner nonetheless, as if doing so could draw something invisible out of hiding. Not that she'd be happy to see it, but being unable to see it while it was there would be worse.

Her mind repeated the information her eyes fed it. *There's nothing there. There's nothing there.*

"He's still there," Stacy said, her voice climbing a bit. "You have to believe me he's there. And he said I better tell him, or he'll get his sister to make me tell."

It's just her imagination, Dess thought, the words popping into her head. Stacy liked to read. She liked to create. She learned to make paper flowers and her own coloring books. She could make up stories to entertain herself. She was stunningly smart and intuitive and willful. And she was still a kid. Her mind could be more than she could corral. But that wasn't the case now, Dess was sure of that. Stacy's eyes told her so, as did the goose bumps on her arms, and the shivers making teeth clack.

"Come on," Dess said, holding out her hand.

Stacy took it and asked, "Are we going to your room?"

"We're going downstairs."

"Dess, please, he's—"

"I know. I don't think you're lying. But he's just a little boy, right?"

"He's mean, though," Stacy said.

"So he's a little bully. We're not scared of bullies, are we?"

Stacy hesitated before shaking her head.

Dess said, "Hell no, we're not. So we're going to walk right by him, we're going to walk out of here, and he's not going to try anything unless he wants his ass beat. And if his big sister shows up, she can get it too."

Stacy squeezed Dess's hand and stood by her. They approached the door, Dess placing herself between Stacy and the corner. She watched the corner for movement, listened for a voice or breathing, anything to validate what Stacy said was there. All she perceived as they made it to the door was that the temperature continued to fall.

She opened the door and as she moved Stacy through first, Dess felt the door hit something before it bumped against the wall, like someone had put their foot at the bottom of it. She hurried out after Stacy and they both turned to see the door start to close. Could have been the push of a breeze if a window had been open. Maybe the house was more tilted than they noticed.

She held Stacy close and braced herself to see and hear the door slam on its own. Instead it remained ajar, and the sound that made her jump came from one floor down. Someone was on the stairs. She heard, "Hey, it's me," and through the thudding of her heartbeat in her ears she almost didn't recognize her father's voice. She turned the flashlight toward the sound of his voice and felt like the world was righting itself when she saw that it was, indeed, him.

"What are you doing?" Eric said.

"I couldn't sleep," Dess said, "and, uh, I went to check on Stacy."

"Did something happen?"

She looked back to the door. It was as she'd last seen it, wasn't it? It hadn't inched any closer to closing? Maybe it had, but just a literal inch, then. Nothing significant enough to justify her wariness of it.

"We just had to get out of there," Dess said.

"I heard somebody," Stacy said.

The expression on her father's face told Dess that he was keeping something important to himself, and that she ought to ask him what he had just asked them. He wouldn't cop to anything in front of Stacy, though. She would have to wait until later.

"If you want, we can all go downstairs," Eric said. "Play some games or something. Then if either of you get tired you can have the couch. And we can all keep an eye on each other just in case. Probably should have done that anyway. First night sleeping in different rooms. I think we're all just a little bit out of our comfort zone."

"Yeah," Dess said, leading Stacy down the stairs, now putting herself between her sister and the room, like a shield.

On the ground floor, in the house's shrunken living room, Eric and Dess let Stacy pick the first game, and she selected her favorite, ABC's. After playing through two rounds they moved on to charades, but after just a few turns of that Stacy was lying on her side on the couch, her head on a throw pillow, eyes closed. Dess took the opposite end of the couch. She would sleep in a sitting position so she could put her head on the back cushion and let her father have the extra throw pillow as he made do with the floor.

"Night, Dad," Dess said.

"Good night."

"Hey. One thing real quick."

"What's that?" Eric said.

Dess double-checked to be sure Stacy was asleep, then said, "You know you're going to have to tell me what happened to *you* upstairs, right?"

Eric sighed. "Good night, Dess."

"Yeah. Talk to you in the morning," she said.

Eric

A whisper drew him from sleep like an alarm. Eric would have mistaken the voice for Tabitha's, but he knew that this was just part of him wanting to hear his wife's voice. This had been a stranger telling him something about dreams. He couldn't recall what exactly they said but suspected it was more threat than warning. Maybe he was wrong, though. Maybe he was just paranoid. Everything that happened in the last year and a half pushed him to employ suspicion as a first line of defense.

He sat up and saw that Stacy was still asleep and that the other end of the couch was vacant, save for a note written in black crayon on a sheet of paper. *Out running. bb. Dess.* He checked his watch. Eight thirty in the morning.

So Dess had gotten up early, ventured upstairs by herself to get paper and a crayon from Stacy's room, wrote her note, and left the house without waking him. If past lives were a thing—*Hell, why wouldn't they be,* Eric thought—Dess had been a ninja or spy in one of hers. He knocked on his forehead with his knuckles and bit down on the word "stupid" before it could get out. He had to do better. That was all he could control. Lecturing her like she wasn't an adult would do no good. It wasn't like he had much disciplinary leverage over her, either. What privileges could he take from her? What else could he do to impart how he felt besides raise his voice, which wasn't his style? In terms of authoritarian hierarchy, they were less father and daughter and more co-guardians. Hell, she had even earned her own money. He couldn't pull rank on her or pull anything away from her. Despite all of that, he was still the parent here. The only one she had left, for all practical purposes. If he let something happen to her, there was no one else to blame. Hell, for all he knew something already had happened to her and he was here wasting seconds he couldn't get back thinking about what he couldn't do instead of just doing better. A spear of guilt gored him as he felt sure that Dess was in trouble. Of course she was. If there was one thing recent history had taught him, it was that fears came true far more often than dreams.

He went to the living room window and saw Dess running hard back toward the house, having rounded the empty orphanage in the valley. He felt his tension soften, but not melt. How many laps did she plan to take? He needed to let her know that she couldn't be pulling stunts like this anymore. He went to the couch and gathered Stacy up. She groaned, hugged him around the neck, and put her head on his shoulder.

"I'm still tired," she said.

"We're just going to check on your sister. I'll bring you right back."

He carried her out the front door and made sure to close it behind him hard enough for the sound to bound through the valley, so Dess could hear it.

A car pulled within about twenty yards of the house and parked. It was a small, nondescript four-door, nothing like the trucks and vans the movers had driven yesterday, or the black luxury sedan Dana drove. Its door opened and out stepped a short, stout middle-aged white woman who looked to Eric like the kind of person who got overcompetitive during a friendly softball game or team-building exercise.

She removed her sunglasses before asking him, "Are you the new keeper of the castle?"

He rolled through his possible responses in his head. Eunice had assured him yesterday evening that no one from town would harass him. "Nobody here is inclined to do such a thing. That's not how we raise 'em in Degener. You probably passed through other towns on the way here that gave you the opposite impression, but here, we don't tolerate that shit."

She'd sounded almost too convincing, which was what had prompted him to test whether Dana might verify what he'd read in that article. In that moment, Eunice had sounded exactly like someone who could strong-arm a group of people into thinking and behaving the way she wanted them to. And yet, here someone was, not quite twenty-four hours after they had officially moved in.

He decided to have faith in Eunice's words and introduced himself in a polite but firm tone. "I am. I'm Eric."

He moved Stacy over to his left arm so that he could shake hands with the woman, who said, "Nice to meet you, Eric. I'm Emily Steen, though most people call me Millie."

"I know that name," he said, and needed only a couple of seconds for it to come to him. "Emily Steen. I read your article about Miss Houghton the other day. I was just talking about it to someone yesterday."

"Really? You read that whole thing and that still wasn't enough to scare you off? What in the world still made you want to come here?"

Eric's eyes narrowed and he held Stacy closer. "What are you here for, Miss Steen?"

The confidence seeped from her face, replaced first by slight bemusement, then a flush of embarrassment that reddened her like a sunburn. "Oh Lord. How did that come off? I hope you didn't . . . I didn't mean . . . Listen, I was just hoping to introduce myself and maybe have a conversation with you. Make sure you know what you need to know about your present circumstances. Is there a chance we could talk just you and I?"

Something about Emily Steen made Eric immediately distrustful of her, beyond the way she had shown up unannounced and spoke of him being "scared off." It could have been that the previous night's events had heightened his already elevated suspicions of just about anything unfamiliar to him. But he was sure that there was something else, and thought back to the article she'd written to determine what it could be.

"You can't give me a better idea of what you'd like to talk about?" Eric said.

"It's related to the house."

"And us being here. Is that right, Miss Steen?"

Emily sighed. "I'm here for your well-being, Eric—sir—I promise. Feel free to call me Millie, by the way."

"I'd rather keep it formal, if it's all the same," he said.

She nodded, bit the inside of her lip. It felt good to Eric that he seemed to have her off-balance. For the first time in a long time he wasn't the one reacting and adjusting. He was out ahead of the conversation, steering it. He hadn't had solid control of much, if anything, since leaving Maryland. Hell, even before then. Now, though, he wasn't just letting this happen, letting this stranger show up, speak their piece, and leave.

"I'll have to ask you to pardon my word choice, earlier," Emily said, "and my impolite arrival, too. Least I should have done is brought a gift, now that I think on it. But, as for the nature of the conversation I'd like to have, I'd really rather not speak of it in front of your little girl here. Some of what I've got to say might not be fit for her ears."

Stacy said, "Are you going to say bad words?"

Eric shushed her and smiled at her despite wanting to keep this woman at bay. Emily smiled too. "No, little missy, I won't."

Eric said, "Miss Steen, I don't think you being here is appropriate."

"Just hold on. It's about Eunice and this house, and making sure you at least have all the information."

"Mm. Does she know you're here?"

"No. I'm one of the few people around here who doesn't run almost everything I do by her first."

"I thought not," Eric said. "And I get the impression you're here to tell me something about her that's meant to get me to leave." Before she could answer, what he was reaching for in his mind came to him. "You know, one interesting thing I remember from that article is that you always seemed opposed to some of Eunice's more tolerant or accepting proposals."

Emily's jaw slacked and she shook her head quickly. "I'm sure I didn't do that at all."

"Not directly, in a roundabout way. You know, pretty much saying, 'I don't mind what happened, I mind the way it happened.' The Juneteenth-recognition thing, for example. That jumped out, you not being on board with that."

"Oh Lord, sir, with all due respect you misread what I was saying there."

"No, I think I got it. You said you were okay with the idea—"

"More than okay—"

"—you just didn't like how it came about. Lots of people take that sort of stance when they don't want to come out and just say what they'd really like to say."

In her eyes now, he saw more than just surprise and confusion, he saw hurt that would be hard to fake. Not impossible, but difficult. She might have been telling the truth—her truth, at least—about him misreading her intentions. But who was she anyway? Someone whose biggest grievances with the woman helping his family amounted to "She oversteps in her successful efforts to make this town a better place." Why would Emily Steen's intentions matter to him more than Eunice Houghton's?

"All I can say to that," Emily said, "is that if you'd read any of my other work—any of it—you'd know that that's not who I am."

"I'll take you up on that. I could use something new to read," he said. "In the meantime, if you don't mind, I am growing a little concerned that you might say something unfit for my girl to hear. If you want to reach out to me in the future, as long as you run it by Eunice or Dana to make sure it's all on the up-and-up, I might be open to a conversation."

Emily looked at him like she no longer spoke his language. This meeting had gone somewhere she hadn't thought it could get to. It had flown free of her grasp when she didn't know it had wings.

She walked away with her head low and Eric thought he heard her muttering to herself. At her car, before she got in, she turned back to him and said, "If I may, just . . . ask Dana or Eunice—whichever—ask them about the memorial. Tell them you heard it from me or not, it doesn't matter. Just mention it to them and see how they act. I think, at minimum, you really should know what's motivating all this."

As she got in her car and started the engine, Eric heard Dess behind him say, "What was that all about? What memorial?"

"Why didn't you like that lady, Dad?" Stacy said. "Because you thought she was going to say cusswords?"

"She just seemed a little rude," Eric said. "It's okay to introduce yourself to your neighbors, but you should at least give them time to have some breakfast, don't you think?"

Stacy nodded. Eric turned to Dess, who asked again, "What memorial? Who even was that? Does she know Eunice?"

Before Eric could answer, Stacy said, "She said her name is Emily."

"Aren't you chatty today," Eric said.

"I'm sorry," Stacy said.

"That's okay. This is just time for me and your sister to talk, okay?"

"Okay."

Dess said, "Just Emily? She didn't give a last name?" She was still out of breath and had more questions than Eric thought she'd have. What was going on with her?

"If she did, I forgot it already. It's not important, Dess. She said she was just here to check on us, basically. But she wasn't with Eunice so I just, you know, played it safe. Told her we were okay so she doesn't need to come back around like that."

"Did you tell her about last night? Did she have anything to say about that?"

"None of that was her business to know. Look, let's get some breakfast first and then talk later. We need to discuss you sneaking out without telling me where you're going anyway. Okay?"

"Yeah, yeah, all right."

Eric knew what that meant. He remembered the first time Tabitha had translated his daughter's words for him. *One "yeah" means yes, two "yeah"s means "not really."*

I thought that was "yeah, nah," he'd said.

That just means "no."

He was surprised she didn't have more of a comeback for him. She wasn't likely to say something too defiant. It wasn't in her nature, and even if it was, she minded her words around Stacy. Still, he expected a small quip. *Yeah, yeah, we'll talk about that, and everything else.* She was past him and moving toward the house before he could really measure what was in her eyes, what he might have missed. Was last night worse than she had let on? Or had something else happened that morning? He thought about how fast she'd been running. She might have just been pushing herself, but she also might have been hurrying to get away from something. By the time he caught up to her in the house, she had put a braver face on.

"How was your run?" he said.

"Pretty good," Dess said, and he knew that was all he'd get out of her.

After they got ready he took the girls into town for breakfast—where everyone who saw them said "Hello," and "Welcome," and smiled their broadest smiles like they were politicians glad-handing during a campaign. Later he called Dana to tell her of Emily's visit, and later still, while Stacy napped, he talked to Dess about what happened to each of them the night before, adding her account to his journal.

Before sunset, he went back into town to use a computer at the Degener Public Library. He found no meaningful search results for any variation on the term "Degener memorial." He then moved on to read some of Emily Steen's work available online. From what he saw of it, she was an ally from before people commonly used the word "ally" in that fashion. That didn't guarantee that her written words were sincere, or that she was the same person now. Still, he might have misjudged her. He should have let her talk. Or maybe his instincts were right and he'd been smart to stonewall her. How the hell could he know, one way or the other?

He wished Tab was with them. She would tell him not to think too hard about all the things he didn't know or couldn't know, and focus on what he knew. What he could be sure of. Focus less on what could go wrong, more on what could go right. He could imagine her saying it, but it wasn't the same as hearing it. Even if she was there to tell him, it might have bounced off him given all that had gone wrong in the last year and a half, and the fickle nature of the one thing that had gone right.

CHAPTER 15

Dess

When she woke up that morning, the silence startled her. She saw her father on the floor, her sister at the other end of the sofa, but didn't hear either of them breathing in their sleep. Dess checked on Stacy first, saw her chest rising and falling even though she made no sound. Next she checked on her father, who was doing the same. He didn't flinch when she approached, showed no sign he heard the sound of the sofa creaking when she got up. He was just asleep. Nothing to be worried about. Still, how quiet he was disturbed her. Like he was pretending he wasn't awake, lying in wait. Maybe he was.

She rubbed her eyes. What the hell was she thinking? Why would Dad do that? Yes, he'd talked with her about sneaking out. It was remotely possible he was baiting her to try again, looking to catch her in the act, but that wasn't his style. He wasn't a schemer.

Well, he didn't used to be. By necessity he'd become a bit of one. That was how they'd gotten a head start out of Maryland and how they managed to get as far as they were now. Scheming, planning, lying, and deceiving, they'd been at it for months. It was hard to imagine Dad deciding to turn that energy against her now in the hopes she'd spring the trap just so he could prove a point.

No, she was overthinking this. Even under normal conditions people slept differently in a new place. This house didn't come close to qualifying as normal. After what happened yesterday with the bathroom door, and then what happened last night, it was no wonder she was paranoid. The house was making her feel that way. She needed to get out for a minute. Get some air, get a run in.

That meant going back to the third floor to get her shoes. She looked at the stairs and was emboldened by how ordinary they looked. Not even a hint of a goose bump rose on her. The daylight helped. Her single-mindedness helped more. The same thing that motivated her to take that offer to run errands for strangers got her going now. If something had to be done, then it had to be done. Thinking on it for too long was just going to raise doubt and invite fear that, while valid, results in inaction.

She was up the stairs and in her room before thoughts of last night could make her hesitant. She slipped into her shoes without lacing them— deciding to do that downstairs. Passing through Stacy's room, she grabbed a sheet of paper and crayon so she could leave a note for her father, in case he woke up before she was back. She didn't plan to be gone long. One lap around the property, into the valley, past the orphanage, and then circle back. Maybe take a second lap if she was feeling good. Given the sleep they'd lost last night and how hard her dad and Stacy seemed to be sleeping now, Dess thought she might get back before either of them woke up.

The wind picked up a bit as she descended the hill and entered the valley. It was welcome, given how warm the morning was, but it made the surrounding woods a little loud for her liking. She didn't know if there were any animals to be concerned about in the Texas Hill Country, and guessed that if there were, Dana Cantu would have warned them. Still, she didn't like the idea of a coyote or even a large stray dog stalking her under cover of rustling trees, so she stuck more to the open field. That put her closer to the orphanage.

From the spite house, it looked far more dilapidated than it did as she approached it now. It was evident that Miss Houghton had landscapers take general care of the area, but Dess didn't expect the orphanage to be almost habitable. It looked like someone had repainted the orphanage's main house just a few years ago. None of its windows were broken, there weren't any shingles missing from its roof, the walls weren't cracked, and the front door . . .

There hadn't been a front door when she looked at it a few minutes ago. She couldn't be wrong about that; she remembered the black space where the door should be sort of making it look like the building was screaming.

That had pushed her to run closer to the trees before the thought of stealthy lone predators or strays pushed her toward the field and orphanage. There was a front door now, though, large, closed, and like new.

She slowed a little and kept her eyes on the buildings as she rounded them. Something else wasn't right. It went beyond the buildings not quite looking as run-down as she expected, or the strange business with the front door. She tried to view it like a puzzle that she was overthinking, something with a solution so simple it's almost a cheat. Pa-Pa Fred had told her a riddle like that when she was a kid. "A man has thirty-six sheep. Three of 'em die. How many are left?"

"Thirty-three," she said, confident it was a trick question, and that the trick was simply fooling her into second-guessing the obvious answer.

"No, ma'am. Twenty-seven," he said.

"What? No way. How?"

He put on that big grin that she never quite trusted and said, "What do you mean? I told you. A farmer had thirty *sick* sheep."

"That's not fair. That's not what you said."

He laughed. "May not be what you heard, but that's what I said. You've gotta always pay close attention."

That was the orphanage now, trying to trick her with sly misinformation, ready to allege she was inattentive.

Chill, it's not alive, she thought. *It's not* trying *to do anything.* She scanned the buildings to figure out what she was missing. She spotted it on the church steeple, as she ran toward the spite house on the back half of her lap. It wasn't something that she had missed, but something that should have been missing. The large cross she saw atop the church hadn't been there yesterday, the day before, or earlier today, before she started her run. She remembered it clearly. The conical spire had looked incomplete to her without a cross. There was no way to explain why one was there now. The door and undamaged exterior could be waved away. The cross couldn't be. Nonetheless, as she stopped to stare at it, she tried to think of how she could have overlooked it before.

A gust stirred the treetops behind her and sent a throng of screeching birds flying. All that noise made her jumpy. Dess turned, ready to see and flee any animal charging out of the woods toward her. She remained tense even when she saw that nothing was running at her, because she had turned her back to the orphanage.

She thought she heard something far behind her. People singing? Chanting? It was either a song or a prayer. *Or just the wind,* she told herself. It was blowing harder, the sound of it rushing past her ears, but that wasn't it. She felt the voices crawling under the skin on her back. She stiffened, gritted her teeth, then made herself turn around because it had to be done. She had to see.

The singing stopped. The cross was gone.

Heart pounding and mind fraying, she backed away from the orphanage. She spared a glance at the spite house to make sure it was still there and hadn't pulled a disappearing act, and she almost laughed at the idea of that house as a sort of haven.

She looked at the orphanage one more time. The main building looked as washed out and neglected as it did from the spite house. Some of its windows that had appeared intact minutes earlier were shattered. The front door was gone again. Not just open, gone. She saw that. She thought she saw something in the dark, open doorway. Was someone standing there? It became more of an impression than something visible with each passing second. The presence of a woman in a dark, long dress, pinned to this site for decades.

"Tell him to leave us alone," the presence said, sounding angry and anguished. When Dess heard those words, too clear to be a hallucination, she turned and ran to the house.

She made it back just as the stranger who had arrived was leaving.

Dess had seen something she didn't like in her dad's expression when she got back. She couldn't figure out exactly what it was at first. All that she'd seen near the orphanage was still too fresh in her mind; she was still working to rationalize it. Were both places haunted, the spite house and the orphanage? The entire estate, from the hill through the valley? Was it just the previous night's encounter somehow lingering with her? That struck her as more likely, but she didn't understand why she thought that. It was like spending one night here had awakened something intrinsic to her, let her see things that would have escaped her before. Was that possible? God, how haunted was this place?

She needed real answers, starting with what was going on with her dad. After taking a minute to collect herself some more, she realized why she didn't like way he had looked. He'd been wearing Pa-Pa Fred's smug, cunning smirk, like he had just won something from someone who didn't know a game was going until they lost. What had he done to earn that feeling, even for a second? Was it something he'd said to that lady, Emily?

Emily.

Dess remembered that name. The lady who wrote the article about Eunice. Emily Steen. Did Dad think she'd forgotten? That she might skip a detail as important as knowing who wrote that article? Of course she read and recorded the name of the person who had strong misgivings about a stranger they were putting their trust in. She'd made a mental note to look up more of Emily's writing on her own when she got a chance, see if she had more or worse to say about Eunice. Now she knew she could do one better and go right to the source if the opportunity presented itself.

How's that for always paying close attention, she thought, then imagined Pa-Pa Fred somewhere on the other side, reading her mind and laughing to show his approval, and also to take a little credit for her acuity.

Millie

*L*ord, how had she screwed that up so badly?

Millie Steen replayed her conversation with Eric for the thousandth time, wondering what she should have said differently and whether it would have mattered. He had read what she'd written about Eunice and that had predisposed him to think less of her. But how could anyone read what she'd written and take it the way that he had?

No, she couldn't do that. *Consider all valid perspectives.* She had whipped together a paper on that subject back in her freshman year of high school, a frivolous, irreverent few pages centered on a character of her own making misunderstanding the word "bad" as it related to her father's favorite song, "Bad, Bad Leroy Brown." She'd written it to reinforce a point she'd argued with her parents about recently, that the most sensible answer could still easily be a wrong answer. Her teacher had graded it a B-plus and held her after class to say, "I know you barely even tried with this one. Imagine how good you'd be if you worked at it." Within days she had gotten started with the school newspaper and wouldn't stop doing the work, at various publications across the country and outside of it, for the next forty-four years. Even after leaving Dallas to retire to her hometown, she felt obligated to write one last piece.

When she had left Degener, the Houghtons were respected and prominent. When she came back, there was only one of them left, Eunice, with whom she had exchanged letters for nearly the duration of her career. Eunice had shown up at a few ceremonies to see Emily receive awards. They had shared drinks at fundraisers and after-parties. Millie used to be one of Eunice's select confidants, and after hearing about the supposed Houghton curse, Millie facilitated Eunice's first meeting with Neal Lassiter, hoping he could gradually steer her away from believing she was destined to die screaming. She'd worried then that she was risking their friendship, but to her surprise it thrived as Eunice took a liking to Neal. What their friendship could not survive was Emily's return to Degener and the full, undistracted realization that Eunice owned the town. Worse yet, that the rest of Degener was too beholden to her and blinded by the prosperity she brought them to care that they lived under another citizen's rule.

So she had written what she'd written, submitted it to *The Texas Tribune,* and accepted the severance of her relationship with Eunice. In hindsight, maybe she should have worked harder to stay in her life. Maybe she could have done better work from the inside, talked Eunice out of some of her worst decisions, such as letting the last couple who stayed in the spite house—the Renners—remain there so long even after it was clear that their health was worsening daily. And now, less than a year later, she brought someone else to the house. A man with children no less. Eunice was letting children live there. She was even further gone than Millie had thought.

Millie did not believe the house was haunted, but there had to be something about it that drove people away from it, and drove them to the brink when they were in it. She'd never seen anything in her work and travels to convince her that the supernatural was real, but she'd seen things that made her think that the nature of some dangers was hard to explain, and that the cost of examining some threats was too great. Was knowing the exact mechanics of how the spite house had hurt the Renners worth creating another set of victims? Hell no, it wasn't.

Jane and Maxwell Renner, a husband-and-wife team of "paranormal researchers," had shown signs of withering within three days of their stay. They had visibly lost weight as though ill, she more than he. Bags dragged their eyelids down, added years to their faces. How they behaved was even more concerning. When they drove into town to eat or seek interviews, those they got close to said they appeared increasingly disoriented, unable to stick to a topic. They smelled like layers of sweat, dust, and must. The last people to see them at Jake's Cakes and Waffles said they came in that morning wearing clothes too heavy for the summer and sat trembling together on the same side of a booth. Max held Jane and talked to her while she looked around like she didn't know where she was. They put off ordering anything for several minutes, then left in a hurry, practically shoving their waiter aside when he tried to ask what was wrong.

That night they left the house and drove to the nearest major hospital, twenty minutes southwest of Degener. Word of what happened to them leaked from the hospital and made it to town. Eunice could intimidate the mayor, the shopkeepers, and even the sheriff into falling in line, but she couldn't squash gossip, especially not when it was this good about something so bad. Each of the Renners had suffered unusual, severe nausea and arrhythmia symptomatic of extraordinary stress. Worse than that were the sporadic spells of aphasia and dementia symptomatic of strokes. Jane Renner apparently endured the worst of it.

If it had all been an act on their part, it had been a convincing one that they never tried to capitalize on. Millie had tried to track the Renners down to speak to them for a follow-up article, but the couple had taken down their website, scrubbed their social media profiles, and changed all of their contact information.

She couldn't let what had happened to the Renners happen again. She had called Neal twice since she came home from seeing Eric. He hadn't answered, so she left voice messages and sent a follow-up text. Eunice wouldn't speak to her, but she still liked Neal. If Millie could get hold of him, catch him up on everything, he could get in Eunice's ear and convince her to stop what she was doing. He wouldn't have to sacrifice his trademark skepticism to believe the house posed a danger based on what had happened to the Renners.

Millie had calmed herself down enough to make a late lunch when she heard a car door close in front of her house. She lived on the northside on two acres of property, amid neighbors who all had a couple of acres apiece as well. There was no mistaking that sound. Somebody was on her property.

She went to the front, looked through the screen door, and saw Dana's car parked in her driveway. Millie stepped outside, stopping at the bottom of her porch steps.

"Hey there, Millie," Dana said after she got out of her car.

"Dana," Millie said.

"I apologize for coming out without calling first. Although to be fair I don't think you can be too mad at me for that. Sort of a pot-kettle thing, wouldn't you say?"

Millie chuckled, though she was not amused. "If you're trying to convince me that it's okay for you to come out here to harass me, you should stop."

"I'm not here to harass you. If anything, I'm here to ask you not to harass Miss Houghton's guests."

"Uh-huh," Millie said. "Does that gentleman know what he's getting into? I mean all of it. What he's getting his girls into?"

"I appreciate your concern, Millie, but this isn't your business."

"This is my community, and you don't get to tell me what's not my business. Your own boss has been preaching how important we all are to each other since way before you got here. Hell, before you were born. Even if I were a stranger, though, I'd still be a person with a heart, and knowing what I know would still make it my business. In fact, looking at it from about as many angles as I can, I don't see how this couldn't be my business. People have suffered in that house, and you know it. Grown men and women who ought to be able to take care of themselves and ought not to be afraid of things that aren't supposed to be real have gone into that house fine and come out forgetting who they were before they went in, or so scarred by it they go into hiding, like they think the house is going to try to find them. I sat by when it was the frauds and thrill-seekers, but this is a family. You're really letting that man keep his girls in there? You know what happened the last time there were kids in that house."

Dana said, "You know what, actually I don't know, because nobody does."

"That's your best argument? That pedantic bullshit? There are lives on the line here. This isn't some damn debate for you to score points on technicalities."

"You're right, this isn't a debate. It's not a conversation, and it's not your concern. I'm only here to advise you—"

"Warn me, you mean. Go ahead and say it."

"Advise you."

Millie came a step closer. "Say what you mean. You and the old lady are putting me on notice."

"Fine," Dana said. "If that's how you want to take it, then that's how you want to take it. You want to find out what 'the old lady' can do when she's really pissed off? Try her."

"I can take whatever she can pitch," Millie said, grinning. "Better me than that family come to harm."

"For God's sake, nothing's going to happen to them. Jesus, what do you think we're doing? You think we want something bad to happen to them?"

"Listen to you. Good Lord. I've heard people all over the world say things like that. Talking about how they didn't want to do all the harm they went ahead and did anyway. Like they could magically 'want' away the consequences of their actions."

Dana threw up her hands and walked back to her car. "I'm through with you. I said what I came out here to say. Don't act like nobody warned you."

"That's right. A warning. Feels better to say what you mean, don't it?"

Dana got in the car and slammed the door. Millie watched her leave. A small part of her tried to argue that she could have been a little more diplomatic.

"Hell with that and hell with her," she said, then went inside to call Neal again, and to consider what other actions she might take.

Lafonda

So you don't know what else she might have told him?" Eunice said to Dana.

Lafonda was close enough to see Dana's jaw tense like she was trying to fuse her upper and lower rows of teeth. "I know what he told me," Dana said. "That isn't good enough?"

"If it were, I wouldn't have sent you to see her. How long were you even there?"

"Longer than you were. Next time send yourself."

Lafonda shifted in her chair and wondered why she was even here. This was not part of her role. Granted, her role was regularly subject to expansion. Just recently, for instance, she'd been designated a one-woman day care for a few hours. She hadn't exactly been fine with it at first, but the kids proved agreeable. Even interesting, the younger one with her inquisitiveness and the older one, Odessa, with her wit. She'd have rather been doing what she'd initially been hired for, health care and personal training, but the other things Eunice asked of her exhibited how much trust the old woman had in her. She cooked, she provided therapy—physical and mental—she listened when Eunice needed to unburden herself or shed a tear, and she encouraged her when Eunice needed to snap out of a funk.

What she did not do before today was sit in on Eunice's one-on-one meetings with Dana. Those were a different line of business, and even though she had suspected Dana had always wanted to creep into her domain, Lafonda had no designs on taking on Dana's role. Why then, today, had Dana asked her to join them? She had even said "please" before La-fonda could tell her "no." It was as close to pleading and bargaining as she thought Dana could get.

Eunice had loaded a response to Dana's last comment and was dying to pull the trigger, Lafonda could see it in her face, the blue-flame heat in her gaze. Before she spoke next, she rubbed her brow and wiped some of the animosity off her face.

"Dana, I almost just fired you."

"For real, this time?"

Eunice hissed her disapproval, and Lafonda realized that, in these meet-ings, these moments weren't uncommon. This reinforced that Lafonda was right to recommend more yoga, despite Eunice's preference for the punch-ing bag. What she really needed was an extended vacation that might turn permanent, ideally on one of those islands she liked to talk about, where people lived longer and stressed themselves less. Lafonda made a mental note to bring that up later when the time was right.

Dana told Eunice, "The only thing you'd have to worry about her saying is something you already got ahead of. Because you told Eric about what happened with the Renners, right?"

"I did. It's one of the first things I told him. I told him twice, in fact, because I reminded him of it again last night."

You're lying, Lafonda thought, and brought her hand halfway to her mouth as if to catch the words in case they came out. Eunice spotted this, but said nothing. Years of hearing people make excuses for skipping a workout or cheating on their meal plan had made Lafonda surprisingly adept at identifying someone's "tell." Eunice's was overexplaining. If she had really told Eric about the Renners, she would have left her answer at "I did." Lafonda knew that. What she didn't know was what exactly Dana and Eunice were talking about.

She had come on board a few weeks after the Renners had left the Mas-son House. She'd overheard their names in conversation a few times and knew they'd left early, their work unfinished, but she hadn't asked about them. She was too busy minding and maintaining her own business. Still, stories about them were in the air among the people of Degener during her first month on the job, and sometimes she'd hear about how bad they looked within their first two weeks of being in the house, how people had known early on that it would be bad for them there.

Sometimes, the fate of the Renners came to Lafonda under the guise of concern and questions. "Please tell Miss Houghton I'm happy to make deliveries for the next people she gets to stay in the house," the grocer told her once. "That last couple looked like they got themselves so busy they forgot to eat when they were there."

When she accompanied Eunice for her checkup, she heard her physician say, "I'm going to write up your prescription so that you have some extra, in case you need to share a few with whoever else you get to stay in the Masson place. The two that just left, if they hadn't been so sleep-deprived, I think maybe things would have gone better."

Lafonda hadn't taken the bait to overshare in the former instance or ask Eunice any questions in the latter. She'd already felt comfortable in her role and in town by then. Eunice could be a little testy when Lafonda wouldn't let her have her way, but she was earnest about being healthy, which made her easier to work for than many of the people she'd worked with and for previously. And she paid extraordinarily well.

Better than that, though, Eunice was good on her promise that the people of this small town would welcome her warmly. Even if they hadn't, Lafonda had been confident she could endure. Her skin was thicker than it was dark, and she was practiced in giving hate the response it deserved. There was no hate to be found in Degener. People were so friendly at first she was sure it was some kind of setup, but she soon learned that it was consistent. Nonetheless, as well as she got on with Eunice and with the locals, she didn't feel comfortable enough to say anything to Eunice about the Renners. It wasn't part of her role here, and what she had heard of it was surely exaggerated anyway. The people of Degener, kind though they might be, spoke of the Masson House as though it were an active thing.

Lafonda, in her interview with Eunice, had called herself a "practical agnostic" when asked about her belief in the supernatural. "I wouldn't spend a night at Triple-Six Lucifer Lane or anything. That's the practical part. Otherwise, though, I've never been moved to feel strongly one way or the other."

Even after hearing of the Renners' hasty exit from the property, she didn't come closer to viewing the spite house the way the locals did. Perhaps if she lived here long enough, that would change. Throughout Degener, people struck her as superstitious more than religious. If she drove past any of the local churches on Sundays, their parking lots might be half full on the busiest days. Decent attendance, but not full attendance. Nonetheless, most of the cars that didn't have a cross stuck to the bumper had one dangling from a string on the rearview mirror. The relatively few people who didn't have one or the other typically wore a cross around their necks, though some of the younger locals were content with a tattoo of a cross on their shoulder, forearm, or wrist. Lafonda could count on one hand the number of people she'd seen in Degener who had none of the above. She imagined most of the houses had at least one wall devoted to a collection of crosses.

On its own, this might not have stood out. But there were also an inordinate amount of good-luck charms, and not little trinkets like a rabbit's-foot key chain or a four-leaf clover. Many people in Degener, men and women, wore jewelry adorned with sigils. Lafonda had looked some of them up online, and they seemed to be symbols meant to ward off spirits. When she realized this, she guessed there must be a store in town that specialized in this sort of thing and everyone was just being supportive, but no, there was no such store. These people had gone out of their way to acquire these items. It was like they all thought they might bump into a ghost, not just at the spite house, but anywhere in town.

Practical skepticism was something she and Dana had in common. Eunice seemed to prefer the company of disbelievers and even debunkers of the supernatural. She counted a famous skeptic among her closest friends. Lafonda surmised, based on what she heard during the interviews with the ghost hunters, that Eunice distrusted many professed believers. And, though she had no real proof of this, she also suspected that Eunice enjoyed feeling like she knew something those close to her did not. Lafonda had thought that was a relatively innocent quirk before.

Hearing Dana state that the Renners hadn't just fled, that something had happened to them, and knowing that Eunice hadn't disclosed this to Eric, made Lafonda think worse of Eunice's fondness for secrets. Without knowing the whole truth of it, though, she could not be sure she wasn't overreacting.

She thought of looking into it on her own, going to Millie Steen directly and asking her about the Renners and any other previous residents of the spite house. She doubted Millie would trust her, though, especially after Dana's visit. She could try someone else in town, but who would talk? Who was going to risk their job at the factory, or their wife's job, or their cousin's? Almost anyone in Degener who didn't work for Eunice was close to someone who did. Even the outliers who had a couple of degrees of separation between their livelihoods and Eunice's business knew she could have them ostracized. Have their customer base dry up, their contract offers passed over. Make it a headache for their permits to get approved, or make sure their leases weren't renewed. Lafonda had heard bits and pieces of stories about that sort of thing when people weren't aware she was within earshot. She suspected this was at least part of what motivated Eunice's generosity. She paid well, supported local business, was a great provider to the town, all of which gave the residents more to lose, and in turn gave her leverage over them.

The same applied to the Rosses. Eunice was giving them a one-of-a-kind opportunity, which meant she could take something from them that they couldn't get anywhere else. Wasn't that enough? She needed to keep them in the dark about what happened to the spite house's previous occupants, too?

"Whatever did happen to the Renners?" Lafonda said, like they were old friends she lost touch with.

Eunice looked at her like she'd forgotten a third person was in the office, then looked away for a second, searching for her response, before answering, "They ended up hospitalized. Exhaustion or some such. The husband turned out okay, but the wife needed more time. She was eventually checked out too, as I understand it. They essentially overworked themselves, didn't eat right or sleep enough. We won't let that happen to the Rosses."

Not one mention of ghosts, Lafonda thought, and that solidified for her that Eunice was hiding something. The entire point of putting people in the house was to gather proof of her beliefs. Once she had sufficient proof, she hoped to get some scientists interested and deeply involved. Surely many brilliant minds would want to devote themselves to the most important discovery in history, and if, in the course of their research, they uncovered a way for her to be rid of the curse, well, that was the true objective. Lafonda was aware of that much.

She glanced at Dana, who peeked back, and in that half second Lafonda understood that Dana invited her to the meeting so she could ask about the Renners and put pressure on Eunice to either come clean or commit to the lie. Dana must have thought it wouldn't be easy for Eunice to lie to Lafonda. Eunice trusted Dana with her business affairs, but the business was just a means to her ultimate goal of not dying the way her aunt died. She trusted Lafonda with her health, with keeping her alive until a cure for the uncommon curse was found. That might take years. She and Lafonda understood this and had a different level of trust because of it. Dana wasn't there during doctor visits, she didn't lay out her prescriptions each morning, talk with her about the vital statistics captured by her watch each day.

Nonetheless, Eunice had lied to her without blinking. The closest thing she had to a confidant, who took the job to replace the previous caregiver and personal trainer, who retired after twenty years. Lied to her like she was a stranger.

"How about this, I'll talk to him again tomorrow," Eunice said to Dana. "Really make sure he's taking it as seriously as he should, and remind him that we'll take his girls in if he asks. Would that make you feel better?"

"I'd be good with that," Dana said.

Eunice looked at Lafonda for her answer. "A reminder can't hurt," Lafonda said. She wanted to say more, press for more, but was still corralling her thoughts when Eunice adjourned the meeting.

She told herself that she would find a way later to bring the subject back up. After their late workout, perhaps, with Eunice tired and her defenses down. Or over dinner, if she got Eunice really rolling downhill telling stories, maybe then she'd be more apt to be honest. But Lafonda did not bring it up again that night. She kept it to herself, running through how the conversation might go in her head because she still wanted to find the right words and right time. That was what she told herself. A kernel of her knew, however, that the real reason she didn't mention it was that she didn't want to hear what Eunice might say.

You didn't really tell Eric about the Renners, Lafonda imagined saying to her. *Why not? And why did you lie about it to Dana? I know you're scared to die, but enough to put someone else in danger? Are you really that scared?*

And if Eunice answered honestly, Lafonda believed she would say, *Yes.*

Max Renner

"Y ou need to eat," Max said again. His heart was beating so hard he thought he might faint. He'd never had to tell her to eat twice before. He rarely had to give her any instruction more than once.

Jane wasn't fully catatonic, which was what made her impossible to diagnose. She was more like an old "Hollywood Voodoo" zombie. She would move on her own to obey orders. If you told her she should go to the bathroom before going to sleep, she would do so. If you told her that she needed to eat, she ate. She even used utensils. But if you told her to walk into traffic—which Max did a few months back—she would stare at you like you were a puzzle she was bored with.

That was how she looked at her bowl of stew now.

How does she know? Max thought.

He had ground up peanuts and put them in her food, but he'd seasoned it well enough to mask the smell or taste. At least he thought he had. Maybe she still sniffed them out. There was no way she could see them, and he told her to wait in the bedroom while he made it, to be sure she didn't see him preparing to poison her.

Eating half of a Snickers bar would be enough to close her throat and send her into shock. Max put about four times that many peanuts into the stew. In hindsight, that might have been overkill. The aroma was too intense and kept her from eating. He only wanted to be sure he put in enough to end her life quickly. There was no guarantee it would be painless, but he wasn't sure she felt pain anymore.

THE SPITE HOUSE   ·   113

He could have made it simpler. After trying and failing to have her walk into traffic, he bought a gun. A black nine-millimeter, semiautomatic. Nothing outlandish. Something to end the facsimile of a life she had left, and end his suffering.

It wasn't just the burden of caring for her. It was what he saw each night in his sleep. Terrible visions too immediate and painful to be dreams. He saw Jane crawling inside the spite house looking for a way out, but confined within its walls. Its windows wouldn't break when she tried to strike them. Its door wouldn't open for her or let her pass when someone else opened it. The floating hallway always called her back to it, and she had no choice but to obey, even though it took another small bite out of what was left of her each time she returned to it. How long until there was nothing left of her?

Too long. He hated himself for thinking that, but it was true. As awful as it was to think of her soul being consumed by that place, it was even worse to think of how long that would take, and what it meant for him. Years of tortured sleep and wearying days. He drove as little as possible now, always fearful of falling asleep at the wheel. Last month he pleaded with the landlord to move them to an apartment on the bottom floor, because he'd caught himself on the verge of nodding off while coming down the stairs. How long before he fell asleep with the stove on? Or passed out on his feet in the shower and cracked his head on the way down?

What happened to Jane—her separation—was indirectly breaking him down, too. Eating him up in its own way, months after he thought he escaped the house. Killing her, then, was more self-preservation than pure selfishness, and there was a clear difference between the two, he thought.

So why couldn't he point the gun at her, even with her back turned? Why did the thought of doing so make him want to throw up? It wasn't just that a shooting would be messier in every applicable sense. It was that there was no real buffer. No step between. His finger on the trigger, causing a bullet to fly through the back of her head. There was some separation between telling her to get hit by a car and her actually following the order. A smaller distance between putting crushed peanuts into her food and letting her eat it, but a distance, nonetheless. He needed that. She wasn't going to give it to him this evening.

Max took her bowl away and dumped the stew into the sink. He could always let her starve, he thought. Or die of thirst, that would come faster. Leave the house for a week or so, let inertia be her killer, and deal with the body when he came back. But that was too cruel, and he knew that the part of him that still held out hope for her would override the part that wanted to move on without her. That same part of himself might have taken over long enough to grab her hand if she dipped her spoon into her stew tonight. It would have pulled her out of harm's way if she had listened when he told her to walk onto the highway.

He went to the fridge for leftovers from yesterday's takeout. He thought about heating it up, then just gave it to her cold. It wasn't going to make a difference to her or him. She'd eat it regardless, and a basic courtesy wasn't going to make up for what he just tried to do. Not even close. His guilt-driven nightmares were already lined up and waiting for him to fall asleep.

Eric

The night arrived too soon, the way all dreaded things do. Eric tried not to dwell on what it might bring. He, Stacy, and Dess cooked dinner together after getting an evening delivery from the grocer. Home-made spaghetti in meat sauce, something simple for their first time preparing a family meal in a proper kitchen, albeit a compact one, in eight months. They still made a bit of a mess, sang some songs while cooking, and laughed together, but ultimately it wasn't the distraction he hoped for. If anything, it brought the darkest part of the night to them earlier. Time flies and all.

Given the previous night's disruption, they were ready to sleep less than three hours after the sun went down. Spending the night together downstairs again was an easy decision. The only one willing to go back upstairs after dark was Stacy.

"I'm not scared anymore," she said. "If that boy comes back, Dess said she'd beat his ass, and his sister too."

Eric looked at Dess. "Is that what she said?"

"She's rephrasing it a little," Dess said, "and I think she must have gotten that one word from you."

"Mm."

He had stopped at a general store and picked up a few board games after visiting the library, and they played for a short while until Stacy yawned one last time and went to her corner of the sofa to sleep. Dess was next, leaving Eric to fight off sleep alone for a little while longer.

He lay back, rested his head on the throw pillow, and wondered how his heart could beat so fast while his brain was so desperate to turn off. The pops and cracks and creaks of the house settling and being pushed by the wind did not appear to bother Dess or Stacy, but they left him twitchy and stiff. He craned his neck to stretch it as though it might turn to stone if he didn't.

How much time passed before he heard the *thump-thump* of footsteps? He thought he might have actually fallen asleep before he heard it, or at least been on the verge. Now he was as awake as he'd be if he heard a smoke alarm, except he felt no urge to leave. He sat up and faced the stairs.

He saw a pair of bare feet on the highest step visible to him. If made to guess, given their size, he would have said they belonged to a woman, but they might have been a man's. They stood out more starkly in the dark than they should have. He thought they carried a bluish, chilled hue that he began to feel the longer he stared.

I'm dreaming, he thought, and a voice came behind his own so close it had to be attached. "There are no dreams in this house." She sounded sad, angry, and afraid, like she needed his help and had asked for it several times already.

The person on the stairs took the next step up, out of sight. Eric stood and started toward them. He paused a moment.

He shouldn't go upstairs.

Why not?

His girls. He couldn't leave them alone.

Why not? They'd stay down here, where it was safe. He would go upstairs to see who or what else was in the house. Wasn't that why he was here? Wasn't that the job? And the sooner he could find out exactly what was happening here and inform Eunice, the sooner he would get to leave and never come back. Avoiding it all didn't do him any good. If he was going to be here, then he should do his job and finish it as soon as possible.

Besides, maybe he'd find what he was really here for upstairs. What he'd run from last night without thinking. The truth might be up there. The truth about what he'd really seen in his grandfather's house years ago, and what it meant about himself and his kids. His youngest especially. He had to find the answers, for his own sake as well as theirs. They deserved to know.

He recognized that this justification did not come entirely from him, and perhaps came entirely apart from him, but it moved him, nonetheless. Brought him to the stairs and up to the second floor, where he heard something above him. Door hinges groaning. More thumping footsteps, moving a little faster, almost as if chased.

Eric went to the third floor, barely feeling his own weight as he took each step. The door to the first bedroom, Stacy's room, was closed. The door to the floating hallway was as open as an invitation. The light was on inside. The voice that told him this could not be a dream moved toward him again. It didn't feel like it was in his head, or like it was just a disembodied voice drifting in darkness. It sounded like it belonged to someone present, and nearby.

When he stepped into the hall, a man cried out in misery above him. Eric was shocked still. He looked up, saw only the ceiling, not the hovering specter that he expected. When he could move again, he turned around to leave, but the hallway door he had come through was closed. When he touched the knob it felt like his hand might freeze to it. He pulled it back and shook out the pain. He tried again and it was even colder. He felt it all the way up to his shoulder, then couldn't feel his arm at all an instant later.

At the other end of the hall, the woman was crying. There was a mix of confusion and fury in her sobs, and in between them he heard her say, "Why can't I get back? It can't keep me here. I have to get back."

He walked toward that end of the hall, hoping that either of its doors might be open, or would let him through. The woman would hopefully let him pass. She came into view more clearly as he came closer. She was crouched on the floor, hair covering her face. Was she digging at something? Looking at something? He got the impression that even she did not know what she was doing, that she wasn't even thinking of what she was doing.

And then, with another step, she was no longer there.

Her vanishing wasn't what made him stop, however. The sensation of someone standing behind him did. Even though he wanted to run, his body turned as if remotely controlled. When he got all the way around, the light died, and he only got a glimpse of what was before him. A man as tall as him, wearing his clothes, wearing his face, reflecting his complete, paralytic terror.

Eric's legs gave out and he dropped to the floor. The oxygen in the hall got thinner, his chest tightened, his mind crushed under wave upon wave of panic. What the hell had he just seen? Why'd he even come up here? Something led him up the stairs. It took hold, removed the idea of resistance, and now here he was.

A scream came from two floors down. Dess. Eric punched his chest twice, trying to get his lungs working properly again, like slapping an old appliance. He was able to take a big enough breath to shout, "Hold on, Dess. I'm coming!"

Fighting through unsteady legs, he got to his feet and ran as well as he could to the far end of the hall, where the doors were indeed open.

When he made it back down to the living room, he saw that the front door of the house was open, and that his daughters were gone.

CHAPTER 20

Dess

*D*ess snapped awake upon hearing something close to a roar come from upstairs. She turned to where her father should be and saw he was gone. Where was he? Was that him crying out? No, that was something else. It sounded unnatural to her. As unnatural as the next thing she heard, a little girl who said, "Ooh, I love it when he's unhappy."

The little girl giggled and Dess jumped up, fully alert and awake. She looked around, saw no one else in the room, then recognized that she didn't need to see a threat to respect it.

She grabbed Stacy, who was still asleep.

"Hm? What?" Stacy said.

"We have to go. Come on," Dess said.

The other little girl, the unseen one, laughed. "Who says you can?"

With her sister in her arms, Dess faced the door, and knew that the invisible girl stood in front of it, blocking it. She felt her terrible, brutal coldness.

"My brother says your father can't leave the hall," the girl said. She sounded like talking mist. "What if I say you can't leave the house?"

Stacy whimpered and hugged Dess tighter, and that brought Dess's anger to life like a summoned monster.

"Let us out," she said.

The girl laughed louder. Dess raised her voice. "Let us out!"

The girl stopped laughing to say, "No. You're ours now."

"Let us out, let us out, LETUSOUT!" Dess screamed, and she rushed the door. A blast of arctic air pushed at her, chapped her skin to the point it almost burned, but she ran through it and outside with Stacy.

The car was locked and her father had the key. She stopped and looked around for where she could go. The orphanage wasn't an option. The woods beyond almost blended with the starless, cast-iron sky, part of a dark wall that was taller than the eye could measure. Maybe she didn't have to go any farther. She and Stacy were out of the house, maybe that was all—

Dad's still inside.

She turned and started to shout for her father but didn't want to startle Stacy. She couldn't set her sister down to go back into the house either. What then? What could she do? For the first time since her new life had begun, Dess felt tears stinging her eyes. They burned when she blinked them back. She wasn't sad, she was angry and growing more furiously frustrated by the second. Why had Dad left them alone in the first place? Where had he gone to get himself lost or stuck?

A figure appeared in the doorway. Dess recognized it as her father, but still felt an impulse to duck behind the car and hide. *It's not really him,* she thought, then pushed that out of her head. There was no reason to think that. A little over a year ago, a similar thought entered her mind when she'd been shocked to see Stacy again, and she was still ashamed of that moment. She couldn't let that happen here, for Stacy's sake if not her own. They were all they had and any mistrust of each other would be their downfall.

"Dad, over here," she said, as though he couldn't see them and wasn't already coming toward them.

"What happened?" Eric said. "I heard a scream. Was that you?"

"We have to get out of here," she said.

"What happened?"

"Please, let's just go. I'll tell you on the way. Let's go."

"Right. You're right," he said, and pulled out his keys.

"Where are we going?" Stacy said as they got in the car.

"Remember the big house we stayed in a couple nights ago?" Eric said. "I'm taking you back there."

Dess latched on to what he said. *You're not coming back here,* she wanted to scream at him, but she held it in. She knew what he would say anyway, she could map their entire argument in a second. He would say he had to come back, if not tonight then tomorrow. She would tell him he didn't have to, and he would say she knew better. She'd insist this place was too wrong, too dangerous, and he would try to get her to pin down exactly what made it more dangerous than what they'd been doing before, the reckless things she'd been doing to earn money, the construction and security jobs he was taking specifically meant for people who couldn't be on a company's books, who wouldn't require any paperwork if they met with an accident or even vanished on the job. Everything about their lives had been a risk since they'd hit the road, from the places they stayed, to the ways they made money, even the simple act of driving.

He would be convincing, yet she would remain unconvinced. She would tell him that those things were different because they were at least known, and the house was something they couldn't understand no matter how open their minds were after all they'd been through. He would just say again that this was their best chance, their only chance, and she'd have no real way of stopping him from coming back. All she'd have was the confidence that she was right, and the frail hope that she was wrong.

Eunice

For Eunice, sleepless nights were a vice as unaffordable as excessive drinking or smoking. She turned off any screens in her vicinity by 8:30 P.M. After this watershed, she also forbade herself any music with lyrics and that couldn't be defined as soothing. She gave herself between thirty and sixty minutes to read in bed, and most often was welcoming sleep before the half-hour mark.

Her head had to be on a pillow and her eyes closed by 9:30 P.M. Any later and it might throw off her biorhythms for the next few nights. She'd spent a fair amount of time learning this about herself and about the benefits of sleep in general, how failing to get enough of it could lead you to an early grave. As such she even used to keep her phones silenced at night. The last of her relatives died decades prior, and there was never any business important enough for her to let it rouse her.

That was before she missed the midnight call from Maxwell Renner shortly before they'd fled the Masson House. She still didn't think there was anything she could have done for them had she answered, but she should have been available to them. It was her business.

So when her phone rang and woke her at 4:14 A.M., and she saw that it was Eric calling, she felt a mixture of frustration and vindication. She wasn't derelict in her duties this time, even though the slight twinge in her chest and tightness in her jaw made her regret feeling so obliged. On answering she thought, *There'd better be something really wrong for you to call me now. One of your girls better be in trouble, or else why are you bothering me?*

"We're headed your way," Eric told her. "I'm cashing in that open invitation for my girls to stay there."

Something was indeed "really wrong," and Eunice felt a rush that she had to quell with a deep breath. If they were coming to her, then something had chased them out of the house. Same as with Max and Jane, except Eric was not hightailing it out of town, he was coming to her. This was a good sign. It meant that the spirits hadn't gone into hiding, and also that Eric was made of sterner stuff than anyone who'd been in the spite house before. He was going to give her a chance to keep him in there.

"You ought to stay here overnight, too," Eunice said. "You sound flustered."

"We'll talk about it when we get there."

After hanging up, she went to Lafonda's room, two doors down the hall, awakened her, and told her what little she knew. If Lafonda had any questions, she kept them to herself, and joined Eunice in action. They went downstairs, prepared a pitcher of water and some lavender tea, things to help ease frayed nerves. Lafonda suggested putting some cookies in the oven, and Eunice said that was a smart idea. Not scratch-made, the quick-bake kind taken out of a package. They might not be done by the time the Rosses arrived, but the aroma would prove pleasant and calming, especially for the little one. It was important to present a welcoming atmosphere, convince Eric with every tool she had that he could trust his daughters with her.

Eunice made sure to be at the door before the Rosses pulled up. She read Eric's dazed expression as he came to the door, Odessa's wide and weary eyes. She felt like she could nearly see what they had seen just by looking at their faces. She was disappointed to see Eric hadn't brought his journal with him. It was difficult not to demand he tell her everything that had occurred in detail so she could write it herself, but she held off even lightly prodding him. It would be imprudent. Now was not the time to show any impatience, give off any hint that she was anything except supportive.

They all spent some time together in the kitchen. She hoped the Rosses might open up to her after settling down, but the most they said was that "things got weird," and "we just had to get out of there."

That was fine. Eunice glanced at her watch several minutes after they arrived, while Stacy and Dess ate cookies. Her heart rate was still slightly elevated. Hopefully none of her excitement was evident in her face or voice.

If Peter Masson and the children—and whoever else might be there— were still stirring, that meant there was little chance they might no-show when she brought Neal and other observers to the site. That was good. Terrific, even. But it wasn't enough. "Little chance" was not "zero chance," and she could get to that, at last, as long as Eric remained in the house.

After breakfast, Eunice took Eric for a walk on the property's trail while the girls stayed in the house with Lafonda, playing some alphabet game they said they would teach her.

"You're looking better today," Eunice said. "How are you feeling?"

"Anxious," Eric said. "I don't want you thinking I'm going to come running to stay here every time things get a little crazy in the house. Last night, I did that for my girls. I can hang in there by myself, you can trust that."

Eunice smiled. "Here I was thinking you'd tell me you didn't want to stay there anymore."

"Most people don't get paid to do what they want," Eric said. "They do the work because they want to get paid. I need to get paid, Miss Houghton. Not the little bit that's kept me and the girls treading water. I need the kind of money we agreed to. So as long as the work won't kill me I'm here to do it."

"I'm glad to hear that, but there is something that I want to share with you that I should have told you before."

"Does it have anything to do with some kind of memorial?" Eric said.

She stopped and stared a moment. Her first instinct was to ask who from town he had been talking to, but she suppressed this. It would sound defensive. He had just expressed willingness to stay. She didn't want to say or do anything to make him second-guess his decision. At the same time, she didn't want to overshare, and didn't like being thrown off course. Who could have mentioned the memorial to him? Surely not Dana. Lafonda, then? She asked that question about the Renners yesterday, and tried to sound innocent in doing so, but Eunice knew that it meant something was on her mind. Should Eunice sit down with her, try to talk it through, or remind her of her role here and why she shouldn't step beyond it? What if that talk didn't go well, and she found she couldn't trust Lafonda anymore? It had taken months to find someone with Lafonda's exact qualifications and disposition. Eunice wasn't sure she had time to find a suitable replacement at this point.

"Emily Steen mentioned it to me," Eric said. "I wasn't going to bring it up, but after last night and after what you just said, I feel like I have to."

Millie Steen. Of course. Why did Eunice suspect anyone else? Lafonda of all people? Getting so close to her goal was making her paranoid. Making her think someone or something was destined to undermine her. If she didn't assert some control over her suspicions, she was liable to run off the very few people she needed with her. Right now, that short list included Eric Ross.

"Follow me," Eunice said, and took him off the trail and toward a naturally footworn path leading to the perimeter thicket.

"The memorial is related to what I was already going to tell you, just so you know," Eunice said. "I appreciate you trusting me with some of your family's history already. I'm sorry for not reciprocating until now. And I'll ask your forgiveness in advance for leaving out some things, but I need you to come by some answers on your own. If I tell you too much it can bias you about what you think is present in that house. Does that make sense?"

"I think it does," he said.

"Good," Eunice said, and looked ahead. The trees appeared to part the closer they got to them. They approached what almost looked like a wooded tunnel. An opening hidden in plain sight, seldom entered yet never too far from her mind.

She began, "At the time of the Civil War, here in the Hill Country, there were many German-Texans, most of whom were abolitionists and Unionists who didn't want to fight their country. A group of them from just northeast of here stopped in Degener on their way out of Texas. Twelve men and boys headed to Mexico to avoid conscription. They were promised a place to sleep and supplies by a man they trusted, my great-great-grandfather, whose name I never speak, who I hope is sitting in the hottest pot in hell right now. He turned them over to a group of Confederate guerrillas. This was in the summer of 1862, around the same time that a similar thing was happening in Comfort and other parts of Texas.

"The Confederates hanged them all. The youngest to die was fourteen. It was a tragedy and a crime, and we've been trying to make amends for it ever since. I wish I could say we were motivated only by doing what's right, but there's an element of self-preservation to all that my family has done in the many years since."

They were surrounded by trees now. A small, round clearing was coming into view ahead of them and in the center of it was a tall stone slab.

"Those men and boys who died that day have plagued my family since," Eunice said. "Really, I believe they're present all over the town. It wasn't just my ancestor who took part in that murder, so it makes sense they would haunt all of Degener. And I have my theories about spirits, how one might attract another, then over time those two attract a small group, and then possibly a larger group. Just like the living, with a relative handful of people starting a settlement where others eventually see that they can thrive. Oftentimes, here, you may notice people glance to the side like they think someone's there, when there isn't. You'll see them look up like they thought they heard someone talking to them. I've made an afternoon out of people-watching at the park on a warm day, counting how many times someone shivers for no apparent reason. Frankly, it's made it easier for me to keep some of the local history secret, so guests in the spite house find out its history on their own. People in town respect me enough to obey my wishes, but I also think they're simply scared to say the wrong thing and cause a spirit to haunt them with the same tenacity as the ones who haunt me.

"Others took part in the killing, but it was a Houghton who betrayed the spirits who cursed my family. Those other men must have been faces in a crowd to them, but my ancestor was someone they believed a friend. The betrayal is clearly the thing they can't forgive. They don't have any power to attack any of us in my family while we're alive, but as we're dying, well, it's hard to describe. They come to us then and the worst part is that we—I—don't know if it's over when we die, or if they get to keep torturing us forever after. I have my suspicions. My mother, in her advanced age, convinced herself that she could avoid the spirits altogether if she ended it quickly enough. She waited for me to leave her alone one day and shot herself in the head. When I found her later, the look on her face was . . . she must have seen something just as she pulled the trigger, right when it was too late to stop herself. I can't believe the fear imprinted on her face after she was already dead. I believe many things are possible, but not that. I have to tell myself that to remain sane."

Eric let a moment pass, silent condolences, Eunice figured, then he said, "So I'm really here to prove the place is haunted so you can talk to the spirits or something? Ask them what's next?"

"Something to that effect. The next step won't really involve you. If you do your part, document what you see, give me something substantial I can take to the ones who'll take over after you, you can walk away after that and never worry about any of this again."

Eric nodded. "What if I wanted to be part of that next step, though?"

"One thing at a time, Mr. Ross. Focus on what you were hired for. When you're done I'm sure you'll want to rest and recover, and we'll both be moving on from each other."

They continued in silence for the last minute of the walk until they reached the clearing. There, Eunice pointed to the gray stone, six feet tall, shaped like a chipped incisor. "Here's the memorial."

Eric approached it while Eunice kept her distance. She knew every name etched into it by heart already. She'd visited it often after Aunt Val died, when her father and uncle followed the guidance of a fringe preacher who told them to pray before it. Pray until they wept and then pray harder, every single day. They did this until more terrible, screaming deaths in the family taught them it was futile.

Eric, grazing the stone with his fingers, said, "Why did Emily tell me to ask you about this?"

"I don't try to understand what motivates her anymore. My best guess is she thought it would force me to tell you my family history. Or maybe it was something else. There was an old incident related to this monument and to the spite house. Maybe that's what she wanted me to tell you."

He turned to her. "I see. Well, if you didn't want to tell me, it would have been easier to lie and say you didn't know what I was talking about, wouldn't it?"

Eunice sighed, then smiled. "This happened in 1969, when my father ran things with a heavier hand than I do now. The memorial was in the city park then. Some people in some nearby towns weren't too keen on anything that called attention to the South's war crimes. I suppose that hasn't changed much even today. One day, our sheriff at the time—my mother's cousin—received word that some hooligans planned to desecrate our monument, after night fell at the park. The sheriff came to my father about it and my father, with the approval of my mother and other local leadership, advised the sheriff to gather some deputies and volunteers and wait for the troublemakers to show up, to show them that we weren't going to stand for such nonsense, but in a way that sent a clear message.

"They caught the bastards, rounded them up, and my father's idea for their punishment was unexpected. Already at that time the spite house was thought to be haunted. Even people outside of Degener knew of it. The rumor went beyond the house having ghosts. They said it would make you disappear if you went inside. How they came to that, I have no idea. Obviously you've been in and out, so you know that much is a lie, but it was all fresh in everybody's minds because its owner died just a year earlier. The story going around was that after he'd been buried some people saw him walking down the road going back to his house, looking grim about it, like he didn't want to but had no choice."

Eunice saw Eric stiffen at this and added, "Even I never believed that one, and I've known spirits are real for most of my life. Anyway, the men who came here to deface the monument were taken to the house and told they could either spend one night there, or several at the jailhouse, but once they made their decision they were stuck with it. They all made the mistake of choosing the spite house.

"Not two hours went by before the first of them tried to come out. They didn't try to sneak out—not that you could. There's no way in or out but the front door, or breaking through a window, I suppose. Either way it would be obvious. Those men tried to walk out the front, right past the sheriffs and deputies and others parked outside. From what I've heard, after our folks raised their guns at them, it really looked for a moment like those men would rather be shot than forced back inside. They kept saying that they wouldn't go back in, that the place was wrong." *That they heard two children laughing and telling them that the house was going to eat them,* she thought, but did not share. "They apologized and begged to go to the jailhouse, as long as they didn't have to go back inside. It took the sheriff threatening to shoot their legs out and drag them back in for them to go in on their own, crying the entire time. These were all grown men. They ended up staying the whole night and all of them came out in the morning. None of them disappeared after all.

"But later, after they got home, one of them, a man named Clyde, kept talking to his family and even his preacher about how he had to go back because he left something in the house. They didn't know what to make of it at first and just told him that it couldn't be that important. He still had his wedding ring, his father's watch, the most important things that he'd had on him at the time. What could he have left behind that could make him think he needed to go back? He couldn't tell them, or wouldn't. He just kept saying he had to go, until one day his wife and children woke up and couldn't find him in their house, and didn't see his truck out front.

"Since he'd talked about it so much, the spite house was the first place they asked the authorities to look for him. Sure enough, his truck was parked right by it, but they searched that house, the valley, and everything nearby, and found no trace of him. People said all sorts of things to explain it away, even accusing some of our good citizens of killing him and stashing the body someplace where it would never be found, but I don't think anyone would have done that without my father's approval, and he might have okayed some intimidation, but he'd have had too much sense to green-light a murder, especially since the message had already been sent.

"Still, it raised enough problems and questions that he and my mother decided to move the memorial onto private property to prevent something like this from happening again. My great-great-grandmother, Beatrice, commissioned the memorial in the first place, so it was ours to do with as we pleased. We brought it here, and now, a couple of generations later, it's become yet another Degener myth."

Eric took a deep breath, exhaled slowly, then said, "Thanks for telling me all of that."

"I should have told you everything on day one. That way when Emily brought it up, you could have said, 'Tell me something I don't know.' But better late than never, I suppose. As long as it's not too late. I hope it's not."

She felt a flutter of fear as he hesitated, then he said, "It's not. This doesn't change anything. I'm going back, I'm getting the job done, I'll earn your money, and then I'm getting my girls as far away from here as I can."

"That sounds like a solid plan, Mr. Ross."

She talked to him about practical matters as they went back to her house. Whether either of the girls had allergies or illnesses she and Lafonda should know about. Favorite foods, favorite hobbies, anything to make sure that their stay was as ideal as could be. He told her some things she'd heard already from Lafonda based on her earlier meeting with the girls. Stacy, like many her age, liked arts and crafts and using her imagination, and was fascinated with books. Dess was an athlete, preferred to be outdoors. Eunice said she would take them shopping, get Stacy some art supplies and Dess some running shoes. Afterward they would go to a park and a museum downtown that they might enjoy, with his permission, of course. All the while, she was satisfied with how open she was with him. No, she didn't tell him about the Renners, but she said enough for him to know what he was going back to, and he was still on board. That probably spoke to his desperation, and she felt some empathy for him, but was happy that he was committed, one way or another. She wasn't going to risk saying anything else that might dissuade him.

That was why she kept a couple of things to herself. Like the full truth about Clyde Carmichael, how the sheriff found him in the floating hallway of the spite house, alive but unresponsive. A blank slate who stared ahead and didn't say anything. How, after consulting with her father, the sheriff received permission to take Clyde into the woods, shoot him in the head, and bury him deep. She used to wonder if that was a sound decision, and what she would do in the same situation.

Thankfully, she'd never been called to do something that severe. The worst she had to do was withhold information about Clyde and the Renners, as well the fact that the city park wasn't the memorial's original location. Its first home was at the spot where the spite house now stood. Peter Masson moved it so he could build his defiant home near the trees used to murder twelve men and boys in 1862.

Eric might have stayed even if he knew all of this. Why risk it, though? Besides, from what she could tell, he was better equipped to handle the house than the people it swallowed up in the past. He had his own history with ghosts at his grandfather's house. That must have inoculated him somewhat. He wasn't an ignorant thug like Clyde Carmichael, or a shallow fool like the Renners. He could endure. And in the event he ended up like Jane Renner, Eunice would increase the payout to pacify Dess and Stacy, as well as dull any needling from her own conscience. Of the many things wealth was good for, one of the most underappreciated, in her opinion, was that it allowed you to purchase self-absolution.

After Eric left to return to the Masson House, Eunice went into the study nearest her bedroom, locked the door, and called Neal Lassiter.

"Hello, hello, Dame Eunice," he said.

"Hello, Neal. You sound in good spirits."

"I was until you uttered that awful s-word."

She grinned. "Get used to hearing it. You have to know that that's what I'm calling about."

"I see. So you're telling me the time has finally come?"

"I think it's right around the corner."

"Hm," he said, then hesitated before shocking her with, "You truly think that poor man and his girls are going to stick around long enough to get you your 'proof'?"

Her smile faded. "You've talked to Millie."

"She gave me a call telling me to give you a call to talk you out of this. I've been meaning to, I just got busy."

"Yes, I'm sure it's time-consuming finding subjects to ridicule for the next season of *The Faithless Egotist Hour*."

She could almost hear him tilt his head and frown at her through the phone. "I'm offended that you left 'Heathen' out of my show's title."

"I offer my apologies, and presume you'll accept."

"When haven't I?" he said.

"Good, because I really do believe this is going to happen this time," Eunice said. "This family is not like the others."

"Of course not," he said, "for starters they're a family, not hack filmmakers or reality show wannabes looking for a shortcut to fame. That should trouble you, Eunice, not make you feel like 'this is the one.'"

Eunice said, "What about it should trouble me? I know that you of all people aren't about to tell me they're in danger because the house could be haunted."

"You have me there."

"I know I do. I suspect that's the real reason why you hadn't called yet. You have to know I wouldn't actually put this family in harm's way."

"I know you wouldn't intentionally hurt anyone."

"And how would I accidentally do it, Neal? Anyway, the children aren't even going to be staying in the house anymore. They'll be staying with me. And their father has agreed to stay in that house—safe and sound—long enough for me to be able to make a believer out of you."

"Well, I hope that day comes soon, because I can't wait to flip you over to the rational side of the world."

"Just be ready to fly down here when I make the call," Eunice said, "and expect it to be soon."

Eric

When he was fifteen, Eric's mother was diagnosed with cancer, and given less than a year to live. That summer, as she seemed to get sicker by the day, his father and grandfather took him to a lakeshore near his house to let him get drunk for the first time, get his emotions out. Mostly, he just wanted to know why. Why her? Why so young? Why someone so good? *Why?*

"I think the same thing all the time," Eric's father said. "All I can do is just remind myself that . . . you know . . . everything happens for a reason."

"Bullshit," Frederick Emerson said to his son, sounding like someone had directed a slur at him.

"Pop, not now," Eric's dad said.

"Yes, now," Fred said. "Don't go filling your boy's head with that bullshit. Things happen for one of two reasons: You either let something happen, or you made something happen."

"Really, Pop? Are you serious right now?"

"I sound it, don't I?"

"So what are you saying?" Eric's father said, his voice pinched a little. "You saying I *let* my wife get sick? You're saying I'm letting her . . . *what* exactly? Huh? What am I supposed to do? What am I supposed to 'make happen,' Pop? I'm not a nurse or a damn doctor. There's nothing I can do."

"You don't know that," Frederick told his son. "You haven't even tried."

Eric's father stormed off then. Walked to the house of the nearest neighbor he knew, about five miles away, and spent the night there before getting a ride home in the morning. The next day, he took Eric's mother to another doctor to get a second opinion. A week later they visited a third, who recommended a specialist on the other side of the country. A month later, Eric's mother was signing up for a drug trial, and being told about other possible treatments her first doctor hadn't mentioned. She lived another twenty-two years, long enough to give Dess good memories of her.

That was when Eric learned that his grandfather's motto had value. It didn't matter that it wasn't one hundred percent true, it mattered that it called you to act. It demanded that you not sit back and trust the world to grant you a single kindness or break. Anything good it gave you could be stolen right back if you weren't vigilant. He knew that too well. His grandfather's truth resonated with him today more than ever. If you didn't at least try to make something happen, you were just letting something eventually happen to you and yours.

Eric stared up at the spite house like it was a giant daring him to move so it could step on him. He was no match for it, but he'd have to face it on his own, and he ultimately had no one else to blame for his predicament. He had let everything happen that brought him to this.

A cool front blew in to finally bring a belated hint of autumn to Degener, Texas. Eric stared up at the Masson House as the wind chilled him in a way that was distinctly natural compared to what he'd felt the night before.

The girls wouldn't be there tonight to distract the house, or him. He couldn't play the ABC game with them, tell them corny jokes while cooking dinner. He would have the house's full focus, and it would have his.

He turned to the buildings in the hollow between the hills. Under different circumstances, Eric would have presumed that a long-abandoned orphanage, with its adjacent empty church and playground, would be at least as haunted as the novelty house overlooking it. Compared to the spite house, however, it looked like a sanctuary. It was a place he could go to for a little bit of peace before stepping back into whatever madness the spite house had planned for him. He could also drive away, go back into town at the moment, kill time at the library or any shops, but he wasn't sure that he'd come back if he did that.

He started toward the orphanage. An unexpected instinct came over him when he turned his back on the house—an urge to dive to the side or duck into a ball, or do both at once. It was as if he sensed a truck bearing down on him from behind. He held still for a moment and let the sensation fizzle out. It might've come from within, apprehension manifested as a physical flight response, but he doubted it. Something from the house had reached out and rung the alarm built into the living that warns them that the dead are watching. Was the spirit toying with him, or did it want something? Did it want him to turn around? Come into the house? Or did it want him to stay away from the orphanage? He believed it was the latter, in part because it gave him more incentive to go there. When he was able to move again, he walked down the hill.

The central building of the orphanage smelled of neglect and reemerging nature. The dust inside tickled Eric's nose. The Houghton family's devotion to the upkeep of the Masson House was not reflected in the condition of the orphanage. It wasn't quite in shambles, but inside it proved far from livable. Shattered slates of ceiling plaster lay scattered on weak, rotting floorboards. He entered through the open front doorway, which was barely holding on to a jamb that was barely holding on to the rest of the building. The walls looked fragile and had water stains that looked like they'd burst into brackish fluid if poked.

There were no furnishings left behind. No writings or markings defaced the walls. No evidence of squatters or vandals, or that the place was abruptly abandoned. The building was in about as ordinary a state of disrepair as it could be.

The narrow entryway fed into a broader, circular foyer. An open doorway ahead led to a long, windowless hallway, while another doorway to the right opened to a brighter, shorter hallway littered with shattered glass from the series of broken windows along its outer wall. To the left of the foyer, Eric saw a wider doorway that led to what he presumed was a dining room, given its proximity to what had evidently been the kitchen. It seemed strange to him, now that he considered it, that so many doors were missing. Was this normal for an abandoned building? Leave some exterior doors to possibly discourage trespassers, but take out the interior doors that otherwise would have no use?

Not wanting to walk across broken glass or trek down an unlit hallway he couldn't quite see the end of, Eric opted to explore the dining area. It was a large space with a higher ceiling than the foyer, and tall windows that faced the Masson House. He pictured being a child here, eating breakfasts with your fellow orphans, the glare of the sun reflected in the windows of the odd house on the hill. And then in the evening, near supper, returning here to see the sun set early behind the broad side of that thin house. Masson built his home to antagonize and torment the orphans and their caregivers. Why? What did he gain from this? Had he simply despised children?

This last consideration brought a microquake up through Eric's spine. He let his daughters sleep in the bizarre, haunted home of a man who might have hated kids, and whose niece and nephew seemed to haunt the house with him. That would explain the phantom children who taunted his girls the last two nights. How had those kids died? What did Masson do to them?

Eric felt a flush of shame and shook his head at the magnitude of his mistake. He shouldn't have allowed Stacy and Dess to spend one hour in that place. He stared up at the house through the windows of the dining hall, protected from its balefulness by the distance. Then he saw it.

A figure stood in the window of the spite house's master bedroom on the top floor. Even from afar and through the glass, Eric could make out enough of its features to know it was a man, older, as gray-faced as he was grizzled. His gaze was made of ice, and Eric felt unnaturally numb, like he'd been pulled from his body and flung into space and was seeing all of this through some form of telepathy. He was drawn closer, close enough to see the years of pain on the old man's face. Pain born of anger, regret, solitude, and fear. So much fear, but that hadn't always been the dominant emotion.

Behind him, he felt a presence in the room, not entirely unlike what he would feel on the frigid nights in the house his grandfather rebuilt, when the fire tried to come alive again. This presence was more unfamiliar, though, and older. As old as the man in the window at least. It moved closer to him and Eric felt its decades of emotions too. He brought his hands to his head, pressed them to his temples, and shut his eyes tight like he meant to squeeze these foreign feelings out of his skull. He opened his mouth to scream, but a presence behind him spoke first.

"Tell him to leave us alone." A young woman's voice. It carried its own echo ahead of it. "Tell him to leave us alone," she said again, a little louder and deeper with age.

"Tell him to leave us alone." An older woman now. Still the same woman? He couldn't tell. His muscles strained when he turned, like he'd lifted a weight right at the threshold of his strength. The room was visibly empty, yet filled by the presence and its voice.

"Tell him to leave us alone."

Did the building shake that time? Or was it just his body shaking, his head rattling? At least he could feel something again, awful as it was. Cold as it was.

He ran out of the building, stumbling a few times as he went, his legs feeling not quite connected to him. The voice followed him, growing older with each utterance until it rasped with the last energy of a bitter, dying person. *"Tell him to leave us alone tell him to leave us alone TELL HIM—"*

He fell to the ground a few feet past the front entrance. A pervading grief and sickness spread through his body. He clenched his fists to dig his fingernails into his palms, physically rejecting any sensation that did not originate with him. He knelt in the grass, gagged and dry heaved, but managed not to vomit.

After the stomach pangs subsided, he remained on the ground for a time, as though praying toward the Masson House. The wind pushed the swings on the playground behind the orphanage's central building. The rusted chains gave off a metronomic creak as they swayed. Eric locked on to the rhythm of the sound, ignoring its sharpness. That steadiness helped to settle him.

A flush of anger came over him as he stood. This was the second time in less than twenty-four hours that he'd let something run him off. Last night he had the excuse of needing to protect his daughters. What was his excuse now? He had come here because he was afraid to enter the spite house again, and ended up so scared he had to find his way out. He made himself turn and face the orphanage, almost took a step toward it. He imagined himself going back inside, a taller, broader, braver version of himself. A man with fists like bricks, a stare that could stop a heartbeat. The man he wanted to be.

He would go back into the building and make something happen. Make the spirit that spoke to him tremble and weep when he bellowed back at it. Make it remember that it was dead, and not like Stacy had been, or like they said his grandfather had been, but forever dead. Never coming back, because it lacked the will to do so. All it could do was shout at the occasional intruder and scare them because they failed to understand how weak and sad it really was. The man he wanted to be would make the ghost cower, run screaming back to its grave. How exactly, he didn't know, but he knew that man could make it happen.

Except that man wouldn't have been here in the first place, because he wouldn't have let Stacy die. Somehow, he wouldn't have let that happen.

Eric shook the grief and shame away before it overcame him, brought him back to his knees. He looked again at the spite house and saw that the old man—Pete Masson, whose life possessed Eric in his sleep the night before last—was no longer in the window. He tried to collect his thoughts, assemble them into something that could make sense of all of this. Provide answers.

That was why he was here, wasn't it? Yes, he and the girls needed the money, but he needed his answers just as much. They left home ultimately because he didn't have a better answer for what they should do after Stacy came back, and that was because he didn't have an answer for how she had come back, or if it was even really her.

He was starting to get some answers about the nature of death and what came after, though. He just had to think about all he'd been through, dating back to when he was a child. The cold was key. He felt it naturally again, outdoors, and noted how different it was from the deep freeze he felt in the orphanage and in the spite house, and in his grandparents' house when the ghost fire burned. He never felt anything close to that around his grandfather, despite the rumors some of his neighbors and even distant family members once spread. That "Ol' Fred" actually died in that fire and that the living version of him wasn't alive at all, but a dead man impersonating a living one. But if he really was dead, the cold would have been all over him and bleeding out of him. You'd have been able to feel it from twenty feet away. That wasn't the case, nor was it with Stacy. The difference, though, was that he'd only heard stories about what happened to his grandfather. Gossip, second and thirdhand conjecture. He knew what happened to his little girl. What she came back from. So for her not to carry the cold of death meant something, he just couldn't yet say exactly what.

The house could still help him with that. There was more than the old man inside. Along with the ghost children, there was the crying woman. Then there was the phantom projection of himself that he'd seen there. Things he didn't understand, but that he could learn from. There was even the myth that Eunice shared with him earlier today, that the house could make the living disappear. If it could do that and also make the dead reappear, as he'd already experienced, then maybe it was a bridge of sorts. Maybe he could use it to find out how some people made it across. How some people came back again. He wanted to be sure that it was really Stacy who returned, not an impostor. And if it really was her, he needed to be sure she wouldn't disappear on him without warning. Without at least giving him a chance, this time, to say goodbye.

No, it was never going to come to that. He wasn't ever going to need to say goodbye, at least not until the day he died. He wasn't going to outlive his child. One way or another, he could not let that happen.

As he approached the house, still weary and aching, he saw the woman from the hall standing in the open doorway. Still blue, her expression full of anguish. Her mouth did not move when she spoke to him. He heard her clearly through the wind and distance.

There are no dreams in this house. Only lies. Lies, lies, lies. They've trapped me here. They'll trap you. His lies and theirs. No dreams, only lies.

If that was true, if the house was full of lies, not answers, then couldn't she be lying to him now? And even a lie can reveal a truth if you find out why someone is telling it.

Eric continued toward the house. He would take his chances with it. The woman retreated before he came to the door and he did not see where she went. He walked up the stairs to the master bedroom. Exhaustion seized him at last, just as he reached for the journal on the bed. Later, he would awaken in darkness without remembering the moments before he'd fallen asleep. He wouldn't remember filling page after page of the journal, but he would remember what he wrote, because it came to him as he slept. Not as a dream, however, because dreams truly did not exist in the Masson House.

Masson

The most frustrating part of getting the men from the AEF to believe him was convincing them that he disappeared at all. As far as his superiors were concerned, Peter Masson died a year before, on the battlefield near Saint-Étienne.

"There must have been a mistake, sir," Peter said to the interviewing officer. "I'm not dead. I'm here."

"Yes, clearly you're here," the interviewer said. "But maybe the 'mistake' is on your end, and you're not who you believe you are."

"I've given you all my information, sir. My signature is on my recruitment card. I can write it for you if you give me a pen, so you can see it matches. I can tell you anything else you need to know. If you send me back home my brother will recognize me within a hundred yards. I *am* Peter Masson, sir."

They eventually made him write his signature on a blank sheet of paper, presumably to cross-check it as he suggested. He never knew what other steps they took to verify his identity. Whether they checked photographs of him that they had on file, whether they interviewed anyone else from the 144th. Whatever they did, they must have been thorough. They were not satisfied that he was Peter Masson until late October, and he did not make his way home until November.

He expected there to be much disbelief when he arrived in Degener. He did not expect that disbelief to be his own. There were strangers in and around his family home, none willing to explain what business they had there, or why expansions had been built. An overly polite woman who met Peter there told him he could find Lukas staying in Degener's lone hotel with his wife and daughter. Lukas was shocked to see Peter in person, but not as shocked as he would have been had he not received a telegram informing him that a grievous error had been made and that his brother was not dead. Still, after such a swing in circumstances and emotions, Lukas was, in his own words, "unsure of what to believe." He was not overjoyed or even relieved to see that Peter was back. Peter understood why this was before even knocking on the front door of their house. The instinct that drove him to come back from the war proved correct. Lukas had jumped at the first opportunity to rid himself of the property meant to stay with their family for generations.

The home that their father left to them—that the Houghtons gave to their father as reparation for the hanging of his great-grandfather along with eleven others in 1862—was being expanded upon. Neighboring buildings put up on either side of it. Construction was close to completion.

The buyer was Everlasting Arms Ministries. They were based in Chicago, according to Lukas, sponsored by a wealthy benefactor. They were looking to expand into more "idyllic" parts of the country, where they could transport orphans from crowded cities to places that looked and felt like they offered a new beginning.

It was a noble endeavor, Peter agreed, and he understood why they found this part of the Texas Hill Country so attractive. But none of that changed the fact that this was still his house and his land, just as much as it was once his brother's. He never agreed to sell his half of their inheritance, and never would. It was their father's land, purchased at the price of their great-grandfather's life. The marker that commemorated their great-grandfather's murder still rested on the hill to the west, for God's sake, overlooking this fresh injustice. To sell their house and land was a betrayal.

Surely the kind sisters of Everlasting Arms would understand the land's importance to him and be reasonable about the mistake they and Lukas had made. Surely, people of the church would have compassion. They could find other land nearby. The Houghtons would help them. Peter would as well. He would make sure to compensate them for having to void the agreement they made with Lukas, as well as for any additional inconveniences, even if it meant providing them free labor until it satisfied however much additional debt they felt they were owed. Even Lukas, eager as he had been to sell the property, would have his eyes opened enough by the blessing of his only brother's unexpected survival to see the injustice that he'd inadvertently done to Peter. Perhaps the orphan children, as well, would sympathize with Peter's right to remain in his home and want not to compound a war hero's suffering.

"You've been given a second life, brother," Lukas told him. "Isn't that enough of a blessing? You want to take this home away from these children, too?"

Peter wanted to choke his brother then. Render him unconscious and then beat him awake. He could have done it. Even as a medic he'd learned ways to defend himself and hurt others while in the army. Lukas had no idea what Peter had been through, and had no right to speak to him about blessings. Not when he stayed home while Peter went overseas and got his hands filthy trying to patch up bodies ripped up by war machines. If anything, Lukas was blessed to have no scruples or dignity, leaving him free to act as he pleased, while Peter was afflicted with a sense of duty and knowing what was right.

It was like they were siblings in a fairy tale with a corrupted ending. Instead of Lukas receiving any well-earned comeuppance, Peter was going to suffer for having courage. *Then the giant seized the hero before he could escape down the beanstalk, and made good on the promise to grind the man's bones into flour for bread.* Peter should not have been disappointed. He shouldn't have dared hope for his brother's understanding, but what Lukas said to him tore something out of him that he had failed to loosen, so it did not come away clean.

"I can't take from them what's already mine," Peter said, trembling, his rage rattling its way out of him. "And I wasn't given a second life. I never died."

"True, but we certainly thought you did. They sent us some poor soul's remains, what little was left of them. They said it was you. We held a service. There's a tombstone with your name—"

"I never died." He swallowed his compulsion to say it a third time. Something within him wanted to scream it a thousand more times. *I never died. I never died.* On and on for as long as it would take for everyone to believe it. Himself most of all, the one person who could be sure that it was a lie.

Stacy

The people she couldn't see were waiting for her in Miss Eunice's house. This time they said things that she could not ignore, and she couldn't make them stop talking.

They waited until she was by herself to talk to her this time. She didn't even have Miss Happy with her. Even though Mom wasn't there, Stacy knew that she'd call it "unsanitary" to bring her doll with her to the bathroom, so she left Miss Happy in bed with her sister.

Dess had said to wake her up if she needed to use the bathroom, but it was only around the corner from their bedroom. Miss Lafonda showed it to them the first night. And Stacy knew Dess was tired, she'd seen her yawning all day. So she slid out of bed and out of the large room they shared, found the bathroom on her own, and was on her way back when one of the invisible people said, *We need your help.*

More than she wished Dess, Mom, or Dad were with her when it happened, she wished Pa-Pa Fred were there. He knew how to be scarier than scary things. She remembered the last time he came to see them in Maryland. He walked her to the store, but when she wanted to cross the street to get away from the neighbor's new, big, angry dog, he told her, "No." The dog bared its teeth, growled, and barked as they walked past the black metal fence that kept it in its yard. It looked like it could slip its head between two of the vertical fence posts and get close enough to bite them, but Pa-Pa Fred told her it couldn't. "Even if it could, I wouldn't let it. Watch this," he said.

Then, still holding her hand, he stooped low and close to the fence, to get face-to-face with the dog. It kept barking and snarling for a few seconds, then got quieter the longer Pa-Pa Fred stared at it. At first, Stacy thought he was making friends with the dog. Then he grunted and quickly gnashed at it, like he meant to be the one to break through the fence and start biting. The dog whimpered and ran away from him. For a second, Pa-Pa Fred looked happy in a way that made Stacy want to run, too. His smile was wider than she'd ever seen, and she noticed how white and large his teeth were. He looked like someone who was only supposed to come out at night, who lived near woods you were supposed to never walk through.

Then he turned to her and was himself again. "See? Nothing to be afraid of. You could've done that."

Stacy shook her head. "I'm not big like you."

"That's got nothing to do with it. What have I told you? You can do anything you want, you just have to make it happen."

Maybe the problem, now, was that she didn't really want the invisible people to stop talking. She felt they were trying to tell her something important. It was the way they spoke, like someone was trying to pull them away or shut a door on them before they could get the words out. And they were asking for help.

Please. We just need you to remember.

They weren't like that awful dog that acted like it would chew through metal to get at her. They weren't mad, and she couldn't even see them. That made them different from normal strangers she knew better than to talk to. How dangerous could they be if they weren't really there?

We're no danger at all. We're just asking for help.

Yes, yes. We only need you to tell us how you—

Shhhh. Careful. Don't scare her.

Too late, she realized giving them a chance to say anything was a mistake. If they could say anything that might scare her, they had to be bad, or at least they couldn't be too good.

She put her hands over her ears, but still heard them. They were so much louder tonight than they were the last time she was here. They whispered so quietly before that she couldn't understand them. Now they sounded like they were right next to her. How could that be? Was it because of what happened in the skinny house? That was the only thing she could think of. Being inside that horrible house made it easier for the ghosts here to talk to her, or easier for her to hear them. Either way, she hated it. She wanted to get away. She wanted to go home.

Remember the water, one of them hurried to tell her as she ran back to the room. The others joined in, saying the same thing over and over. As much as she didn't want to hear them anymore, she was just as curious to know what they meant.

Remember the water.

That felt like something she needed to do. Maybe it'd be an answer for why things had been so strange lately. Why she hadn't seen or spoken to Mom for so long. Something must have happened to explain that, and also why they had run away from home. Something really bad that Dess and Dad weren't telling her.

Her hand was on the doorknob. She could open the door, go back into the bedroom, and wake up Dess. Then the people she couldn't see would leave her alone, or Dess would make them leave her alone, like she had with that boy and girl in the skinny house. But what would happen after that? Things would keep being strange. Mom would keep being gone and Dad and Dess would keep saying Mom would be with them soon, even though it was already too late to be soon.

She closed her eyes and saw the water. She could smell and taste it. She felt herself floating in it. She couldn't remember everything about it, but she knew that Mom was still with them the last time Stacy was in the water like that. It had been a fun day. A surprise. And now she remembered it was also the last time they were all together.

After that, she thought there had been a car ride, but that was fuzzy to her. The next thing she clearly remembered was walking down a street. Walking home.

Something happened when they went to the water that day. She had to find out what.

Yes, one of the people told her.

There's water here, another said. *Do you know how to get there?*

She did. There were two ponds along the big walking trail outside. If she followed the trail she would find one of them, and maybe being near it would help her figure out what the people she couldn't see were talking about.

Eric

Eric's eyes opened to concentrated darkness. There was an element in the room, a force of reality, consuming any light and warmth with the hunger of a black hole. To call it Death was inaccurate. It existed before the Life that birthed Death. It was the original state of nature. Unlit blankness. Nothingness. Eric knew that if he could crawl from the bed and fumble his way to the windows to get a proper view, he would see that Nothingness all around the house.

Getting out of bed seemed impossible, however. He sat up, surprised that he still held the journal and pen. He turned on the lamp on the nightstand, expecting it not to work, but it gave him enough light to see what was in the journal. The handwriting was his, but looser, a little harder to read. Like he'd written it under duress and a tightening deadline.

His unwitting, automatic writing captured Peter Masson's story up to the point that Eric had lived it. As Eric read it, something shifted to his left, in a corner of the room. He looked at the crowded shadows there and knew something hid within them. The cold intensified, making it difficult for Eric to speak through chattering teeth.

"Y-y-you d-died," he said. "Y-you died and came back. H-how did you do it?"

Peter Masson remained silent and hidden, but Eric knew he was there.

"You just couldn't let them take your land? Was that it? Do you even know how you did it or was it just like an accident? Come on, say something, damn it. What are you scared of?"

The quiet and cold brought Eric's anger up to the same level as his fear. He felt less like he was back in the room at his grandparents' house, afraid of fire and shadows, and more like he was channeling his grandfather.

"Whatever you think might happen if you talk to me, start saying too much, it'll be worse for you if you stay quiet. You think I don't know you're there? I know. And I know your name. You're Peter Masson. You died in the war, you were blown apart—"

The old man groaned from his corner, but still did not reveal himself.

"You were blown apart," Eric said, shaking now. "You *died,* Peter. And then you were alive again. I know it. I just saw it all in my dream. I *lived* it."

"There are no dreams in this house," the woman said. The iciness she added to the room pushed a shocking chill into his bones and teeth. Eric winced, but kept his focus. He wasn't going to break now.

Perhaps there were no dreams in the spite house, but there were other things. Lives and memories that you could step into. He'd done that twice now.

"No, no, no. That's not true. You're wrong." She was close to him, maybe even close enough to touch him if the freezing sensation that numbed the right side of his body was any indication. "It's all a lie," she said. "He couldn't come back. No one comes back. If you could, I would. I've tried. I've tried I've tried—"

"It's not a lie," Eric said.

"You don't know. You don't know."

"I do," Eric said.

"How? How, you liar? *How? Hhh*—?" A hissing gasp cut her short, like something sucked her out of the room. The chill vanished as well. Masson's presence lingered long enough to whisper, "I'm sorry." Then it was gone and the lamp's light could reach the corner Masson had occupied.

Eric felt light-headed and nauseous. He tried to get out of bed anyway and after failing at that he sat back against the headboard and imagined how terrible it must be to exist as Peter Masson now did, and as the ghost woman did. Stuck in relentless desolation. Not like his baby girl. Stacy was warm with life. She had pulled herself out of death's grasp and he was starting to think that how she'd done it was a mystery that could be saved for later. What mattered more was whether she legitimately came back. There seemed to be precedent. Peter Masson apparently came back, which lent much more credence to the rumors surrounding Eric's grandfather. Both lived to be old men after returning, too. So it was possible that Stacy was here to stay, Eric thought. Presuming that she was herself, and not something in disguise, a changeling wearing her like a skin. Another question he needed to set aside. One thing at a time.

Above all else, at the moment, he wanted to believe that Death—a conscious and active force—wouldn't up and discover she was missing someday and try to take her back. His grandfather lived long enough to meet his two great-granddaughters, who, incidentally, would never have been born if he had remained dead. And Masson lived at least long enough to build this house. How long after that? Eric thought he could find out. In the morning, if he didn't feel too sick to move, he would do just that.

Eunice

he Houghton Estate had little in the way of security. It never struck Eunice or any of her predecessors as necessary, despite their fear of death. The town itself was all the security they needed. The sheriff's office favored them. The small-business owners favored them. All the people who enjoyed the fruits that they provided favored them, if for no other reason than that it was in their best interest. So it wasn't until Lafonda moved in and insisted that a security system be installed for her own peace of mind that Eunice bothered with one, which she quickly found annoying, given that it announced the opening and closing of any door that led to the outside. She let Lafonda activate it only at night when no one would be coming in or going out.

When the voice announced, "Back Patio One, Door Open," it cut clean through her sleep. Eunice woke with her heart pumping. Surely no one had broken in. That would be absurd.

Or would it be? A parade of strangers had come through her house for job interviews and she turned down all but one of them. Someone from one of those little "ghost hunter" groups might have taken the rejection poorly, come here to get payback.

She opened her phone and checked the security app. Right away it showed her the live feed from the camera where there was movement. It was outside by Oscar's pond, named for her cousin. There was a small figure standing in the gazebo in the center of water just deep enough for an adult to drown in, if they couldn't swim.

For a second, her mind still cloudy with sleep, Eunice thought she was watching Oscar's ghost relive his final moments. Then she realized who the figure really was. The little girl. Stacy.

Eunice threw on her robe and house shoes. She thought she heard movement from Lafonda's room but did not wait for her. She left her room, hustled down the stairs and out the same door Stacy had used.

She appeared to be leaning out over the pond when Eunice saw her, though she was still far away enough that she couldn't be sure. "Stacy! Stacy, dear, stay where you are!"

When Stacy turned to her, Eunice could still not quite make out her features and a horrible thought pinned her in place like a dead bug in a display case. *It's a trick. A trap. They've outsmarted you. That girl is just bait to lure you out and now they're going to get you. After all this time, you let your guard down and this is it.*

It was the cooler outdoor temperature combined with her inability to make out the girl's face that brought her to this grim, false conclusion. The certitude of her impending death fell on her like an avalanche. She wanted to swing her fists and claw her fingernails at the invisible avengers who would swarm her, but soon realized that the chill spared her bones, much less the deeper parts of her being that would absorb the subzero radiation of the dead. This was just natural, autumn air. The product of the season and the night. It wasn't related to what she had feared since Val died, and feared even more after Oscar died.

Can't risk it, Eunice thought. *What if you're wrong? They'll have you.*

Stilled by fear, she glanced at her watch to check her pulse, see if it was irregular. It was slightly elevated, nothing alarming, though. No indication of a looming heart attack. Beneath the numbers, something else caught her eye in the glare of her back patio lights. Her company's name etched into the watch's face. ValTuf. She could almost feel her aunt Val's hand on her shoulder again. It felt protective. Even empowering. Facing down the unimaginable, Val still tried to shield Eunice from harm.

Eunice wasn't that brave, but she could match that defiance. She'd spent her life eluding death and destiny. Avoiding risks to her health, as well, but not at the expense of her ultimate goal. If she let fear get the best of her now, all her patience and persistence might go to waste. There was a perfect tenant in the spite house, at last, but if Stacy got hurt on her watch, Eunice wouldn't be able to convince Eric to stay. She knew the chill in the air wasn't the ghosts. She *knew* it. The only thing keeping her from going for the girl was cowardice. She couldn't let that be what condemned her.

She walked toward the gazebo. "I'll be right there," Eunice said. "Don't move."

But by the time Eunice crossed the bridge Stacy had moved away from the open space and into the center of the gazebo. The little girl's eyes shimmered with worry.

"I'm sorry," she said as Eunice came toward her. "I know I shouldn't be here, but they told me to."

"It's okay. I'm just glad you're not hurt," Eunice said, crouching and hugging her just to reassure herself that Stacy was a real, physical thing. Not a spirit in disguise. Then it hit her what the girl had said. *They told me to.* She pulled back and stared at her for seconds that spread like a bloodstain on cloth.

"Are you going to tell my dad?" Stacy said.

"Who are 'they'?" Eunice said, unable to keep all of the sharpness from her tone. "You said 'they' told you to come here? Who?"

The girl drew a deep breath, as though bracing herself to be disbelieved. "I heard people in the house. I went to the bathroom and they started talking to me. I was scared. I was going back to tell my sister, but they asked me to help them. They said they were sorry for scaring me. I didn't say anything back because I don't talk to strangers. But then they said I should come down here to the water to see if I could remember. I don't know why I listened. I just felt like I had to." Tears came to her eyes. "Am I in trouble? Are you going to tell my dad?"

Eunice took a moment to work up a smile and sweeten her voice. "No, no, dear." She heard Lafonda's feet crunching up the pathway behind her, so she spoke loud enough for Lafonda to hear how she wanted the situation handled. "We won't even tell your sister, just in case she might tell your father. You're not in trouble. I saw you out here and I got scared for you. I know this pond isn't very wide, but the water is deeper than it looks. It wouldn't be good if you got in."

"I didn't want to get in. I just wanted to remember."

Eunice looked back at Lafonda, who stood on the bridge. Lafonda mouthed, "Is she okay?," and Eunice nodded, though she knew her eyes said otherwise.

"What are you trying to remember, Stacy?" Eunice said.

The girl's mouth hung open for a moment. Finally she said, "I think I forgot something really important."

She thought about pressing the girl for a real answer, but knew it wouldn't do any good. With Lafonda there, it wouldn't look good, either. It would just give Lafonda something else to question later, while Eunice's own question for Stacy went unanswered. Besides, she wanted to get the girl back inside in case her sister woke up. Tomorrow, she'd bake the girl some brownies or more cookies, get her in a more comfortable, trusting state, then ask why she had really come out here. What exactly "they" had told her.

Eunice stood and handed Stacy off to Lafonda. "Would you mind sleeping in Miss Lafonda's room the rest of the night? That way we don't have to wake your sister if she's still sleeping. I think she could use the rest. In the morning we'll have Miss Lafonda make your favorite, and when your sister comes down we'll tell her you got up early because you smelled it cooking, and nobody will be in any kind of trouble."

"Thank you," Stacy said.

Eunice looked to Lafonda and said, "How rude of me, Miss Lafonda. I didn't even think to ask you about this. But you don't mind having a guest for the night, do you?"

Lafonda had a hundred questions etched into her expression but managed to suppress them and put on her kindest voice. "I don't mind at all. It'll be my pleasure."

Eunice followed Stacy and Lafonda as they walked to the house. She stopped at the door and waved for them to go on.

"I just need a moment," she said. When Lafonda looked hesitant, she added, "I'll be fine. I'll take a little something to help me sleep when I get upstairs and I'll be all right. Go ahead."

No child had lived at the Houghton Estate since Eunice was young. There was a reason for that.

Left alone, Eunice looked back to Oscar's pond. A vision of him in the water came to mind. It wasn't a memory. No one saw him enter the water that night. He snuck out late when everyone was asleep, just like Stacy.

No one was ever sure of why he did it, although Eunice thought she knew, which was why she didn't picture him falling into the water by accident, but going in deliberately. Not quite appreciating how cold the night was—how much colder the water was—until it was up to his chest. Even then, for a few seconds, he probably tried to keep swimming.

He'd been a frail and undersized boy. Clumsy, awkward, and asthmatic, all of which hurt his chances of making friends even more than being the outsider from up north did. His father—one of Eunice's paternal uncles—sent him down from Connecticut in the hopes that the warmer climate would be easier on his lungs. Eunice was the only person Oscar's age who paid much attention to him at school. Outside of school, he was confined to the estate.

A few boys befriended him just prior to Christmas break. Eunice found this suspicious. She was mindful and protective of her older, bigger, yet somehow "little" cousin. Aunt Val would have wanted her to look out for him. So she made it her business to listen in on what the other boys said to Oscar. She heard one of the boys tell him, "My father was like you when he was young, but he made himself strong by swimming in cold rivers in the winter." Had she realized Oscar might take this comment seriously she would have spoken to him, dissuaded him, or at least warned her parents to keep an eye on him during that harsh December.

He must have believed putting on a sweater and coat would insulate him. Instead, the added layers probably made it harder for him to get out of the water when its temperature drove the air from his chest. The extra exertion, no doubt, contributed to the asthma attack that killed him.

A groundskeeper found Oscar in the morning, lying on his side next to the pond, his clothes wet, his lips blue and drawn back in a grimace, his eyes open so wide it looked like he didn't have eyelids.

Eunice gleaned much of this through eavesdropping on her parents' discussions in the weeks that followed. One discussion in particular stood out.

Her father, remorseful for allowing his brother's son to die under his care, refused to believe that their familial curse accounted for the fear frozen on Oscar's face. "He's a boy," her father said. "*Was* a boy. He's too young for them to have come for him."

"There is no such thing as too young," her mother said flatly, like an old professor dismissing a wrong answer she'd heard a hundred times before. At the time, Eunice had thought her mother cruel, in part because she wanted to believe her father was right, which would mean her youth granted her temporary immunity from the curse that made Val's death so horrible. She also thought her mother should spare her father such harsh

THE SPITE HOUSE · 153

sentiment, no matter what the truth was. Later, with better understanding of all her mother went through, she understood why her mother said that. Eunice also understood why she had no younger siblings, and resolved to never become a wife or mother herself.

"You can't know that they came for him," her father had said.

"You can't know what I know," her mother answered. "You'll never know what it's like to feel a body turn to ice as it's being born. I'm sorry for this loss. I'm very sorry for Oscar. But hiding from the truth does no good. You hid it from me and let me marry into it. Now it's mine as much as yours, and I can promise you that there is no such thing as too young."

Dess

The first thing she noticed when she woke was Miss Happy, lying alone on Stacy's side of the bed. She sat up, looked around the large room for Stacy. Her blood was rushing, heart thudding like she was pushing through the last 400 meters. Was her worst fear coming true? Stacy gone, vanishing as inexplicably as she returned? Dess shook her head. After how far they'd come and all they'd given up. All she needed to do was keep her sister safe, and now she didn't know where she was.

The door opened slowly and Lafonda came in with light but urgent steps. "Hey. Get dressed and get those running shoes on. I've set you up to meet with someone about—"

"Where's my sister?" Dess said, almost like she thought Lafonda might be holding her hostage.

"She's downstairs. I made her some pancakes. She's fine. She is now, anyway, but last night something happened. She was sleepwalking or something and got out to one of the ponds out back."

"She *what*?" Dess said.

Lafonda said, "Hey, voice down. We can't wake Eunice up."

"Why?" Dess said, nonetheless following Lafonda's instruction to lower her voice. "What are you talking about? What's going on?"

"Your sister got up last night and went outside."

"Is she okay? Where is—"

"She's fine now. She went to one of the ponds but we got to her before anything happened. Well, Eunice got there before me, but she froze up for a second. I don't know if she was second-guessing how to help, or just didn't want to, or—"

"Why wouldn't she want to?"

"Because she believes in ghosts that want to kill her, Odessa. I think she might have been scared. Or I could be wrong, but just the fact that I'm thinking it makes me question if you're as safe here as you should be. On top of that, your sister went out because she said she heard voices telling her to do it. I don't believe in ghosts, but I also don't think she just made all that up. Anyway, Eunice had her stay with me instead of bringing her back to your room because she said she didn't want to wake you up, and that didn't sit right with me either. Something's up and I don't like it. I know your family's not exactly in a position where I can just call child services or something, but I can't just do nothing."

Dess said nothing to refute this, and Lafonda nodded at her silence. "Right. So I've had me a busy morning trying to come up with an idea. Eunice took something to help her sleep, so she'll probably be out a little later than usual, but not too much, if I know her. So we don't have a whole lot of time to make this happen."

"Okay, make what happen, though?" Dess said. "You want me to meet somebody?"

"Would you please just let me tell you?" Lafonda said. "Look, something happened with the people who were in that other house before y'all, and I don't think Eunice told your father about it. I don't know what all there is to it, that was before I came on board, but it's come up recently and I think you ought to know about it. All I can tell you is what Dana told me today, that there was a couple there before y'all, and the wife ended up hospitalized. Dana knows more but she's at the factory office and she can't get out of her meetings to come talk to you before Eunice is up. Or if she did, someone at the office would tell Eunice about it later and that defeats the whole purpose of us trying to do this without her knowing. But there's somebody else who she thinks can fill you in. The lady who came to the spite house the other day, her name's Emily Steen. She's a local and little bit of a big deal down here from what I gather."

Dess went to the armoire to grab some clothes, then to the closet to change. Lafonda followed her to the closet doorway, where she waited with her back turned. "Yeah, okay," Dess said. "Okay, so that was her at the house. She's a writer, right? I read something she wrote up about your boss. It didn't seem like she was a fan."

"Their relationship is tricky from what I gather. It was never my business, but it's apparently bad enough now that Emily doesn't trust me by association. I asked her to come get you to talk to you, I told her it was safe, but she thought it was some kind of setup or something. Like we're going to trap her, I guess. I don't know. It probably didn't help that Eunice sent Dana after her the other day."

"What?" Dess said, incredulous, emerging from the closet dressed save for her new sneakers. She sat on the bench at the end of the bed to put her shoes on.

"Not like, 'after her,' like a mob hit," Lafonda said. "I shouldn't have put it like that. It was just to have a talk, but—"

"Lafonda, Lafonda, just tell me what's up. What am I doing? I'm down to do it if it'll get us through with all of this quicker."

"I think it will."

"Cool, then I'm down. What is it?" Dess said.

"Emily's agreed to pick you up off-site," Lafonda said. "Not too far away. Right down the road."

"But you don't want to take me there yourself."

"I can if you want me to."

"Yeah, nah, I think I get it. Don't want to get caught taking me. But what exactly are you worried Eunice would do if she found you out?"

Lafonda shrugged, let out a short coughing laugh. "You know, a week ago I'd have said 'nothing.' I wouldn't even be doing this, I suppose. But after the last day or two, and after last night especially, her wanting to hide what happened from you, I don't know. I'm sure she wouldn't do anything too bad, but there's a big gap between 'too bad' and the right thing."

"Yeah, I see," Dess said. Now she understood why Emily Steen viewed Eunice and anyone who worked for her with suspicion.

She didn't have any concrete cause to have faith in Emily, either, but considering the risks, she didn't find it too reckless to run out and meet with a woman who, at minimum, cared enough to show up at the spite house to give them some information. Dad ran her off, but even on the way out she'd shared something with him. She'd mentioned that memorial, which he might not have followed up on yet. He was so focused on the money that bigger-picture things were escaping him, like his own well-being and simply staying alive. Or maybe the money was the bigger picture to him, and he thought that if it came down to his survival versus the girls being set for life, the latter was more important. He was being foolish if that's what he thought. She and Stacy needed him more than the money.

She shouldn't have let him go back to that house. It clearly wasn't harmless after all. It put a woman in the hospital. And Eunice had known about that and kept it to herself. Now even Eunice's own people were doubting her judgment and morals. Dess had to do something.

Lafonda's directions were easy. Follow the long driveway off the estate and onto the connecting road, then turn left and follow that to the nearest crossroad less than half a mile away. Emily would be parked there and standing outside.

"She'll wave when she sees you," Lafonda said. "If anything comes up, I'll call you, but I think Eunice will believe me if I just say you went for a run. Just try not to be too long."

On her way out, Dess stopped to check on Stacy. She didn't ask about what happened the night before, because she knew if she heard the slightest bit more about it she would want to stay, and that would be—as Mom would have told her—short-term thinking. Once Eunice was up, this opportunity would be gone. Lafonda and Dana were willing to help her behind Eunice's back, but with her awake and watching, maybe not so much.

She brought Miss Happy down with her and gave it to Stacy, which put a bigger smile on her face than the pancakes already had. "This house is big. Don't lose her."

"I won't," Stacy said. "Thank you."

"I'm just going to go out for a run, all right? You be good for Miss Lafonda. Listen to her like she was me, okay?"

"I will. She's going to let me see the library today."

Dess said, "That sounds awesome. Have fun, I'll be back."

Then, despite telling herself not to, she hugged her sister and said, "Love you, Staze." It might give away that things weren't exactly as normal as she was making them seem, since they didn't hug every time they might be apart for a little while, but "Odessa Ross"—real name Desirae "Dess" Emerson—could not help herself. She didn't want to think about it, but things seemed to be coming to a head, and there was a chance she might not get to see Stacy again after she left. That wouldn't really happen, but just in case—just in case—she wanted to make sure it wouldn't be like the last time she thought she'd never see her sister again. This time she'd get to hold her and tell her she loved her while Stacy could still hear it.

Millie

What would she do if this turned out to be a bait and switch? If La-fonda said she was sending the girl but instead Eunice pulled the sheriff out of her pocket and sent him to pick Millie up? Jail her for a day on some horseshit charge—trespassing or harassment. She wouldn't put it past her former friend. And what would she do if something like that did happen?

Reset and try something else, Millie thought. There wasn't another option. She wasn't going to stop at doing half of a right thing. She wouldn't allow herself to be content with saying, "Hey, I tried," if Eric Ross got hurt. She was involved now, like she should've been before.

The children were out of the house, at least, but from her conversations with Dana and Lafonda this morning, Millie was under no impression that the situation was that much improved.

It was early, still, but the sun was out and made the day feel more like spring than autumn, neither of which really existed in full or for very long in this part of Texas. Parked where she was, on a road as open as this, it was silly to think that the sunlight left her any more exposed than an overcast day would, but that was nonetheless how she felt, and it made her antsy. For the tenth or hundredth time she checked her watch.

"She'll be here when she gets here," Millie said to herself, then looked up to see someone running alongside the road, far enough away that she couldn't make out any features. Emily raised her arm and waved at her like she was alerting passing drivers of an accident ahead.

Dess picked up her pace when she saw Emily's signal and didn't appear to be too winded when she got close enough to say, "Are you Emily Steen?"

"Yep. I take it you're Odessa."

"I am."

Millie motioned for her to come around to the passenger side. "Get on in."

"Where we going, Miss Steen?"

"Lord, not you too. Your dad called me that, but I'm pulling rank here as the elder. It's Millie, or Emily if you absolutely must, but none of this 'Miss' business."

"Okay, Millie. Where we going?"

"My place if you're good with that. Just a quick drive to the northside. I don't trust anywhere else. Eunice has eyes all around."

"I see. So you meant that stuff you wrote, then. You think she's like a dictator or something."

"You read the article too?" Millie said. "Look, just so you know, some of what I wrote in there, I know how it might have looked on the page. I wrote that for a specific audience, not anticipating all of this, obviously. And I know this is one of those things where if you have to call yourself something, then maybe you're not really that thing, but I want you to know I'm an ally. You can check my history on that."

Dess looked at her with scrunched confusion. "Okay."

Millie sighed. After Dess got in, Millie started the car and made a U-turn to drive back home. She felt her forehead dampen with sweat. Why was she so nervous? Why was she struggling to say the simplest thing?

"Never mind all that," Millie said. "I'm just in my head about this because I got off to a bad start when I tried to talk to your dad."

"You're off to a great start now," Dess said.

"Funny. I know I must sound foolish to you. 'Ally.' Do y'all even still say that, or did you replace it with something new?"

"Y'all?"

"People that are younger than me."

"I can't speak for that many generations, Millie," Dess said, smirking.

Millie let her jaw drop in mock offense but genuine surprise. "Oh, you're quick. That was pretty good. I think I'm going to like you."

"If you can tell me something that'll help my family out then I promise to feel the same way."

"Fair deal. There's a lot to get into. Any place you want to start?"

"Yeah, what's really up with Eunice. I left my sister back with her and Lafonda. Before we get too far, I want to know how far gone she really is. What's her deal?"

"She's got an odd history and I think it's starting to make her crack. She wouldn't hurt your sister, though. Now that y'all are out of that house I think you're safe. I'm more worried about your dad still being in there."

"Why? Can what's in there hurt him?" Dess said. "Lafonda said that a lady who stayed there before ended up in the hospital."

"That's true."

"But she lived, right?"

Millie said, "As far as I'm aware, yes. Listen, though, there's a lot to get into, like I said. Let me just start with your first questions about Eunice."

And so Millie told Dess of the Houghton family history and hex, as told to her by Eunice herself several years ago.

Dess

When they made it to Millie's house, Dess first asked if she could be excused to use the bathroom. She needed a moment alone to process what she'd heard. She did not question whether Eunice Houghton was really cursed or just thought that she was. That was irrelevant, and she was certainly in no position to doubt someone else's experiences with the uncanny. What she did question was Millie's reassurance, as well as Lafonda's, that Eunice didn't present a direct danger. Someone under that much pressure, that desperate to live, might do anything. And there was her sister, living proof that death didn't have to be final. What if Eunice found out about that? What might she do then?

How would she find out, Dess thought, and felt a modicum of relief when she couldn't think of an answer. Stacy wouldn't tell. She'd shown no signs thus far of even knowing what had happened to her, much less how she had come back.

When Dess came out, Millie called to her from her living room. She sat in a chair and offered Dess a seat on the couch, where between them, on the end table, sat a bottle of whiskey and a quarter-full tumbler for each of them.

"You don't look twenty-one," Millie said, "and you also look more like you'd pick a sports drink over liquor ten times out of ten, but I figured it'd be rude to just pour myself some and not offer any."

Dess sat down, picked up the glass, sniffed it, and pulled back from the burn that went up her nose. "Ugh, that smells like fuel."

"Don't it? That's basically what it is. I know I can't run without it."

They shared a small laugh, then Millie said, "Okay, let's talk about the house now."

"Let's do it," Dess said.

"The house and that whole area where the land dips between the hills, that belonged to Eunice's great-grandparents. They gifted it to the Masson family as a bit of penance for the big betrayal and the execution. Pretty much tried to buy their way out of their curse.

"Where that old orphanage is, that was the Masson family's home. Adler and his wife had a son who fathered two boys, Peter and Lukas. They weren't quite Cain and Abel, but they were different enough for problems to arise. Luke, the older one, had no affection for family history. Peter, on the other hand, thought living on that land honored his murdered ancestor."

After a sip of whiskey, Millie continued. "After their father died, Luke and Peter were the sole inheritors of the land. Luke wanted to sell it, Peter wanted to build out more on it. They spent some years arguing over what to do with it before World War One interrupted the argument.

"Peter joined the army as a combat medic. That way he could demonstrate his Americanism, like his ancestors tried to, and show that he could be proud of his German heritage and still be true to Old Glory.

"Luke got himself exempted from service somehow. He stayed home and Peter went to war. Now, a lot of what I've said so far is oral history, but Peter going to war is on the record, and so is this next part. Around October of 1918, Luke received a telegram saying his brother was killed in action. The army delivered Peter's remains, which weren't much and weren't fit for public viewing. A service was held, a box was buried, and that was supposed to be that. With his brother buried, Luke managed to sell the property."

"Even with the war on, he got a buyer?" Dess said.

"Oh, yes," Eunice said. "The saying goes, 'When there's blood in the streets, buy property.' That probably isn't fair of me to imply about the buyer, though. It was a ministry called Everlasting Arms from Chicago. They operated a few orphanages up north but were looking for a more rural locale, and fell in love with the Masson land. It worked out well for Luke, the only problem being that his brother apparently wasn't dead after all."

"I was waiting for something like that," Dess said.

"Sure. He couldn't have built that house if he died over in France," Millie said. "There'd been some kind of mistake. That sort of thing wasn't too uncommon back then. When he got home, Peter was mad about the sale and the construction. About a year had passed since he was supposed to have died, and most of what they were adding on to the house for the orphanage was done. The first group of kids were moving in. Kicking them out and forcing the orphanage to give the land back wasn't going to happen. Peter tried anyway, though. Man had tunnel vision. All he could see was the land he thought still belonged to him. He'd been through hell overseas. His heart was set on home. He was determined not to let anyone take it from him and didn't care what anyone else thought of it.

"Thing was, nobody was going to help him move an orphanage off the land, even though he promised to help them look for a new area nearby. He didn't have anyone on his side to help him take it to court. So he decided to take things into his own hands.

"He built the spite house in 1925. He built it to cast a shadow over the valley. But to do it, he had to move the memorial. And he built his house at the spot where those men and boys were hanged."

Dess shuddered and Millie shook her head. "I know. Saying it out loud makes me mad at myself for letting you stay there. All I can say is I've never really believed in ghosts. But there's something about that place, isn't there?"

"Yeah, there really is."

Millie nodded, then went on. "So, that's also why the house is built the way it is. That was the only way to fit it in that space without crossing his property line or teetering over the lip of the hill. It wasn't the most convenient place to live—you've been inside, you can vouch for that—but he went with it because he wanted the sisters of Everlasting Arms to see his strange, pathetic house and feel guilt for denying him what was his. He wanted the children to look up and see it and feel intimidated. At that point he just wanted other people to be miserable along with him."

"And he really lived there?" Dess said. "He didn't just build it for show and move somewhere else?"

"No, he really lived there. With his bedroom windows facing the orphanage, and all his lonesome hatred facing it too."

"He wasn't alone though," Dess said. "When we were in there my sister said she heard a little boy talking to her, and on the last night I heard a little girl. Were they kids from the orphanage?"

Millie sighed and tilted her head back, stretching her neck as if to loosen throat muscles exhausted from storytelling. "Oh, the kids. That might be the strangest part of—"

Dess's phone rang, cutting Millie off. Dess looked at the caller ID, expecting to see Lafonda's name, or Eunice's. Instead she saw the name DANA CANTU in big white letters against a blue backdrop. She answered, "Hello."

"Hey, are you okay? Where are you?" Dana said. She spoke quickly and sounded out of breath.

"I thought Lafonda told you where I'd be—"

"You're still with Emily?"

"Yeah?"

"Do you know where Lafonda is? Did she go with you?"

Dess stood, her heart suddenly thudding as though she were at the starting blocks, ready to race.

"No. Are you at Eunice's house? She's not there?"

"Well, they're not downstairs and nobody's answering me, but there's some car parked out front."

"Whose car? What's going on? You can't find my sister?"

"I can't find *anyone*. I'm going to call Eunice's phone aga—"

A sound between a gasp and a scream came through the phone, loud enough to make Dess jump and for Millie to hear it.

Dess called out, "Dana? Can you hear me? Dana?"

Millie stood and came closer to hear the clumsy, slapping noises of a struggle come through from Dana's end of the line. Grunts and clipped shouts. Two voices, neither forming discernible words. One voice belonged to a man.

With one last, hard bump the call ended.

Lafonda

In all the time she had spent with her, Lafonda never saw Eunice stay in her room this late into the day. On a few occasions she'd stayed in bed an hour past her preferred breakfast time, always to make up for the rare restless night, but she would still be up and about shortly after the sunrise during the daylight savings season, and before the sunrise when the clocks fell back. Granted, the previous night had broken her routine, and she'd taken a pill to help her sleep, but Lafonda still hadn't expected Eunice to take this long getting her day started. She was simultaneously glad that Eunice was taking her time—giving Dess more time to spend with Emily—and also worried about Eunice's health. Her job was still to keep Eunice active and well, no matter how uncomfortable she felt about recent events.

Eunice was awake now, at least. She just hadn't left her bedroom. Lafonda checked on her four times after Dess had left. Eunice grumbled, "I can hear you out there," the third time Lafonda came to the door, and this last time Eunice said, "I'm getting ready, Lafonda. For heaven's sake, give me a little time to get myself together."

"All right. I'm going to leave the door cracked if you need to shout for me," Lafonda said.

"Fine, fine."

Lafonda went back to check on Stacy in the second-floor library, one turn down a short hall to the right of Eunice's room. She brought her to the library after breakfast. When she first went in, Stacy walked all around, staring up at the bookcases wide-eyed like she was seeing stars in the sky for the first time.

Little Stacy Ross was growing on Lafonda. Last night's strangeness aside, she seemed like a good kid. She was quick with a "thank you," and you didn't have to tell her anything twice. Lafonda cautioned her against taking any books from the lower shelves without asking first. Stacy put her hands behind her back and kept them there as she went around the library, not even tempted to touch a book without permission.

Now Stacy sat in a club chair much too large for her. She'd propped her little doll beside her. In her lap was a hardback book of classic myths and fairy tales that she'd asked Lafonda to take down for her. It had a full-page picture of a wood engraving for every story, and a handwritten dedication to Eunice on the flyleaf that read, "From Val, for your birthday." Stacy said aloud that all of these things were "so cool," then promised to be "extra careful" with the book.

Lafonda watched her turn each page like it would either blow away or crumble to dust if she didn't handle it right. She found this adorable, yet something about Stacy's reverence for the paper made her a bit uneasy. For a moment she felt like the girl was making a show of being so well-behaved and innocent. *Like she's trying to trick me,* Lafonda thought, then tapped her forehead three quick times, an old habit for when she wanted to knock a dumb or otherwise unwelcome thought out of her mind. How paranoid could she be right now? It was one thing to be a little on edge given what recently transpired, to be suspicious of her very wealthy and very determined boss, and something else to think a seven-year-old was masterminding a devious plot.

The distinct crack and creak of the front door opening and moving on its hinges stole her focus. It sounded different from the upper floors of the house than it did when you were right in front of it. Harsher and more aggressive, like someone had pushed through it fast enough to be on the other side of the door before anyone could stop them from coming through. It was a strange feature, more of the house than of the door. The acoustics of the building brought the sound noisily up the central stairs, down every hall and into every room. It was as if the house were its own giant alarm with no regard for who might be entering, whether it be intruder, invitee, or inhabitant. Eunice had said time and again that this was a deliberate feature of the house when she'd tried to convince Lafonda that a modern, proper security system was unnecessary. The compromise they had come to, installing the security system but keeping it off during the day, had left them both a little dissatisfied. Eunice was quick to say how creepy it was to hear the system's disembodied voice announce when it was being turned on or off—to say nothing of when it declared a certain door or window was opened—while it took Lafonda months to get used to the idea of living in a house full of luxuries and lax security.

She said to Stacy, "I think Miss Dana just got here. I'll be right back, okay?"

"Okay," Stacy said, barely looking up from the book that held her rapt.

Lafonda wanted to meet Dana downstairs, duck into one of the rooms that kept conversations secret, or go out back with her to talk about everything, make sure they were on the same page. The discussion they had over the phone that morning went so fast Lafonda couldn't remember all that she'd said to Dana. And she still wanted some clarity on exactly what happened to that couple. The Renners. Did they have physical injuries, or was it more of a panic attack situation? She wanted to know if the house somehow posed a threat. If it did, she'd have to talk to Eunice. She couldn't continue working for someone who was endangering others without giving them information that might lead them to opt out.

She expected to see Dana at the foot of the central staircase, waiting for her to come down, but Dana wasn't there. Lafonda looked to the right, toward the open door of the drawing room. "Drawing room" still struck her as a strange room name, as did many of the room names in the mansion. She supposed it was one of those divides between a normal person and a rich person that the normal person could not bridge unless they lived long enough with or as the rich.

In every other house Lafonda had been in, rooms had common, simple names. Dining. Bed. Bath. Laundry. Living or family. If there was an office, it was likely a converted spare bedroom. You might have a sunroom if you were well off. The Houghton Manor, however, had all of these as well as a great hall—which she was currently in—a stateroom, an outer parlor, an inner parlor, a theater room, three studies, a private chapel, an upper and lower loggia, multiple antechambers, and more, not including the library. Even the bedrooms were officially "bedchambers," and had a grandiosity befitting the title. Lafonda believed she'd done rather well to memorize most of the room names, as well as how to get to one through another and then another and into the next without always having to track back into a hallway. She was never interested in looking up what each room name meant, though, at least for those that didn't strike her as obvious.

Looking at the open door of the drawing room, she pondered the room's original purpose. She'd been in it a few times, and as far as she could tell it was just a gloomy micromuseum dedicated to Eunice's great-great-grandmother, Beatrice. Three massive portraits of the Houghton matriarch decked the walls of the drawing room, one that captured Beatrice in her twenties, another from when she was middle-aged, and a third that immortalized her later years. Furniture and décor that was handpicked by Beatrice during her extensive travels, mostly conducted during her fifties, filled the room. Rugs from South and Central America, authentic china, pottery from Africa, Baroque chairs she had picked up in Italy, more. All set in a room without windows and, more conspicuously, without any tangible remembrance of Beatrice's husband.

Lafonda made the mistake of asking about Eunice's great-great-grandfather once. Eunice answered, "We never speak of him," seeming to forget there no longer was a "we" when it came to the Houghtons, just her. The refusal to speak his name made him feel more ominous and present to Lafonda, somehow. If ghosts existed then surely he was made into one by his family's campaign to forget him, and Lafonda sometimes wondered if he might be lingering somewhere in the house. She'd felt it most in that drawing room, which she never liked looking in the direction of, much less entering. Eunice would visit the room for maybe half an hour once a week, and while Lafonda primarily thought of it as a tiny museum, she believed it was a place of reverence for Eunice. A small, private sanctuary where she could pay her respects, seek guidance, meditate, or whatever else she felt she needed to do to maintain her mental health.

Eunice hadn't visited it for a few nights, however, so why was the door open now? Even if she'd been in recently, she never kept the door ajar out of concern that it might later ease shut in the night and awaken the voice of the alarm system. Dana wouldn't go in there. She found it eerier than Lafonda did, had said as much before.

So why was the door open? It was as if someone did it to lure her there, or distract her.

Go upstairs. Something isn't right.

It was too late. She felt a presence behind her, a shade at her back. A sinking sensation drew her insides toward the floor. She did not want to turn around. Maybe if she'd done that a moment earlier it would have been safe, but now it was too late to turn around, and also too late not to.

She pivoted slowly, expecting to see the hazy image of Beatrice's husband hovering above the bottom step, directing his anger at whoever was nearby for all the years he'd spent being forgotten. A great scream would leap from her throat at the sight of him, and she might pass out where she stood.

What she saw instead brought a more primal and practical fear that cramped her muscles. A short, brown-haired man with a patchy beard stood before her. He pointed a gun at her chest and held a finger to his lips. He had stern, weary eyes, and a quivering grip on the black pistol.

Lafonda's fledgling scream deteriorated on its way up and came out as a death rattle. *At least it's not a ghost,* she thought. *I'm going to die,* she thought. *I'm going to miss everyone,* she thought. *I'm not going to miss anything, because I won't be anything. I don't know that. I'll know very soon. Oh God. Oh dear God oh God.*

The man stepped toward her, moved behind her. He must have been hiding behind the staircase. Now he had one hand on her shoulder and the gun at her back. He leaned in close and spoke quietly. "I don't want to hurt anyone, got it? If you do as I say, no one will get hurt. I don't want to shoot you, but I will if you scream or do anything stupid. But I don't want to, got it? You got it?"

Lafonda nodded. She'd worked in an emergency room before transitioning into private care and personal training, and even in her current field she'd been in situations where a life was in the balance, and one couldn't afford to waste much time second- and third-guessing what to do, what to say, what they heard and what it meant. This was not quite the same as the circumstances she'd been in before, but not so different that her brain might lock up and make her useless.

"There's a little girl here, isn't there?" the man said. He sniffed in short, rapid breaths, sounding like he'd run up and down the stairs several times before hiding behind them. He had the tangy smell of sweat on him. He looked just a little too stocky to be a long-term drug addict, Lafonda thought, but also too tired and jittery not to be under the influence of something. All of this was presumptive, but she'd have time to reconsider those presumptions after she survived this ordeal.

"Hey, you need to answer me," the man said. "There's a little girl in this house, isn't there? Look, I'm not going to hurt her, but I need her. I need her help. She can help my wife, that's why I'm asking about her. That's all, you see?"

"There's nobody else here but me," Lafonda said.

"That's a lie. Don't lie to me."

"Just take whatever you want. There're lots of valuable things—"

"I'm not here to rob you, goddammit. Listen to me. You are going to get yourself hurt, and the old woman hurt, too. And the little girl, too, by mistake. By *mistake* if I start shooting and I don't know where she is. Now I know you're lying. I know Eunice is here. I've been here before, I met her back when she had the other one before you. Letty. Letty was the one before you. You know that, don't you? So you know I'm not lying. I know what I'm talking about. I know the old woman's here, and I know that a little girl is, too. So don't lie to me about that anymore or you're going to make me do something I don't want to do."

"If you shoot me, they'll hear it," Lafonda said. "Then they'll hide in a room and lock themselves in and call the police. If you really have been here before you know how big this place is. There're a lot of rooms they can hide in."

"Listen, lady, goddammit, I am not playing around. You really want me chasing them around here and shooting this place up to flush them out? Does that sound safe? Are you even listening to what you're saying? To what *I'm* saying? I don't want to hurt anybody, but you're going to turn this into something it doesn't have to be."

He pressed the gun harder into her back, and her understanding of the situation told her that the time for talking him down was over. "They're upstairs," she said.

"Where upstairs?"

"Eunice's room. Do you remember where that is?"

"No. Walk me up there. And don't get stupid."

She moved forward, taking each step with deliberate care to show the man that she was not thinking of running. He kept a hand on her shoulder and raised the gun to the nape of her neck. At the top of the stairs she turned right in a stiff way that she hoped would make him feel as if he were partially steering her. He'd told her to lead, but she thought it would be best for him to feel as though he were still in physical control. This was important as they passed the open door of the library. He wouldn't see Stacy if he glanced inside. The chair she sat in faced away from the door and covered her, and she was as quiet as an actual librarian. But if she sneezed or coughed, or if her page-turning was just a bit louder than Lafonda thought it was, then this man would go inside to investigate, and Lafonda had no plan for what to do if that happened.

She resisted the urge to hold her breath or turn her head away from the library's doorway as she passed it, to do anything different from what she'd been doing. Her pulse picked up and she feared the muzzle of the gun would register this like a stethoscope, or that her smartwatch would blink on and ask, "Would you like to record an exercise?" It was one thing to "act casual," which she already didn't know how to do, but a different thing to "act as scared as you already are, no more so." She had no way of knowing whether she kept herself from signaling to the man that anything was amiss, even after they passed the library and came to Eunice's door. He could shove her into Eunice's bedroom, shoot them both, and then double back to the library to find Stacy if she had tipped him off. She tried not to think of this. Her legs might give out if she latched on to it as a true possibility.

The door to Eunice's bedroom was ajar. Lafonda gave a courtesy knock and waited for Eunice to respond, "Yes?"

"It's me again," she said, a little louder than she would under normal circumstances.

"I know it's you. What is it now?" Eunice said. As Lafonda pushed the door open the man did indeed shove her ahead, so hard that she almost fell to the floor, saved only by putting her hands out on the chaise longue a few feet from the bed.

This is it. He's going to shoot us. She turned to see the man pointing his gun away from her, holding it low and with both hands like the center stick of an airplane he was pushing into a dive. She followed his gaze to what grabbed his attention. Eunice stood just outside her bedchamber's bathroom, still in her sleeping gown and robe. If any shock had ever shown on her face upon seeing the gun, Lafonda had missed it. Eunice glowered at the man and cocked her head like she was looking for the right angle to take before lunging into an attack. She took a small step forward, and the man took a larger step back before the gun reminded him that he was the only armed party in the room.

"What are you doing here, Mr. Renner?" Eunice said.

Hearing that name made Lafonda feel sick, and for the first time she believed that he wasn't some local, drug-addled black sheep there to rob them, someone who'd been spying on them for a few days and baked up a master plan where he'd use Stacy as leverage to be sure Eunice gave him the most he could get. No, he really was here for Stacy.

"Where's the little girl?" Max Renner said. "I know she's here. I'm not here to hurt anyone, but I need to know where the girl—"

Lafonda shouted, "Stacy, run!" She did not know what made her do this at this moment. Even as the words came out she thought she might be doing the wrong thing. Making the worst choice that she could. It didn't even feel like a decision, more like an action she had no real control over, like waking up every morning. Something you weren't doing a moment before and that was already behind you by the time you realized it had happened. "Run away right now! *Run!*"

Max looked around the room and waved the gun like he expected a small group of commandos to come out from trapdoors beneath the rugs or a false wall hidden by the bookcase. *He's going to start shooting,* Lafonda thought once again, but was at peace with it this time.

Stacy heard her, she was sure, and she had an unaccountable confidence in the little girl to evade capture for however long she needed to. There was no logic behind this feeling, no reason to be convinced that Stacy hadn't frozen with panic in the chair upon hearing Lafonda tell her to run, nor any reason to believe that Stacy would not run toward Lafonda's voice instead of away from it, except that she was a bright kid who didn't need to be told anything twice, and who snuck out of the house last night, making it all the way to the gazebo before anyone got to her.

Besides, logic did not reign over this moment. Logic could not account for how Max Renner even knew Stacy was here, much less why he was so determined to find her. But here he was, looking for her.

Lafonda looked again to Eunice, who had trepidation in her eyes, but it was painted over iron. She had a rigidity to her that Lafonda hadn't seen before. Her lips were parted, baring her teeth. Lafonda thought of the story Eunice told her of her aunt Val. The way her aunt raged in her final moments. The implication that the heart attack was only one element of what claimed her life that day on the hill. Lafonda wondered if winter would flood the room now, with their deaths imminent.

"Why did you do that?" Max said. "Why did you do that? I told you I wouldn't hurt anyone."

"You have a fucking gun," Lafonda said.

"I'm not going to use it on her. I can't. I need her help. I told you this!"

"You shouldn't have come here, Mr. Renner," Eunice said, slowly and deliberately, like it was the last thing she ever meant to say.

This is too much for her heart, Lafonda thought. *She's going to drop dead before he can pull the trigger.*

"You shouldn't have brought us here," Max said to Eunice, shaking the gun at her with one hand.

"I made an offer. You and your wife made a choice. I'm sorry for what happened to her, but—"

"No! You're not sorry. You just wish we would've stayed longer, but you're not sorry about what happened. You should've told us about that place—"

"I told you there was something there."

"We didn't think it was real," Max said.

"And I'm to blame for that?"

Max bit back whatever he meant to say next, wiped his face, and gathered a fraction of composure.

"If you're really sorry about what happened to Jane, you'll help me," he said.

Eunice said, "I'm not letting you take that girl. She's my charge, and I need her. If that's why you're here, I'm afraid there's nothing I can do."

Max chuckled. "You're 'afraid'? No, no, you're not afraid. Not enough. Not yet."

He stepped toward Lafonda, grabbed her by the arm, and pulled her to her feet. He put the gun to her temple and told Eunice, "Who else has to suffer over this because of you? How afraid are you really? I know you're afraid to die. Afraid of your little curse. You think it's going to go any easier on you if you make me kill this woman because you won't help me?"

Eunice inhaled deeply through her nose to speak, but Max cut her off. "Don't. Before you say it, I'm going to tell you both one last time, I'm not going to hurt that girl. I can't. I need her to save Jane. But I don't need either of you, get it?" He traced a small circle against Lafonda's temple with the point of his gun. She shivered at this, but kept her eyes on Eunice, pleading with her not to trust this deranged man, not to sacrifice Stacy's safety for hers.

"You mean what you're saying, don't you?" Eunice said. "Fine. Let's see about finding her, and we'll talk more about this from there."

"Okay, now we're talking. Now you're being reasonable," Max said, a sudden lightness springing through his voice. He sounded relieved. Bordering on hopeful, like it was the first hint of good news he'd heard in years. "Let's go. You first. You're going to call out to her and tell her it's okay to come out."

"I'll scream again," Lafonda said. "I'll keep telling her to run. I won't let you—"

Eunice put her hands up in the universal sign language of peaceful negotiation. "Miss Lafonda, it's all right. I know this man. I know he's desperate. I know he's doing something foolish. But I know why he's doing it, and I believe him when he says he won't hurt Stacy. And I don't want him to hurt you, either. Now I need you to please trust me. Please."

Once more, Lafonda scanned the old woman's face. It was hard to read, but she seemed to have a plan. Maybe it was as simple as stalling. There was no way she was really going to let Max take off with Stacy, was there? If nothing else, it would destroy any chance she had of keeping Eric Ross in the spite house, ruin everything she had worked for. But if she could buy some time . . . Dana would be here soon and when they heard Dana come in, they could scream for her to call the sheriff. That had to be it.

Even if she was wrong, and Eunice really did plan to let Max abduct Stacy, Lafonda knew she couldn't help the girl at all by dying right now. So she didn't object or resist as Eunice led Max Renner out of the room and toward the library.

Stacy

"Run" means run and hide.

Dad and Dess worried that she might not appreciate the importance of the "drills" they ran with her. In empty parks, in shopping centers near closing time, in multilevel parking structures, even at a local carnival once, when there were hardly any people there, they practiced what Dad described as "hide-and-seek, but serious."

"If I say run, it means run and hide until one of us comes to get you," Dad said. "If you hear us calling for you, you come right out. I'll only ever say run if it's really serious. Something very bad has to happen for me to tell you this, and I might not have time to say all of this to you then. That's why it's so important for you to take this seriously, okay?"

There were things about this she didn't understand. What kind of "very bad" thing could happen? For any other emergency, Dess and her dad wanted her by their side. Even going about everyday activities, one of them always remained nearby and would check on her if she stayed too quiet for too long, even when she was in the same room with them. Almost like she might disappear if they didn't look at her or speak to her often enough.

What she did understand was that the drills were very important to Dad, and to Dess, too, so she listened.

As soon as she'd heard Lafonda shout, "Run," Stacy dumped the book out of her lap, hopped down from the chair, and ran for the nearest door. Had she been facing the hallway door, or if it were closer, that's where she'd have gone, but her practice, the drills she'd treated so seriously, taught her to go for what was closest and not to turn back or even look behind her unless she absolutely had to.

The nearest of the three doors she faced was to her right, between a pair of tall bookcases. The door, too, was tall and she worried when she pulled the latch down that the door would be too heavy for her to open. Instead it pushed open almost on its own as soon as the latch bolt released. She slipped through and shut it behind her.

She was in an antechamber that had a fireplace, a large round table, and several chairs along the walls beneath multiple massive paintings and portraits. The size of the Houghton Manor, a source of wonder less than a minute earlier, made her dizzy. The antechamber's ceiling, as it was in every other room, was too high. The floor tiles were too wide and too long, and there were too many of them. The people in the portraits were too big to fit more than half their bodies within the frames that surrounded them, and if they could have pulled themselves free from their canvases they would have emerged as giants.

Stacy wanted to crawl up to the base of the big round table and pretend it was a good hiding space. Knowing that this was a bad idea, she next wanted to drop to the floor and cry. That was before the voices of the people she could not see returned.

Keep running.

Keep going.

Get away.

Don't get caught.

Trust us.

Run, girl. Run!

She ran across the antechamber, away from the voices as much as whatever Miss Lafonda told her to run from. But the voices followed. At the other end of the antechamber she pushed open a door and stepped into a bedroom.

The storage bench at the foot of the bed made her freeze. The gray rectangular box was just big enough for her to fit inside, and its lid was open.

You can hide there, one of the voices told her. She shut her eyes tight and held Miss Happy tighter and shook her head hard at this. Behind her eyelids she could see something that felt like a memory but that couldn't be a memory, because she was sure it hadn't happened to her. She was lying down inside something soft but small, like a tiny bed with walls around it. Her eyes were closed but she sensed her surroundings in her mind.

She saw Mom and Dad approaching her. Dad held Miss Happy then, in this fake memory, and he started to give her doll to her but then pulled it back and whispered, "No, no, no." He and Mom then kissed Stacy on the forehead and walked away, and she'd felt sad because they were sad, and she'd wanted to get away from that feeling.

She opened her eyes to escape this vision, then turned away from the storage bench. In the far corner of the room, near the door that led to the hallway, she saw a tall, linen-lined wicker basket and ran to it. This was a better place to hide. It wouldn't be as dark on the inside as the bench. There was no chance that its top would lock or be too heavy for her to open once it was in place. She would not feel trapped inside.

Stacy climbed into the basket and sat down, hunching over as she set the lid in place. Through the walls of the room she thought she heard someone call her name. The people she couldn't see never called her by name. This was someone who was really there. When she heard them again she knew that it was Miss Eunice.

Had Dad and Dess asked Miss Eunice and Miss Lafonda to practice emergencies with her? If so, why didn't they let her know? It confused and frustrated her, having to wonder whether these other grown-ups had permission from her dad to run their own "drills." Without knowing that, she couldn't even know if this was a real emergency, or a made-up one. It did not help that the people she couldn't see were still talking to her.

Stay where you are.

Don't listen to her.

Don't trust her.

Don't help her.

They did not like Miss Eunice. They said the word "her" like they wanted to spit it out of their mouths, and it almost made Stacy feel sick to hear it. She knew that she needed to listen to what Miss Eunice was saying, however, so she made herself focus on doing that.

"Can you hear me, Stacy?" Miss Eunice said. "Wherever you are, just stay there. If you have found a place to hide, don't come out, no matter—"

A man's voice interrupted her. He was so angry and loud that Stacy couldn't understand him. Miss Eunice just spoke over him. "Don't come out for us. Wait for help to get here. I've already called—"

The man shouted Miss Eunice down again, and Stacy heard at least one word he said very clearly this time. He used the word "kill." Stacy whimpered and thought, *Why is this happening? I want to go home. Why can't we just go home? Why?*

She asked her dad "why?" the first time he told her that "run" means "run and hide."

He got very serious with her, used a heavier voice that made him sound a little like Pa-Pa Fred when he was fed up with something, and said, "Stacy, you know better than to question me, don't you?"

The Pa-Pa Fred voice scared her just a little. Pa-Pa Fred had never talked to her like that. He was always happy and encouraging with her. But she overheard him talk to Dad and Grandpa that way a few times, and it always sounded like Pa-Pa Fred became a different, meaner person when he talked like that. She didn't like it.

"Yes, sir," she said. "I know better, I'm sorry."

"It's okay," Dad said, sounding like himself again. "Just trust me. I know what's best."

She trusted Dad, even though he and Dess sometimes didn't want to answer her most important questions. Maybe they were as afraid to say the real answer as she was afraid to hear it. *Because of you, Stacy. We left home and can't stay anywhere and can't see Mom again all because of you.*

All of it was her fault. She'd done something that she couldn't remember doing and made all of this happen. Now, because of something else she was doing—hiding—a man was shouting at Miss Eunice and saying he was going to do something bad to her. The same man scared Miss Lafonda into telling Stacy to run. Miss Eunice said she had called for help, but that might put whoever was coming in danger, too. Who did she call? Miss Dana? Someone else?

"Dess is coming back," Stacy said, then put her hand over her mouth to prevent another accidental outburst. Still, it was good to hear her own voice—one she could be sure to trust—over all of the others she was having to filter, navigate, and pinpoint. It gave her a small amount of confidence, which saved her from breaking into tears when she heard the man shout again—closer this time—and heard Miss Eunice cry out. She sounded like she was in pain. She heard and felt the thump of something hard hitting the floor. Miss Lafonda cried out next and there was another hard thump that shook the wall beside the basket. They were right outside the room.

"You're going to make me do something I don't want to do," the man said.

"The sheriff's already on his way," Miss Eunice said.

"Stop lying!"

"I pushed the button on my bracelet soon as I saw you, you fool. It goes right to the sheriff. I've just been waiting for him to arrive. He's got to be close now. Tell him, Lafonda."

"She's right," Miss Lafonda said.

"Okay, so you're going to make me shoot it out with him?" the man said. "You think I won't shoot him if I have to? I already told you I'm not leaving without the girl. This is your last chance to help, or else I'm going to kill you, too. Both of you."

Hearing this alone might have prompted Stacy to do what she did next, or her concern for Dess coming back to the house to deal with the dangerous stranger. What immediately motivated her to climb out of her hiding place, however, was the vile glee she heard in voices of those she could not see.

Yes!

Kill her!

Do it!

She's ours.

The last one.

Dead and ours at last.

Stacy could not know why they were saying this, but she knew that what they wanted must be wrong. Just like their attempt to make her remember what she'd forgotten was wrong. Everything about them felt wrong and evil.

They did not return their attentions to Stacy until she was already out of hiding and opening the bedroom door.

Wait!

Don't!

He'll hurt you.

Stacy entered the hall and shouted, "Stop! Don't hurt anyone!"

The three grown-ups in the hall turned and looked at her. The man tried to put on a friendly mask, but all of his madness showed through it. Miss Lafonda looked like she might cry, and also like she couldn't decide what to do next. Miss Eunice grimaced, clutched at her chest, and dropped to her knees. The face of her wristwatch brightened and turned red. A sound came from it like an alarm. *I'm too late,* Stacy thought. *She's already hurting, and it's my fault.*

The stranger approached Stacy, putting his gun behind his back and out of her sight after he extended his free hand to her.

"Hey there, Stacy. It's Stacy, isn't it? My name is Max. I know I might look like a bad guy, but I'm not. I just need you to come with me to help me with something. It's about my wife. I think you can help her. Will you come with me to help her, please?"

Stacy willed herself not to tremble, and not to look away or even blink. She stared at him the way she'd stared at the big sharks behind the glass when Mom took her to the National Aquarium. The sharks scared her so bad she wanted to run outside the first time she saw them. But then her mother reminded her that they couldn't get to her, and she felt possessed by the urge to be bigger than her fear and show the sharks that she had no reason to be afraid. No glass stood between her and this man who wanted to harm two people she liked, however. Which meant she needed to be even braver in front of him.

"You can't hurt Miss Eunice or Miss Lafonda anymore," Stacy said. "And you better not hurt my sister if she comes back."

"I don't want to hurt anyone, I promise," Max said. "I just need help."

Stacy reached out and grasped Max's hand.

"Hold on," Lafonda said, but Max was already walking back down the hall toward the stairs with Stacy in tow. "I said hold on! Where are you taking her? I'm going with you."

Lafonda took a step after them but Max turned to her and did something that made Lafonda stop moving and catch her breath. Stacy could not see what he'd done, as he held her close to his left hip, blocking her view. She imagined it had something to do with the gun in his other hand. She knew enough about guns to know they were dangerous.

"Sorry, you had your chance to be helpful," Max said. "I'm not taking any chances with you now. You stay here."

"Where are you taking her?"

"Ask Eunice, if she makes it. I'm sure she can figure—"

The creaking and closing of the house's front door interrupted him. Stacy heard him catch his breath, felt him shiver, felt a fizzy panic take over her insides. Her sister was back. That was it. Dess was here and now Max would threaten her. Max promised he didn't *want* to hurt anyone, but he didn't promise to never actually do it. And Stacy knew Dess would fight him the moment she understood what was happening. She also knew that fight would end badly one way or another.

It's too late. It's my fault.

Max nodded for Lafonda to go to Eunice, who sat on the floor, back to the wall. Eunice breathed deeply and steadily, and fixed Max with a look that Stacy didn't know a real person could make. She only ever saw that look on villains in cartoons, in the moment right before they try one last time to kill the hero and get themselves killed instead. It transformed her face, her whole personality. She was not Miss Eunice right then. If she could stand up, she would become the Dark Queen of her great-but-haunted castle.

Downstairs, footsteps echoed. They sounded strange to Stacy, and a thought popped into her head. *Dess doesn't walk like that.* Dess stepped lightly wherever she went because of the dance classes Mom encouraged her to take. The person who came in downstairs sounded like they wanted to knock holes through the floor.

From downstairs, Miss Dana called out, "Eunice? Lafonda? Are you up there?" Stacy felt a guilty sense of relief. She might still get Max away before her sister came back.

Max motioned for Eunice and Lafonda to enter the bedroom Stacy had been in. Neither said anything, and though they moved slowly they followed his instruction.

"Eunice? Lafonda? Odessa?" Dana sounded like she was coming back to the central stairway. Max looked for a place to hide when he heard Dana on the first step, and he chose the library, bringing Stacy with him. They waited at the edge of the doorway, just out of sight. Stacy did not know if she should shout a warning or stay quiet.

Dana spoke to someone else as she came to the top of the stairs. "Hey, are you okay? Where are you? You're still with Emily? Do you know where Lafonda is? Did she go with you? Well, they're not downstairs and nobody's answering me, but there's some car parked out front. I can't find *anyone.* I'm going to call Eunice's phone aga—"

She was just beyond the library, likely headed to Eunice's bedroom, when Max made his move. Still holding on to Stacy with his left hand, he stepped out and threw his right arm around Dana's head, pinning her phone to her ear for a moment. Dana pushed at his arm, turned and slapped at him. Max cried out in shock, matching Dana's own cries, then shoved her backward with his shoulder to give himself space to swipe at her face. The back of his hand struck her chin, knocking her into the wall, then onto the floor. She landed just after her phone did, its glass face cracking as it flatly smacked the tile.

When Dana looked up, holding her chin and wincing, she saw a gun pointed at her. She squinted at the gun at first, like she couldn't tell what it was, then her eyes widened.

"Max? What the hell are you doing here?" she said.

"You. You're coming with us," Max said.

"What are you talking about? What are you doing—?"

"Shut up and get up. Do as I say and I won't have to hurt anyone."

Dana stood up with her hands raised. "Okay. Okay."

Max made Dana walk ahead of him at gunpoint while he escorted Stacy downstairs. Stacy felt like she was holding his hand tighter than he held hers. She looked back once as they neared the front door, almost glad when she didn't see Miss Lafonda or Miss Eunice behind her. If either of them were there, she might have released Max's hand to run back to safety. Only it wouldn't have been safety, it would have started everything over again.

As she came closer to the door, the people she couldn't see got louder.

Wait, please!

Don't let him take you!

Don't leave us!

Help us!

You have to tell us—

Please!

How did you get back?

How did you get back?

How are you alive again?

It was hard to ignore them, but she did as well as she could, not by blocking them out, but by opening her ears to them all at once, so that they drowned each other out. She could not have done this for too long. When they made it outside and the voices scattered and flew into the open air,

Stacy couldn't help but be glad to be out of the house, even though she was being taken away by a bad person.

A car was parked close to the house, still running. Max said, "Stacy, you can get in the back, okay? You'll get to meet my wife. Her name is Jane. She's quiet right now, but she's nice, I promise."

He then got close to Dana and whispered something to her, and Stacy could not tell what he said to her but saw Miss Dana nodding quickly.

At the car, Max opened the back passenger-side door, where there was a woman lying down like she didn't want to be seen.

Max said, "Jane, sit up, honey," and the woman lifted her head and obeyed his order without looking at him or anyone else.

To Stacy he said, "Get in. It's okay, she's my wife. She doesn't want to hurt you either." Stacy climbed in and sat next to the red-haired woman, who didn't seem to notice anything was taking place around her. Max opened the front passenger door for Dana and made her get in before he ran around to the driver's side, got behind the wheel, and drove away from the house.

During the drive, Stacy could not look away from Jane, who stared ahead, blinking every seven seconds. Stacy kept count. She reminded Stacy of one of her old dolls from before she helped make Miss Happy. Jane could breathe and move on her own and looked alive, but Stacy thought Jane's actual life was missing from her, and this made her sad, like she could understand what that was like.

She reached out and touched Jane's hand to let her know someone else was there. Jane's pinky flinched on contact, then went still, and she did not move again until they got where they were going.

Dess

Dess and Millie arrived at the Houghton Estate to find Lafonda and Eunice seated together on the top step of the front porch. Dess opened her door before Millie's car was at a full stop. She ran toward the women and said, "What happened? Where's my sister?"

Lafonda looked up with an apology in her eyes, and Dess thought she might throw up. "Somebody came to the house. A man came here with a gun and he took her."

"What? Took her where?"

"I know where," Eunice said, having to catch her breath after she spoke. "I just need a little more time to recover, then I'll get the sheriff. He'll get her back and he'll get Max too. He'll get him, that son of a bitch."

"No, no, no police," Dess said. "Shit, shit, I don't know what to do."

Eunice said, "I understand why you'd be worried, but trust me, the sheriff will just do what I tell him. He won't be looking into whatever it is that you-all might have done, or what you're running from."

"Have you called my dad? I keep trying him but he isn't answering."

Millie stepped forward and said, "Hon, I think Eunice might be right, and you know I hate to say that. But if we're talking about some man with a gun—"

"It was Max Renner," Eunice said.

"Oh hell," Millie said. "Damn it, Eunice, I told— You know what, not the time." She turned to Dess. "Honey—"

"Just let me think a second," Dess said. "I need to think."

Lafonda said, "Odessa, what is there to think about? Saving your sister has to be the priority here."

"You don't understand. It doesn't do any good to save her if someone ends up finding out about Stacy," Dess said. The tears flowed now, and her voice cracked. "You have to believe me. For the love of everything, please. It's hard enough for me to trust any of you. If anyone else gets involved then . . . Shit, I don't know what to do."

"What do you mean?" Eunice said.

Millie put a hand on Dess's shoulder. "Hey, look at me. Just talk to us, hon. Tell us what's going on. Help us understand."

Dess composed herself as well as she could and said, "Stacy died a year and a half ago."

A fattened second of silence passed between everyone before Eunice spoke up. "What do you mean she—?"

"I mean *died.*"

"Like she flatlined and got resuscitated?" Lafonda said.

"Like she died and was buried. We held a service. We had an open casket. We all saw her inside. We all cried and tried to pretend the preacher's words meant anything. We all said our last goodbyes like she could hear us. I kissed my baby sister on the cheek and told her I was sorry. I didn't even know why I said it. I was just sorry that she was gone. I was sorry for any time I didn't spend with her, or if I ever kicked her out of my room or didn't take her to the park when she asked me, or anything. Then we all went and watched her get lowered into the ground, and then I spent the next few months wondering how the rest of the world was still going on when my sister wasn't here anymore. And I was just getting used to the idea of feeling like that for the rest of my life when she came back."

Eunice's eyes were wide now, her mouth agape. Millie stared at Dess like her young friend had ranted in an invented language. Lafonda held her hands near her mouth as if she meant to recite a secret prayer.

"I still don't understand. What do you mean came back?" Millie said.

"Look, I'm telling you everything," Dess said, any semblance of composure crumbling again. "You wanted to know, I told you. This is why we left home, because my sister came back from the dead like she'd never left. We couldn't stay home around all our neighbors and family and friends who knew she was dead. That's why we've been on the run like fucking criminals. That's why my dad's in that fucking house to make this fucking money so we can just stop running. It's all to protect Stacy. Don't you see? What happens if somebody else finds out? What happens to her then? You gonna promise me that your sheriff wouldn't tell anybody, Eunice? *Nobody?* What if you're wrong? What happens then?"

Eunice, using Lafonda's shoulder to balance and prop herself, got to her feet.

"Eunice, you can't be up," Lafonda said.

"I'm fine."

"You need to go to the hospital. You might have had a heart attack."

"I would know if I was dying, you ought to know that." She turned to Dess. "I do honestly feel that I can guarantee your sister's secret would be safe. My man is loyal. But it's not my place to force that decision on you. If you want me to call him, I'll do it. If not, I won't, and we'll think of something else."

Millie said, "I've got a gun under the seat if you'd rather we take this on ourselves. Just a six-shooter, not something built to take out an army, but it's sufficient for this."

Dess looked at her with surprise.

"It's Texas, dear," Millie said. "Even us old bleeding hearts keep reasonable protection."

After wiping her eyes and face with her hands and then collecting herself, Dess said, "All right. Let's go get her. You said you know where he took her?" she said to Eunice.

"The spite house," Eunice said. "I'm sure of it."

Dess thought, *Is that why Dad isn't answering? Did that man catch him there? Is he okay?*

"We have to get over there," Dess said.

"I got you," Millie said. "Lafonda—"

Eunice said, "I'm coming too." She looked to Lafonda before she could protest. "Maybe he'll take me in exchange for Stacy. Even if not, this is my mess. I've no right to sit it out."

Lafonda sighed. "We'll go in my car. Better to have one extra in case someone needs to drive to get help."

"Let's go," Dess said.

Less than a minute into the drive, Millie said, "You can talk about it if you need to."

A weight slid off of Dess's shoulders. She looked at her new friend, said, "Thank you," and told her as much as she could before they arrived at the spite house.

Dess

*D*ess didn't have nearly enough time to tell the full story, and there were many details she wouldn't have shared even if she had the time. Like how vicious the arguments between her mother and father got after Stacy died. How some of her family members seemed to choose sides in the wake of her parents' separation. How she and her friends drifted apart while she was stuck in the crushing gravity of grief.

Where it started, though, was at the lake on a warm day in spring. For three weeks it had felt closer to mid-June than late April, so her parents decided to go to the water. Later, when their fights would descend into pointless pettiness, they would each blame the other for deciding to go to the lake that day. As if assigning blame could make sense of what happened. Dess was sure that neither of them believed their accusatory volleys. Her father confessed as much to her while they were on the road. As for her mother, she hadn't spoken to her in a year now.

Their relationship had frayed months before Dess joined her father on the road. Dess struggled to forgive her mother for some of the things she said to her father in anger. She got nastier in their fights over Stacy. "You let her go in the water. You let her get sick. *You let this happen.*" She knew exactly what she was saying, knew how those words would tear through him. Still, Dess kept enough faith in her mother to believe that she'd only been lashing out. Mom couldn't believe Dad was responsible for what happened.

Her parents taught Stacy to swim when she was a toddler. The waters in the lake were close to still, and relatively cool, despite the warmer weather.

Not brisk enough to be uncomfortable, though. Especially not for Staze, who loved the water and was overjoyed to be swimming so early in the season, even if it would be a few months before their first trip to the coast, which she looked forward to the most. For that Saturday in April, the lake would suffice.

The lakeshore and waters weren't crowded, to their added delight. Few other families took advantage of the weather that day. Three or four weeks later, there would have been far more competition for space on the beach and in the shallower ends of the water. As it was, there were enough people for all of the parents and older children to keep an eye out for everyone's youngest without getting into anyone's way.

The clouds that passed through threatened no rain and seemed to arrive just to provide a short respite from the heat. The humidity was low. The day could not have been more ideal.

It was not until Monday that it became clear something was wrong. Stacy first complained of her head hurting on Sunday night. By the morning she was running a fever and could not keep her breakfast down. Her mother wondered if she'd gotten too much sun on Saturday and hadn't spent enough time under the canopy they had brought.

Her symptoms alone would have been alarm enough for her parents to get her to the hospital, but she also sounded disquietingly unbothered when she reported her pains. "My head hurts really bad," she would say, wincing like a light was in her face, but not crying or even sounding urgent. She wasn't a whiner by nature, but that didn't explain her stoicism. She was still a kid, and kids couldn't hide their misery when they were sick. Stacy, though, sounded like she was sleep-talking through a drug-induced dream. At times she seemed not to realize that her parents and sister were there at all.

On the way to the hospital, Dess and her mother sat next to Stacy in the backseat while her father drove. They talked to her to try to keep her awake, keep her responsive. Dess was terrified that Stacy would stop answering them, shut her eyes and never reopen them. They were all scared of that, she supposed, all except for Stacy, who was barely even there.

At the emergency room, Stacy was taken to the back without waiting. The family was allowed to go to a smaller waiting area behind the first two sets of double doors, but not into the room where staff would be working to save her life. Dess and her parents sat together in the waiting area, expecting every nurse and doctor who walked by to be the one who would approach them with information on Stacy. When a sullen-faced doctor finally did approach, Dess saw in her eyes that the news was as bad as it could be.

It wasn't heatstroke, as her mother had feared, or anything else that they could have accounted for. *Naegleria fowleri* was a "brain-eating" amoeba that can lurk in freshwater lakes and rivers, and that could enter the body through nasal passages. The only quality that exceeded its deadliness was its rarity. Fewer than one hundred fifty people in the United States had been infected with it in over fifty years. It was like Stacy got struck by lightning while hiding in a basement. Like this thing was a hunter determined to kill her.

The days between Stacy's death and her "homegoing" service somehow moved lethargically for Dess. Her parents had to occupy themselves with the unsavory tasks of notifying family members and coordinating the service. Dess had no such obligations, which gave her ample time to dwell within doleful memories and regrets, field clumsy condolences from friends, and be alone in a quarter-empty house that felt emptier.

After the funeral she found herself increasingly frustrated by the lack of anyone to bear the guilt for Stacy's death. She hated to think it, but often wondered if things might have been easier if Stacy had died of heatstroke, or had drowned when they were all distracted. They would have cause to blame themselves, then. They could punish themselves and each other and then look for a path to forgiveness. Because the guilt and fury and accusations still existed, but without cause they did irreparable harm. They fractured her parents' marriage.

Beyond the worst of their arguments, where each held the other liable for their loss, they could not agree on how best to mourn or honor Stacy. Mom needed to purge the house of any "inessential" reminders. Clear out Stacy's bedroom, donate her books and clothes and toys, and keep only photos and maybe a few specific, personal items, like Miss Happy. Dad needed to keep Stacy's room pristine and every single one of her belongings in the house, and also to find some other way to keep her name alive.

Dad first looked into creating a small nonprofit in Stacy's name to raise awareness about the thing that killed her. Mom pointed out what must have already been apparent to him: He'd get no traction seeking funding to fight an illness that killed fewer people in over half a century than heart disease did every few hours. Calling attention to the threat of *Naegleria fowleri* amounted to starting the Stacy Emerson Fund for the Prevention of Exceptional Misfortunes.

He next explored other memorial opportunities focused on general assistance for sick children. He also considered purchasing a star to be named after her before seeing that this was a scam. He approached the local public library system about how much he would have to donate to have a section of a library dedicated to her. He looked into dozens of options and could not determine which was the right one.

Maybe if Mom had worked with him—and especially if she had guided him, given how much more sensible and decisive she could be—Dad would have found his direction. Or if Dad had been more willing to compromise, had given Mom more time to navigate her mourning, they never would have separated. Instead he pushed his way, and she pushed her way, and after a few months Mom moved into an apartment one town over.

That left the house half empty, and with the amount of time her father spent in his room on his laptop researching, Dess might as well have been living on her own. She enrolled in summer school to earn the credits to graduate early, at the end of the fall semester, and made plans to leave home after Christmas. She had a few friends whose parents would let her stay with them until she went to college. Other friends who graduated the year before and shared a small apartment said she could crash in their living room. She had options if she wanted to get away from the house and the direct shadow of her kid sister's death. That was her plan, but it changed in early August, when Stacy came home.

Dess and her father spotted the little girl walking alone in their neighborhood after dark. They were close to home after a rare night of dining out, trying to have a semblance of a pleasant evening, when they saw her on the sidewalk headed toward their house. The girl wore the same dress that Stacy had been buried in. She walked the way Stacy did when she was excited, each step almost a hop. Even from behind, before they could see her face, her identity was unmistakable. But it had to be a mistake. Stacy could not be there walking alone at night. When they pulled ahead and saw the girl's face it would be someone else's because it couldn't be Stacy's. It was, though. It was her.

Dad pulled over, got out, and ran to the girl. Dess was right behind him. The girl smiled Stacy's smile and jumped into her father's arms the way

Stacy did. When she spoke to them with Stacy's voice she didn't ask why they left her someplace to walk home by herself, nor did she tell them where she was coming from. She asked where Mom was.

"She's away right now," Dad said, sounding robotic. Sounding programmed.

"Oh. Okay," Stacy said. "Can I ask what's for dinner? I'm really hungry."

Months later, Dess still carried guilt over the twinge of terror she felt at hearing this. *She's a monster,* she first thought. *She's not really her. She's something pretending to be Stacy. That's the only explanation. Or else me and Dad just went crazy together.* But when they got her home that night she didn't go for their throats or demand a glass of blood instead of water. She ate the pancakes Dad made for her, because that was her favorite.

"Pancakes for dinner?" she said. "Really?"

"Pancakes whenever you want," her father said. He still sounded flat, but Dess understood it was because he was working to keep from screaming out in joy, or from insanity, or both at once. She felt the same thing. A bubbly madness. Glee heaped upon hysteria. The world stopped making sense and that should have been cause for concern, but not when the nonsense broke so beautifully in your favor. Stacy was with them again. Eating dinner like a living person. Laughing at her own jokes. When she excused herself to go to the bathroom, Dess almost lost her mind laughing.

"She has to go to the bathroom," she said after Stacy stepped away. "That's a real thing, Dad. That's not like a ghost thing. That's a real thing."

Her father shook his head. "This isn't real. This isn't possible."

"It's real, Dad. I'm really here, I'm seeing this with you. Her plate's empty. Somebody just ate that food and it's her. She's here."

"I know. I know. But, Jesus Christ, this is impossible."

What neither of them dared speak of was the possibility that—even if it was real and not a shared delusion—this was temporary. Tomorrow morning, or the next day, or the day after, they would wake up and Stacy would be gone again. This was merely a small reprieve. A flash of generosity from some incomprehensible force too far removed from humanity to understand the potential for cruelty in its charity. Because once Stacy was gone again it would be like they'd lost her for the first time. However many centimeters they had crawled away from their initial grief, they would lose them and be right back where they started. They had no time to prepare for her reappearance and would be unprepared for her next absence.

Aware of this, neither Dess nor her father slept that first night. When Stacy said she was tired, they felt an urge to prevent her from going to bed, remembering that night in April when the illness seemed to make her drowsy before taking her. They stayed up late with her, playing the ABC game and listening to music and watching her favorite shows, until finally she could not resist sleep any longer.

When she got to her room and saw her favorite doll resting against the pillows, she went up to it and said, "Bedtime, Miss Happy." Dess felt any lingering doubt wash away.

She and Dad stayed in the room with her as she slept that first night, barely passing a word between them. Dess spent almost all night on her phone, searching for whatever she could find about people returning from the dead. She imagined her father was doing the same.

When Stacy woke up the next morning, Dess felt a dangerous optimism stirring. *She's back for real,* she thought. *This isn't a one-off thing. She's going to have her whole life back.* She didn't share these hopeful thoughts with her father. She let him be the first to broach the subject of Stacy being with them permanently, two weeks after she first returned. Only he did not sound as positive about it as Dess had expected.

"We have to figure out what we're going to do if she's really back," her father said.

"Dad, I'm starting not to think it's an 'if' anymore."

"Right. Then we have to figure out what to do."

"What do you mean?" Dess said, although she didn't need an answer. She knew.

"How long do you think we can go like this?" he said. "You and I know that this is a miracle. The ultimate miracle. But if anyone else found out, I don't know that they all would feel the same way. They might think she's something else."

Dess remembered her own first thoughts upon seeing her sister alive again. *She's a monster. Something pretending . . .*

"That might not even be the worst of it," her father said. "The ones who do think she's a miracle girl might get more obsessed with her and be more dangerous than the others."

"So we can't let anyone find out about her."

"Right. But how do we go about that? We can't just keep her hidden in the house forever, but we can't let her be out and about where anyone might recognize her either."

"You think we have to move?" Dess said.

Her father raised his eyebrows and glanced away, then answered properly. "Not quite as simple as that. We have to think long-term. What if she ever gets sick again? Not like what happened before, I just mean the flu or pneumonia or anything normal where she still needs to go to the hospital. How are we going to hide who she is then? What do we do about school? Even homeschooling has paperwork involved. If she's really going to get a new beginning, we've got to get her a whole new identity."

Dess scratched her head like she was digging an idea out. "You know, Dad, maybe it's time to let Mom know about this. I get why we waited, we had to make sure it was really real. But she deserves to know. She also could probably work this out better than we could."

Her father sighed. "I've been thinking about that. I just don't know what happens if we tell her. I don't know if it's the best idea."

"Come on. Why not?"

"I'm not saying never tell her. You're right, she should know. Maybe we should have told her already. But it's not about the way things should be, it's about the way things are and what would happen. How do you think your mother responds to this? I'm asking sincerely, that's not rhetorical. I know I have my concerns, but if you honestly don't have any, then I'll figure out the best way to break it to her. I'll do it, I promise, if you don't think anything would go wrong if we told her."

This isn't fair, putting it on me, Dess thought, and almost said. But then she reconsidered. Her father was treating her like an adult, letting her weigh in. He wasn't lying when he said his question wasn't rhetorical. He needed a second opinion and would've welcomed a dozen more if not for the one certainty he currently held: They had to minimize the number of people who knew that Stacy was alive again.

The only other person they could afford to share their secret with was her mother. How would Mom respond to finding out Stacy was alive? Hell, how should they even let her know? If either of them tried to tell her about it before letting her see for herself she would think they were crazy, wouldn't she? Who wouldn't?

The only option was to just show her, then. No sufficient warning, just bring her over and bring Stacy out to see her. She wouldn't be able to deny what she saw. Not at first, at least. But there was a real chance that Mom wouldn't accept what her senses told her. If they brought her over they wouldn't be able to let her out of sight until they were sure that she didn't have any doubts left. They would have to take her phone from her, in case she wanted to call other family members to tell them about this miracle, letting too many people in on the secret. Or call the authorities to report that an unforgivable hoax was being perpetrated against her estranged husband and surviving daughter, or that her grieving husband might have abducted someone's child who looked like his deceased daughter.

It wasn't a stretch to believe Dad was the victim of a heartless con. In Mom's eyes, the way he grieved was unhealthy enough for it to teeter into obsession with a little push. The easy conclusion to reach—much easier than the idea that death actually wasn't permanent, or that a child could resurrect themselves—was that Dad had submitted some information to the wrong website while researching ways to honor Stacy, landed on some vile con man's mark list, and fallen blindly into a trap. There was precedent for that sort of thing. Outside of religion and folklore, there was none for Stacy's return.

Worse, Mom might think that Dad found some kid who looked like Stacy and kidnapped them. The kid might be playing along because they were scared. She might have to walk a hundred miles to come to that conclusion, but how much farther did you have to walk to get to the idea that raising the dead was a real thing? Hell, that wasn't even a walk, it was leaping off a cliff and trusting gravity to ignore you. It was insane. Yes, Dess and her father had taken that leap, but neither could explain why. Maybe they just felt like they didn't have much choice. Maybe they both intrinsically understood that Stacy heading home meant that she was going to knock on the door and keep knocking until they answered or let the morning come, let someone else find her out there. And that one way or another they'd be responsible for what happened to her next.

Mom didn't have those same conditions. She was already out of the house. She could come back and stay, help them figure out what to do next. Or she could leave. Keep it to herself or tell others. Think the best or the worst. There was simply no way Dess could know how her mother would react.

She wanted to believe that Mom would accept this miracle for what it was, embrace it, but she knew that there was a chance Mom would reject it. A small chance, perhaps, but a real chance. The question, then, was whether it was worth the risk. She wasn't sure. Why couldn't Mom have just been with them when they found Stacy?

It came to her then, and a measure of peace settled over her. The real question wasn't "Should we tell Mom?" It was "What would Mom think is the best thing to do for Stacy?"

Dess said to her father, "I think if Mom was in our shoes and we were in hers, she'd say the risk was too high to tell us. She'd put Staze first, and wouldn't chance it."

Her father's shoulders slumped and his head bowed. When he looked back up, she saw the glint of the tears he'd dammed up still in his eyes. She took a breath to keep from breaking down. He must have expected her to say something else. *We have to tell Mom. We should have told her the first night. It's the only right thing to do.* He looked almost like he needed to hear that, like it would refill his depleted reserves of faith in this all to work out.

"Okay then. So we're back to the original question," he said. "What do we do long-term?"

They discussed this and kept coming back to the same conclusion as they thought up one counterargument after another. They would set the conversation aside for days at a time, then pick it up again to see if it might lead somewhere else. It never did. All the while they kept Stacy indoors and felt guilty for it, even though it was for the best.

Stacy never complained when told she couldn't go outside, see her friends, see Mom or anyone else. All she did was what she was asked to do. She was the same mindful, bright child as before. The only noticeable change to her was confirmed a couple of months after she came home. One day, her father had Stacy stand against the wall where her height was last notched a few weeks prior to the visit to the lake. She was half an inch taller now. Just like any other living child, she was growing. When he shared this with Dess, they both cried.

Not only was Stacy back, her life was back. All of her tomorrows. Only she didn't have a future there at home. The conversation, as far as weighing their options, was over. Leaving was the only choice.

Once this became inarguable, Dess and her father tried to come up with a plan. He would pay off his car and buy another, cheaper one with cash. Something none of their relatives or friends would know about, and therefore something they couldn't describe to authorities, if and when it came to that. Dad would leave word with his family that he and Dess just needed some time away, and would be back soon. No one would have reason to disbelieve this at first. Still, some family members were liable to text or call within a couple of days, just to check on them. When they received no response, or once they found out he and Dess had changed their numbers, they would get worried, and suspicious. They might wait another day or two after that, but soon they would try to file a missing persons report, and if they ran into any roadblocks regarding that, they might go as far as to hire a private detective to track them, or investigate on their own. One way or another, they would look for him and Dess, and that meant they needed to be careful. It might also mean staying on the move for a while.

They had advantages. Any authorities or detectives looking for them would be looking for just the two of them, not a third person. And they both knew that a missing persons report for two black adults—with no evidence of foul play, at that—wouldn't gain national attention. They could make it work. Just to be safe, they would adopt new names. If anyone asked, Dess would now stand for "Odessa," not Desirae. That way Stacy wouldn't have to learn to call her something new. Stacy wouldn't take a new name at all. She had enough questions about all of this as it was, they didn't want her wondering why she couldn't be herself anymore, and they didn't want to call her anything that might even hint at her not being herself. Her father adopted the name Eric for no better reason than thinking it would be easy for him to remember, he said.

When Dess asked where they might end up, her father said they'd settle down at the nearest safe place, but suggested it would be hard to find one. There was one place he saw as a backup plan, though. The city where his grandparents once lived. Her new namesake. "It's as far away as we can get where I'll still kind of know my way around," he'd said. "I think we should head in that direction. If something better doesn't come along before we get there, that'll be our last resort."

"You don't think anyone would know you there?" she said.

"No. I haven't visited since I was a kid, and all the folks that knew your grandpa and his parents are either too old to remember me or dead themselves by now. Nobody will recognize me."

"And nobody in the family is going to think to look for us there?"

"They might. That's why it's a last resort. Like I said, we only make it there if nothing better comes along. We play it by ear, see how things are going. Hell, with any luck at all, Odessa is one of the first places they think to look for us. We shouldn't be anywhere near it for a while, which should give them more than enough time to come, see that we aren't there, and then leave to look elsewhere."

She didn't trust him, but couldn't pinpoint why. He wasn't telling her something, she was sure of that. What could it be? What ulterior motive could he have for wanting to go to his grandparents' house? She couldn't think of one. God, she couldn't start thinking this way. Bad enough she'd basically given her mother a vote of no confidence. She couldn't start doing that to Dad, too.

Her father, by way of a trusted coworker at his cybersecurity firm, bought a few necessities, including a new car under his new name, and some ID cards that wouldn't fool any cops, but would probably pass muster with anyone behind the counter at a motel that accepted cash or prepaid cards.

When all of the arrangements had been made, they left under cover of night and vowed to stay on the move and stay vigilant for as long as necessary, until they could be sure Stacy would be safe.

Eric

Sixteen hundred miles northeast, in a cemetery close to the home he'd made with Tab and the girls, there was a quartzite tombstone with his daughter's name etched into it. Beneath that stone, buried in the earth, was a small pink coffin. Since Stacy's return, Eric had asked himself many questions. Seeing Masson's grave answered one, but added another in its place: Was there still a body in her grave?

He tried telling himself that this didn't matter, but he couldn't suppress it or his other remaining questions. What exactly was she? A spirit that somehow gained a body? Was she completely herself, freed from her grave without having to disturb a blade of grass on her burial site? If so, why? How?

Peter Masson had two graves. One tombstone, topped with a marble angel that stood almost eye-to-eye with Eric, marked Masson's death date as September 29, 1918. The other, a granite nub, said he died on October 7, 1963. The first grave had apparently never been disturbed, the body beneath it never disinterred. A monument to a mistake that hadn't actually been made.

Were Masson's war-torn remains still underground? Eric wondered. Or had his ghost reconstituted a healthy body from what had been buried, as well as the pieces left behind on the battlefield in France? If he could find that out, it would help him understand what Stacy was as well.

These questions ran themselves ragged in Eric's head until another pulled itself into the clear. *What about Masson's niece and nephew?*

Those kids were as present in the house as Masson and the woman were.

Where were their graves? Why wouldn't they be buried near the relative who cared for them? Could it be because Masson did something to them? It seemed unthinkable. The time he spent reliving Masson's life, feeling his thoughts and emotions, gave Eric no indication that Masson was capable of such evil, but what did he know? The war could have changed him, the trauma eroding his decency and sanity over time. Or maybe it had to do with coming back to life. The determination to fight off death and seek revenge or righteousness consuming you until you were barely the person you were before. That was what some people used to think of his grandfather, Eric remembered. After the fire, some said he was a changed man, and others responded, "Well, of course he is. Someone tried to kill his family and he almost died. That would change anyone."

"Oh no," the gossipers said. "That's not it. Ol' Fred is a different kind of different."

Not for the first time, Eric thought of something he hated to think about. An early Sunday morning when he was visiting his grandparents. His grandmother brought him to church before service started so he could help fold programs and clean pews. She dropped him off in the lobby and told him to wait while she went to the restroom, but he drifted into the nave when he heard two older women mention his grandfather.

"I'm never gon' get used to seein' Ol' Fred in here," one woman said. She and her friend sat at one of the front pews, their backs to the nave's entrance. She spoke a little louder than she needed to. Eric could see a large white hearing aid in her right ear. "Never, never, never."

"Well if he's here, at least that means there's no devil in him," her friend said, matching the first woman's volume.

"Yeah, you say that."

"I know it. God won't let a devil into the church."

"God wouldn't kill a man and let something come back pretending to be human, either," the first woman said. "You know, sometimes I test him. I call him anything but Fred to see if he'll correct me. He don't. You know why?"

"'Cause he's being polite," the second woman said.

"'Cause that ain't his name. 'Cause the real Fred died in that fire and some devil took his spot."

"So you say."

"I keep telling you."

"And I keep hearing you every Sunday, and praying you don't scare yourself any sillier with these ghost stor—" She stopped, shivered, and turned to see Eric in the aisle. He must have gotten too close, made a noise. The way she shivered, though, wasn't like she was cold. It was like she felt a bug deep in her ear. Eric remembered his grandfather saying that when you shivered like that, it meant someone had walked on your future grave.

The two women stared at Eric like he was doing something odd and vaguely menacing. Holding a lit match and letting it burn to his fingertips, or shaking a jar with a wasp in it and teasing at opening the lid, all with a smile on his face. It unnerved him to see how unnerved they were. What did they think he was going to do? Run and tell his grandfather? And then what? What did they think "Ol' Fred" could do to them? Part of him had been tempted to run and tell his grandfather on the spot just to see what would happen. To see if he could really give them a look that made the buzzards follow them. The thought made his heart race with an emotion that confused him. An unsavory but undeniable pride in the slightest possibility that his grandfather could do such a thing. He couldn't stop smiling about it all through that Sunday's service, and had nightmares about large scavenger birds devouring helpless old women for a week after.

Now, it was something Eric had to consider about his daughter. Could she do some of the things they said his grandfather could do? Might she be even stronger, since she not only had come back from the dead, but was the child of someone who should have never been born?

Peter Masson's house should have never existed, and now it was a magnet for the otherworldly. It was sentient in its own way, made up, as it was, of the lost lives that were trapped within it, and maybe it had drawn Eric to Degener in the first place. That was the best Eric could make of it. That the spite house caught his eye and lured him in to get closer to him and his daughters because of what his grandfather passed down to him. They weren't supposed to exist either. Just like the house, they were here because of a man who refused to stay dead.

Frederick Emerson had something in common with Peter—a consuming anger that twisted a righteous cause. The difference was that Frederick got what he came back for, because that was the kind of man he was. Eric remembered the stories about how his grandfather had made sure that each of the men who burned his house down with him in it met a bad end. A late-night car wreck, a hunting accident, a perfectly bad fall while doing roof work. Each man's death looked like random misfortune, but everyone who knew him knew Ol' Fred made it happen. Eric was moving past wondering how it was possible for his grandfather to do what he did, and instead was focused more on why he lacked his grandfather's will and strength. If he could go back, he'd ask the old man to teach him every-thing. Teach him to make things happen.

Eric wasn't in a position now to know all that his grandfather knew, but he could look into what had happened to Masson's niece and nephew, see what role they played in all of this, what answers they could provide. After his visit to the cemetery he went back to the Degener library, where the librarian looked at him almost the way the old women at his grandparents' church had years ago. She had more sympathy in her expression, though. A hint of guilt, too? Like she'd lied to a homeless man about having no change to spare. Did he look that much worse to her now than he did two days ago?

Regardless, she helped him find obituaries and records that confirmed Masson's second burial, as well as the fact that his first wasn't undone. However, she said that there weren't any records about the passing of Mas-son's niece and nephew, much less their funerals.

"That's always been one of the things about that house," the librarian said. "One day those kids were just up and gone. They probably ran away. I remember my poppa having some stranger theories about it, but he grew up in that orphanage around older kids who swore they knew the real truth, so who knows?"

"What was the 'real truth'?" Eric said.

"Oh, nothing for you to worry about. Old nonsense." She dodged eye contact and touched the back of her neck like she thought a fly was crawl-ing on her. "I'm sorry I brought it up."

"How sorry would you be if something happened to me or my kids because you were too scared to tell me the truth?" Eric said. "Or is all the hospitality and concern around here just a show? None of you really care, do you? It's just me and my girls in that house on our own. Can't even get a simple, hon-est answer out of the kindly local librarian. How do you think that makes me feel as a father? I'll go ahead and tell you. It makes me really fucking anxious. It makes me think the people here, smiling in my face and telling me not to worry when they know damn well that there's plenty for me to worry about, are setting me up. And if it was just me, I wouldn't mind so much. But you and everyone else here knows that I've got my children with me."

He leaned forward, almost halfway across the desk, dropped a fist onto it. Not quite a punch, but a strong enough knock to make the librarian flinch. "To tell you the 'real truth,' right now I'm so anxious I feel like I should do something to show people how seriously I take my daughters' safety."

In the brief silence that followed, he replayed in his mind what he had said. The words meant less to him than the voice that spoke them. He hadn't done an impression of his grandfather's voice, he had channeled it.

The librarian stammered, then glanced around and noticed what Eric already had. They were alone in the library. Someone else might show up at any second, but that could be a second too late if he were to come across the desk, menace her because she wouldn't talk. Then make good on his veiled threat whether she talked or not.

He wouldn't do that, of course, but she didn't know that. All she knew was that he was Eunice's guest, which meant she probably couldn't even kick him out of the library or say she'd call the cops without getting the old woman's permission first. She was more powerless than him from every angle, and they both knew it. This didn't make him feel any better. This wasn't like when he took over the conversation with Emily Steen. In fact it made him a little sick, but it was practical and proactive. He didn't expect her to start suddenly giving up Degener secrets, but she would go home and dwell on this interaction. Maybe tell her husband about it, but probably not even that, because if he told anyone else then it might get back to Eunice, who wouldn't take her side regardless of what she heard about this exchange, because the town librarian had immeasurably less value to Eunice than Eric did.

Next time they talked, he might push things a little further. Tell her that either he could let Eunice know that the lady down at the library had hinted at a "real truth"—see how the queen of the town responded to that news—or he could keep it all to himself if she would just tell him what that real truth was.

For now, he backed away from the desk and said, "Anyway, thanks for your help today."

"Y-you're welcome," she said, as though fighting a program that commanded her to say it.

Eric gripped the steering wheel like he meant to tear it off. His dread of returning to the house brought this on, but also his frustration and embarrassment with being so afraid. What he'd done at the library was a small start. Practice, really. He'd been far too reactive to everything to this point. Even to Stacy's death. He was never going to get a real grip on this situation until he did more to get ahead of it, and he couldn't start doing that until he had a better grasp of what Eunice fully expected of him before she paid him.

Had he uncovered even half enough proof of the haunting to satisfy the terms of their agreement? He knew the full name and story of the man who built the house. Knew Masson went to war, died, came back, died again, was buried twice. How much more would she want to know to consider his work done? Did she need the specifics about the niece and the nephew? Would that be enough? They hadn't laid any of that out. He hadn't pushed hard enough for answers—even when they met and talked by the memorial—because he didn't think things would move this fast. He had been prepared to go sleepless, to be disturbed, but not to pass out and walk through a dead man's past. Not to feel like he was coming apart, never to be whole again. The way the librarian initially looked at him and spoke to him let Eric know it wasn't just in his head. He looked as ill as he felt.

It was savvy on Eunice's part, he had to admit. Letting him commit to finishing the job without pointing out where the finish line was. She could drag this out if she wanted, keep him working for a per diem that was still better than a month's pay under the table at some construction site. And then there was the payday awaiting him if he saw this all the way through, the kind of money that could let them buy land, buy some much-needed privacy. The kind of money that could buy Stacy a new life, set her and Dess up for the rest of their days. Eunice could withhold that ransom for months if she saw fit.

He needed to call Eunice, tell her what he'd found so far and pin down exactly how much more he needed to do to get his money. That was what his grandfather would do. Eric's father, God bless him, was more mild-mannered, and Eric still had more of that in him than he cared for. Frederick wouldn't have been half as patient. The first time Eunice admitted to with-holding information she should have shared in their first meeting, he would have told her, "It'll cost you more to keep anything else from me." He'd have told her that there was nothing he wouldn't do to protect his family. He would crawl out of Hell and send an old woman back in his place, if he had to. Frederick would have understood then what Eric was just realizing, that he could have used his dire straits to gain some leverage. Eunice knew he was in a desperate situation, but desperate men could be dangerous. If there was one thing Eric had on Eunice, it was that she feared for her life almost as much as he feared losing Stacy again. He had missed earlier chances to let her know what he was willing to do. Next time he talked to her, he'd make sure she understood. And, hell, why wait for the next crazy thing to happen before he reached out to her? He hadn't checked on the girls yet today, anyway. He'd give her a call now, let her know they needed to talk.

Eric kept one hand on the wheel and took his phone from his pocket with the other. It was dead. Of course it was. He couldn't remember the last time he'd plugged it in. A simple thing that he'd been disciplined about since going on the road, and it slipped his mind like it was something he forgot to grab at the grocery store. He wondered if Dess had called while his phone was off. If so, she was likely worried enough to come back to the house to check on him. That was the last place he wanted her to be. He hated to think of her worrying about him. Daughters weren't supposed to worry about their dads.

The drive back to the spite house felt shorter than it should have. He was off the paved street and following the winding dirt road toward the house before he was ready to be. When he pulled into the clear, near the house, he would have enough room to make a U-turn, and he told himself that's what he would do. Go back to town and get some food, walk around some, maybe find a coffee shop where he could get in someone's ear and see if they might give him some more information. Something about Masson's niece and nephew that could help.

That plan evaporated when he saw three cars parked near the house. He recognized everyone who stood outside the cars, staring up at the Masson House. There was Eunice, Lafonda, Emily Steen, and Dess.

Stacy wasn't with them.

Was she somewhere else with Dana? Why wouldn't she be with Lafonda instead? Why were any of them here? What in the hell was going on?

He pulled to a fast stop and jumped out of the car. His first instinct was to shout at all of them. Where the hell was Stacy? Had they left her somewhere? Had they *lost* her? His heart was pounding. For the love of God, he'd left her in Eunice's care for *one night* and already something was wrong. He might as well have kept her with him in the spite house. The primary thing keeping him from screaming at Eunice was suppressing his urge to throw up. Because as pissed off as he was, he was even more anxious. A sickening nervousness filled him from his gut to his throat.

When he got close enough, he saw that Dess had her most resilient face on, which meant she'd been crying recently. The roiling fear in his stomach turned painful. Fire and fangs tore through every emotion but despair. Eric braced himself to hear the worst news he could hear about Stacy, and to relive the worst moment of his life.

After they explained everything—Max's arrival, Stacy's abduction—Eric was fully possessed by such fury that it seemed to have come from a primordial time. A wrath that was the grandmother of survival. That long ago forced the Earth to give rise to animals so that it would have something it could inhabit. It was accompanied by the precursor to human fear—the raw, preservative utility of necessity.

Much of what Eunice and Dess imparted glanced off him. The man's name and the fact that he'd been here before didn't matter. Eric didn't care that Dess had revealed Stacy's big secret, and he wasn't upset right now about Eunice's lie of omission. Nothing mattered beyond the simple fact that some bastard stole his baby girl and brought her here. That man was holding her at gunpoint inside the house. Eric could only think of two things, *PROTECT* and *KILL*. Not merely the words, but the actions. Gradually, more cogent thoughts regained purchase in his mind, but still worked in service of the two primary drivers.

PROTECT.

KILL.

"I need to go in," Eric said.

"Hold on," Eunice said. "You don't want to do anything to make things worse."

"Sorry, I should have been clearer," Eric said. "I'm going in."

"Dad, we don't know where he is in there," Dess said.

"I'll find him," Eric said.

"He has a gun."

"And Stacy. That's why I'm going."

"Then I am, too."

"No."

"Dad—"

"We've got a better chance if just one of us goes. He might panic if he's outnumbered. We can't risk that. And of the two of us, you know I'm not letting you go."

Dess looked at him like she wanted to hit him, and that brought him an ounce of peace. It told him that if he failed at this then his older girl would go in and save her sister.

Emily stepped forward and said, "We all know you're concerned, Mr. Ross. I can't begin to imagine. But are you sure that's the safest thing to do?"

"No. The only thing I'm sure of is that my daughter needs me."

Emily nodded and said, "Won't argue that. I got a gun in my car if you want it."

Eric considered the offer. "If I had ever fired one before, I'd take you up on that, Millie. Can't afford to fuck that up on my first try, here, though." He looked at Dess and said, "I'll be back with her."

"I know you will," she said.

From one of the master bedroom windows of the Masson House, a shaded figure watched Eric approach. Eric felt something different in the coldness of its gaze this time. It was far less hostile and more concerned. Possibly afraid.

The front door opened as he reached for the knob. A little white girl in an outdated dress stood just inside. A younger boy stood beside her. Both smiled. Eric paused briefly, then went in as the children turned and ran from him, fading fast with each step until only their laughter remained.

Eric didn't register the door shutting behind him. He stood still and listened. When the children's laughter dissipated, he heard a man's muffled voice coming from upstairs.

Max and Jane

Earlier that day, two hours before sunrise, Maxwell Renner woke up in his small, spartan apartment in East Texas to see his wife standing above him in bed. This alarmed him, because he hadn't told her to get up, and Jane Renner wouldn't do anything without him telling her to.

Jane's mouth was pulled into a tight grimace, like she was smiling through an electrocution. Her eyes bulged, her fists were clenched. Max pushed himself back against the headboard, his heart beating faster than ever before.

Of course she came to life again now. After he once again tried to get her to kill herself. Not after any of his better days, when he made sure she ate well, read to her, tried to play cards with her, cleaned up after her. No, it had to be now, when she had cause to kill him.

Tiny, astonished breaths slipped out of his mouth, each meant to hold words—questions, reassurances—and instead carrying clicks from his tongue and throat.

"Finnnnd me," Jane said through her clenched teeth. Her voice, unused for months, strained under the stress.

"What?" Max said.

"Come back," she said, then dropped onto him, hands at his face like she meant to snatch off someone's mask.

"Jane, stop! I'm sorry!"

"I caaannnnn come back," she said, ignoring his apology. "The chillll-drennnn told me it's reeealll." Then she poured her thoughts and emotions into his mind, and he took it all in. He had no choice. She gave him all of her agony and loneliness and confusion and desperation, but more than that, the revelation that she was not beyond hope. There was a way back.

He saw flashes of images and faces, heard the dead and the living who'd been inside the house recently. More than any others, he saw the face of a little girl, and understood she was the one who could help him to help Jane. Then the nightmares would stop, and his burden would be lifted.

"Eunice hasssss the girl," Jane said, her voice fading, her face beginning to relax, placidity coming over her. "Eunice has her," she said, softer this time, like she was talking in her sleep.

So the old woman had this little girl. Sure she did. Eunice was scared and selfish and conniving enough to let people go into that house without really warning them. Not just saying that it was haunted, but that it was *hungry*. Max wouldn't put it past her to use someone's kid to get what she wanted.

He held Jane's limp body close, rocked back and forth, and cried. "Okay. Okay. I'll do it, babe. I'll go. I'll go. I'll go."

He repeated this like an incantation until it chased away the part of him that begged him not to return to Degener. That told him how foolish he was to linger in Texas so long, pretending he would someday summon the courage to drive to the Masson House to save his wife. Who was he kidding? He didn't even have the guts to go public with what happened. He never wrote about it online under a username, scared that it would put him on the spite house's radar. That it would find him. Take him, too.

Now he was going to go back? No, he'd be better off going to the closet, getting the gun, and shooting Jane now, so he could be done with this and go on with his life.

He shook his head. He wasn't going to do that. He loved her. More than that, he owed her.

"I'll go," Max said. "I will go." An hour later he was on the road, with Jane in the backseat and his gun in the glove compartment.

The last purely lucid observation Jane Renner made—before the spite house tore her soul from her body—was that she understood why Eunice Houghton preferred handwritten journals. It was easier to track the degradation of a person's sanity through their handwriting than through the words they wrote. What she'd written in her journal was alarming, but how she'd written it was worse.

"Something here," in large, jagged letters on one page.

"Has taken part of," slightly smaller on the next page.

"ME," in capital letters on the third page, "and won't give it back" scribbled across the fourth.

Days earlier she noted that *There are no dreams in this house,* something she wrote down on two more occasions while she was still her undivided self.

The closest thing to an unclouded thought she'd had since the divide wasn't fully her own. It belonged in part to the children that she once laughed at. The girl and the boy who had been here for decades and who whispered to her that the house could make her disappear. When she first heard them, she laughed them off as products of her imagination. When the house pulled her apart, the children did some laughing of their own.

Most recently, however, the ghost children told her something useful. That threatened to make her hopeful. They said that the dead did not always remain dead. That the little living girl who had just been in the house had died and come back.

Why can't I get back?

Find the girl and ask her, the children told her. Yes, find the girl, seek her help. If Peter Masson wanted to help Jane, he'd have already done so. He couldn't even be moved from his self-made prison on the top floor. But that girl could help.

Then the children of the house did something even more wonderful and terrible: They used their energy to push her out of the house, across the icy, dead space between herself and her body, and let her pretend to almost be alive again. They gave her the words to say and just enough energy to speak them. Then, when she'd done what they wanted, they drew her back into the house.

She laughed madly then, and the awful sensation of making sound without having lungs felt new again, because she had lungs a moment ago. Or was it already a day ago? A month? Time was a different thing to the dead and even the half dead. It was one of the many differences that made her ache, made her restless, angry, even spiteful.

Her laughter gave way to wailing as she returned to walking the hall where she'd parted from herself, and the stairs that sometimes seemed to number in the thousands, and every space and corner of the Masson House that she was compelled to haunt.

Stacy

The man, Max, was getting upset with her, even though he didn't want to show it. Stacy could tell, because he was talking louder, and he kept stopping himself to take a step back after she said something he didn't like.

I didn't do anything, she wanted to scream at him. Dad and Mom had taught her to respect adults, but this was different. This was a bad person. Maybe he wasn't always this way, maybe wanting to help his wife made him be like this, but this was who he was right now. He hurt Miss Eunice. He had pointed his gun at Miss Dana and talked to her like he would hurt her even worse if she didn't do what he said.

When they got to the skinny house, Stacy was glad to see that Dad's car was gone. If he had been there when Max got there it would have gone very badly. If Max tried to hurt her dad she didn't know what she would do, but it would be terrible.

She didn't understand what he kept asking her to do. "Show her how to come back," he said.

"Back from what?" Stacy said.

"You know," he said, close to shouting. "Back from the other side."

"I don't know what you're talking about," Stacy said.

"You *do*. Back from the dead. Show her how."

All Stacy could do was shake her head at him. He was saying things that didn't make sense. When things died they didn't come back, everyone knew that. Mom and Dad taught her that when Pa-Pa Fred passed. They could live on in your heart if you loved them, and they could watch over you until you saw them again way later, but they didn't just come back like they were gone for a trip. That's not how it worked.

Maybe if Miss Dana were there she could make him make sense, but he took her to the top floor when they got to the skinny house and told her to stay there. "I'll hear you if you try to leave," he said. Stacy heard Miss Dana say, "Just don't hurt the girl. You'll be sorry if you do."

He made a growling sound at that, then took Stacy down to the dark hallway that went to the bathroom, where he told his wife to stay. Stacy was the only one there with them now, but she still wasn't talking. She just stood by the door, waiting to be told what to do. She didn't even look like she knew where she was.

"Look," Max said, wiping his forehead, "just tell us whatever you did to come back."

"I didn't do anything," Stacy said.

"Yes, you did! Stop saying you—" He stepped back again and put his hands on his hips. He had tucked his gun in his pants behind him after telling Miss Dana to stay upstairs. When his hands moved to his hips, Stacy thought he might reach for it, threaten her with it. He didn't do that, though. He wasn't that bad of a person. Not yet.

"Okay, let's just start over," he said, and once again they started over, with him struggling to sound friendly and gentle, and her still unable to understand how she was supposed to help him.

"Did I tell you I was in this house before?" he said. She nodded. Either he thought she was too dumb to remember something he already told her, or he was so upset that he forgot what he said. She noticed before that grown-ups got that way sometimes. When she was in school her teacher would get so mad at some of the boys who really misbehaved she would start to write the same words from a lesson on a chalkboard right under where she wrote it the first time. This was worse, though. Her teacher would at least catch herself halfway through. Max just kept going, telling her again about the time he met Eunice and agreed to live in the house, and how things started to go wrong.

"So listen, I get it that this isn't easy for you," he said. "Believe me, I've been through something very tough and scary myself. So has my wife. What she's been through is a lot like what you went through, except she's still going through it, and she's not even supposed to. Do you understand?"

She hesitated, not sure which would make him madder, saying yes or no. "No" would upset him right now, but "yes" would make him upset later when she still couldn't do what he wanted her to. Before she answered, though, she heard footsteps coming up the stairs. Max heard them, too, and stopped talking. He even held his breath. He turned around to his wife and put a finger to her lips, as if she might say something.

The sound of the footsteps moved past them and up to the top floor, where Dad slept on the first night they were here. Max exhaled and said to his wife, "Do you know who that is, Jane? Can you see them?"

She continued to say nothing, and Stacy's eyes got wider. Max had to know his wife wasn't going to talk to him. She hadn't said or done a thing this whole time. Stacy figured out that that was what she needed help with. So why was he acting like she might answer him now?

A coldness like a mist moved into the hall. It made the light a little dimmer and turned it a shade of blue. Max rubbed one of his arms.

"Jane?" he said. "What's happening? Jane? Babe, if you're here at all right now, if you can hear me at all I need your help. I need your help to help you."

His hand went behind his back and Stacy moved away from him. He did not grab his gun, though. He stood still, his breathing getting quicker. With his back turned she couldn't tell, but Stacy thought he might be crying.

The footsteps came back down the stairs to the third floor, where Stacy was. The door to the first bedroom opened and someone walked in. They were talking and it sounded to Stacy like they were saying a prayer. The voice was low and deep like it didn't want to be heard, and it was muffled by the wall, but Stacy knew it was her father's. It was the only thing that kept her warm.

"Daddy, I'm in here!" Stacy cried.

The voice paused, then answered, "I'm here too."

"Hey," Max said. "Hey, listen. Sir? Sir, listen, this isn't what you think!"

Her father continued his prayer and Max shivered. Even his wife started to shake, unable to ignore the cold, which Stacy knew was getting worse even though she felt like a blanket protected her from it.

Max punched the wall and shouted, "Hey man! Whatever you're doing, stop. Just stop! This isn't what you think it is. I wasn't planning to do anything bad. And I really don't want to hurt your kid, but you're scaring me. And if you don't stop whatever it is you're doing, I swear to God—"

Behind her, a woman wailed, and Stacy dropped to her knees and covered her ears. Max did something similar. His wife stayed standing and trembling, then took in a big breath that sucked in the wailing sound. Her face showed surprise and she looked alive for the first time since Stacy first saw her. Jane looked at her hands like she'd never seen hands before. Max saw her reaction and said, "Jane? Oh my God, are you really—?"

Then the children giggled, the sound bouncing up and down the hall.

Quietly, Stacy said, "Please, Dad, please get me out, please."

Max and Jane said nothing until the light flickered. Jane made a short gasping sound and between one of the flashes of light and darkness disappeared from the hall.

Max got up and stepped toward where she'd been. "Jane! No, no, no, no, n—"

When the lights went all the way out, he stopped saying words and just started grunting and breathing heavily like he wanted to take in all the air he could before he went to a place where there wasn't any air. Something fell hard to the floor and Stacy heard Max struggling and making little whining, pleading noises. Then he gave out a final cry that faded into an echo, then into nothing.

Stacy waited for whatever made Jane and Max disappear to come after her next. She thought about how unfair it was that her father was so close but still couldn't save her. That whomever he was praying to wasn't answering him. Maybe because she didn't deserve to get saved.

I didn't do anything, she had said, had wanted to scream. But maybe she had. The voices at Miss Eunice's house wanted her to remember something. The vision she shook away when she saw that open bench—the sight of her parents walking up to her while she was lying down in a box. Sleeping inside the box. Why would she have been sleeping there instead of a bed? Why would she have been dressed so nice to go to sleep?

It didn't make sense, just like being stuck in that dark place away from her parents and sister didn't make sense. Being in the dark here made her remember how it felt when she got lost and found her way home. It felt like she was deep underwater, where it got so cold it should have been impossible to breathe, except she didn't need to breathe. She didn't need light to find her way up either, not at first. She just needed to keep swimming and fighting until eventually she saw a light, and then keep going until it got closer. When she finally saw a light, that was when she realized somebody had been helping her the whole time. She'd fought hard, and was getting tired, but whoever was helping her didn't let her quit. They made her think of what Pa-Pa Fred told her.

She wanted to get home. The only thing that could stop her was getting tired. That was how she'd gotten lost in the first place. Getting tired, falling asleep so hard that Mom and Dad let her sleep in her nice clothes, in a box. No, it wasn't just a box. What was it?

Stacy shook her head hard. She didn't want these memories. She refused them. They were lies. This house contained evil things that told lies so well they made you think they were your own thoughts and memories. It wasn't true. It couldn't be.

The door at the end of the hall opened and the light came back on. Stacy saw her father and wanted to run to him, but hesitated, because he did not look happy to see her. There was a stern look on his face. Something was wrong.

He held out his arms for her to come to him. "It's okay, Stacy. I'm here. Now you get up, you come right over to me, and *do not look behind you.*"

Eric

Eric didn't know what he would do until the moment he entered the house.

PROTECT. KILL. That was as far as he thought it out. Then he heard someone upstairs. A man talking. A man long dead.

He'd lived chapters of Peter Masson's story for the past two nights. He knew the man's voice. He heard Max Renner's voice as well, but he was oddly less important than Masson right now. Eric knew he could not negotiate with Renner, and didn't want to directly confront him and risk something happening to Stacy. He might be able to appeal to Masson, the man who built the house and surely understood how it could do the things it did. How it made certain doors stick when it wanted to trap someone. How it made some people disappear, like the man from Eunice's story, Clyde Carmichael. How it could make you see your doppelgänger, like Eric had in the hall on their second night in the house. Masson might even have mastery over all of that. If he did, or if he knew anything that could help now, Eric would find a way to make him talk. He failed at that last night. Today would be different.

Eric chose not to rush up the stairs. It would be impossible for him not to be heard, so he wasn't concerned with softening his footsteps. Instead he wanted to be sure his pace wouldn't cause alarm. Rapid, stamping footsteps could give the impression of an incoming attack. They could be mistaken for more than one set of footsteps. They could inspire a cornered, armed man to make a rash decision. The kind that he'd beg to be forgiven for at a trial months later, while still deflecting blame for his unspeakable crime. *I wasn't thinking clearly. I was scared. I heard their footsteps and I knew I was out of time. If they'd just left me alone for a little while longer, then I wouldn't have done it.*

As Eric passed the third floor, Max stopped talking and Eric could only hear Masson's troubled muttering above him. Eric saw that the door to the first bedroom was closed, as well as the door to the floating hallway. It should have been more tempting to open either door and see what was on the other side, especially since the electric tingle that stretched from his nape to his heels told him that Stacy was behind one of those doors. Probably in that damn hallway that even Dana felt anxious about, and that the phantom woman—Jane Renner—lured him into two nights ago. Where he briefly saw himself standing *apart* from himself.

He kept going upstairs to the master bedroom. When he opened the door, the room's cold retreated from him. To his right, in his periphery, he saw Dana standing in the corner behind the door like an intruder waiting to attack. When she saw him she looked less relieved than suspicious, as if unsure if he was really himself.

"Where were you? This man has your daughter," Dana said.

"I know. I'll get her. You can get out. The way is clear." She hesitated and he told her, "You'll just be in the way. I've got her."

Dana went past him after he stepped aside. The cold pulled away from him again when he moved farther into the room. He took another step and it retreated once more. Then again until it packed itself into the corner on the other side of the bed. There the density of the cold formed an elastic wall that let Eric come forward only so far before it pushed him back. The nausea born of being in touch with death boiled within him, burned and scraped, but he did not buckle to it now as he had at the orphanage.

Eric stared at the corner. No human form appeared there for several seconds, but at last Peter Masson could remain unseen no longer. He sat on the floor, knees held to his chest, a small and frail old man whose words were still indiscernible.

"I see you," Eric said. Masson either could not hear him or chose to ignore him. "I know you," Eric said. "I told you last night, I saw it all. I know why you built this house. I felt your pain, all of your anger and hate. Only thing I don't know is what happened to those kids."

Masson shook his head at this and rocked in place.

"Whatever happened," Eric said, "whatever you did, this is your one chance to make up for it."

"I never hurt them," Masson said. He'd been saying it the whole time, but now at last he spoke forcefully enough for Eric to hear him clearly. "I never hurt them. I never hurt them."

"Like you never died?"

Masson groaned and dipped his head lower. "I never hurt them. I never hurt them."

"This is your chance, Peter. You can't bring those kids back, but you can save my daughter. You can do something. Or you can stay up here forever, stuck in your own guilt for whatever you did. It'll be a lot worse for you if you do nothing. Help me save her, damn it."

Masson lifted his head, stared through Eric, and said, "I can't even leave this room! I can't do anything. I can't. They won't let me. They won't forgive me. And I never even did anything." Through hollow, echoing sobs he returned to his mantra. "I never hurt them. I never hurt them."

Eric understood then that he was appealing to the wrong spirit. Masson built the house, but over time "they" ran the house. The children.

When he got back to the third floor, he went through the door to the first bedroom. Eric did not genuflect, shut his eyes, or clasp his hands. He did, however, speak with reverence he had not proffered to Peter Masson. He did not patronize the spirits of the children by forcing solemnity into his tenor, but he spoke deliberately and with a hint of gratitude, as though he owed them in advance for help he wasn't sure they would provide.

"I know you're here, I know you can hear me," he said. "I don't know what you want from me, but I have to believe you don't want to see another child suffer here."

The room grew no colder and Eric wondered for a moment if he was wasting his time. If he should instead go back outside and ask Millie Steen for her gun, and see if she might come with him, too, as backup.

Then he heard Stacy through the wall. "Daddy, I'm in here!" Hearing her dug hooks into Eric's heart and reminded him that he could not afford any doubt or indecision or carelessness. He had to make this happen.

He held back tears and rooted himself to where he was. "I'm here too," he said to Stacy. Then he continued his plea to the children. "Help my daughter. You can keep me if you want. You can ask me to do anything, tell me to do anything, I'll do it. I swear. I swear on my soul that I will. Just please help my daughter. I'll do anything you ask if you help her."

He repeated this last sentence as he felt the temperature plummet and heard Max Renner telling him to stop. He said it again and again as he heard things happening in the hallway on the other side of the wall. Awful-sounding things, but things that did not touch Stacy, that only made Max and his wife scream and cry and struggle. He was sure of this, because he felt almost like he was part of the energy that attacked the Renners. That raw fury that had seared *PROTECT* and *KILL* into his consciousness was in the hallway with the children, perhaps even fueling them and the house as they snatched Max's and Jane's lives and souls. When their screams stopped, his anger dissipated, and his only thought was of Stacy.

Eric went to the stairwell and opened the door to the floating hallway. Inside, at first, he saw only Stacy. Then his eyes adjusted to the dimness and he saw someone behind her. A man whose stance matched his, whose eyes and skin and clothes were his as well, but whose expression was full of hate and horror and, worst, despondency, like he was staring at someone who abandoned him to die alone years before.

When Eric held out his arms and motioned for Stacy to come to him, the doppelgänger mirrored him.

"It's okay, Stacy," Eric said, "I'm here. Now you get up, you come right over to me, and *do not look behind you.*"

Stacy did as she was told and ran into his arms. "I've got you," he said. "I've got you."

He said this to her all the way down the stairs and as he approached the now open front door, right up to the moment something kicked his legs out from under him and he fell forward, half tossing Stacy toward the door like someone was there to catch her and take her the rest of the way. His eyes never left Stacy's as they both fell. She hit hard but got up quickly. *Tough kid,* Eric thought. *I love you so much, Stacy, I hope you know that. I hope you never forget that. Now get the hell out of here and don't look back.*

Stacy still faced him, so she didn't see what Eric saw through the open door. Dess, Lafonda, and Millie all ran toward the house. They ran as though the door might shut on its own and refuse to open if they didn't get to Stacy fast enough. For all Eric knew, that was exactly what would happen.

"Get out," Eric shouted, almost like he was angry with her. "Stacy, get out now!" He tried to stand but couldn't. An impossible weight and cold pressed on him and he felt like he was turning into both ice and stone at once.

Stacy backpedaled toward the open door, her expression crushed by fear and grief. Eric felt his heart breaking. She shouldn't have to see this. She'd been through too much already.

She yelled, "Don't hurt him," at something, then turned and ran out of the house, where Dess waited for her.

The door slammed shut and the world lost its light and color. The weight on Eric's back lessened enough for him to turn over and see what Stacy had seen.

A young girl of maybe eleven or twelve stood at his feet. Her younger brother was right behind her. Peter Masson's niece and nephew glowered at Eric and said nothing, as if waiting for him to explain himself and beg forgiveness for trying to leave without fulfilling his end of the deal he'd just made. *I was just getting her out,* he thought, but felt too tired to say. *I would have come back.*

Then it came to him again, the same as the night before, the great deep sleep that delivered him fully into the emotions and remembrances of those who once lived in the house, and who still occupied it well after their lives ended.

The Children

heir uncle Peter did not want them. Eleanor was sure of that. She wasn't as naïve as he thought she was.

"I'll be caring for you and Owen now," he said when he came to pick them up and bring them back to Texas. He expected them to believe it, too, that his aim was to actually care for them, not just legally abduct them. Rob them, in their time of grief, of what small joy they had left.

They were staying with their elderly cousins Jonas and Johanna in Alabama, before the storm that took their parents struck. Father sent for Mother a few weeks before. He wanted to show her the city where he planned to build their newly acquired assets into a true fortune. West Palm Beach, Florida.

The Miami area's land-boom period was waning even before a devastating cyclone had crippled it two years earlier. Its economy further faltered after a run on the banks a year after that storm. This made it "ripe for redevelopment," according to her father.

Eleanor was happy for her father's enthusiasm, but not about potentially moving. They didn't know anyone in Florida. Their closest relatives lived in Mobile, Alabama, more than six hundred miles from West Palm Beach. Cuba was half as far from West Palm Beach on a map.

Their cousins in Mobile, Jonas and Johanna, were more like Eleanor and Owen's great-grandparents. They were twins, one a widow and the other a widower, who lived together in Johanna's house in northern Mobile. They also took frequent trips to Jonas's beach home in Beldame.

Eleanor and Owen were at the beach house when the storm that drowned their parents struck Florida. People knew for days that a storm might be coming. That Friday's newspaper reported the cyclone killed twenty people in the West Indies. Johanna and Jonas still went ahead with the trip to Beldame. They said they only had so many summer days left and planned to make the best of each one.

More fatalities were reported in Saturday's paper, and "HURRICANE MENACES FLORIDA" was the front-page headline on Sunday morning. Nonetheless, Eleanor felt no concern for her parents. The islands where people died were less advanced, less fortunate places where people lived in less stable homes. West Palm Beach was a more modern city that smart people flocked to and poured money into, according to her father. Surely they learned from the previous storm and rebuilt stronger houses afterward.

Her faith proved unfounded. Although the vast majority of the dead in Florida were migrant workers who lived in the lowlands near a place called Lake Okeechobee, many also died in West Palm Beach. Eleanor held out hope that her parents were not among the dead until their bodies arrived for burial in Mobile, one day behind Uncle Peter.

"Why can't we stay with our cousins?" Owen asked when Uncle Peter told them that they were going to come live with him.

"They are older," Uncle Peter said, not bothering to lower his voice even though Johanna and Jonas were only one room away, and likely heard him through the open door. "They need to be resting in their later years. Not chasing and bothering after you two."

"We aren't a bother to them," Eleanor said.

"Good. I trust you won't be one to me now that I'll be caring for you."

Eleanor's parents had raised her too well to say what she thought: *If you really cared, you would let us stay here for as long as we could, with people who love us.*

Four months after taking them to Degener, Peter had to bring them back to Mobile. Johanna and Jonas had died within a few days of each other. They shared a single service and were buried on the same day. Eleanor heard someone at the service say that the twins seemed lost and hopeless after the children went away. As they were lowered into the ground, Owen cried aloud, "It's not fair." Eleanor hugged him and agreed.

Indeed it was not fair that their uncle had done this to their cousins, who she knew had not truly succumbed to illness, but to loss and loneliness.

Their uncle did not want them. So why did he take them in?

He certainly hadn't built his emaciated house with the intention of ever having a guest, much less raising children in it. It appeared the only reason he'd delayed at all before coming to get them was because the house needed renovations to accommodate them. Uncle Peter gave up his third-story bedroom and workspace to Eleanor and Owen, moving himself to the top floor that had previously been his study. A month later, construction was finished on the jettied washroom hallway built to give his niece and nephew some semblance of privacy.

Eleanor eventually learned from the kids at Everlasting Arms that the top floor should have been called "the scowling room." The orphans swore they saw him there most mornings and most evenings, standing in the window and glaring at them for hours. One child overheard a Sister say, "That man haunts that house." From there "the Ghost Man" joined his previous nickname of "Scary Old Peter," and that was before the orphans found out about his plot and tombstone in the cemetery, and the accompanying lore of his return from the dead.

The orphans saw Eleanor and Owen as outsiders, even though they shared the tragedy of having no parents. The children of Everlasting Arms were united in their fear of the spite house. Eleanor and Owen lived inside it, along with its strange, hateful owner, and that eclipsed any commonality.

Still, the orphans tolerated Eleanor and Owen as objects of subtle ridicule, because to fully shun them would have upset the Sisters. Sometimes that tolerance leaked into shows of courtesy and affection—a shared piece of fruit, or invitation to join them in a game—before the orphans would remember that Eleanor and Owen lived with the Ghost Man. Then the taunting would begin again.

They always met with Eleanor and Owen in groups of three or more. Eleanor turned twelve not long after arriving back in Degener for the first time since she was a baby, but carried a cynicism well beyond her age. She wondered if even the orphan children understood why they felt compelled to always outnumber the two Masson children. "Your uncle is dead. I saw his grave. I touched the marker."

"You live in a ghost's house."

"If you live there, how do we know you're not dead, too?"

The orphans had more in common with Uncle Peter than they realized. He didn't like Eleanor and Owen either. He fed and sheltered them, but hardly said a word to them beyond what was absolutely necessary.

"Dinner," he grunted at them each night when food was ready.

"Breakfast," each morning, said almost grudgingly, like a judge ordered him to make sure he gave the children a chance to feed themselves.

Never so much as "Come and eat." Never a mention of what he made. Just an austere announcement, as if he didn't really care if they ate or chose not to.

On most Saturdays, Uncle Peter went into town and came back with what they needed from the general goods store. He would also bring home an even sourer mood than what he'd left with. The rumor that the orphans picked up from eavesdropping on the Sisters was that Scary Old Peter spent part of the day visiting a lawyer in town, trying and failing to devise ways to evict them and reclaim his family home.

Uncle Peter's vindictiveness contaminated the walls, fouled the floors, molded the wood, and grayed the windows of the house. The building reeked of his anger. It made Eleanor restless at night, wondering when Uncle might go mad and do something awful. She often heard Owen stirring in his sleep as well.

One night Owen knocked on her door, then entered her room before she answered.

"Can I sleep in your bed?" he said, and took her silence and shift away from the center of the bed as a yes.

As they lay there, Owen on his side and Eleanor on her back, an unexpected thought popped into her head. Before she could think better of it, she said, "Don't you think it might be fun to play a joke on one of the children from the Arms?"

Owen didn't answer for a long time. Had he never answered, she might have let it go, and all that followed might never have happened. Or maybe it would have only been postponed.

"What kind of trick?" he said after so much time passed she thought he had fallen asleep.

"They all think that Uncle's dead and the house is bad and we're bad for living in it, don't they? They're scared of us, even though they act brave around us because there're always so many of them around. But what if we caught one of them by themselves and made believe like we were just as bad as they say we are? We could pretend to drag them into the house, and tell them it really is a ghost house, and that they were right all along, we're ghosts who've been pretending to be alive. We'll say that once they get in the house they'll disappear, and no one will ever see them again unless they learn to be nice to us. Then, if they're nice enough, we'll teach them how to be like us. Ghosts pretending to be alive."

Owen shuddered. He pulled the covers tighter around his shoulders and pressed his head harder into the pillow. "I wouldn't like that trick. It's mean."

"No it's not. It would be fun. And even if it is mean, it's fair because of how they treat us."

Owen stayed quiet until Eleanor fell asleep, which took some time, as she had to quell a newfound resentment she felt for her younger brother, whose rejection of her idea made her feel even less seen and loved than Uncle Peter and the orphans could.

"You don't have to believe me. That doesn't stop it from being true. This house really can make you disappear."

"Stop saying that," Owen said, on the verge of tears. He had heard this same thing from Eleanor every day for weeks. She was getting meaner, and he didn't understand why. He was starting to hate her for it. Not the childish hate that's just a word directed at foods they don't like or a parent who has told them no. It was legitimate hatred that was a coin's width away from love.

It was mid-January. Christmas came and went without Santa finding them. The Sisters from the orphanage brought small gifts, but Owen couldn't live off that single act of tenderness for the next twelve months. He needed Eleanor to be loving and consoling again. He hated this new version of her who hissed, "Be quiet," or, "No one wants to hear it," when he said he missed their parents and cousins.

He especially hated her taunts about the house. She kept saying it could make someone vanish if they stayed in it too long.

"You need to let me teach you how to stop it from happening before it's too late," she said. "If not, you're just going to be gone one day."

"You're lying," he said, his voice cracking. "Prove it."

"I can't demonstrate it myself," Eleanor said. "You'll just say it's some kind of trick I pulled to fool you. But if I showed you with someone else, you'd believe it then."

"I told you I'm not doing that."

"It would be very easy, Owen. We pull one of those rat children from the orphanage into the house—"

"I'm not doing that."

"—and once you see one of them vanish, you'll believe it's true. And once you believe in it, you'll know how to make sure it doesn't happen to you."

Owen pushed away from his chair at the small rectangular table in the corner of the kitchen. As he ran to the stairs he heard Eleanor call after him, laughter in her voice. "Oh come on. Where are you going?"

He ran to the third floor and went into the hallway. He shut the door behind him and locked it from the inside, then ran to the other end of the dark hallway to lock the door at that end as well. He made it there just ahead of his sister, whose longer legs let her make up for his head start faster than he anticipated, though not fast enough.

She tried to open the door, and when she couldn't turn the handle she knocked so politely it had to be another taunt. "Owen, what are you doing in there?"

"Leave me alone."

"You know you shouldn't play around in there. What if that floor gave out?"

"Stop messing with me."

"I'm serious," she said, and she did sound serious. But he couldn't be sure that wasn't a trick. "You need to come out. You're not supposed to *stay* in there. You're supposed to just walk through. I don't think it was built for someone to stand around or sit in the same place for too long. I mean it, Owen. If something happened to you in there I would be sick. I'm sorry for how I've been behaving. I'm not really mad at you. It's this house. It's those other children. It's Uncle. It's everything that has happened to us. I'm as sad as you are about all of it. Remember when you said, 'It's not fair,' at our cousins' funeral? You were right. And I haven't been fair to you either. I'm sorry."

He knew she was sincere, and reached to unlock the door, but something happened. In that moment, in the darkness, the anger and bitterness that drove his uncle to build this house—that drove him to steal his brother's children from a place where they were happy—seeped into him. He understood why Eleanor was so cruel to him, why their uncle was so callous to both of them. He understood the appeal of spite. Being mean because it was all you had. That emotion and revelation poured from every board and nail of the house and washed through him. It made him feel sick, frightened, and empowered all at once. He felt like he might wet his pants, but also like he might have the ability to fly or make himself grow big enough to be a giant who could make others feel small and weak, instead of him always feeling like that way.

He even felt like he could do the thing Eleanor liked lying about.

"I'm going to stay here and let the house make me disappear," he said.

The door handle rattled. "Owen, I'm serious. Come out, now."

"Be quiet. No one wants to hear you."

"Owen, I'm—"

"'Owen, I'm serious,'" he mocked. "I'm serious too. I believe you now. And I don't want to be here anymore. So I'm going to make myself not be here."

He walked away from the door and from the sound of her calling his name. He went to the center of the hallway to lie down. He surprised himself by how deeply he meant what he said. He didn't want to be here, but he didn't think he could take himself to where he wanted to be, back with his parents, or at least with his cousins. As emboldened as he felt, he didn't believe he could reverse time or death. He didn't even think he could truly escape where he was. But he could make himself invisible. He could disappear. That might not make him feel better, but it would make his sister feel worse. That was good enough.

In a different house, one with a natural right to exist, and uncharged by the omnipresent vindictiveness of a man who tore the veil between life and death, what happened next would not have been possible. But this was not a different house.

The cold smothered Owen. He curled into a fetal position and thought of his mother. He inhaled deeply and drew more of the cold inside him. He did this all with the natural, wordless knowledge of an infant who knows how to feed, who knows it must cry to be heard and thus attended to, who knows of certain essential things without awareness of knowing anything.

Eleanor managed to pick the door's lock with a butter knife. She stepped inside, turned on the light, and found the hallway empty.

Masson

Between his veteran's benefits from the war, the money he reluctantly accepted from Luke's sale of the land, and some shrewd investments, Peter Masson had a small fortune to his name and never needed to work again. This suited him, because working meant being around others, and he couldn't stand most people.

Coming home after getting goods and groceries was the worst part of his week. It was the farthest he would be from the next time he'd have cause to leave the house. He hated his creation as much as he needed it. He wanted to tear it down with his own hands but could not imagine living anywhere else. It was as if the house owned him, not the other way around.

He never bought more than he could carry alone. It was always enough. Eleanor and Owen didn't eat much, and even if their usual appetites doubled in the week ahead, he could always do with less so they could have more. He did it before.

He did much for his brother's children, he believed. He gave them a place to call home. Abnormal as it was, it was something permanent, not the fleeting situation they had in Alabama. While no one could have predicted that the twins would pass when they did, it had been obvious to Peter they weren't long for the world. That left him as the children's only suitable guardian. The children suspected he had other, less noble reasons for taking them from the place where they wanted to stay, but what other reasons could he have? Did they think he'd taken them in simply to spite Lukas posthumously, by proxy of his children? Absurd.

Beyond basic necessities, he gave Eleanor and Owen an outside chance at reclaiming the inheritance they shouldn't have lost and would never have known about if they never came back to Degener. He was still waiting for the appropriate time to make them aware of this. Someday soon, he was going to tell them their complete history. What their ancestor died for, what the Houghtons did to repay them, what their father sold and surrendered. What the Houghtons, with all of their might and influence, refused to help him retain.

He might never get a legitimate chance to undo the iniquity done to him, but he could ensure the children understood what was rightfully theirs, and instill in them the verve to fight for it. *Someday,* he used to tell himself, *as soon they're old enough, I'll tell them everything, and they'll understand better than Lukas ever did.*

Someday never came.

The day that they disappeared, Peter came home to find Eleanor sitting by herself at the kitchen table. She looked like she was asleep. Her head rested in the crook of her folded arms. Her body did not jerk with sobs and her voice did not hitch with them either, so Peter was surprised to see her face soaked in tears when she lifted her head and looked at him.

"Something happened," Eleanor said.

He set the groceries down. She had a bad dream, he presumed. Or one of the orphan children said something especially terrible to her. If that was it, then enough was enough. He was going to speak to the Sisters about it. He had seen Eleanor look sad before, but never distraught like this. Not even at the funerals for her parents and cousins.

"What happened?" he said.

"Owen is gone."

"What do you mean?"

"He's gone."

"What are you saying? He ran off?"

"No," she said. "He was upstairs in the hall. That stupid hall you built. He locked himself in and wouldn't let me in. I upset him. I said awful things."

Peter sighed, relieved that he wouldn't have to go chasing after Owen in the woods, thinking of a fitting punishment for when he found him. "So he's just upstairs. You worried me, Eleanor. You shouldn't say he's 'gone' if he's just trying to hide from you—"

"He's not hiding, he's gone. Can't you ever listen for once? He's vanished. He's *missing*."

Peter's blood started to race. "So he did run away?"

"No. He was in the hallway. He wouldn't let me in. He said he was going to disappear. He said he didn't want to be here anymore. And then when I got the door open, he wasn't there. He couldn't have gotten out without me seeing or hearing, even when I came to the kitchen to get a knife—"

"A knife?" Peter said.

"Just to open the door with," she said. "Not a sharp knife. Don't look at me like that. I know what you're thinking, I can see it in your face. I wouldn't do anything to hurt him. I love him. Not like you."

Peter stared at her. "We'll address that little comment after I get your brother."

"I told you, he's gone. I've already looked for him."

As he marched to the staircase, Peter called out to Owen, told him to come out of hiding. "I mean it, boy. If I find you somewhere after I've told you to come out, you're going to be in a world of trouble."

He went downstairs first, to sweep the building from the ground up, not wanting to get caught upstairs in case his nephew was on the ground floor where he could run outside.

There was nowhere for the boy to hide downstairs. Peter walked back up to the second floor, where Eleanor watched him without helping. He looked everywhere he could think of, including the pantry, which was much too shallow to hide a boy of Owen's size. On the third floor the only viable hiding spots were Eleanor's armoire, the hallway, and the bathroom. Peter did not find Owen in any of these places.

He checked his bedroom last. He did not find Owen in his wardrobe or under his bed. Peter thought he must have somehow missed him, and returned to the first floor to cover the house again, calling out Owen's name more angrily now.

When the boy did not turn up after the second search, Peter went to Eleanor. "You need to tell me the truth about what happened."

"I told you," she said.

"Did he really run off, Eleanor? You've had me searching inside this house the whole time, I could've been out there finding him."

"He was in the hallway. I told you."

"What did you get the knife for? Did you do something? If it was an accident, it's fine," he said, though his tone and volume indicated it was far from fine. "You just need to be honest with me about what happened."

"He disappeared," Eleanor said. "It's not my fault. The house made it happen. *Your* house. This is *your* fault. Why did you make us live here?"

"Eleanor, we don't have time for this. Your brother is missing."

"You don't care about that. You don't even want us. You just want to hurt Daddy, and he's not even alive anymore. So you took us here to make us as miserable as you. You're only made of hate, just like this house. What is wrong with you?"

"Enough!" Peter said. He took her by her shoulders and shook her. He never laid a hand on either child before this, but he also hadn't encountered a moment like this. Owen was gone, and Eleanor was saying things she couldn't possibly believe. Horrible lies. She must have done something to her brother and was trying to pass her guilt on to him. That was the only explanation. She was smart enough to know why he took them in. The twins died just months later, and all that talk at the funeral of them dying of loneliness without the children was nonsense. They were old. He'd recognized that and made the only sensible choice.

Yes, there were other, more distant relatives he could have handed them off to. Or he could have bought a more traditional house for them to live in with a hired caregiver. He had the money for that. So why didn't he do it? Why was he asking himself that now? It wasn't important. It was all rooted in a lie. He wasn't hateful enough to want to hurt Lukas, much less his niece and nephew. There were sound reasons for all he'd done. Tradition and justice and righteousness. Any suggestion to the contrary was a lie. He was not a hateful man. He was a *wronged* man, damn it, and he built this house to remind people of that, not just to anger them because he was angry. She was wrong about him. Wrong, wrong, absolutely wrong. And a liar. Maybe worse. What did she do to her brother? What would it mean for Peter if Owen was hurt?

"Do you know what you've done, Eleanor?" he said. "Do you know what they'll say of me if your brother's been hurt? Do you understand?"

He shook her harder with each question, once so fiercely that he lost his grip. Her temple cracked against the edge of the hardwood table as she fell.

Eleanor slumped to the floor in a way that looked sickeningly familiar. He'd seen it too often in the fields in France to forget it. He'd been trained on what to do when he saw it, and that training brought him to his knees and his fingers to her left wrist. Her pulse slowed and weakened under his fingertips. He reached for his waist, for one of the pockets of a medical belt. Ammonia aromatics might rouse her, and with that accomplished he could then address her head injury before any swelling or discoloration started appearing.

He had no medical belt, though. No ammonia, or any of the other supplies that he'd kept on him in the field where he fought to saves lives, but ultimately could not save his own.

No, no, I never died.

And you never hated Lukas for what he did, either?

Another voice that mimicked his thrust that question into his mind. It was heavier than his own voice, though, and frighteningly dark, like a cliff's edge you couldn't see at night. It was the voice of the man Eleanor said he was. The man everyone else in Degener thought he was. The spiteful man. The man who claimed to be driven by a need to honor his murdered ancestor, but who was instead consumed by rage he wished to make contagious. A man whose enmity was too big for him, so he built a house to contain it all, and that still wasn't enough.

"Do you know what they'll say of me?" he had yelled at Eleanor seconds ago.

Worse things now, the other voice told him. It seemed to come from within and also all around him. Like the house was speaking to him, and was also a part of him. *When they find her like this, what will you say to them? They'll say you hurt the boy, too. They'll say they're only surprised that it didn't happen sooner. Even if they prove it was an accident, they'll still say you're guilty. They'll see you for what they've always known you to be.*

Not if I save her, he thought. He got up and rushed downstairs. Once outside, he ran downhill toward Everlasting Arms, where he could see the nuns supervising some of the children in the play area. They could help him save Eleanor. The orphanage had to have emergency supplies for when one of their children got hurt. It wasn't too late. It wasn't.

Halfway to the orphanage, he stopped. *You should go back and bring Eleanor with you.*

No. It's not good to move someone who's suffered head trauma.

You know that. The Sisters don't. They'll wonder why you left her behind. It will look suspicious to them. Go back and get her. You'll have to move her eventually anyway.

There was no real sense to this, yet Peter followed the advice of this other voice. He went back into the house and took the stairs hesitantly. A glacial coldness surrounded him. It brought to mind something he worked very hard to block out. The memory of his own death, which he often revisited in his sleep, and which he considered a product of an injured brain, nothing more. Here he was, though, reacquainted with the coldness of death, which was comparable to nothing but itself.

That other voice—the voice of the house—must have known this was waiting for him. That was why it told him to come back inside. When he came to the kitchen and saw that Eleanor was missing, it said to him, *She's gone, but she's still here. You won't find her. Just like the boy. If you went to the Sisters and told them Eleanor was hurt, then brought them back to this, you know what they would say. Even if they can't prove you did something to the children, they'll tell everyone about how you ran for help and brought them back to an empty house like a madman. They will conspire with authorities to get you locked away in a sanitarium. And then they will have this house taken down, and that can't happen. Now you'll have time to think of a simple story about sending the children away.*

"Where are they?" he screamed at the house.

Here with me.

"Who are you?"

Stop pretending not to know. I am what brought you back to life, and I am in turn what you have brought to life. I am something that shouldn't exist, because you should not have returned. The children understand it now, and you should see what that has done for them. They understand how much more there is to this house. Right now they're moving through doors and halls that you can't see because you are still lying to yourself. It is time to stop saying you never died. Stop denying—

"Stop it! Stop talking to me. I have to concentrate. I have to find my brother's children."

You know you won't find them. But they might find you.

Peter searched the house for Eleanor, retracing what he'd done to look for Owen. He shouted loud enough to drown out the voice of the house, loud enough to be heard by the children in the orphanage's playground, and by the Sisters supervising them, although they could not make out what he was saying. He went on like this for hours, until he ripped his voice to pieces and his legs and lungs burned from climbing the stairs.

Exhausted, Peter collapsed to the floor of his bedroom. With his ear to the floorboards, he heard something downstairs. Eleanor and Owen were laughing. Were they toying with him all this time? Was this some devious game?

Their laughter came up the stairs. It echoed strangely, alternating between sounding closer and farther away. When it came to the bedroom door he found the strength to get up.

When he opened the door the laughter stopped. He should have at least heard or seen the children running down the stairs. He did not. The worst of it was that this did not surprise him.

He retreated to the far corner of the room on the other side of his bed, as far from the door as he could get, and sat on the floor. His sanity would not begin to stitch itself back together until the next morning. Until then, he repeated the only words that could give him any solace, and that kept the voice of the house at bay. The lie that was most important to him at the moment. "I never hurt them. I never hurt them."

Dess

Something in the house held the front door shut. Dess handed Stacy off to Lafonda shortly after the door swung closed. Now she felt the doorknob resisting when she tried to turn it.

"It won't open," she said. She slammed her shoulder into the door twice. "It won't open! Help me! We have to get him out!"

Millie joined her first, then Dana. Together they pushed against the creaking door. Behind them, Lafonda stayed with Stacy while Eunice surveyed everything from near the cars.

The door buckled, then flexed outward as something on the other side slammed into it, staggering Dess, Millie, and Dana. As Dess moved toward it again, the knob turned and the door eased open.

Dess saw her father facedown and was fortunate to have only an instant more to wonder what she and Stacy would do if he was dead. When Eric stirred and tried to get up, she hurried to his side. He grabbed her arm as if it were a rope keeping him from a steep fall. She did not mind the pain. His eyes were wide and she knew that in his mind he'd been gone for far longer than the handful of seconds she'd spent trying to get to him.

He tried to speak. His mouth fell open and a choking noise came up from his throat. Dess put her hands to the side of his face. She stared a measure of peace into him and said, "Dad, it's all right. You're back. This is real. I'm really here, you're really here, Stacy's outside and we're all going to be all right. We just have to leave. You ready? Can you stand?"

He nodded and she helped him up. Dana let him lean on her as they walked out. Millie stayed at the door, her back against it and feet planted hard, pinning it to the wall in case it tried to swing shut on them. She let the others leave first, then followed. The door did not close behind them.

Gathered near the cars, Dess and Stacy hugged their father while the others huddled around them. "What about the Renners?" Eunice said. "Are they still in there?"

Eric shook his head. "Gone." He sounded parched, but Dess noticed that he didn't look as distressed as he had just seconds earlier. He almost looked aloof, like he'd taken a strong anxiety pill that just kicked in.

"What do you mean 'gone'?" Eunice said.

"Like that story you told me about the man who came back to the house in the sixties. Clyde. It's the same for the Renners. The house has them. They're in there, but they're gone."

There were follow-up questions in Eunice's eyes—in everyone's, Dess saw—but they all spared him immediate questioning.

"All right, I'll have the sheriff bring some people by to search, just to be sure," Eunice said. "We'll talk more about it later. For now, I think we could all use some rest. You're all welcome to come back to the mansion."

At this Stacy let out an uncharacteristic, scared whine and held her father even tighter.

"Yeah, nah, how about Millie's?" Dess said, looking at the woman whom she felt an outsized trust in. She'd been ready to go into the house guns blazing to save Stacy. Dess would always be grateful for that. "No fresh, bad memories tied to your place yet."

"Good point," Millie said. "Everyone who wants to come is invited. My bar's stocked up for anyone who needs a drink. Lord knows I do."

They piled into the cars they'd arrived in, leaving the Renners' car behind. Soon the Masson House and land were silent, still, and not at all empty.

Eric

"Well," Millie Steen said, "apparently ghosts and shit are a real thing." This broke an extended silence and got a polite laugh out of Eric, and brought a smirk to Dana's face. Eunice remained quiet.

Eric knew he should be more anxious than he was. The girls were asleep in Millie's spare bedroom. He stayed with them and watched over them until he was sure they were out, which didn't take too long. Exhaustion weighed on all of them more than their lingering fears that this ordeal somehow wasn't over. Once they went to sleep, Eric asked Lafonda to look in on them while he stepped away. He needed to finalize things with Eunice.

He asked Dana and Millie to join him in the living room as witnesses to the discussion. Not that their presence would make this more official, but he wanted them there just the same. He wanted Eunice to know how little he trusted her.

They sat in the living room looking at each other before Millie made her comment.

"You should have known they were real," Eunice said to Millie. "I told you a long time ago."

"Yeah, you did," Millie said, sounding like she had a witty retort loaded. If she did, she kept it to herself and said, "You told me."

"Did you tell her everything, though?" Eric said. "Or did you leave out the most important thing? Could be that's why she never believed you."

Eunice sat up straighter in her chair, and just that little movement made her wince. It was evident to Eric that recent events had drained Eunice, just as they had him and his daughters. The key difference was that Eunice knew ahead of time how bad things could get and didn't warn anyone. He had little sympathy for her.

"I can understand why you'd be angry," she said.

"I'm not angry," he said.

She waved a hand. "Upset, then. You know what I'm saying."

He smiled. "I do. And I acknowledge your best effort at an apology, even if I'm not ready to accept it. My baby got taken by a gunman today, after all."

"I assure you I had no idea that would happen. There was more I should have told you, I'll admit, but I couldn't have anticipated that."

"Definitely more you should have told me," Eric said. He drank the whiskey Millie had poured for him earlier. "Like how this was less about finding proof than it was about switching the house all the way on."

Eunice flushed red. Was she more angry or ashamed? "I don't know what you mean by that."

"You do. And I promise you, I did it. The house isn't going back to sleep anytime soon. So what's your next step exactly? I need to know so I can wrap up my part in this."

"Your part is over. I don't ask any more of you. You'll get your full pay-out, and we'll even help you find a permanent place to stay. Dana will meet with you tomorrow to go over the details."

"I'm glad to hear that," Eric said. "But you're not the one to tell me when it's over, now. I made a promise to Masson and to the kids. Eleanor and Owen."

"Eleanor and Owen," Eunice said. "That's them. I used to hear my mother pray for their spirits by name."

"So you know I'm not making it up," Eric said. "They helped me save Stacy, so I made a deal with them, and I need to see it through. I promised to give them a chance to confront their uncle. He's been hiding from them in the house all these years. They want to see him. They want him to grovel for their forgiveness, and they want him to tell the full truth about everything. His whole story. I promised I'd get him to do that."

"And how are you going to keep that promise?"

"I told Masson it was his chance to unburden himself and finally rest in peace," Eric said. "I also told him that if he did this, there was a chance the last living Houghton might show up for it, and maybe he could get an apology out of her."

Eunice nodded and looked energized. "That settles it. I'll be going inside."

Dana said, "You can't be serious. That place is dangerous."

"I know that. I've known for a long time. That's why I've always sent others in my stead. But I'll only get one chance to do this right. I can't afford to wait, or trust it to anyone else. I don't have much time left."

Millie said, "And let me guess, you're not going to go in alone. After everything that's happened, you're going to let other people go in there? You should burn the damn thing down."

"And anger what's inside?" Eunice said. "Release those spirits? No one knows what will happen if I do that. That's the reason why I've done all of this, because there are too many unknowns. But if we make it known to the world that all of this is a 'real thing,' as you said, Millie, and we do it in a way that can't be denied, then it will be the most important discovery in human history. We'll have the attention of every brilliant mind looking for a new frontier. Every billionaire looking to pour a fortune into being able to say, 'I did it first.' Every religion with deep pockets looking to use it as proof that they're right. Every government or institution that wants to research it on the off chance they could monetize or weaponize it. And I don't care what motivates any of them. I don't care if they're competing instead of collaborating, they'll still be working toward new, deeper discoveries, and they'll be able to do a thousand times more than what I can do on my own. And then maybe, finally, one of them will find out how I can escape this curse."

She was breathing harder and reached for the bottle of water near her. When she struggled to twist the cap open, Dana reached over and did it for her. After a few sips, Eunice was able to continue.

"I'm calling in a few favors to have a news crew at the site in less than a week," she said. "I've already told Neal to be ready when I call him."

"Lord," Millie said, "you're going to bring him into this, too?"

"That was always the plan," Eunice said. "People will insist anything is fake these days, no matter how convincing the footage. Some won't believe what they see unless someone they follow or idolize tells them it's real. If Neal says it's real, or if he at least won't commit to calling it fake, people will listen to him. Even other skeptics will listen. It's the only way this works. I have to bring him in."

"I'll be there, too," Eric said. Dana and Millie looked at him, stunned and perturbed. Neither had the nerve to chastise him after what he'd been through, however.

"You don't have to do that," Eunice said.

"Again, that's not your call."

"I see. Can I ask you something? You said the children wanted their uncle to tell the truth about everything. What exactly does that mean?"

"They want him to admit that he died and came back," Eric said.

Eunice leaned forward. "And they'll want to know how he did it, too?"

"Yes. I thought that would get your attention. That could give you another option if your big plan doesn't pan out. And now you might see why I'm so eager to do my part. I'm going to make sure you hear it from him, so you don't get any ideas about coming after Stacy someday, now that you know about her."

Eunice reared like she'd been slapped. "I am sincerely sorry for failing to tell you everything you deserved to know, but I can't believe you think that means I would do something so much worse. I would never do anything like what Max Renner did today."

"Sure. Listen, when you pin down the date you're going back in, let me know," Eric said. "Thanks for having us, Millie. Talk to you in the morning, Dana." Then he went to the spare room to be with Stacy and Dess.

Dess

Four days later, Dess was starting to believe her father was not completely himself. He moved stiffly, like he'd aged a few decades since first arriving in Degener. Nonetheless, his demeanor was that of a man with few worries. He hummed sometimes as he moved about the two-bedroom suite Eunice rented for them. They were on the outskirts of San Antonio, but he took them into the city—downtown—every night to eat, surrounded by tourists and locals. His desire to keep a lower profile was gone.

Only in his sleep did he seem troubled. From her bedroom, Dess could hear him pacing, groaning, crying. She checked in on him the first night, saw him sleepwalking and knew better than to wake him. In the morning, she told him that she saw him up, eyes closed tight, sweat beading on his forehead, his face crunched in pain. She saw him take a step, stop, gasp, turn his head like he was scanning the room even as his eyes were closed. She watched him go through these and other motions for most of the night, accounting for her tiredness the following day.

"You don't worry about me. I mean that," he said, although he spoke like he didn't mean anything that he said these days. She couldn't help trying to check on him again the next night, but the door to his room was locked.

After a few days of this, she told him, "When Eunice does her whole séance thing, if it goes like she says it will, we should come up with a plan to call Mom."

"You think so?" he said.

"Yeah. It should be safer then, right? Everybody will be paying attention to what's going on with that, with the house. And I bet it'll get a little cha-otic for a while, too. So even if Mom, you know, reacts badly and tries to tell people about it, I think it'll get lost in all the noise, if it gets any attention at all. Plus we'll have the new place out in Cali. We don't have to tell her about that. We can still lay low. But, Dad, I'm worried about you. If something happens to you, I can take care of Stacy on my own, but just 'cause I can that doesn't mean it's the best thing for her."

"Or for you," he said. "You're right. We'll figure out a way to tell your mom and hope for the best." He smiled. "Can you imagine how happy Stacy would be to see her again?"

"She wouldn't be the only one," Dess said. Honestly, though, she'd be too nervous about what could go wrong to be as overjoyed about seeing Mom as Staze would. Unlike Dad, Stacy seemed to be herself. She was a little more reserved with strangers now. When waiters or waitresses at restaurants spoke to her beyond asking her order, she was guarded with them. She didn't make her little napkin bows or flowers anymore. Other-wise, she was okay. She didn't struggle to sleep or suffer nightmares about her kidnapping or the spite house. Granted, she didn't like sleeping alone either. Next week, when they got to the new place in California, Dess would see if Stacy wanted to sleep in her own room or continue sleeping with her big sister. Then she'd have an even clearer picture of how well Staze was holding up. For now, though, she felt confident that Staze would come out of this tougher and smarter.

Dad was something else. Dess couldn't shake the frantic look on his face when she got to him after he was trapped inside the house. How he grabbed her arm like his life depended on it. It concerned her that he didn't want to talk about it, that he walked around as though he'd never been that person, even for an instant, much less the careful man he was before they arrived in Degener. That, plus the sleepwalking, made her think he was suppressing something and it wasn't good for him.

Even when he spoke of the house—of Eunice's séance—he made it sound like a tourist attraction he was mildly curious about.

"Should be interesting to see how it all plays out," he said.

"Yeah, nah, 'interesting' isn't the word I'd pick," she said. "It doesn't worry you at all?"

"A little, just because it worries you. But I've been through the worst that place can do and I'm still here. What else is there to worry about?"

There wasn't much she felt she could say to that. What was the point of trying to convince him to be more afraid? Maybe she would feel more secure if he were less secure, but was that what she wanted? No, of course not. He was right, he survived the worst of it. Maybe he hadn't come out as well as he could have, and certainly not the same as before he went in, but he survived. She had to be happy with that and do her best to believe that the spite house couldn't hurt them anymore.

Eunice

There had been much to do in the six days since she last stood in the shadow of the Masson House. Eunice finished it all with time to spare.

She called the sheriff and directed him to be sure no trace of the Renners remained on the property. That included disposing of Max's car. It wasn't the first time he'd done something illegal at her request, although this was a little more extreme than the minor intimidations he was accustomed to. Still, he'd known the legacy of Degener sheriffs long before taking the job, and did as instructed. But he told Eunice afterward that he was never going into the spite house again, and wouldn't subject his deputies to it either. She didn't ask why. She just said it shouldn't be necessary going forward.

She let Dana see to the particulars of the Rosses' financial affairs and green-lit a larger payout than she originally planned for. Eric's comment about her coming after his little girl stung. She hoped her extra generosity made him feel ashamed for accusing her of having designs on Stacy. Maybe she would seek some time alone with Stacy in the future, to see if she could get her to open up, to talk about how she made it back from the other side. Of course that was still possible, provided her initial plans fell through, or even if they didn't. There was no sense in letting a potential resource go completely unevaluated. She hardly thought that made her predatory.

The morning after Max Renner's stunt, Eunice started calling in her favors, holding people accountable to old promises. Her first call was to Neal, who she knew would raise no objection. Next, she called a few local news producers who she knew would make excuses. They had no one to spare to cover the story. It was too short notice. If she could just give them until next month.

A producer in San Antonio agreed after she reminded him of all she'd done to get his sons accepted at her alma mater. He sent a small crew, but didn't agree to a live broadcast. He promised that if the footage was in any way usable, it would be televised and featured heavily on the station's website. That was good enough. All she needed was independent, reputable videography. A local broadcast to generate early buzz would be a bonus. Neal would be the primary reason the story went international.

In the midst of this she also managed her health and caught up on sleep. Lafonda still would not let her engage in any vigorous exercise and insisted Eunice schedule a doctor's appointment to confirm whether she'd had a heart attack or, as Eunice insisted, "just an anxiety attack."

"After I'm done with this, I'll get checked," Eunice said. In truth, she worried that she would back out of her plan if she found out her heart was weaker and damaged. She might get too scared to go inside, to be sure that things went as planned. What then? Wait until she recovered? What if it took a year or more for her to feel healthy enough? The house might get quieter then, and she'd have to hire someone else to reawaken it. She had no qualms about that, or about withholding information again to be sure they weren't scared off early. She wasn't happy about doing that to all the people she'd done it to—Eric most of all—but she'd keep doing it as long as it was necessary.

The biggest issue with starting over was the unlikelihood of finding another Eric and Stacy Ross. It was a miracle that they landed in Degener, almost as if the spite house had reached out into the world and handpicked them. Not only were they on the run and desperate to take her offer, they were already in tune with the other side. Eunice knew how exceptional they were. They brought more out of the house in a few days than the Renners had in close to a month.

No, she couldn't let this moment pass. And it was already in motion. Neal had arrived the day before. The reporter and cameraman from San Antonio agreed to arrive hours ahead of the event. Millie decided she wanted to be there, as did Dana. Lafonda asked if Eunice wanted her there. "It's fine if you'd rather wait outside," Eunice told her.

Dana did not say why she wanted to attend, but Eunice suspected it was for the same reason as Millie. "I can't let you do this to Neal without being there myself," Millie said. "And if Eric is going to be there, he should have someone there looking out for him."

Not wanting to give her impetus to write another hit piece, Eunice agreed to let Millie come. Another renowned and reputable witness would prove beneficial, and it wasn't as if Millie might catch her in the act of manipulating or misusing Eric in some horrid way.

In fact, as the week went on it became apparent that Eric would be a no-show. She called him several times, and each day he answered, but never communicated a sense of urgency or anticipation when she verified the date, time, and expectations with him.

"I'll be there," he would say one day, "I'll see you there" the next.

"Eric, if you'd rather not come back, just tell me," Eunice told him that morning, when he still hadn't come to her mansion. "I understand. I won't hold it against you or try to undercut our deal over it. You have my word."

"I'll be there, Eunice. I have to be."

Now, the night was here, but Eric wasn't. The sheriff assigned two deputies to wait outside in case something went wrong. It looked good for the news crew, who planned their exterior shots and took people aside one by one for interviews. Millie and Neal talked outside while Lafonda and Dana kept each other company. Eunice wished Eric had told her he didn't want to go through with it, but she'd meant it when she said she wouldn't hold it against him. Just looking up at the spite house made her pull the collar up on her jacket. Its chill was not nearly as severe as what she'd felt when Aunt Val died, but it was nonetheless recognizable to her. If this was what it was like out here, how strong was it inside? The house was as active and awake as she expected it to be. Eric didn't have to be there to keep it "switched on," as he put it. He'd done all she could have asked of him.

Eunice checked the pulse indicator on her watch and was glad to see it in a manageable range. The longer she stood here staring at the house, letting it intimidate her, the more time her heart would have to catch up to the trepidation in her head. She had waited long enough. She had waited years. It was time to get this done.

She called out to the others, "Are we ready?"

Millie and Dana hesitated. The two who knew. The others quickly gathered what they needed and followed Eunice into the spite house.

The interior was not as cold as she expected. That made her pulse quicken. Maybe Eric was more essential than she thought. But the house had been active. The sheriff had said he wouldn't go back inside, so something must have scared the hell out of him.

That was right after everything happened, Eunice reminded herself. *Of course it was buzzing then. Now you've let it sit alone too long. You've let it go dormant again.*

No, that couldn't be. It couldn't be dead quiet now, less than a week after the Rosses left. Unless . . .

What if it was sated? It took the Renners when they came back. What if that was all it wanted? That might be why it let Eric go. Nothing to do with a deal he brokered with the children. The house simply didn't have room or use for him. Now it was going to hibernate, and she arranged all of this for nothing. It was colder inside, yes, and the cold appeared to shift around, like it was stalking prey for sport, but that wasn't going to convince anyone that the house was haunted. Damn it, she should have had people on standby ready to go sooner, no more than a day after Eric left the house. She could have gotten Neal a private jet from anywhere in the country. Could've pressed one of the television producers harder and earlier, had a crew reserved and ready. Why did she think she could wait this long for the house to still be as alive as she needed it to be?

She took a deep breath. *Relax, be patient. This will happen. You'll make it happen if you have to.*

"So we're just waiting, right?" Neal said.

Eunice looked at him, then the others. Neal stood against the wall opposite the couch, where Dana and Millie sat together. The news team set up just inside the door, obviously not expecting any emergencies that would demand a fast evacuation. Eunice stood in the center of the room. Seconds turned into minutes with no one saying anything, but with Neal's impatient sighs growing in frequency.

"Are you supposed to do something to summon the ghosts?" Neal said.

"I'm already doing it, just being here," Eunice said. She raised her voice slightly, as if announcing herself to the house as much as to the rest of the people in the room. "I'm the last member of the Houghton family, and at this place, in the midst of the American Civil War, a dozen men and boys were hanged in a horrible crime because they were betrayed by one of my ancestors. My family tried to make amends but they could not protect us from the curse put on us by those who died. So we tried something else. We gave the land up to a descendant of one of the hanged men, but things did not go as we'd hoped. Since then, this land's history has only gotten worse, with this house being the worst of it. I believe this house has wanted someone from my family to be here in a moment like this, when it has its eyes open. I believe that it knows this is the last chance for the ancestors to confront someone who shares the blood and name of their betrayer."

Eunice's heart was racing; she didn't need to check her watch to know that. It felt sore, too, like an overworked or bruised muscle. She was taking a gamble. The curse never directly killed anyone in her family. The stress of knowing about it likely contributed to some heart attacks and suicides, but the ghosts couldn't kill. They only swarmed and horrified those already dying. What if it was different at the scene of the original crime, though? What if the site, or the house, gave them power they didn't have elsewhere?

In the silence that followed her speech, Eunice thought she heard men screaming somewhere outside of the house.

"Anyone else feel that?" Dana said, zipping her jacket all the way up.

Millie nodded, brought her hands up to her mouth to warm them.

Eunice felt an awful exhilaration, like she was the passenger in a car moving much too fast, taking corners without slowing, weaving between other cars, narrowly dodging disaster by inches and milliseconds. When she heard someone on the stairs behind her, she became so light-headed she almost couldn't feel the strain in her chest.

She turned and saw Eric come down the stairs.

"When did you get here?" she asked him. He didn't say anything and didn't quite look like himself. He was more intense than he'd been before. Angrier, maybe. She had apologized for not being forthright with him, and for what Max Renner did, even though that wasn't her fault. What else could he be angry about?

"I thought you weren't coming," she said, then heard Neal behind her say, "Eunice, what are you doing?"

"You don't look well," Eunice said to Eric. The hardness of his glare couldn't hide the fatigue in his eyes. Had he lost weight? Over the phone he sounded at peace. It stunned her to see him in this condition. Had the house done this to him since he'd arrived? When did he get here? How long had he waited for them upstairs? "You should leave, Eric. I told you, you don't have to be here."

Neal said, "Eunice, you're worrying me. This isn't funny."

"Eunice, who are you talking to?" Millie said.

Hearing this, Eunice glanced back at the others, who stared at her like she was holding a knife to her own throat.

"I'm talking to Eric," Eunice said, closer to a question than a statement. In response Dana's eyes got wider, and Millie just shook her head. Neal moved closer to her, but cautiously. He was shivering and she saw a confusion in his eyes that made her smile, despite her mounting fear. Her friend Neal Lassiter, confident king of skeptics, was struck by uncertainty for perhaps the first time since he was a teen.

She turned to Eric again and saw someone else in front of him. An old man kneeling, his head bowed, his hands on his head as if to keep his skull from exploding.

"Forgive me," the old man said. "Forgive me, forgive me, forgive me please. Let me go, please. Let me just go. I'll help you. I'll do anything. I can help you. Please, please forgive me."

"What is that?" Dana said. "Am I the only one hearing someth—?"

The children's laughter cut her short. Eunice felt the cold encroach on her. It was electric, radioactive, so cold it burned. The children laughed harder. At Eunice, at the miserable old man who must have been their uncle Peter. Or were they laughing at something else? Something very soon to come.

That distant screaming Eunice thought she'd heard a moment ago was closer and louder now. Flying through the night, toward the house. Eunice's heart was in a vise. Her legs weakened. She heard people calling her name. Not just the living people in the house with her, but those on their way, and who were not alive.

Amid the distant chorus of the dead calling out to her, she did not hear her mother, father, Cousin Oscar, Aunt Val, or any other member of the family taken before her, and she did not know if this was a godsend or an omen.

"Eric"

He was the secret-keeper. The one who never told his wife or children the story about his grandfather and what that could mean about him, what it meant for all of them. He was the one who didn't tell his older daughter why he planned all along to get back to his grandparents' house in Odessa, Texas. That is, until he happened upon a place with even older ghosts, and more of them.

He was the part of Eric who didn't trust that Stacy was really alive again. The one who could not accept the answers he was given, who was obsessed with finding answers that would ensure he could keep his daughter safe. Even learn to bring his girls back from the dead, if it came to that. He was willing to give up his own life to find out. But the girls still needed him out there, in the living world, as much as they unwittingly needed him here among the spirits. So he gave all that he could spare—the part of himself that Eleanor and Owen taught him to surrender.

The house had started to pull This Eric away from him on his first night inside, without him realizing it. The children and the house recognized what they needed from him, long before he realized what he could get from them, or that he would even *want* anything from them. They were patient, opportunistic, and vicious enough to make other spirits tremble. They seized him just when he needed them most. And they showed him how power could be drawn from anger. That power allowed them to do so much more than haunt and frighten someone, which was all most of the dead managed to do. Even the souls that cursed the Houghtons ultimately

THE SPITE HOUSE • 253

did little beyond wait for each family member to die, then terrorize them at the moment of death. They could have done worse things to truly enact their vengeance if they knew how, but those men allowed their rage to dominate them, when they could have let it empower them. The children were different. They could draw a living, breathing person into the dark and keep them there forever.

This part of Eric that made the deal with the children was made up of all his anger, his necessary secrets and distrust. He had more in common with his grandfather, who came back to ensure his family's protection and wreak his vengeance. His grandfather defied death to show how deeply he refused to forgive. And This Eric did not forgive, either. Not Eunice Houghton, who hid things from him while encouraging him to stay in Degener, putting his children in harm's way. Not Peter Masson, a coward who—in life—tried to disguise selfishness as a virtue, and took two children away from a place they loved, then failed to protect them. Worse, he refused to act when he could have saved Stacy. If Peter had done what he should have, Eric would have made his deal with him, instead of with the children. He more than earned what awaited him, in Eric's eyes.

Finally, this part of Eric could never forgive his other, living self. The part of him, he was sure, that had let everything happen, instead of making something happen. This Eric believed that none of that remained with him.

The very first thing This Eric did once he was free of his other self was to find Masson and say, "You don't have to go on like this. It doesn't have to stay this way."

Masson did not respond. He stayed in his corner, repeating, "I never hurt them."

"All they want is an apology, and for you to tell them how you came back," Eric said. "Then you can go. Don't you want to? Aren't you tired?"

"I never hurt them."

"Like you never died?" This Eric said. "Just give them what they want, Masson. Tell them you're sorry, and tell the truth. Then you can leave. Let them have the house. They already control most of it. You've been holding on to this one piece of it and you don't even want it. They want it all. Give it to them. Give them their apology, be honest about what happened to you, and they'll let you leave."

This went on for days, Eric as persistent in his mission as Masson was in his denial. Eric did not care about lying to the dead old man. The house and the children wanted their uncle out of his sanctuary in the bedroom, the one place he was safe. They wanted his spirit in full the same way they had Max and Jane Renner, and Clyde Carmichael. They would have Eric's remnant as well if he could not do as promised. And then he wouldn't be free to roam the house, examine its captives, seek his answers. He'd be bound to the house and its true owners—Eleanor and Owen—in a deeper and worse way than he already was. He could not let that happen.

When Eunice finally entered the house, Eric felt her arrive. He broke Masson by saying, "The last living Houghton is in here now. She's brought people with her. You can tell the children what they need to hear and then tell the world what the Houghtons and this town did to your family. This is your chance at peace and justice. Forgiveness and righteousness. You built this house so that no one would forget what was done to you and your family. The Houghtons pretended to care, then didn't lift a finger to help you keep your father's home. They let this town spread rumors that you were a madman who killed his brother's children. That you're the reason this house is evil. You have a chance to confront the last one left and make her tell the truth. You're going to let that pass?"

This brought a small light to the old man's dead eyes and he lifted his head to face Eric. "The last Houghton is here?"

"You know she is. But she won't stay long. This is it. You can stay trapped here forever, or you can have your reckoning with her, then be at peace."

Then Eric was on the stairs, moving down, his footsteps thumping without his feet landing. It was still very strange, being a spirit divorced from its body. But he was consumed by what he was here to do. Just as Eleanor and Owen were consumed by their hatred. And Peter himself was consumed by his fear. Eric thought that this was what allowed him to hold on to consciousness and sanity. His focus kept his sanity from being ripped apart by the impossibility of his existence, like Jane Renner's.

When he came down the stairs and saw Eunice, Eric felt afraid at first because he knew that she could see him. He didn't yet know how to control who he appeared to. The children knew. He would learn from them over time. Now, though, he was visible to Eunice because she was closer to death than she realized. He could see the life leaking out of her in curling wisps.

When did you get here? she said. *I thought you weren't coming. You don't look well. You should leave, Eric. I told you, you don't have to be here.*

But he did. When he had told her that, she hadn't understood what he meant. She would soon.

He was among the dead now, and the emotions of the house fully infected him. When Masson appeared downstairs with him, the old man's fragile defiance crumbled to remorse and terror in an instant, and Eric knew that meant the children were present as well.

Eleanor and Owen laughed at their uncle's pleas.

"I can help you," Masson said.

"We don't want your help," Eleanor said.

"We want you," Owen said.

"Please, let me help you," Masson said. "I swear I'll help you. If you give me time, I can remember. I can tell you."

Eunice, through clenched teeth, hissed at the old man, "Tell them."

The people in the room looked at each other, bewildered. The children continued laughing.

"Hurry and tell them, for God's sake," Eunice said. Her hand went to her chest and she clutched the front of her shirt like she meant to tear it off. "Hurry! I need to know."

"I need time," Masson said. "I just need time to remember."

"There is no time! They're coming, damn it!"

A rumbling energy shook the house. Eunice cried out in pain and fell to the floor. Before any of the living could get to her, Eric moved forward and picked her up. When Millie, Dana, and the others stopped and stared, he knew they still could not see him. They only saw Eunice suspended just above the floor. It hurt him to hold her, but he did it without thinking, forgetting that she was beyond saving and, moreover, not worth it. It was a lingering piece of his other self, something that it would call decency but that he knew was purely weakness. He wanted to drop her, but couldn't, because as angry as he was, he did not hate her with the purity that the children did. He knew he would, eventually. The bit of humanity clinging to him would fade as he learned from the children, observed how they toyed with the souls they would soon collect.

Eleanor and Owen had given themselves to the house completely and bonded with it. They were fueled by the hatred that originally cursed the land. The malice that pooled in Degener, Texas, leading men to commit mass murder, and go unpunished. And the rage that led murdered men to seek vengeance beyond death. On it went, through Peter Masson, into the house he built, and into his niece and nephew. The children did not just hate their uncle and the Houghtons, but the men who cursed and haunted the Houghton family, too. And they had spent a century growing stronger, planning their chance to make them all suffer.

This Eric knew that Eunice was doomed. Death wasn't the end of her pain. She belonged to the house, to the children. He couldn't save her, but he might save her cause. She floated in his grasp, the camera capturing it all. Bottomless fear contorted her face until she found a scream she didn't have the strength for, and she let it go as she died.

The storm of rage that encircled the house rushed inside as Eunice died, then became something else when it tried to abscond with her spirit. No longer a multitude working together, but a compressed and horrified *one*. A singularity of despair. The children still laughed but that sounded like screaming now, too, and Eric felt like the last man in the world on the last night of the world, watching the sun burn out. Because there was no one else there who shared his perspective, who felt sorrow for all of the dead. None of the living, scared as they were, could be as afraid as he was of the children.

Eunice, the vengeful twelve, and Peter Masson were all sucked down into the darkness of the house. The children gleefully followed to drink in their fresh terror and agony, and they took with them all of the noise and almost all of the cold, save for the chill that still emanated from the specter of Richard "Eric" Emerson.

With everything quiet again, Millie Steen found the courage to approach Eunice's floating body. Dana reached out to stop her and said, "Don't," but she walked up and took the burden from Eric's arms.

He sighed and she stepped back quickly, like she heard him; then she turned to the people blocking the door and barked at them to move. She ran with Eunice outside, and the others followed.

This Eric's phantom pain subsided now, and the overwhelming emotions of all the others spirits departed as well. The quiet gave him a moment to remember his purpose. He had fulfilled his end of the deal made with Eleanor and Owen. He was now free to watch how they controlled the house, and roam all of its spaces. He could dig through its secrets. Listen to what it might know about the dead, the returned, the bridges and doors that connected life and death. Learn how to walk through those doors with purpose, cross those bridges back and forth at will. It would take years. He had that. He wouldn't age here, not the way his living self would on the outside. Time would feel weightless to him here. He also knew he would not pursue this completely alone.

By making Eunice's death the spectacle she wanted, he ensured others would come to the house. Lives that the children might take, which gave him more chances to see how they did it. And even if those others never arrived, there was someone else he knew would always be with him.

His living self, the part that left him behind, dreamed of him already, and always would.

Eric

At Dess's insistence, Eric watched the footage of what transpired at the Masson House when Eunice died. They watched it together once, on one of the many cable news broadcasts turning the video and its aftermath into a twenty-four-hour story. He saw Eunice calling his name, talking to him as if he were there when he wasn't visible on camera or to anyone else in the room. He watched her cry out and collapse, then appear to levitate for several seconds before finally succumbing to her heart attack.

There was debate about the video's authenticity. It wasn't surprising. An old multimillionaire obsessed with the afterlife faked her death along with footage meant to prove the existence of the supernatural. It wasn't the most ludicrous conspiracy theory you could find online. As Eunice had predicted, however, Neal Lassiter vouching for what he saw gave the video enough credence to be treated seriously by most.

"I can only report what I observed," Neal said. "That's the scientific, rational approach, and what I observed is exactly what you see in the video."

That was his official statement on the matter. All he had said since was that he had lost a friend and would appreciate everyone respecting his privacy. Maybe in a month or two he would retract that official statement, start looking for "logical" answers to what he witnessed. Dana said she didn't think it was likely, though.

Busy as she was, Dana made sure to call Eric after Eunice passed to assure him nothing had changed. He would still have the full financial support promised to him. She had a question for him, as well. "Eunice thought she saw you in the house that night. She even spoke to you. Do you have any idea why?"

"No clue," Eric said. She might have guessed he was lying, but she didn't press it, and he didn't care one way or another as long as it didn't impact their agreement.

"Neal is going to pull together a team to do some more research in the house," Dana said. "Eunice earmarked some funding for him, and it's all he can talk about whenever I talk to him."

"You're telling me this because?" Eric said.

"You're connected. And Eunice, bless her, she kept things from you. I don't want to do that."

"Mm. How are Lafonda and Millie?"

He was glad to hear they were doing well, in light of everything, and Dana was glad to hear that Dess and Stacy were happy with their new home.

Stacy was going to start school after the Christmas break. She was eager to talk to kids her age again, make some friends. She liked being near the coast, too, although Eric told her that these beaches were better suited for hanging out and watching the water instead of getting in. Lots of smaller rocks hiding around the big rocks, he told her. The currents were strong too, making it too risky for swimming. She seemed to understand.

He took her to the beach a day after they moved to Northern California. He wanted to see how it felt, watching her come close to untamed water. Wondering if there was some invisible threat out there that could take her away again. Small butterflies fluttered in him when Stacy came within about twenty feet of low tide. Before he could call to her to come back, Dess did it for him. It felt good to be a little uneasy. The part of himself that he surrendered to the house held most of his stronger emotions, but he was glad it wasn't stealing his worry. He still needed to be able to watch out for his kids.

Eric was also glad to be done wondering what Stacy was, or how she re-turned, and back to thinking about more practical things. How would she do in school? What was Dess going to do with her life now? She had been willing to sacrifice so much to help give her sister a chance at a future. Now they both had that chance. They were going to grow older, have complete lives, maybe kids of their own one day.

That thought brought a smile to his face. If he could hold on long enough, he hoped his grandkids would look up to him like he used to look up to his grandfather, and that he would get a chance to tell them exactly how unique and gifted they were. The power they could access if they needed to.

He didn't know how long he had, however. The difficult nights threatened his health. What would happen to the girls if he died in the next few years? Could he claw his way back to them?

Dess took charge of reaching out to Tabitha, letting her know they were safe, laying the groundwork for a reunion as a contingency, in case Dess checked on him one morning and found him dead cold and gone. It wasn't something he cared to think of, much less talk about, but he knew it was important to be prepared. Still, he had reason to believe he wouldn't die soon.

His other half was having too much fun dragging him back into the house each night via dreams that weren't dreams, because, as he well knew, there were no dreams in that house. His other half would figure out soon enough that it would have to pace itself. Eric's muscles and joints ached, his eyes felt sore from how little rest he got, and he was always a little chilly, even when he was sitting in the sun. He was up to two energy drinks per day to stay awake as long as he could, and that couldn't be great for his heart. If things continued like this, he might not make it to his next birthday. And that was not what his other half wanted. It wanted him to have a long lifetime of misery and anxiety—of his heart skipping every time he caught himself nodding off. Of being forced back into that house night after night, venturing so deep into its shadows that he was sure he'd never make it back to the light. His other half would have to scale back how often it drew him in if it was going to prolong this for decades. Eric was sure it was smart enough to recognize that.

Every time Eric joined his other self in the house, he felt how glad it was to have him back. Not because it was lonely, or missed feeling alive and being whole. No, it was glad that its living self hadn't truly escaped the Masson House either. Eric knew that even when his other half reached the end, discovered there was nothing more to learn, no more power to grasp, it would keep looking. It would keep tormenting him with its restlessness. It would never stop.

Out of spite.

ACKNOWLEDGMENTS

To my brother Marvin, and my sister-in-law Yolanda. The trip to come see you in 2019 gave me motivation to finally finish what I started. Thank you. Love you.

Thanks to my agent, Lane Heymont, for believing in this book, facilitating this journey, and consistently coming through when you say you will.

Thank you to my splendid editor, Daphne Durham, her assistant, Lydia Zoells, and everyone else at Tor Nightfire who brought *The Spite House* to life.

Thank you to the Black Bar Mitzvah team, Jay Ellis, Aaron Bergman, Sydney Foos, and Alexis Dinenberg, for your faith in the book. Likewise to Katrina Escudero with Sugar23 for your work in making it something that much bigger.

Thanks to my parents, brothers, aunts, uncles, and cousins for putting up with me being way too into scary stories for just about my entire life.

And thanks to Karla, the first person to hear every bit of good news I've had to share along the way. Love you.